Daughters of God

Praise for Jerry Marcus

Shoshana's Song
ISBN 978-0-941394-08-6
Finalist in the 2013 Arizona-New Mexico Book Awards

"Masterfully told coming-of-age story...Jerry Marcus interweaves discussions of faith, marriage, intellectual freedom, and the roles of women throughout their lives. It will help both young and mature readers explore how women gain strength in their faith journey."
Mary Lou Henneman, *Congregational Libraries Today,*
Church and Synagogue Library Association

Broken Trust
The Murder of Basketball Star Jack Molinas
ISBN 978-0-941394-06-2

Great book...
Sam Amico, *ProBasketballNews.com*

Jack would have loved how you portrayed him.
Bill Tosheff, 1951-52
NBA Co-Rookie of the Year

"As the film *The Lion King* vividly portrayed the conflict of good and evil…Marcus' works [also] praise noble souls and expose all that is ignoble in our rich, powerful and sensual modern world."
Rabbi Yaacov Fogelman, *The Bulletin,*
Philadelphia's Family Newspaper

The Last Pope
ISBN 978-0-941394-02-4

"Creative and provocative suspense-filled novel."
The Chicago Tribune

"A great plot."
Naples Daily News, Florida

"An intellectual thriller."
Marquee, San Diego

"A provocative tale that kindled my imagination..."
Mary Harris, Minister,
United Church of Christ
Boonville, Missouri

"Gripping!"
Anne Gerber, *Chicago Columnist*
Lerner Newspapers

The Salvation Peddler
ISBN 978-0-941394-01-7

"A master of the suspense novel."
Abilene Reporter-News, Texas

"I enjoyed The Salvation Peddler." President Bill Clinton

Abraham, Isaac, Jacob and Zev
ISBN 978-0-941394-00-0

"A significant, moving novel…An important addition to books about the Holocaust and Jewish people."
American Jewish Congress

"An extraordinary book."
Dorothy Fuldheim, News Analyst
Scripps-Howard Broadcasting Company

"Original and compelling"
The Chicago Tribune

Daughters of God

Jerry Marcus

Brittany
PUBLICATIONS
LTD.

Brittany Publications, Ltd.
Chicago, Illinois
www.brittanypublications.com

This book is a work of fiction. References to real people, events, establishments, organizations, or locales are intended only to provide a sense of authenticity and are used fictitiously. All other characters, incidents and dialogue, are drawn from the author's imagination and are not to be construed as real. Any resemblance to actual persons, living or dead, is entirely coincidental.

Inquiries should be sent to Brittany Publications, Ltd.
brittany@powercom.net
www.brittanypublications.com

Our books may be purchased in bulk for promotional, educational, or business use. Please contact the Brittany Publications, Ltd. Sales Department by email at brittany@powercom.net.

ISBN 978-0-941394-09-3
Library of Congress Control Number: 2015952558

Printed in the United States of America
Set in Baskerville

Cover design by Shawn Biner, Biner Design, Milwaukee, Wisconsin
Interior Design and Typography by Brittany Publications, Ltd.

First edition, 2017

Dedication

In memory of Max (Larry) Gold and Danny Tramutola. Their commitment to fairness and justice enabled them to make a real difference in the many lives they touched.

Nobody has a more sacred obligation to obey the law than those who make the law.

— Sophocles

Acknowledgments

My sincere appreciation to
Marion Estelle Gold—
For her creative suggestions and encouragement.
I also want to thank Diane DeRoy Crawford—
For her thoughtfulness and friendship.

Marion and Diane have my respect,
admiration, and gratitude.

Three Suggestions

by Anne Marisse

Don't believe the tales they tell you,
sunlight is around the corner
of your mind.

Ideas
are the stuff dreams
are made of—
have one
today.

In daring
we exchange the wandering
for the glorious wondering;
So reach out
for chance rings
beckoning
on life's merry-go-round.

Chapter 1

She was so frightened. Angela Robinson stared at the television screen with disbelief as the governor of New York State stood before the public. Morris Green was pleading for understanding, forgiveness, and privacy. He had just confessed to having *human frailties*. Governor Green, his wife Sally at his side, was resigning after admitting to a long-term relationship with a young woman working for one of New York City's low-profile, but high-class escort services.

Max Gold, a crime reporter and columnist for the New York tabloid *Public Corruption*, was covering the story. This was his specialty. Exposing politicians, clergymen, and others who dictated the law to their constituents and professed morality to their flocks, while they violated all their own directives. Unfortunately, they usually had easy access to skilled and influential attorneys who, more often than not, succeeded in having all the charges against them dismissed. At worst, they received abbreviated sentences.

Max knew that Morris Green fit this profile very well. A son of privilege with a family that is part of the American dream. Green, a former attorney general, gained his reputation by going after the powerful and never caring about the little people he hurt, always justifying whatever means he used to accomplish his goals.

Now he was hiding behind his wealth and his wife. It didn't matter what he was putting her through. Her loyalty to him was something the masses would admire. Max was sure that the governor thought, if his wife could forgive him, someday the people of New York would, too!

As soon as he finished speaking and stepped back from the podium, a young reporter in the front row called out to him.

"Governor Green, Governor Green! That's all you have to say?"

The governor had promised his attorney and his wife that he would not take any questions, so he surprised them both when he turned back to the podium.

"No, young lady… That's not all I have to say! What's your question?"

"Kathleen Murphy, *Daily Post*. You attribute your behavior to *human frailties*. Is that enough of an explanation to the people who voted for you?"

"I don't want to put my family through an ordeal that was not of their choosing. Is that good enough for you, Ms. Murphy?"

"So are we are to believe," Murphy persisted, "that one of the most ambitious politicians in our country is resigning because he doesn't want to put his family through an ordeal?"

"That's what I said," Governor Green snapped back at her. "It's up to the people, not you, to decide whether or not they accept my explanation. Is there anyone else who doubts my sincerity?"

The room was quiet for a moment, surprised by the governor's outburst.

"I have a question," came a voice from the second row.

The governor grinned for a moment in Max Gold's direction. "Okay. What's your question?"

There were whispers around the room as Max Gold stood up. They all knew that the governor was not a big fan of his work. Max had a reputation for independence, known to avoid being friendly or soft with the people he covered. The story around the local newsrooms was that on the day Max interviewed for the job at *Public Corruption*, he told the editor, "I learned from one of my old journalism professors: Don't be patronized and taken in by those you interview. Objectivity is not something to be trifled with."

Max glared right back at the governor. "Some people would say that your actions are the highest form of hypocrisy. How do you respond to them?"

"I would agree that my behavior was disappointing and shameful. Not only have I caused my family great suffering, but I violated the trust of the millions of New Yorkers who believed in me. Now it's time for me to repair my marriage and show the public I have learned something from my transgressions."

"Don't you view what you did as a crime? In the past, you have prosecuted others for basically the same behavior you now admit to."

"In the future, I hope to respond to all questions and to set the record straight."

The red-faced governor smirked at Max Gold for a moment, then waved at the audience and walked off the platform, as additional questions shouted from the audience went unanswered.

Max's gut told him, as big as this story was, it was only the tip of something even more reprehensible. As a highly experienced and astute journalist, Max instinctively knew it was up to him to uncover what really happened—before Morris Green began his comeback. Max shuddered when he envisioned this disgraced governor standing on a platform, the cameras rolling, his wife beside him—and surrounded by the clergy of many denominations—beginning the speech that would restore his reputation and power.

Right now, at this very moment, Max took an oath to himself: "I, Max Gold, will do everything in my power to find out the real story. I know it is a task that needs great attention to detail, and dedication on my part not to allow any politician to get away with crimes against those they were elected to serve."

❧

Not all witnessed the scene in the same way. The Laughing Angels knew that it was only a matter of time before the governor made a comeback. After all, recent history proved that disgraced politicians, even a former president, often find the inner strength to overcome the scandals and crimes they committed, as well as the bad publicity. They cackled hysterically as they listened to Max Gold's oath. *One more faithful and good citizen*, they thought, *doomed to betrayal by the elite and powerful.*

The Righteous Ones, who believed fervently in the goodness of people, would not give in so easily. They beamed with pride as they watched Max do his best to make a positive difference. In Max's name, they approached God, and asked for assistance.

The Laughing Angels continued their wicked laughter as the Righteous Ones waited for the Supreme Being to respond. There was only silence.

Chapter 2

Four weeks had passed since Morris Green's resignation. He was keeping a very low profile, not seen in public nor giving any interviews. This was his time to plan a strategy, to find a way to keep out of prison and go on with his life.

As Max began to assemble his notes on the governor, he recognized an underlying theme throughout his political career. This former prosecutor had always believed that he was above the law. Moreover, Green was willing to make excuses for some members of his staff, and others in his inner circle—probably to buy their silence for his own transgressions. But he showed little understanding or compassion for those who held points of view different than his own.

As a prosecutor, Morris Green was known for his brutality. Max knew of more than one instance when Green threatened innocent and vulnerable witnesses with jail time, if they didn't testify against what he called the "big fish." Unfortunately, Green was never concerned with the safety of these individuals after they served his needs. It was not his concern if they were in obvious danger of being threatened, maimed, or possibly murdered by the people they testified against in court.

This complex man had his own enemies, but even they played it safe around Green, and with good reason. Many, including Max, suspected that Green kept a file of damaging information on as many influential people as possible, including judges, his own colleagues, and some well-known television executives and journalists. What Max did not know was that a deal had already been made between the prosecutor's office and the governor's legal team. After all he had done, there would be no jail time for Morris Green.

Max knew the governor was not the type of person who would allow himself to slide into the abyss. His family was accustomed to celebrating his accomplishments. Setbacks, although this one self-inflicted, were just a prelude to new opportunities. Another chance, to pick himself up, and strive for the glory.

The women in Morris Green's life, his wife and Julia, his eldest daughter, were ready to support him as he ascended to the mountaintop. This time, however, they would not allow him out of their sight. On his own, they sadly knew, he was not trustworthy.

Sally Green was determined to protect her investment. She had confidence in her husband's political potential. It didn't matter that Morris was corrupt to the core. Even though she had known that for years, she still gave up her own prospects for a successful career to be Morris' wife and the mother to their children. Her priority was their survival and way of life, and their daughters' futures.

The Laughing Angels had seen this scenario before. Disgraced politicians wanting to be understood and forgiven for their transgressions. Morris Green never doubted that the prosecutors would be lenient on him. They presumed that the governor would eventually make a comeback and somehow manage to keep his status in the community. What chance did Angela Robinson, the young woman from the escort service, have against the rich, corrupt, and powerful?

No doubt, the Laughing Angels contemplated further, the Righteous Ones would wait for God to intercede, while the corrupt continued with their evil ways.

The Righteous Ones sadly realized that the Laughing Angels might be right. Without God's intervention, it was a no-win situation for them. They understood that the governor would do everything in his power to withstand the charges leveled against him, even if it meant rewriting history. People like Morris Green were able to survive their immoral behavior with irrational justifications. Ironically, their lack of morality gave them the strength and fortitude to continue and even flourish.

However, they were not ready to admit defeat. The Righteous Ones sat at God's throne waiting for some direction. They believed that Angela, even with all her problems, had more integrity in one finger than the governor had in his entire being. Surely, Angela would not be forgotten. Even after all her transgressions, God would realize she was worthy of redemption.

Chapter 3

Angela had no place to hide. Her life was now part of the daily and weekend discussions of right and left-wing news analysts, and the jokes of late night talk show hosts and comedians. She was also the number one subject on the editorial pages of liberal and conservative newspapers. Even her parents were not talking to her. She had violated all they considered to be holy. *It was ironic,* Angela thought, *that her parents had more compassion for the governor, and his wife and daughters, than for their own daughter.* This is what the Laughing Angels lived for. All the pain and heartache that occurred between parents and their children.

Angela was disappointed with herself for going so far astray. *Maybe,* she thought, *it was partially due to the breakup of her first romance in high school.* It had devastated her. She stopped believing that any one person could give her all the love she needed. From that day on, sex and love became confused, bargaining chips to be used whenever it suited her purposes. She had felt free to pursue her own goals. Now she feared that same freedom might strangle her, turn her into both the villain and a victim.

Angela knew it would not be long before television producers were competing to give the governor his own talk show. But she was not the pushover Morris Green and others thought she was. Perhaps the Laughing Angels had miscalculated this young woman. The Righteous Ones stood at her side as she looked at her reflection in the mirror. She saw the beginning of a new day.

What right do these people have to judge me, Angela thought.

Down the road, she saw a very good life for herself. She would need to take small steps towards her future, making it easier to build a meaningful existence on a solid foundation. Someday, she hoped, the truly respectable people would appreciate what she had gone through, and honor how she had turned her life around. No longer would each morning be full of dread. Yes, some of the malicious gossip would continue, but that was to be expected. The charlatans, religious and political hypocrites of the world needed her, and other women like her. They came out from behind their pulpits and places of political power to vent their hate in newspaper columns and during talk show television appearances—all while they hid their own dark secrets.

Angela would show them. She was determined to fight for her survival. She began talking to God, but never seemed inclined to pray to a Supreme Being. It was as if she considered herself on equal footing with Him. Her goals would not be dependent on either religion or God, but only on the light that comes from within. She would not be swayed nor intimidated by ancient beliefs and traditions. What mattered most to her was the truth. Angela had learned the hard way that life was not fair. All the pain and resentment she felt needed to be turned into positive action. Angela was ready to change her life, first to survive and then to thrive.

The Righteous Ones also saw the light at the end of the tunnel. Angela moved away from being preoccupied with fear of her death. She was determined to make a concentrated effort to think about a better tomorrow.

Chapter 4

Max wondered if the governor was brooding at home and feeling sorry for himself, plotting revenge upon his enemies, or getting ready for his next challenge in life—most likely doing all three. At least for the time being, Morris Green was making an effort not to be so visible.

Max had written many articles on politicians just like Green. They all had one thing in common. None showed humility until their crimes became public knowledge. Then, out would come the public relations firms to get the cameras rolling, pull in any and all of the favors owed to them by friends and colleagues—even enemies—and use every trick in the books to save their careers and retain their power.

Like those before him, Morris Green assumed the public was forgiving. Sally and Julia were falling into line, and the rest of the family took their cues from them. He had confessed just enough to maintain their support, so they would smile bravely at the cameras, and convince the public that he could be trusted.

Given some time, the voters of New York, as well as the rest of the country, would believe that Morris Green was still a winner, one who could handle adversity and bad publicity, and still have the strength for a comeback. Max knew that most of the press would be pushovers!

Max, however, would not be so easily convinced. All the mercy in the world would not change certain facts. As a prosecutor, there were too many times in the past when the governor shot off his mouth about how the powerful got away without being punished for their crimes. This was now also part of Green's profile.

Max thought it best not to delve into the governor's motives. He wanted to tell the story without searching the psychological reasons for Green's behavior. Let that be a task for someone else. Let the psychologists and psychiatrists blame Green's actions on his mother or an abusive father, and absolve him for all his failings. Why not? It was Angela, the young escort, who they could throw to the wolves. After all, the governor and his family were part of the American dream, and they must be allowed to continue their charade at all costs.

But what about Angela, Max thought. Could he gain her trust enough to tell her side of the story? Up to now, her voice had not been heard. Max was able to convince the escort service to call her on his behalf. He had interviewed Leslie Stevens, the owner of the service, a long time ago, and she trusted him. Leslie said that Angela was not hardened like many of the escorts. She still had an "innocent soul," as Leslie called it. The Morris Green story caused Leslie to close down the service, which up to then had been so secret, it didn't even have a name and was not listed in the phone book. But for many years, the unlisted phone number was discreetly passed around in political circles, from New York to Washington, and Chicago to California.

As soon as Leslie confirmed the meeting with Angela, Max began feeling anxious. If Leslie was right, and Angela Robinson was an "innocent soul," would she be naïve about the consequences of telling her side of the story? He didn't say anything to Leslie, but experience taught him that even the most innocent-sounding people could also have a dark side. What might have gone wrong in Angela's life? Why was she working as an escort? *Whatever it was,* Max thought, *she still deserved to be treated fairly and not demonized in the press, as some were willing to do.* He was also worried what the so-called "Friends of Morris," and others who had something to hide, could do to her. Unfortunately, Max was all too familiar with how well-connected business leaders and politicians, even a president—who led what Max called "shadow lives"—managed to survive the scandals, while the women involved paid a very high price. Maybe, this time, with their lives.

Max and Angela met in her small studio apartment. She was dressed modestly in a pair of navy blue slacks and a long sleeve white blouse. Wearing little make-up, Angela appeared even younger than her twenty-one years. There was something very wholesome about her.

"Please sit down. I'll get some coffee," Angela said.

As she was pouring the coffee, Max could not help noticing a sweetness about Angela. But he also knew that looks could be very deceiving, so he would not let this stop him from asking hard questions.

Then Angela took Max by surprise by asking, "How long have you been a reporter?"

"More than thirty-five years."

"Did you ever want to do anything else?"

"Not really. Even as a kid, when I got a job delivering newspapers, I was fascinated by how eager my customers were to read the headlines on the front page. From that time on, becoming a reporter… That's all I wanted to do. I'm still addicted to the job."

"Why do you want to write my story?"

"I want to tell your side of it. So far, all the public has heard are the *mea culpas* from Governor Green. I think there's more to this story. In all truth, I was a little surprised that you agreed to meet with me. Wouldn't you rather just move on with your life?"

"Maybe, that's the only way I can," Angela answered very deliberately. "I can't allow people to continue talking about me, without them having any idea what I'm really about. These men could literally be getting away with murder, while their wives look sadly at them in front of the cameras, blame the 'other women' for leading their husbands astray, and then move on without any interruptions to their lavish lifestyles."

Angela's determination took Max by surprise. He respected what she said, but also wanted to be sure that he wasn't being used for some unknown or even heinous purpose.

"Angela, I understand how you feel. But don't you think *getting away with murder* is a bit strong?"

"No, I don't," Angela responded emphatically. "One of the escorts, my friend, is missing—and I think the governor has something to do with it."

"Did you report her disappearance? Maybe she just had change of heart and wanted to move on with life—just as you want to do."

"I did call the police. Unfortunately, the police didn't seem to be concerned. Like you, they figured she just moved on. But I know she wouldn't do that. Not without saying something to me."

"Wait a minute…"

"No, you wait a minute, Mr. Reporter. None of these young women had anyone looking out after them. Many of us don't use our real names, and we keep our jobs with the escort service a secret from our families! The only person who knows our real names is Leslie, and she keeps all that information locked in a safe somewhere. We even used special cell phones Leslie provided, so she could reach us at any time. All I know is that my friends are missing, and I think there was some foul play!"

"You said *friends*. More than one escort is missing?"

"Yes, more than one." Angela's eyes glassed over with tears. "Three escorts that I know of are missing. They stopped returning Leslie's calls and I never saw any of them again. I think even Leslie thought they just decided to call it quits."

"Okay," Max said. He suddenly felt sorry for his remark. "I didn't mean to sound cold or cruel. I really want to hear your story, the whole story. I want to tell the public your point of view. I agree with you about how politicians manage to get through scandal after scandal without being held accountable. The police should have taken your concern seriously. So let's just say you're right, and there is some foul play going on. Without any solid evidence, don't you think these accusations might get you in trouble?"

"I think I'm in more trouble if someone doesn't write about this."

"What do you mean?"

"Over the last two years, Governor Green *dated* all of the girls who are missing."

Max sat there in stunned silence. His mind was moving fast, from one possibility to the next. All this time, Max worried that Angela would not realize that telling her side of the story would ruin her chances of changing her life—but she was worried her life might be over.

Chapter 5

Angela gave Max much more to think about than he expected. If she were right, if Morris Green was somehow involved in murder, this was big—maybe too big. Thoughts raced through his mind. Was he too old to take on such an assignment? Was he too frail to go up against such powerful people? He could not go to the police, and he certainly did not want to give this story away to another reporter. If Angela was right, telling anyone about her suspicions would definitely put her life and his in jeopardy. And what about the three missing escorts? How could he follow up on that lead without knowing their real names?

His next step was to call Leslie Stevens again. Maybe she would let him see that secret list of names—at least tell him the real names of the three women Angela said had contact with the governor. When he called, Leslie reluctantly gave him their names, but no contact information.

Even I don't have that, she had said—*and don't call me again.*

Leslie had sounded very nervous and in a hurry. The next day, when Max did try to reach her, the phone was disconnected.

There was only one person Max trusted enough to ask for advice, Detective Tony Pinella. Politics and murder. That was Tony's specialty.

Now retired and living in Newport, Rhode Island, Max knew that Tony was still haunted by his involvement as lead detective in the murder case of Veronica Blake, the wife of the renowned evangelist Jason Blake. Like Governor Green, Jason Blake set his sights on the Oval Office. When his wife Veronica was murdered, Tony was sure Jason was somehow involved. All the evidence, motive, and opportunity pointed to him. But Tony had it wrong. He finally solved the case, and got the real killer, but never got over how he had missed the obvious for so long. He was too sure that Jason Blake murdered his wife.

When Tony answered the phone, he was greeted by a familiar voice. "Hey you old run-down detective, how are you spending your time?"

Tony answered with that deep-throated laugh in his voice Max liked so much.

"Hey, yourself, you old newshound! I certainly don't have to ask you the same question. I've been reading some of your articles on Governor Morris Green. Sounds like quite a character. What's he really like?"

"I'm glad you asked, Tony. That's why I'm calling."

"I'm listening…"

"I thought you might be interested. How about I head out to Newport and discuss it with you in person. Is that okay with you?"

"Okay? That's great! When can you get here? How long do you plan on staying?"

"I've gotta put some notes together and make a few calls, but I can be there by Monday morning, say 10:30 or so. I'd like to stay a few days and pick your brain, if that's all right. Is there a motel nearby your place?"

Tony let out another of his guttural laughs. "It's more than all right. I'd be honored. And forget about a motel. You're staying at my place. There's plenty of room, and I welcome the company."

"I appreciate the offer, Tony. Are you sure? I know how much you like your privacy, and I'll be keeping strange hours."

"I won't take no for an answer. Want to give me a hint about what you've got on the governor?"

"Um… not on the phone. Let's wait until I get there and I'll tell you everything I know so far."

"Sounds pretty serious. You be careful, Max. See you Monday!"

Max put the phone down and gave a sigh of relief. Tony had the wits, experience, and many old friends from the various police departments around the country. Those contacts could help them get information discreetly—without tipping off Green. Tony was a detective through and through. Max just hoped he would not be jeopardizing his old friend by getting him involved in what could be the story of the year.

Chapter 6

Tony was glad that Max called. He had moved to rural Newport, hoping to rid himself of the nightmares, to erase the evil memories about the murders and other cases that still haunted him. It was not long before he realized that reading, fishing, and eating—even trying to meditate—were not enough. There was no getting away from it. Tony Pinella was a detective through and through, and getting back into the action was a way he could actually make a difference in people's lives.

"I'm back! *Detective Pinella* is back and glad of it," he yelled as he took a bowl of cold cooked pasta out of the refrigerator. All the energy and anticipation he felt made Tony feel pangs of hunger. He laughed when thinking how, even as a young child and then as a teenager, food always helped him when he felt nervous or depressed—or wanted to celebrate happy occasions.

Pleasant memories of Tony's childhood came back to him. The wonderful aromas coming from the kitchen where his mother and grandmother spent so many hours cooking. He warmly recalled how they always insisted he come to the table with clean hands, a good appetite, and that he say a prayer before digging into his food.

Tony's prayers today were more secular than religious. He wanted to bring justice to all those who suffered at the hands of others, to bring some peace to their families. There was plenty to do, as he contemplated his return to the action. It was like the old days, beginning a new school term, starting fresh with pads, pencils, notebooks, and pens. After all the years of being a police officer, and then a detective, he was about to face one of the greatest challenges of his lifetime.

One of the reasons he retired shortly after solving the Veronica Blake murder case, was his very painful acknowledgment of all the times that justice did not prevail. Even when it did, it was often too late for the victims' families.

He had witnessed murderers dismissed on technicalities. Judges who cared only about the literal law—and not the spirit of the law. Instead of holding members of the law enforcement community and attorneys responsible for their mistakes, they were willing to allow murderers and drug dealers to go free, to wreak more havoc on the public. *It just was not right,* Tony thought.

He suddenly yelled out to his late and beloved mother: "Mama, please forgive me. I have many questions about God and religion, but I still believe in *your* eternal life. Each and every day, I thank you and papa for all your sacrifices and love. I'm not hostile towards religion and God. I'm still a good Italian Catholic who loves his family and traditions. It's not me who has violated the sacredness of our commandments and traditions. Just look at some of the leaders of our faith and the answer is quite evident. Please, mama, please help me be strong enough to fight against all that's unholy, so that the truly holy people may live their lives in peace and safety."

❧

The Laughing Angels were excited to see Tony back in the game. They were always impressed with how his mind worked. He would make life more interesting for them. They knew how memories of his past investigations still haunted him, especially the murder of Veronica Blake and his arrest of the young Stacey Johnson Blake. In those days, Tony thought it was God who was always playing tricks on the faithful. He even wondered if God were psychotic, something he also knew his mother would never have tolerated in the home of his youth.

They had to admit, Tony was a fighter for justice and truly understood hypocrisy in all its forms. The Laughing Angels would have to be on their toes to beat him at this game. He was a formidable adversary, one who was committed to uncovering the truth—even the truth about God.

The Righteous Ones also had mixed feelings about Tony's return to the fray. Although they knew the detective tried to believe in the goodness of people, he never lost sight of the evil that looms over the horizon. He did not even give God a break. He wanted to hold the Supreme Being accountable for all those who professed to be holy in His name, while covering up their immorality and crimes.

Chapter 7

As Max approached Tony's house, feelings of anxiety and respect came over him. There was no doubt that Detective Tony Pinella was a legend, but what if he could not do the job anymore? They had both gotten older, and Max was very aware how much even he had slowed down. Just rushing to the bathroom numerous times a day was enough to distract his attention for long periods of time. He always wanted to be sure that a rest room was close by—something his younger colleagues did not fail to notice!

At least, he laughed to himself, *Tony Pinella would understand!*

Tony greeted Max with a very warm handshake. Max thought Tony seemed much older than three years ago, the last time they had seen one another. But Max also recognized that he still had a twinkle in his eyes, indicating that this old detective still had his wits about him.

"It's good to see you, Max. Let me take your suitcase and come on in!"

Max could tell that Tony had done an enormous amount of research since their last phone call. There were neat piles of paper spread around the floor of the small living room, with sticky notes in different colors on top of each pile.

Tony set Max's suitcase down in a corner of the room. "You must be thirsty after your trip," he said. "Why don't you sit down on the couch, and I'll get us some lemonade. Or would you prefer coffee?"

"A cold lemonade would be great," Max answered.

Tony headed for the kitchen and quickly returned with a pitcher of lemonade and two frosted glasses. He placed the tray on the table in front of the couch, poured the lemonade, and sat down next to Max.

"Now let's get right to work," he said. "I'm looking forward to working with you on this case. Exactly what do you want from me?"

Max was glad to see Tony so eager. He took one large gulp of the lemonade.

"You got it, Detective. Basically, my research can only go so far. However, before we really dig in, I need to be sure. Do you really want to leave your retirement and get involved in a murder case? We'll be stirring up a lot of dirt and blowing it towards some important people. If I'm right, things could get pretty ugly."

Tony laughed, and then gave a big sigh before he spoke. "Look, I'm not sure that retirement is good for my health either! Since the O.J. Simpson case, former prosecutors, even judges, have been lining up for the television cameras and flooding the public with their shallow opinions. That's what's making my blood pressure go up."

"You certainly are right about that, Tony. As soon as they got a grip on television, they were determined to become permanent fixtures."

"Let's see if we can prevent the good Governor Green from becoming the next go-to expert," Tony said somberly. "I found your news quite troubling that Green had… let's call it *a very personal connection* to each of the three missing escorts. Of course, at this point, I'm not jumping to any conclusions. We certainly need to investigate this further. First, it's going to be very important to see if there are any patterns to the disappearances that link directly back to Green. And, of course, I'll need to be discreet."

"What else does your gut tell you?" Max asked.

"I can't say now. A case like this can go in so many different directions. What made it harder was that the missing escorts didn't use their real names. Now that we know who they really are, it will be easier to find them, or to know if anything has happened to them."

"There's still a lot of work ahead of us, Tony. Angela told me that, as far as she knew, all three escorts were pretty discreet about their personal lives. For the one woman whose disappearance she did report to the police, they concluded she had just moved on, and left it at that."

"Unfortunately, that would be the attitude of many police officers, especially the lazy ones. Until I can find some strong evidence that there was more than the escort service to connect the three women, and prove they all had the same link to the governor, they might still say it's just a coincidence."

Max pleaded with Tony for a better explanation. "Do you believe that it's just a coincidence that three escorts are missing at the same time? That no foul play is involved?"

"Not really," Tony said. "What I mean is that we have a lot of digging to do and could use a real break along the way."

"So you'll work with me on this?" Max asked.

"Try and stop me! Years of experience taught me that using coincidences as an explanation isn't an effective way to conduct police work. Like you, my gut tells me there's something else going on here. Let's see what we find out. At the very least, maybe the governor, or someone working for him, might have paid off the escorts who Angela says are missing."

"So where do we go from here?" Max asked.

"Let's follow all the leads we have. You might want to talk to Angela again, and I'll look deeper into Green's life.

Right now, I'll only travel if necessary. Otherwise, most of my work will be done in the comfort of my study. The most important thing is to stay discreet, as hard as that might be. If the governor is involved, and his cohorts get wind of our investigation before we have the solid evidence we need, the troops will gather around him—and our work will be in vain."

"Understood!" Max said.

After a couple of hours sifting through the paperwork Tony had gathered, it was more and more evident to Max that Tony was really on top of things. If there was a definite link to Morris Green, Tony would find it!

Tony stood up and stretched his back.

"We've been at it awhile, Max. It's just about time for dinner, and we never even ate lunch. I may not be a great cook, but my tuna salad is pretty good. How about it? I never gave you a chance to unpack after your trip. My extra bedroom is just down the hall, next to the bathroom. Why don't you take your suitcase in there, and meet me in about fifteen minutes or so."

"Thanks, Tony. I am hungry!"

When Max returned to the room, Tony had already set the small table in a dining area off the kitchen, and was just bringing in the food. Max was surprised at the sumptuous spread Tony had arranged.

"Now that's a tuna salad," he said. "Don't tell me you also baked that steaming Italian bread?"

"I cannot tell a lie," Tony said. "There's a great Italian bakery in town, and all I did was pop the already-baked bread into the oven for a few minutes. But the salad, now that was my own doing. Hope you like black olives. That's the way my grandmother used to make tuna salad. With black olives, fresh green, red, and yellow peppers, and just a hint of a strong mustard mixed with an Italian olive oil."

"Looks great! Let me at it," Max said with enthusiasm.

Max and Tony ate heartedly and caught up on some old acquaintances and friends. The camaraderie they shared brought Tony back to his early days on the police force, before he became such a loner. When they began discussing old cases, and the challenge they now faced about the missing escorts—and the potential link to Morris Green—Max and Tony realized there was no way to escape the truth. They had seen some of the most evil sides of human nature. They maintained their inner strength by learning to live one day at a time. Otherwise, the chaos in their lives would have destroyed their spirits.

When the conversation stopped, Max noticed that Tony seemed lost in thought. He looked up at Max with great sadness in his eyes.

"Who knows what the governor has done?" he asked.

Max nodded his head in agreement. He wondered if bringing Tony out of retirement was good for him, but not so good for Tony. At the same time, Max was grateful that he had the great Detective Pinella working with him on this disturbing case.

After they finished eating, Tony stood up and stretched.

"Okay, Max. Enough brooding for the day. Let me show you some of Newport. It's a nice peaceful town. In many ways it's paradise."

"Great! I would like that."

Chapter 8

Max and Tony spent the next couple of days reviewing all the information Tony had collected so far, and putting their plan of action together. Max knew that Tony was right. Morris Green had many powerful friends, including on the police force, who had much to gain by protecting him—and just as much to lose—if that link to the missing women was uncovered. If they were not discreet, not only would they be endangering their own lives, but Angela's as well. They needed to have solid evidence before making any direct accusations.

A few weeks after Max's visit, Tony received a telephone call from one of his trusted friends in the New York City Police Department. So far, all the investigations into the disappearance of the three young women had brought no worthwhile information. There had been no purchases on their credit cards, no contact with their acquaintances and friends, and no credible eyewitnesses who claimed to have seen them.

While all this was taking place, the former governor of New York was gaining confidence about a comeback. His wife Sally was beginning to show her face increasingly in public, and it seemed only a matter of time before the popular couple and their daughters returned to their prominent social circles.

On the other hand, Angela's life was not going as smoothly as she hoped. Although, at first, she had shied away from publicity, soon it became very clear to her that there was no way of stopping the constant chatter about her. That's when she began entertaining the possibility of a book contract, and was ready to sign on the dotted line for a very lucrative amount. Unfortunately, the publisher's office was in one of the several buildings owned by the governor's parents. When word got out about the potential book, it was easy for the elder Green to make sure the publisher withdrew his offer. Others followed suit, and the offers to Angela through her agent came to a rapid halt. Moreover, Angela's agent dropped her completely, stating there was not enough of a story to warrant his time and effort.

Angela was crushed. While she always had mixed feelings about being exploited for profit, she felt frustrated and angry that Morris Green and others like him always seemed to win. *Maybe someday,* she thought, *the truth would come out—and she hoped she would have some hand in telling it.* But how? Unless the real story became public, she feared she would also disappear—and there was no one who would even care or notice. She began to hyperventilate and her heart pounded with fear mixed with anger.

The Laughing Angels loved this. They were proud of how the rich and powerful were able to manipulate events and people. Nothing and no one was too sacred for them to destroy. They cackled with delight. Poor Angela was no longer confident she could make it on her own. So much had gone wrong in her life, and there was no question she had wasted a great amount of her potential. Maybe now she would understand what the Laughing Angels thought all along—that being a good and loving person would not pay off.

The Righteous Ones thought Angela deserved another chance. This time, they pleaded on her behalf to God. He did not appear to be listening and their request was not even acknowledged. It did not matter that their tone revealed a sense of urgency, that they even raised their voices, seemingly unafraid of offending the Supreme Being—something that was very unlike the Righteous Ones.

They continued their vigil. Angela's survival was very close to their hearts. It disturbed them how the powerful would usually get all the assistance they needed, and those like Angela would be allowed to flounder and ultimately fail. Like Angela, the Righteous Ones were feeling so invisible and powerless. Few, if any, suspected they were considering a revolution against the Almighty. The poor, downtrodden, and powerless were all part of the faceless people. How could the Righteous Ones abandon them, even if God turned the other way?

The Laughing Angels felt vindicated and were about to celebrate, when out of nowhere came that familiar thunderous noise and bright light. They looked at Angela and saw that she was no longer breathless, and even had a confident smile on her face. She was reciting the prayer of mourning, not for a relative or a friend, but for herself. Angela was burying her old life as an escort—and as a victim.

For the first time in a long time, it was the Righteous Ones' turn to rejoice!

Chapter 9

The governor was feeling strong again, confident that all the bad press was behind him. He was eager to be interviewed by friendly reporters and sympathetic radio and television show hosts. He now proudly roamed the streets of New York without a worry, going to his favorite restaurants with his lovely and devoted wife by his side. His eldest daughter was back in her social sphere, no longer sitting alone, crying in her room.

Tony and Max knew that it was likely Morris Green had gotten away with a crime. Angela had been trafficked out of state for the purpose of prostitution. No matter what the governor claimed, he broke the law and should have been prosecuted. Instead, he was regaining his influence and distancing himself more and more from his so-called weak moment of disloyalty to his wife and family.

All this, while Tony and Max worked in the shadows, following up on any information they could find on the three missing escorts. Their first lead came two weeks later, when Max saw a police report out of Chicago. Stephanie Taylor, age twenty three, was found beaten, strangled and stabbed to death in her studio apartment on the 5800 block of North Kenmore Street in Chicago, Illinois. From the little evidence they found, the police thought it was a robbery or a relationship gone terribly wrong.

Tom Hoffman, the manager of the building, had told the detectives that Stephanie had been living there for the past three months. She was working full-time at a small local bookstore on Illinois Street in Downtown Chicago, and taking a couple of evening courses at Roosevelt University, also downtown. From all indications, and so far as he could see, Stephanie lived a somewhat quiet life, juggling her time between her job and school. He did not recall her having any visitors. But about a week or so ago, he recalled someone came around asking whether she was a tenant in the building. All he could remember was that it was someone wearing jeans and a hooded sweatshirt. Pressed by the police, Hoffman admitted that he was busy picking up a pile of junk on the curb outside the building from an overturned garbage can.

"I barely looked up at the person," Hoffman said. "I just said *yes* and went on working. Maybe if I'd paid more attention that poor young woman would be alive."

Right now, there were more questions than answers. Hoffman's working with a police artist on a sketch was a total failure. He could not even recall if it was a man or woman, or what the voice sounded like. It was clear, Hoffman would be an unreliable witness, and based on the time of death and Hoffman's confirmed alibi, he was ruled out as a suspect.

Something about the report bothered Max and he showed the photo of Stephanie to Angela. "That's her! That's my friend Joni," she cried.

At this point, only Max, Tony, and Angela knew the truth. Stephanie was Joni's real name, and one of the three Leslie had given to Max. She was one of the escorts that had dated Morris Green.

In times like this, the Laughing Angels loved to roam the universe with very self-satisfied looks on their faces. All the talk about how the powerful would pay for their crimes was a big joke to them. *Only a fool, or one who was willing to ignore all rational evidence,* they thought, *could believe the justice system was fair.*

The Laughing Angels and the Righteous Ones saw the world from their own vantage points. While they both saw human nature creating conflict and chaos, the Righteous Ones continued to believe in the possibility of the soul's beauty and goodness. Even when they were angered by God's refusal to intercede, they truly believed that God created a world where everything is possible—good and evil.

Chapter 10

Max was pleased when Tony decided to take a six-month rental in the Bensonhurst section of Brooklyn, New York. Even with all the modern tools of communication, both of them knew very well that Newport, Rhode Island, was not the ideal place from where to conduct Tony's research and to investigate Stephanie's murder, nor what happened to the two remaining missing escorts. Tony also needed to be in New York, where the governor and his family still lived, and where the escort service had been operating before it was closed down. Moreover, he could keep a low profile and still have access to certain members of the New York City Police Department, something that Max had to avoid in order to keep his fellow journalists from thinking something was up. His meetings and discussions with Tony were planned in a clandestine manner, sort of a cloak and dagger situation. This was Max's story and he intended to keep it that way, at least for right now. Angela's life, and his and Tony's lives depended on it.

On the day of Tony's move, Max was guest speaker for a journalism class in Poughkeepsie, New York. He had been invited by Professor Audrey Wilson, an old friend, who turned to teaching after a very long and esteemed career as political reporter for *The New York Daily News.*

While the students were interested in his older articles about evangelist Jason Blake and basketball star Jack Molinas, they were more curious about Max's more recent articles on Morris Green.

One student was particularly perceptive. "What's the common thread to all these stories?" asked Connie Fabrizio.

"They all gave me horrible nightmares." Max answered without a smile. It was obvious to the students he was serious.

"Why is that?" another student called out.

"Each of them had so much potential," Max answered, "but seemed never able to overcome their evil inclinations."

"What do you mean by that?" Connie asked.

"They all believed that rules do not apply to them. Morris Green's case is the highest form of hypocrisy. When Governor Green was New York State's attorney general, he was a merciless prosecutor, punishing others for breaking the same law he is guilty of—and they all paid a heavy price."

"That's nothing new," Connie said with some resignation. "The rich and the powerful get away with so much. It's pretty difficult to believe in the fairness of the justice system."

Max smiled. He knew it would be hard to argue that point—and the murmurs of her classmates around the room showed that they obviously agreed with Connie. On one hand, Max was gratified to see that these young men and women would not be easily swayed by the words of the powerful and rich. He could only hope, when they went on with their careers in journalism, they would stay strong enough to draw a heavy line between the rhetoric spewed by most politicians—and the truth behind their words. But Max also realized he had to be careful not to hint that there was more to come in the Morris Green situation. These students were smart, and the last thing he and Tony needed was for one of these budding journalists to start asking questions that might draw him into accidentally saying too much.

The questions kept on coming and no one seemed bored with neither the answers nor the exchanges. As Max often told colleagues, "There is nothing like speaking to journalism students. They still need to believe in the objectivity of the press, and the possibility of making a difference. And so do I!"

The next comment and question came from Audrey Wilson. "Let's bring the discussion back to the Morris Green situation," she said. "I'm curious. What do you think, Max? Do you think he'll make a political comeback?"

Max responded cautiously. *Keep it light,* he thought to himself. "It's unlikely," he said. "But one never really knows with politicians. I've underestimated them in the past. My guess is that one of these days we'll see Morris Green hosting a talk show, probably with a pretty co-host at his side. Then, who knows? Maybe he'll throw his hat back into the political ring."

There was a mix of agonizing groans and sarcastic laughter in the room. It was obvious to Max that these astute students, and their professor, knew that he was right on target about the talk shows. This painful awareness of how the world works was a constant challenge to their idealism.

All eyes turned to Audrey Wilson as her laughter stopped and she fixed her eyes on Max. "I've heard from a good source that Tony Pinella, who broke the Blake murder case, is looking into a Chicago murder that might tie back to the same escort service where Angela Robinson worked. Do you know anything about this, Max?"

Max was not sure how to respond to Audrey's question. Any information that came out too soon would seriously jeopardize the work Tony and Max were doing, as well as Angela's life.

How Audrey knew about Tony's role was a mystery to Max—and of concern. He could only guess that, despite all their caution, some of Tony's nosing around had already rattled some very powerful people. Maybe someone who was close in some way to the professor.

Audrey waited for an answer, and then repeated her question. "So, Max? What do you think? Is there some connection?"

"I'm sorry, but I really can't answer that question."

"Is that because you don't know the answer?"

Max spoke more emphatically than he intended. "I didn't say that! It's just something I'm not in a position to discuss."

Not to be dissuaded from her question, Audrey persisted. "Come on Max. We're all colleagues here. When do you think you might be able to talk about it?"

The students listened attentively and were surprised, as well as mesmerized, by their professor's boldness. Max seemed to be glaring at her. Then he spoke slowly, and very deliberately. "Now, *Professor*, you know very well that a good journalist is careful what they say about an ongoing investigation. We need to be sure about our facts. At this point, I don't have an answer for you."

Audrey stood up and looked around the room with a wry smile. "Well class, let this be a lesson to all of you. Not all questions are answered, sometimes with good reason. But that's no excuse not to ask them. You still learn something. For example, our esteemed guest did not deny that Tony Pinella is involved in the investigation. He merely said the investigation is ongoing."

Audrey had made her point. On that note, the discussion ended to great applause from the eager students. Max thanked the class, shook hands with Audrey Wilson, and made his exit.

As he left the school, Max could not help thinking about Audrey's questions. She had good instincts, and she certainly sensed there was more to the Morris Green story than Max was willing to tell. He and Tony already suspected there was an association between Stephanie Taylor's murder and Governor Green. Could there also be something more sinister behind Green's resignation? Was it more than a personal crisis? Could there be some sort of national security implications? Was he putting his own life in danger? He would have to be more careful if anyone else asked him about Tony, or about Stephanie Taylor's murder.

Max did not sleep well that night.

Chapter 11

The next morning Max called Tony and told him about his intense session with the students. He was worried his enthusiasm might have caused him to say too much.

Tony laughed. "I understand your dilemma. I always felt that way after you interviewed me during the Blake case!" He chuckled a bit more. "Don't worry about Professor Wilson. When you mentioned you were going to speak to her class, I checked her out and she's clean as a whistle where the governor is concerned. She was a great journalist and interviewed me several times during the Blake investigation. She most likely assumed we knew each other. You handled her just fine. Like you, I think there is a link between Stephanie Wilson's murder, the escort service, and Governor Green's resignation. But it's too soon to make that public."

When he got off the phone with Max, Tony began mumbling to himself. He did that often when he was alone, trying to keep his mind open—and maintain a fresh outlook on the investigation. He did not want his assessment of the situation and the evidence to have any boundaries.

Tony had his own nightmares. He saw the faceless people everywhere. That's one of the reasons he was so eager to assist Max in this case. Looking at the world, especially in his golden years, Tony grew increasingly angry about how the rich and powerful, especially politicians always got their way. They had no interest in living on an even playing field with the average public.

The voices of the Laughing Angels taunted him frequently. "Why should politicians look at the faceless people," they sang. "After all, the powerful are so good at covering up their tracks and misdeeds. If necessary, they can always hide behind religious pronouncements and prayers. Why waste your time trying to change reality?"

How they loved skirmishing with Tony. Now he had a new murder to solve, and he would challenge the Laughing Angels as few could. The Morris Green investigation held even more promise for the Laughing Angels than the Jason Blake case.

Tony was more determined than ever not to let the Laughing Angels win. He was back in the fray, standing up for all those faceless people—and that kept him strong. He remembered vividly what life was like when he was searching for the murderer of Veronica Blake, wife of evangelist Jason Blake. All the twists and turns, for so long never seeing any glimmer of hope. Finally, his persistence, as well as a few lucky breaks, gave him the answers he needed to find the murderer.

Tony was unwavering in his confidence. There would be justice for Stephanie Taylor. She would not be faceless. The Laughing Angels would not win, even if it took Tony's last breath.

Chapter 12

Max wanted to be sure that he kept the heat on Morris Green, while keeping his and Tony's suspicions a secret. He began writing a series of exposés and opinion pieces on how Morris Green and his multimillionaire parents were getting involved in a variety of charities, particularly religion-based charities—Catholic, Jewish, and Protestant groups. Large donations were also going to major health care associations and hospitals, all eager to send out press releases about their good fortune, and, of course, lavishing praises on Morris Green. Even several well-known evangelists were on the Greens' donations list. After all, didn't they preach the loudest about forgiveness?

Morris Green appeared on their nationally televised sermons and local special events in New York, pleading for mercy and understanding. At the local events, with his wife and daughters at his side, Green challenged the people of New York to overlook his imperfections and think of all the good he had accomplished on their behalf as both attorney general and governor. That the good done by him and his administration to weed out crime and punish the guilty far outweighed any harm caused by his personal transgressions. His family, who had been hurt the most, forgave him. God forgave him. Would not the people forgive him?

Max was personally outraged at Green's epitome of *chutzpah* at these events. He knew that Morris Green never believed any of his actions were mistakes or poor judgment, as he liked to call them. Green's only real regret was being caught.

Max's columns followed every event. He challenged the public to see through the charades, to see how it was only greed that convinced charity executives to overlook the so-called transgressions of the ex-governor. For many of the charities, less than twenty percent of the money donated made its way to support the actual goals of the charity —whether it was medical research, education, or help for the poor and downtrodden. The rest of the money went to pay for the high salaries of executives, fancy cars, and a variety of other perks.

Charity board members also enjoyed the prestige of inviting friends to lavish luncheons and black-tie only award galas, honoring the Greens for their generosity, and hoping the attendees would donate their own money—in addition to the five hundred dollars or more they paid for their dinner tickets.

Green's parents, along with Morris Green and his wife and daughters, were always at center stage to accept their awards, with the eager press following close behind them.

In his most recent column, Max wrote that Morris Green considered himself fortunate to be created in God's image. He believed his actions could not negate this fact. After all, there was never any intention on his part to cause distress and shame for his family and his followers.

In his heart, Max felt that, like God, Morris Green did not want to be held accountable for his actions.

Some readers attacked Max for his lack of compassion for the Green family. One reader wrote: *As a society, we have a responsibility to honor the rich and be thankful for their generosity.* A few elaborated and complained that he was *too tough on the pillars of society.* One claimed to know that Max had skeletons in his own closet.

Max's editor was glad to see that the piece struck a cord with readers, and supported him. When a major advertiser complained about the column, she did not retract it, but asked Max to write a rebuttal, which he did:

Max Gold, Crime Reporter Responds to Readers' Comments

I appreciated all the comments from readers following my recent columns on Morris Green. While many agreed with me, it seems I hit a real sore spot with just as many readers, especially for those affiliated with charities that have dinners to honor the rich for their generosity.

Yes, there are many fine charities and generous donors in our society who do an honorable job of giving shelter to the homeless, feeding the poor, and supporting critical health care research. But there are many more who hold large, expensive and lavish events, who also pay their executives outrageous salaries and fund-raising bonuses—instead of using the larger percentage of donated money to help the poor, the downtrodden, and the sick—to directly support the work of the charities they represent!

Too often, it doesn't even seem relevant who is being honored, or whether or not they came by their wealth honestly. The executive directors of these charities, along with their boards of directors, rarely ask the questions that might stand in the way of collecting the checks, or that might cause donors to cancel their pledges.

It's been said that if Hitler had given money to certain members of the clergy, they might have given dinners in his honor! Think about it.... While horrific atrocities were taking place all around them, didn't Hitler gain the silence of some churches and their leaders just by offering his protection? Power and status were more important than the lives of the innocent.

Yes, some may take offense at my words, and have even threatened me. But, as a journalist, it's my responsibility to the public, and to myself, to dig for the truth. Because as long as I'm writing this column, I will not stop speaking out on the important issues of the day. I will not be intimidated by charity directors and their privileged board members, politicians, and others, who feel offended by the truth.

Please remember, before you donate to a cause in your honor or the honor of a loved one, before you buy that dinner ticket to see a celebrity or politician honored, look closely at what percentage of each dollar actually goes to directly fund the charity's purpose—and how much is paid in salaries or other perks to administrators and board members. Also keep in mind that some very wealthy and powerful people will try to take attention away from their scandalous behaviors by making large donations to charities—hoping to regain their lost respectability.

When a charity representative comes to you during a time of grief, they know you're vulnerable. If you want a deceased friend or family member to be eulogized or honored, don't you want it to be truly because your donation helped to do more for society than to help the organization's director live a luxurious lifestyle? Or to support the hidden agenda of the person being honored at a dinner?

Some may say I'm being unreasonable and unfair. No doubt this column will result in more angry letters and threats. But I'm trusting that even more people in our fine community will be as outraged as I am, and may write that I haven't gone far enough in my criticism. To the latter I say, don't worry—I have lots more to say on this issue, and I will!

Chapter 13

Tony was drinking his morning coffee as he read Max's rebuttal. His head began to pound and he felt a heavy pain in his chest. Although Tony agreed with most of what Max had written, he also realized there was no escape from the realities Max described with such obvious anguish. With all Max's good intentions, Tony knew that the powerful would continue in their *goodness charade*, as he called it. *Why,* he thought, *would anyone expect anything different?*

Tony needed a break. He poured a fresh cup of coffee, and went outside for some fresh air. As he sat on the stoop of his temporary Bensonhurst apartment building, many wonderful memories of his youth returned. Unlike other neighborhoods, Bensonhurst had not changed much. He watched as boys still played on the street. In Tony's time, it was stickball. He recalled those days with a joy, when the younger and older boys played sports together. How the older kids were kind, helpful, and generous with their time, always including Tony and his friends in the games. Sports on West 12th Street were a prelude to adulthood. Anyone from the neighborhood who wanted to participate was given the opportunity to play. It was different now. The world's playing field was not even close to equal. Too many were taken advantage of by the powerful and rich, who had their own agendas—goals that were far from charitable.

Tony wished he could turn back the clock. *There must be a way,* he thought, *to retrieve the past without threatening the present.* Names of friends and neighbors from the early years came rushing back to him. Neighbors worked hard to earn a living, yet still found ways to help each other.

Harry's father was a tailor. Steven's mother and grandmother knitted blankets for every new baby on the block. After high school graduation, Steven opened a small clothing store, and now owned franchises of *Steve's Clothing to Go* throughout the North and South East. John's father and mother owned the local pizza parlor and gave out free slices to the children whose parents couldn't afford such treats. John inherited the business and added more space for what is now the popular *Bensonhurst's Homestyle Italian Cuisine*—bringing people from Manhattan, and even as far as Upstate New York, to Bensonhurst on Friday and Saturday nights. It takes weeks to get a reservation! Mary went to City College and now is a professor of economics at Hunter College. Mary's sister, who always loved bright clothes and red lipstick, stunned the neighborhood when she became a nun. Sarah's father owned the *Supernosh Kosher Bakery*, and her mother treated all children on the block to delicious fruit-filled Hamantaschen cookies every Purim. Every week, her father brought bags of bagels, rolls, and bread to the local charities that helped feed the poor. Sarah is a well-respected doctor at a large hospital, and had opened a free clinic for the homeless in lower Manhattan.

Tony sat on that step with tears in his eyes as he remembered how all the parents on the block—most of them immigrants, or the children of immigrants, from Italy and throughout Eastern Europe. Children were taught the importance of learning and earning a living, and the beauty of friendship and helping their neighbors—and, yes, giving charity to the needy.

It did not matter that for more than twenty years, he had not seen even one of them. A strong emotional bond still existed. Tony thought how those days helped shape how he viewed the world. Those early friendships from his youth formed memories and life's lessons that remained in his heart and mind forever.

Their lives are part my legacy, Tony thought. *A legacy that cannot be broken.*

Tony yelled out, "What if Morris Green's world began sitting on a stoop in Bensonhurst? Not in the halls of private schools, ivy league colleges, and social events closed to all but the wealthy."

❧

The Laughing Angels were amused when Tony looked around to see if anyone heard his outburst! Even they worried if he was crazy altogether! After all, wouldn't most people trade places with Morris Green and choose to live a life of privilege and wealth? Being successful and rich should not make anyone feel guilty. After all, isn't God impressed by those who claim to be self-made, as long as they give thanks to *Him* for all their blessings?

The Righteous Ones looked upon Tony with tears in their eyes. They understood the pain and frustration he was feeling at that moment. Tony lived by the old saying that *if you save one life, you save the world.* It was one of the reasons he went into law enforcement—to help people. As a young officer, he worked closely with youthful offenders, trying to show them there was hope for a better life. Nevertheless, the Righteous Ones also knew there were far too many in the world who thought just like the Laughing Angels.

The Laughing Angels roared with laughter at how this once-great detective's mind twisted and turned. They rejoiced that Tony was not the only one carrying so much baggage. Max was also a wounded soul. Neither Tony nor Max could ever go back to their youthful and blind idealism—no matter how much the Righteous Ones prayed at God's throne.

Chapter 14

Another missing escort was found murdered. This time in Paradise Valley, considered one of the finer neighborhoods bordering Scottsdale, Arizona. Valerie Powell was found on her twenty-third birthday in the apartment she shared with Nancy, her twin sister.

Max obtained a photo and showed it to Angela.

"Yes," she said with tears welling up in her eyes. Valerie was *Vickie*. Another escort who Angela was sure had spent time with Morris Green.

According to the police report, Nancy Powell said she went straight home from her job as a nurse at Paradise Valley Hospital. She was very excited about the birthday dinner she had planned for her twin sister and their mutual friends.

Nancy told the police, "When I arrived home, the apartment was very quiet. I expected to hear music playing and Valerie singing. Val loves to sing," she said, and began to sob. "She always sings while getting ready to go out. I called out for her, and when she didn't answer, I just knew that something was very wrong. It wasn't like Valerie not to be primping for our celebration—and I knew she wouldn't just leave the apartment without leaving me a note."

Nancy's worst fears were realized when she found Valerie lying in the master bathroom, in a pool of blood with a knife in her chest. A neighbor, Estelle Shipman, who lived down the hall, heard Nancy's screams and ran to see what was happening. As she banged on the door to the apartment, she could hear Nancy crying out for help. Nancy told the detectives she remembers staggering to the door and opening it, before collapsing into Estelle's arms.

Shipman said Nancy was crying hysterically, "Please, please call 911! My sister, my sister. Someone killed my sister!"

According to the newspaper, when Detective David Kagan questioned Shipman, she said the girls were always very quiet and polite. She knew that Nancy was a nurse and generally left the apartment very early in the morning, always returning about four or five o'clock in the afternoon. She thought Valerie worked as a model or some important executive job where she had to travel.

"She always dressed in the latest styles and traveled frequently, even on weekends. And there was always a chauffeured limousine to pick her up," Shipman said. "I noticed her clothes because they were in such contrast to Nancy's, who was either in her nurse's uniform or jeans. Neither of the girls entertained much at home," she added. "And, when they did, it was usually with a group of young women their own age."

When Max told Tony about Valerie Powell, Tony called David Kagan immediately. David and Tony had worked together on the Veronica Blake murder and the scandal that surrounded it. That had been an arduous battle and had a deep emotional impact on both of them. Shortly after the Blake trials were over, David decided he had enough of city living in Detroit, and moved to Paradise Valley, Arizona.

He told Pinella, "I've had enough of the snow and ice. It's time for some palm trees and desert sun!"

Although he planned to retire, David's reputation for being an ace detective made him a welcome addition to the Paradise Valley Police Department as an independent *on-call* investigator.

David's phone rang just as he was reading his own words about the Valerie Powell murder in *The Arizona Republic.*

"Hey, old buddy… How would you like a hot lead on the Powell case?"

When Tony told him about the potential connection to Governor Morris Green, David said cheerfully, "I think you could use a little sunshine, Tony. How about coming out to the Valley of the Sun? It will be Kagan and Pinella again, fighting corruption and solving crimes."

Two days later, Tony was on an early morning flight to Arizona. The sooner he met up with David, the sooner they could wrap the noose around Morris Green's neck!

It was during the long plane ride that Tony thought about getting in touch with Arizona award winning investigative journalist, Janice Crawford.

Based on Crawford's articles and several books on crimes involving women, as well as her interest in Arizona politics and knowledge of the Phoenix area, Tony knew there was no better person to assist in his investigation of this latest murder. He respected David's investigative abilities, and had confidence in his own skills, but the potential for politics interfering was always a possibility.

Crawford was known for her intense research and had her own resources. Her book, *Murders on the Reservation*, won awards because she dug more deeply into the evidence than the original investigators. It was Crawford who proved that the original suspect, who was convicted and sentenced to death, was actually innocent. She finally solved the case by showing how some very powerful local politicians had manipulated the evidence. Crawford had solid personal contacts within City Hall, and she knew how to get information that would never turn up, even during the most intensive investigation.

Tony thought it would not take much convincing to gain Crawford's help. After all, the potential link between Governor Green and the escorts had all the makings of a true crime book—politicians, hypocrisy, corruption, sex, murder, and, possibly, one of the greatest political cover-ups of modern times. He got goose bumps just thinking about the possibilities.

Better yet, Tony thought as he dozed off, *I'll write the book myself!*

The Laughing Angels rode right alongside Tony, roaring with laughter at the thought of this cantankerous old detective writing a book. They wondered if they would have a feature role in his current case, just as they had in *The Salvation Peddler*. They snuggled up close to Pinella as he slept, to whisper in his ear. But he was busy dreaming of his portrait on the back cover of the book jacket, and what he would write as he autographed thousands of copies.

In Tony's dream, he was just about to have his photograph taken next to Richard Crenna, who would portray Tony in the movie, when he was awakened by the voice of the flight captain: "Welcome to Phoenix and the beautiful Valley of the Sun. The time is twelve noon and the temperature at the airport is 106 degrees."

"Boy, it's hotter than hell in this town," Tony mumbled as he exited the plane and was hit by a blast of the hot desert air. He headed straight to the nearest men's room, and then to the baggage claim area, where it was a twenty-minute wait for his suitcase. Finally, bags in hand, Tony headed to the taxi line for another twenty-minute wait.

The plan was for Tony to meet David at his apartment in Scottsdale, not far from the murder crime scene and the Paradise Valley Police Department's headquarters. Tony wanted to stay at a hotel near the airport, but David had suggested he stay at his large, three-bedroom apartment.

Tony would have the privacy of his own room, and they could share David's home office. Tony also could easily walk around Old Town Scottsdale or the nearby Scottsdale Fashion Center, when he got restless—something David also remembered Tony liked doing when embroiled on a difficult case. Tony hesitated, but when David insisted, Tony did not have the heart to deny his request. He sensed that David seemed to want the company—and they had been great friends back in the day, sharing more than a few life and death experiences.

Finally, he was second behind a group of six people, and Tony was directed to the third cab on line. His carry-on hanging off his shoulder, and lugging his larger bag behind him, Tony mumbled to himself how much he hated traveling. He grumbled even more when the taxi driver did not even get out of the cab. He just popped open the trunk and waited for Tony to lift his own heavy suitcase. Once inside the cab, Tony rolled up the windows in the back seat and asked the driver to put on the air conditioner.

"Don't work," the driver answered in an abrupt manner. "Where to?"

After whispering a few more obscenities under his breath and re-opening the back seat windows, Tony said, "Just take me to the Cibola Apartments on East Chaparral Road in Scottsdale."

David was standing outside the building when the taxi arrived. He greeted Tony with a big hug, and then retrieved the suitcase from the taxi's trunk. When the driver told Tony the fare was twenty-six dollars, Tony counted out the exact amount and handed it through the window on the driver's side. "Next time, get your butt out of the car to help with the suitcase—and fix your damn air conditioner!" he said.

David laughed. *That was Tony,* he thought. *Just like old times.*

As soon as David opened the door to his apartment, Tony felt a blast of nice cold air. "That cool air sure feels good. Damn it, Kagan!" he joked. "Why didn't you tell me it was so hot in Arizona?"

"It's the desert, Tony," David laughed. "What did you expect? Snow flurries? Listen, old buddy. You've had a long trip, so let's get your bags inside, and I'll get you a cold drink to sip while you unpack. You even have your own bathroom. Why don't you get out of those hot clothes and cool off in a nice long shower. We can talk over a snack. We've got a lot of work ahead of us, and we're expected at headquarters later today."

"That sounds good to me, except for the *old* part!" Tony said as he pretended to take a punch at David.

After Tony showered and put on a pair of lightweight pants and a shirt, they sat down in the small dining area where David had put out a platter of bagels, lox, coleslaw, and cream cheese, one of Tony's New York favorites—and super-strong coffee.

"I got the bagels at *New York Bagels,*" so you would feel at home, David said.

With one hand on a bagel and the other reaching for the coleslaw, Tony said, "This is perfect! Thanks, Kagan. And thanks for remembering I like coleslaw on my lox! Now tell me about the case. I'm eager to get started!"

While they ate, David updated Tony on the Valerie Powell murder case. Tony could not help thinking how good it was to see David again. As well as hoping to solve the Chicago and Paradise Valley escort murders, and maybe linking both cases directly to Morris Green, Tony made a mental note to stay in touch with David after the job was over.

David looked at his watch. "We better head over to the Paradise Valley Police Department. You need to meet Police Captain Juanita Lopez. She's personally supervising the case at your police commissioner's request."

"Sounds good to me," Tony said. "I've heard good things about her. I understand the commissioner knew Lopez back when she was a rookie cop."

"That's the story. She's good. A real no-nonsense professional whose earned a lot of respect around here. I'm sure you'll like her. I'm also sure she's done a pretty thorough background check on you! She knew we had worked together on the Blake case, even before I was told our departments had formally arranged to join forces on this case."

"Well, then, I guess we better be on our best behavior," Tony laughed.

After the short ride to the police station, Tony and David went straight to Captain Lopez's office, where Tony received a warm welcome.

"I'm very happy to meet you Detective Pinella," Captain Lopez said as she shook Tony's hand.

"Thank you, Captain Lopez. I really appreciate the opportunity to work with David, I mean Detective Kagan, and I'm eager to get started."

"Please... sit down. "

Captain Lopez gestured for Tony and David to take a seat at the small conference table in the Captain's office.

"I know Detective Kagan is anxious for you to see the crime scene. So I won't keep you too long. I just want all our cards on the table. It's not often we have an opportunity to work in concert with the NYPD. I've heard good things about you, Detective Pinella, and have worked long enough with Kagan to feel confident that both of you are highly dedicated to the truth. By that I mean, I feel secure that neither of you will take any shortcuts during the investigation that might jeopardize its outcome. There can be nothing that comes back to haunt us in court. The potential link of the two murders to a political motive means that all eyes will be on us—and I don't mean just by the press and public."

In a very firm voice, Captain Lopez went on to explain. "While Paradise Valley has its share of escort services, along with our Scottsdale neighbor, we're not exactly the murder capitals of the country. City officials from both towns are concerned that this murder—and the fact that Valerie Powell was an escort—might hurt the area's popularity as a family vacation spot. That said, I strongly caution you both to tread carefully, especially if any of our own politicians or community leaders were involved with Valerie Powell."

Captain Lopez leaned across the table and looked at David.

"Kagan, I want to be straight with you. When my commanding officer told me about his call from Police Commissioner Sean Brennan, he asked what I thought about having Detective Pinella work with us. At first, I wasn't sure. This case might be loaded with political dynamite that could blow up both our careers. I've gone out on a limb to agree to Detective Pinella's intervention on this case, so I'm trusting both of you to handle the interviews delicately and with the utmost discretion. Bottom line, I want the truth. And I want you to get at that truth in a way that will allow a successful prosecution of whomever is responsible for Valerie Powell's murder."

David looked earnestly at Captain Lopez. "You can count on us, Captain. We won't let you down."

"Okay, then, we're all set. Detective Pinella, nice to have you on our team. Go to it. Just keep me in the loop so there are no surprises."

After they left Captain Lopez's office, David took Tony to the crime scene and briefed him further on the evidence gathered by the CSI team. By the time they left Valerie's apartment building, the sun was just beginning to set. David could see that the long flight, desert heat, and time change had taken its toll on Tony.

"It's been a long day for both of us. How about we head back to my apartment and call it a night?"

"Good idea," Tony answered.

When they returned to the apartment, David asked Tony if he were hungry. "I can rustle up some grilled cheese sandwiches and a salad, or grill some fish out on the terrace."

"Thanks, David. You go ahead and make something for yourself. To tell you the truth, I'm kinda tired. If you don't mind, I'm gonna finish unpacking, take another shower, and hit the sack early. But thanks again for everything. I'm sure glad to be here instead of a hotel. It's great to be working with you again."

David sensed a bit of sentimentality in Tony's voice. "It's good to see you, too, my friend. Get some sleep. We've got quite a day ahead of us."

Chapter 15

Tony was tired, but his mind was racing. He remembered his first meeting with the famous evangelist, Jason Blake. From the outset, Tony believed that Blake was responsible for the death of his wife Veronica. In all likelihood, Tony thought, Blake had hired someone to do the job. He was not the type to get his own hands dirty.

Despite its successful outcome, this case was not Tony's finest moment. Over and over again, he had been fooled by the young and beguiling Stacey Johnson—who had married Jason Blake not long after Veronica's murder.

It was easy to be suspicious of Jason Blake. Although he had been one of the greatest evangelists of his time, he was rarely viewed as a sympathetic character. Many outside his ministry considered Blake to be a charlatan and not trustworthy. Reaching the truth in his wife's murder had been a painful and introspective journey for Tony, and the most difficult case of his career. When the evidence finally fell into place, it became obvious to Tony that Stacey had played all of them. She changed Tony's life forever, and although he did not know it yet, Stacey—who was serving time in a mental institution for the criminally insane—would continue to play a role in Tony's life, even as the Morris Green investigation grew deeper and darker.

Tomorrow would be another long day, but one that Tony was eager to start. He was so glad to be working once again with David Kagan. David and his brother Steve shared a special talent when it came to mediating violent situations. They were both police officers in Detroit, Michigan. At different times during their careers, they both also had worked under Tony. He drove them hard, because he knew they had what it took to be great detectives, but also needed some serious experience to hone their investigative skills. The brothers were grateful for how much Tony taught them, and not just about policing.

The three men became close friends, always striving to bring pride to their families, to the Detroit community, and to the Detroit Police Department.

Tony had also grown close to David and Steve's parents. Rhoda and Charles had worked very hard in their small luncheonette. It was a local gathering place where people who worked in the area went for their morning coffee, neighborhood friends stopped for lunch, and even the teens stopped for a soda after school. The Kagans focused on providing their sons with a secure life and a good education. Faith also played an important role for the Kagans. Both boys went to Sunday school so they could learn more about Judaism and be prepared for their Bar Mitzvahs when each turned thirteen.

In their free time, which was not in abundance, the boys would help out in the store. They were a source of great joy and *nachas* to their parents. That pride grew even greater when both their sons decided to join the police force. They were especially glad to know that Tony was such a positive influence on their sons. For Tony, it was a home away from home. The Kagans were so much like his own parents. They treated him like a son, and David and Steve were like kid brothers to him.

Then came the news that shattered the Kagan family, and cut deeply into Tony's heart. Two fourteen-year-old girls were taken hostage by a deranged man who had been hiding just outside the Blessed Mary Catholic High School. He had surprised and grabbed both girls just as they were leaving the school after choir practice. It was at the end of a short winter day and the school was surrounded by darkness.

Steve was on patrol just down the street and saw some students running from the school, screaming for help. He immediately called for backup, but when he saw there were hostages in imminent danger, Steve's instincts took over. He knew he had to act quickly. Waiting for backup was not an option. He carefully approached and took a shot—aiming for the man's left shoulder so the girls would not be hit. His shot hit its mark, wounding the man just enough so he let go of the girls, who quickly ran to safety.

Before Steve could get another shot off, the hostage-taker got a clear view of Steve, and his aim was solid. Steve was killed instantly by a bullet that went straight through his heart. A heart that was mighty enough to save the lives of the two girls, who would now live to enjoy another day. A heart that beat inside a hero, killed in the line of duty.

The synagogue service brought together residents from throughout the community, along with friends, fellow officers, as well as officers from all over the state. The two girls Steve saved came with their parents—all to express their appreciation and sympathy. They mourned him like he was one of their own.

As Tony finally dozed off, the Laughing Angels danced around his bed. Morris Green might be the most formidable challenge ever faced by Tony. The detective was good, but influential politicians like Green might be better! He was powerful, and just as others like him, the governor had the remarkable talent of surviving one scandal after another. Political despots were never afraid of judgment day. They paid lip service to the Supreme Being, only as a tool to keep others from knowing their true natures.

The Righteous Ones prayed that Tony had not met his match—that once again he would find the inner strength to achieve justice.

Chapter 16

Unknown to Tony, Stacey Johnson Blake knew all about the escort disappearances and murders. During these many years, although still restricted to her room, she had grown calm enough to have limited privileges. She was allowed to send and receive mail, and to read books and newspapers brought to her room by an attendant from the institutional library. The only restriction was that her mail had to be carefully read by her psychiatrist before it was posted.

Stacey was captivated by the news and had her own theories about the case—and the involvement of Governor Morris Green and his family. But on this evening, she grew especially restless when she read that her old *friendly nemesis* (as she called him), Tony Pinella, was on the case. This was the first time in years she wished she were free, working side-by-side with Tony, instead of trying to trip him up at every turn.

Stacey could not sleep. Although it was after ten o'clock, she sat down at the small table next to her bed, and using only the small night lamp composed a letter. She described her observations and dream-like visions about the escort murders. She placed the six-page letter into an envelope, and sealed it. Then addressed it to Detective Tony Pinella.

She shut the light and went back to bed, but still could not fall asleep. She grew more and more agitated, began pacing in circles around the small room, and then screamed loudly: "I'm back, Detective Tony Pinella. And it's only a matter of time before they let me out of this place!"

As the night nurse rushed to Stacey's room, she called for an attendant to bring a sedative. It had been years since Stacey had exhibited such an outburst. They found Stacey on the floor—on her knees, staring up at the ceiling. With tears in her eyes, she cried out, "God, please show mercy on me and all your daughters. Don't we deserve your compassion? Is the evil I committed worse than those of your sons? Are we not also worthy of your forgiveness?"

The nurse wrapped Stacey in her arms, and although she seemed to be quieting down, gave her the sedative injection anyway. The attendant lifted Stacey off the floor and placed her gently onto the bed.

"Please mail this for me," Stacey said quietly, pointing to the envelope. "Promise me, please," the tears still in her eyes.

The nurse took the letter and said, "I promise, Stacey. I promise."

"Should we restrain her?" the attendant whispered.

"No. She's calmed down and will sleep the rest of the night. She hasn't been this stressed in a very long time. Maybe it was a bad dream. Let's just keep checking on her every fifteen minutes throughout the night to be sure. And I'll make sure the doctor speaks to her in the morning right after breakfast."

They stayed just long enough to be sure that Stacey was soundly sleeping. As they left the room, the nurse handed the envelope to the attendant.

"Don't forget to show this to the doctor before you mail it," she said.

They never heard the cackling of the Laughing Angels, who were delighted with the prospect of working again at Stacey's side to torment the great Tony Pinella. When they saw the attendant put the envelope in his pocket, they knew he would forget to show the letter to the doctor.

They were right. The next day he found the letter in his pocket, put a stamp on it and mailed it.

When Stacey awakened very early the next morning from her drug-induced sleep, she lay in bed looking up at the heavens. Worried the attendants might hear her, she whispered softly, "Why should I praise you, God? I can't glorify you for a few good things when I see so much evil all around me. This is what I do have to say to you. If the Vatican is able to redeem itself from all the evil *it* has committed, why shouldn't I be given the opportunity to get out of this forsaken place? I confessed my sins and paid a price with my freedom. How many bishops or priests went to prison for committing *their* sins?"

The Laughing Angels sat in the corner of Stacey's room and roared loudly with laughter, awakening the Righteous Ones from their slumber. "What do you say now, you righteous fools? Do you still think your God looks out for all his children? Or just for the rich and famous?"

"Don't blame God for the evil in the world," the Righteous Ones proclaimed. "In times like this, we should pray to the Almighty with *more* fervor. Don't only accept the commandments of God—embrace them!"

Neither the Laughing Angels nor the Righteous Ones noticed that Stacey was not listening to any of them. She remained quietly on her bed, as though preparing for the world to come. She loved her own ideas of infinite possibilities. A place without holy books. A place without her overbearing father and evangelist husband telling her what to think, what to do. *Where were the clergy, and where were all the other disciples of God,* she thought, *when Western World leaders decided not to bomb the train tracks during World War II—the tracks Nazis used to bring millions of innocent men, women, and children to hell, to their death? Where was God when His people were shoveled into the ovens?*

Stacey heard the sound of her own voice break the silence as she yelled out once again to God. "Why do some people follow the person they call your son? All his good intentions change nothing. If you really are his father, why do you let him lead others astray? Why not give *me* the chance to make things right? Why? I don't understand. If we really are *all God's children*, then I am your daughter—God's daughter. Why not give me the chance to lead the masses to righteousness? In your honor, I will succeed where others have failed."

The Laughing Angels and the Righteous Ones watched as Stacey fell silent once again. She smiled and seemed to be listening to someone. Was God speaking to Stacey, or was she hearing the imaginary voices of her past?

Chapter 17

During the next few days of working and living together, Tony often heard David walking through the apartment talking softly to himself. At first, Tony thought maybe David was praying. He did mention being very active in his local synagogue, and the rabbi encouraged members of his congregation to also be proactive in the community. Tony learned that David made regular visits to the homebound elderly, participated in food drives, and was active in a special youth program designed to reach out to troubled teens. He even started a program for young adults who felt a need for spiritual awakening.

Tony thought now might be the time for the personal discussion he wanted to have with David. "You certainly are juggling a lot of activities in addition to your caseload. How do you handle it all?"

David grew somber. "People need help, Tony—and not just staying safe from crime. Sometimes the elderly and the disabled only need someone who takes the time to share a friendly cup of coffee. I want them to know that someone is here for them. As for the teens and young adults, I want them to know that law enforcement is more than just finding the *bad guys*. It's caring about people, how they live, work, and—yes—even their need for inner strength."

"You're a good man, David Kagan," Tony said. "When I retired and moved to Rhode Island, I pretty much wanted the solitude. The Jason Blake situation took so much out of me. Now the escort murders! Young women who must have given up on so much of their lives to even be in a situation that caused their brutal deaths....

You've really given me something to think about, something more I can give to society. Thank you, old friend!"

"Hey, any time," David said. "It feels good just talking to you about all this. Helps me keep everything in perspective. So does going to synagogue! How about attending a service with me tomorrow? Are you ready for a little more spiritual enlightenment?"

"Sure! Why not?" Tony said. "Got an extra yarmulke hanging around?"

❧

The Laughing Angels were surprised at how philosophical Tony had become. This was a new side to him. Yes, they knew he was a thinking man. That's what made him such an interesting adversary, and a good detective. Always looking at the facts. Who did what and why? Tony was not usually preoccupied with the philosophy of life. Certainly, no one would ever have described him as *intellectually elite.*

Tony was more of an *everyman*. He would consider the facts of a case, but was also vulnerable to his emotions. That was clearly evident in how he handled the Jason Blake case, and his feelings about Stacey Johnson Blake. He almost blew that one because of his apparent sensitivity towards Stacey.

The Righteous Ones realized they had underestimated Tony and, perhaps, others like him. Tony caused the Righteous Ones to consider that those devoted to scholarly pursuits and academic exercises were not the only ones with an ability to understand the human condition.

The Laughing Angels worried about these new conclusions and the potential outcome. With more people like Tony in the world, political and religious leaders would be held accountable for their actions. Where would that leave the Laughing Angels?

Chapter 18

The next morning, Tony awakened to a beautiful, cooler than expected Saturday. Tony was looking forward to accompanying David to synagogue for the weekly Sabbath service at the *Chabad of Scottsdale*. He was familiar with the *Chabads*, an orthodox group known for their user-friendly traditional prayer services, with spirited singing, and interactive and thought provoking discussions that generally appealed to all backgrounds and age groups.

"When I first moved out here, I really missed going to synagogue," David said. "I tried services at a few temples, but they were either too casual or very orthodox, and I just didn't seem to fit in. I was more interested in community service and keeping in touch with my Jewish roots than I was in communicating with nature in the desert, or fundraising at black-tie dinners. When Rosh Hashanah and Yom Kippur approached, I frankly felt homesick and a little lost. I mentioned it to one of the other officers on the force. The next week, I received a handwritten note from the rabbi of the local *Chabad* temple, with free tickets to the High Holy services, and a personal invitation to his home for dinner when the Yom Kippur fast was over. I met such wonderful people and learned so much about the programs for the elderly, young adults and children, that I began attending Friday night and morning Sabbath services whenever possible. I especially like the concept of *Chabad*, because the word itself is a Hebrew acronym for wisdom, comprehension, and knowledge. *Lubavitch* is the name of the town in White Russia, where the movement was based for more than a century. In Russian, *Lubavitch* means the *City of Brotherly Love*. It fills an important need for me, and helps me feel closer to my family and to my roots."

"I didn't know about the origin of the name," Tony said. "But when I was a kid in Bensonhurst, before moving to Detroit, I had a friend in the neighborhood who invited me to a *Chabad* youth function during Chanukah. I innocently asked if he was trying to convert me, and he said, *Hell, no! We're going to eat potato pancakes and sing a few songs. You don't even have to understand Hebrew. And the rabbi's wife makes great cookies.* It left an impression on me. Also got me hooked on potato pancakes smothered in apple sauce!"

"That's a great story," David said. "I'm sure we can drum up some potato latkes while you're here! Now, are you up to a walk? I no longer drive on the Sabbath, but it's only about two miles to the synagogue."

"Sure, let's do it!"

After the words left his mouth, Tony wondered if he could really walk two miles! What he did not tell David was that walking had been a little difficult lately, and sitting for so many hours on the flight to Phoenix did not help. On the plane, and even last night, his legs hurt, and he was a little unsteady walking to the bathroom. His feet felt spongy—at least that was the way he had explained the strange sensation to his doctor several months ago. Dr. Simpkin said it was probably peripheral neuropathy, a result of Tony's long-standing back problems. Recently, there were times when the discomfort was so severe, Tony wondered if he should return to Newport and his retirement. But he quickly dismissed that idea. His desire to solve the murders gave Tony the strength to continue. He could not, would not, let Morris Green get away with murder. He owed that to Angela and to the escorts who lost their lives, and to Max.

As they started out for the synagogue, Tony was surprised at how well he was walking, easily keeping up with David's quick and steady stride. His feet were sturdy and his balance was fine. Maybe David was right. There was something special about the dry Arizona air and beautiful desert surroundings that was invigorating. On the other hand, maybe it was being in the company of a dear friend, who was eager to share an important part of his life with Tony. Either way, after walking two miles, Tony was glad to reach the beautiful synagogue and sit down, and looking forward to the Sabbath service.

Tony looked around at all the hopeful faces. It was an orthodox service, so the men and women were seated in separate sections. He estimated there were approximately three hundred people in attendance, people of all ages and most likely of diverse beliefs. He figured that some attended an orthodox service because that's what they did as children. Others, even if they were not observant, wanted their rabbi to believe strictly in the traditional commandments of the Jewish faith. Of course, for many in the congregation, Orthodox Judaism was simply their personal preference.

The Righteous Ones were very pleased with David's attachment to his faith. They wanted to rejoice, but suddenly felt too weak to do so. All those beautiful souls they had failed to save were warning the Righteous Ones it was not their place to celebrate. Yet, those same souls were proud that David wanted to experience pure Judaism. For David, that meant doing his best to observe the commandments. For many of the others, it was a tall order, especially for those who, for so long, had not adhered to their faith.

Tony enjoyed the singing, even without understanding the language of the prayers. He was deeply moved by the blend of voices—men and women, young and old—all singing in unison.

Memories of his childhood returned. Catholic services were in Latin, and Tony did not understand a word! He thought it was better that way, more mysterious and inspiring just to hear the sounds of the voices and the melodies rather than hear the message. This made it easier to believe in the sacredness of the message and the infallibility of the pope. While it always pleased Tony's mother that he attended church services with her, she reacted without restraint when he commented that *what the church does best is reinvent history*. He could still feel the sting of her slap across his face when he voiced that opinion, only now with the affection of her touch and concern.

The Laughing Angels looked on with delight. So now Tony was an historian as well as a detective—evaluating good and evil in the church, the hypocrisy of religion, and even his own reactions to his mother's slap across his face.

Sitting at the back of the synagogue the Righteous Ones cried out, "Oh, merciful God, please give the people a sign to help them believe in your greatness. Why let them doubt your omnipotence and benevolence? Show them you are a just God who has faith in mankind."

"Oh, my," one Laughing Angel said mockingly to the other. "A miracle is taking place. Finally, the Righteous Ones are giving God a challenge. Do they really think He plays any part in world events? Will God pass or fail, or will He be given a grade of incomplete on this test?"

Chapter 19

The congregation appeared comfortable and relaxed, anticipating an inspiring and enlightening message.

Rabbi Charles Newman was fifty-one years old and very well respected throughout the local community. Somehow, he managed to keep the twinkle in his eyes that so inspired his flock, despite seeing his own days of hope dwindle two years ago. That was when his wife and ten-year-old daughter were killed in a traffic accident on a late Sunday afternoon while returning home from the Scottsdale Fashion Square. The driver of the car that hit them head on was a 26-year-old stockbroker, who survived the crash. One of the police officers at the scene, a member of Rabbi Newman's congregation, told the rabbi that the driver of the other car was under the influence of alcohol, after spending a few hours with friends watching a game at one of the popular sports bars in Downtown Scottsdale. Bill Sheehan was entering the mall parking lot on the wrong side of the lane, just as the Newman's car was exiting.

"Today's sermon is about the Va-yeshev, the Torah weekly portion. My aim is to provide an understanding of why the Torah is so important to Judaism, to our faith. I am taking the liberty of sharing from the writings of Rabbi Reuven Tzvi Ben Yehoshua, of blessed memory. Rabbi Reuven Tzvi was a remarkable man, a scholar, and a true gentleman. It was because of his influence on my father, that I was brought up in Orthodox Judaism… and what led me to have the privilege of being your rabbi. Rabbi Reuven Tzvi beautifully explained why Joseph is much more than a man who wore a coat of many colors."

"In respect to this learned and wonderful man, I will quote from portions of his writings directly:

One cannot read the beautiful story of Joseph without being enthralled by it. The moving drama grips you from incident to incident, from scene to scene, from mood to mood, as you see the wonderful story unfold itself, amid the changing fortune of the youthful and princely Joseph who alternates between honor and degradation, between joyous success and the dreary pit, all the time never relinquishing his fond dream, until finally he becomes the great ruler of Egypt and all pay him homage, and he, returning good for evil, bears no malice but becomes a source of succor and solace for his family and for all the world.

And indeed, it is not only the person of Joseph that was garbed in a glorious coat of many colors, but it is the entire story, the entire drama of Joseph that is wrapped in a coat of many colors, the somber shades of adversity and tragedy, the bright hues of good fortune and success, and the royal and regal tints of honor and acclaim. Look for any color, from the darkest to the brightest, and you will find it in the story of Joseph.

No wonder that our Rabbis saw in the fascinating and multi-colored story of Joseph a foreshadowing of the moving, and variegated history of our people, and they offered this bold and sweeping generalization—Come and see, all the evil and all the trials that come to Joseph likewise befell Zion, and all the good things that occurred to Joseph likewise happened to Zion. And our Rabbis trace with painstaking care the various events in Joseph's life, and disclose their counter part in the life of our people. In the trials of Joseph they see the trials of Israel. The nations in the world have tried in two ways to deflect us from our course. At times, and this has usually been the case, we like Joseph have been maligned and dishonored, cast into the various prisons that the nations have conjured up for us, suffered their blows, and yet like Joseph never relinquishing our dreams. And on other occasions they have sought to entice and to woo us with honeyed words and sweet phrases. Even at times when we have enjoyed comparative freedom and prosperity, coaxing us and cajoling us to give up our true identity, to surrender our soul so that we may live together in perfect harmony and bliss with those among whom we reside, without differences and distinctions."

Rabbi Newman paused for a moment, looked out over the congregation, and smiled.

"The learned Rabbi Reuven Tzvi wrote of the temptations that Joseph faced when he was brought to Egypt and sold to Potiphar, the chief-executioner of Pharaoh. Recognized as no ordinary slave, Joseph soon is entrusted with the management of the entire household. Joseph has great ambitions and dreams of success. At last, it seems that the entire world is open to him. But like many of us in life, just when we think our dreams are all within reach, and like Joseph, we may be faced with many temptations—temptations that also come with great risks.

"At those greatest moments of temptation and decision for Joseph, Rabbi Reuven Tzvi wrote, and I again quote: *At that moment of temptations and trial there appeared to him the picture of his father Jacob in all its sanctity and clarity, and immediately Joseph ceases to hesitate and waver, for he knows where the path of godliness and righteousness lies. He remembers the teaching of his father Jacob. How many times has he heard from him—Hear, O Israel the Lord, our God, the Lord is one. Joseph finds new courage and strength to withstand temptation and to face what the future may hold for him...the day in question, when this occurred, happened to be Shabbos (*the Sabbath)*—and he came home to do his work, and what work did he have to do on Shabbos? He studied and reviewed what his father had taught him. The young Joseph in a strange and new land, separated from his father and home, dreaming of material success and fame, remembers what his father taught him, and in his hour of trial and temptation his father's vision brings him strength...*"

As Rabbi Newman moved from behind the *bimah* to stand closer to the congregation, he explained, "It was during that moment in Joseph's life that the Torah tells us he withstood temptation and thus preserved his Jewish identity and dignity. Throughout the history of the Jewish people, and yet today, we are faced with temptations—some of those temptations accompanied by threats that try to break down our strength and faith. Threats of being different and excluded, during times in our history, even threats of torture.

"Let me conclude with another quote from Rabbi Reuven Tzvi: *Jewish existence is predicated upon knowledge; its greatest threat is ignorance*."

David turned to Tony and softly explained, "The next point in the Sabbath service includes the *Musaf*, a blessing vocalized by the Cantor that includes a prayer for the Holy Temple in Jerusalem. There is much more to it," said David, "but for now I'll just let you enjoy the voice of our cantor."

There was not a sound in the congregation when Cantor Maurice Gross began to sing. His voice was so clear and melodic, that it brought Pinella to a great moment of spirituality he had not felt in years.

After the *Musaf* service, Rabbi Newman came forward to make some announcements about the events taking place at the synagogue during the coming weeks. He also congratulated several new parents, and expressed sympathy for those who had lost their loved ones.

Tony was still thinking about the beautiful voice of Cantor Gross, when the rabbi said: "We are proud to have with us today a visitor from the world of law enforcement—Detective Tony Pinella, a good friend of our esteemed member David Kagan. Your presence among us today is an honor, Detective Pinella. Especially to those of us who are amateur sleuths and enjoy reading true crime novels! By the way, Detective Pinella, I have read *The Salvation Peddler* several times and even used it as a reference in sermons that discuss how religion sadly can be twisted and used as a force for both good and evil in our complex society. Thank you for visiting with us today—and thank you for your fine service to the communities in which you have served."

As Rabbi Newman gestured towards Tony, David poked Tony in the shoulder, so he would stand up and acknowledge the rabbi's introduction. Blushing a vivid red, Tony rose from his seat and gave a hesitant wave to the rabbi and the congregants.

When Tony sat down, the rabbi nodded in his direction and then continued speaking: "And now, let us all commit ourselves to the example set by Rabbi Reuven Tzvi Ben Yehoshua. If we do that, we will have the possibility of a fulfilling life, and someday be part of the world to come. Good Shabbos to you all."

Chapter 20

The day after returning to Bensonhurst from his week in Arizona, Tony heard from Max that the body of the third missing escort, Amanda Wilson, had been found early that morning. She evidently had been stabbed to death, but the police were waiting for the coroner's report. So far, the only lead was Wilson's old boyfriend. Her friends said he had been threatening Wilson for months.

Now there were three dead escorts, all young women about the same age. Max was trying to get more information, in hopes of having an article for tomorrow's newspaper.

Tony was frustrated that even after a week in Arizona, and one more young woman murdered, he still did not have enough evidence to link Morris Green to the killings. The only winners so far in this tragic game were the lawyers, Morris Green, and even Green's family who were protected by most of the press—who portrayed them as the only victims of Green's *inappropriate behavior*, as he called his relationship with Angela.

Tony believed that Angela was still alive only because her case was played out in public. Her story was in the headlines, thanks to Max, while the other escorts had managed to hide from public view—probably too frightened to contact the police. Angela was not going to play that game; she went on the offensive, not willing to be victim to power, politics, and money.

❧

The Laughing Angels roared with delight as they danced around the room. "Poor Tony Pinella," they cried out with glee. "Poor Tony, poor Tony. He still believes there is justice in the world. That in the end, attorneys, politicians, and the almighty dollar will not win over righteousness. Doesn't he realize that each and every flaw in the human condition is an advantage for us? Doesn't he realize that virtue and morality are only God's experiment—a game designed to entertain the Almighty—a game that is doomed to failure?"

The Righteous Ones listened, their heads bowed in sadness and shame, as they waited and waited for God to respond. There was only silence.

Chapter 21

Early the next morning, Tony sat at the small table in his kitchen, drinking a cup of coffee and chomping on a bagel as he opened the morning newspaper. He was still tired from the past week, and the long and uncomfortable trip home. The front page carried the most recent sports triumph and the national political news of the day. Tony quickly turned to the National News & Analysis pages, where he hoped to see Max's article on the latest killing. There it was… As he read Max's description of the most recent murder, Tony felt a chill throughout his body. Max always made readers feel as if they were experiencing the event itself, and the brutal murder of Amanda Wilson was no exception. Tony felt so sick. He ran to the bathroom and vomited up his half-eaten bagel.

He remained in the bathroom, sitting on the floor, feeling too weak to move. *Police work never seems to get easier,* he thought.

One murder after another is a heartache that takes a toll that cannot be measured. Tony thought about the families of these young women, probably still little girls in their parents' eyes. *Losing three young women to such violence, he thought, is just another reminder of how vulnerable we are to the choices we make in life.*

It seemed there was no room for even one mistake, and Tony was determined that Morris Green would pay dearly for his mistakes—in this case more than one!

Feeling a little stronger, Tony returned to the kitchen, poured another cup of coffee, and sat quietly while staring out the window onto the street. His experience with David at the *Chabad of Scottsdale* flashed through his mind. The words spoken by the rabbi, and the emotion expressed by the congregation, were undoubtedly moving. But as inspiring as the words coming from the pulpit might be at certain times in our lives, Tony could not help wondering if religion was more the problem than the solution. In his life, he had seen so many lost souls. He thought, *What if true morality had nothing to do with the various religions, and all the claims their leaders made about God?*

Deep down, the Laughing Angels were captivated by Tony. Even with his dedication to the religion of his mother, his life experiences did not allow him to take as the *whole truth* the words of those who professed to have a pipeline to God. He thought all beliefs should be questioned, even his own.

For the second time, Tony began reading Max's article:

Who Killed the Daughters of God
Max Gold, Crime Reporter

Stephanie Taylor—Beaten, strangled, and savagely stabbed in her Chicago, Illinois, apartment. Valerie Powell—Found in a pool of blood with a knife in her chest in Paradise Valley, Arizona. Amanda Wilson—Also found stabbed to death in New York City. They all worked for the same escort service. They are all gone forever. They were all murdered. They were all daughters of God.

All the screaming, crying, and prayers, will not bring back these three murdered young women, who had only three things in common: They were all pretty, all young, and they all made the same terrible mistake in their short lives—they worked for one of the more high class escort services in the country. A service that provided beautiful young companions to some of the most influential and wealthiest men in New York City. Politicians, lawyers, real estate tycoons—and Governor Morris Green, who recently resigned from his position because of (and I quote) inappropriate behavior. That service is now closed, but no doubt there are other such businesses to fill the social and sexual needs of those who can afford it. Some of these wealthy and powerful men will one day have buildings and maybe an airport or two named after them.

No one will name a street or an airport after Stephanie, Valerie, or Amanda. What were their hopes? To earn enough money to one day go to college? To pay off a college loan? To support a young child? Or maybe to secure their independence as they grew older?

As a very young and evidently very naïve young reporter, I used to believe that all are treated equally under the law. Even when I began covering the crime beat, I wanted to tell the public how the good guys won and the bad guys got busted. But my idealism diminished as each year went by. Oh, yes, our fine law enforcement officers did their jobs, and I respect them for it. Then the legal system takes over. The bad guys are no longer just the evil masked men who robbed banks, murdered innocent people as well as each other, and then went to jail. More and more, law enforcement is faced with having to ferret out bad guys in the finance industry. You know, the ones who wear custom-made suits and cater to the rich, cheat the poor, the middle class, and even their rich friends and colleagues. These newer bad guys are very diverse. Some are from modest means, then made big names for themselves as lawyers or business tycoons—and then ran for public offices. Others were born into political families or were trust-fund kids. Regardless of how they started, they were drawn into the world of politics, where they were courted by lobbyists, big donors, and even foreign leaders. Some took their responsibilities to the people and our country to heart and did good works.

Ah, but there are many others who began to feel above the laws of our land—and no longer responsible for their actions, their choices and mistakes, nor their *inappropriate behavior.* They are the elite of God's children!

Not so for Stephanie Taylor, Valerie Powell, and Amanda Wilson. *No… Not them.* I feel an extra sense of loss when these young women are not treated by the public, or by the law—even in death—as God's children. Their tragic lives will become the butt of jokes at water coolers around the country, and by late night comedians, and the hosts of talk shows. For news anchors, these daughters of God will be known only as escorts living in the shadows of life.

Amanda Wilson's body was found on the lower east side of Manhattan. She had been viciously stabbed five times. While no one has been arrested yet, the police are searching for her ex-boyfriend. Friends said he supposedly had an intense argument with Amanda only a few days before her body was discovered.

The police have not said so during the press briefings, but my sources tell me there is evidence that may link the three murders—a pattern beyond the known fact that all the women worked for the same escort service—a service with a very private list of clients. Could that be just a coincidence? Maybe each of these women posed a threat to someone. A threat so damaging they all needed to be silenced. Are there more women with a story to tell? Are they in danger, too?

Amanda Wilson, 24-years-old, was buried yesterday. Her parents, Greg and Carol Wilson, and Amanda's younger sister and brother, said their tearful goodbyes to their loving daughter and sister. They thought the world of Amanda. They loved listening to her sweet singing voice. She was saving up to take professional voice lessons. Now her voice is forever silenced.

Amanda had plans for a better life. She loved learning new things, her parents said—always searching for some meaning in her life. Her family and friends will remember her as a giving and compassionate young woman.

Like most of us, Amanda made some good choices and some bad decisions. Unfortunately, the public will only remember her as an escort who got herself killed. Amanda deserves better…

Chapter 22

The tempo of his life always quickened when Tony worked on a big case. The last few weeks reminded him that he was tired of all the tedious work that went into these investigations. At the same time, Tony was determined to solve the escort murders, and to give their families some closure. It was frustrating that there still was no public admission from the police that the killings were connected. Without solid evidence, Max and Tony agreed that Angela needed to stay out of the news, or her life would be in danger, too. So far, she was all they had to connect Morris Green with all three murders. Leslie Stevens, owner of the now shut-down escort service, disappeared altogether—hopefully, safely living in another country. The police were not even looking for her and were denying any connection between the escorts—other than their professions.

Feeling exasperated, Tony began looking through the pile of mail that he had left untouched for several days on the kitchen counter. He was shocked to see an envelope with a return address from the John Henry Hospital just outside Ferndale, Michigan. That's where Stacey Johnson Blake was housed in the psychiatric research wing. *How the hell did she get my Bensonhurst address*, he wondered, as he tore open the envelope. Then again, he knew Stacey was smart and certainly conniving. *I better sit down for this one*, he thought.

As Tony began reading Stacey's letter, it was obvious this was not a deathbed confession, and certainly not an effort to mend their relationship. The tears in her eyes when he arrested Stacey had soon turned to a venomous glare when she was found guilty of murder—*but mentally ill.*

As he read further, Tony was shocked that Stacey was offering serious advice about the escort murders.

Dear Tony,

Are you surprised I'm addressing you as "Tony," instead of Mr. Pinella. I think I've earned the right because of all the pain you caused me. But don't worry Tony. I'm not writing to admonish you. I know that in your heart you regret very much what you did to me. No need to ask me to forgive you. As the former wife of Jason Blake, I know that's the Christian thing to do. Evidently the psychiatrists here also believe in absolution, or they wouldn't spend so much time telling me I have to accept the responsibility of my sins, so I can leave the sanctity of the psychiatric ward and be put in a cold dank prison cell!

So now that I have your attention, there is something very serious I want to discuss with you. I have been reading the newspaper articles about some escorts who seem to be popping off one-by-one. I've even discussed the murders with some of the psychiatrists and nurses who work here.

Don't be so surprised, Tony. I think it's part of the therapy here. Get the crazy woman to talk – tell the authorities she is back to reality, then send her back into society. Just don't let her live in my neighborhood or let her near my children.

Well, now that I've forgiven you, I'll get to the point. I know you need my help to solve these murders. Consider it part of my therapy – but you don't have to take me home to live with you. Only joking!

Okay. I'll be serious. From what I've read in the Max Gold articles, even though the cops aren't saying so, you and Gold are convinced that one person is responsible for the three murders. Going after Amanda Wilson's old boyfriend is just a waste of time, and you know it! That guy broke up with Wilson when he found out about her side job, and moved forward with his life. Besides, what motive would he have for killing the other two escorts? It certainly doesn't make sense to me, and I'm supposed to be the crazy one!

Tony, don't get me wrong. I'm certainly not an expert on this subject – and I have nothing against escort services. But I suspect the local police have been given pretty strict instructions to look down another path, rather than to concentrate on the escorts' customers, who may be men in "high places," if you know what I mean.

I've had enough therapy here to realize I've had a few problems and did some awful things. But I can easily justify why I killed Veronica Blake, and a few others. Let's face it, Tony. Are you sure you know my whole sad story?

But let's get back to the present. Coming out of retirement probably was a mistake for you. You're a tired old man who needs some help on this case, and I can give it to you. All you need to do is visit me at my temporary home, here in Ferndale, and we can discuss the case. I'm permitted to have visitors, and I have a feeling that confronting you will be high on my psychiatrist's list of challenges. They may listen in to our conversation, but anything we say is privileged (or so they tell me).

I believe I know who the murderer is. If you want to know, too... come to Ferndale.

I look forward to seeing you soon.

Stacey Johnson Blake

Tony read Stacey's letter three times and then set it aside. He did not know what to think. He still felt guilty about how long it took him to learn the truth about the entire Blake situation, and the impact it had on Blake's sons and on Blake and Stacey's daughter. If he had worked faster, maybe he could have saved them all some anguish—as well as more murders.

Tony also realized that underneath the insanity, Stacey was a smart as well as beguiling woman. She certainly was devious enough to understand a murderer's mindset. Her letter showed she was very astute in realizing the direction Max and he were going with these murders. Maybe, at the very least, there was something she would say to provide some insights.

He would give it all some thought. If Stacey's psychiatrists thought it would not hurt, maybe he would take that trip to Ferndale, Michigan. Maybe…

Chapter 23

After avoiding the police for more than a month, Larry Daniels, Amanda Wilson's ex-boyfriend, was located and arrested for her murder. Max and Tony were surprised at Wilson's arrest. They thought he would only be taken in for questioning. Up to now, they had found no reason to support his arrest—and the police were under strict orders not to reveal any information to the public. This raised their suspicion even more that politics were involved.

In the meanwhile, splashed all over the entertainment section of the newspapers—as well as the gossip columns, was word that Charlie Davis, a popular talk show host on cable television, and his co-host Barbara Elias, were being replaced by ex-Governor Morris Green and Pulitzer Prize award-winning writer Gail Dickson. The Green-Dickson Hour would have a roundtable format, with the ex-Governor Green and Dickson moderating discussions with well-known professionals from the worlds of politics, law enforcement, and journalism. It was the talk of New York and the rest of the country's television-viewing audience. Green and Dickson would provide the public with inside views on crime, corruption, and hypocrisy within the national and international scenes.

Potential guests were lining up to appear on the weekly one-hour show, despite his recent notoriety. Green was setting the agenda for shows that would belie his personal weaknesses. Guests were put on the spot by questions from Green and Dickson that clearly emphasized Green's public support for feeding the hungry, making sure people of all incomes had decent places to live, and assuring that the social security system remained strong. He was also lobbying for a single-payer healthcare system for all citizens—including members of congress.

Then, Dickson suddenly resigned from the show with no other explanation than she wanted to spend more time with her family. Rumors surfaced in the gossip columns that she either got tired of being treated like second fiddle to Green, or that she became worried that her award-winning reputation was being tarnished by working with a known womanizer and political hypocrite.

Even that did not hurt Green's popularity. He remained a popular talk-show hero for supporting the *public good*, while Dickson became persona non-grata, fortunate to be hired for periodic guest appearances on a few talk shows.

It was just one more lesson for Tony and Max how hard it would be to connect Morris Green to any role in the murders!

❧

The Laughing Angels delighted in Green's hypocrisy. He was their true hero, living a double life and being so adept at fooling the public. He had even convinced his wealthy friends to back his cable television show with hefty endowments, while his own parents kept a very low profile, all the time wondering how their smart, talented son could have gone so far astray— and embarrassing his beautiful wife and daughters. *Wait until they learn the truth*, the Laughing Angels thought.

The Righteous Ones looked on with great sadness. Morris Green had thrown away his unlimited potential. Once, they believed he was a great statesman, who might one day lead all the people as its president. The Laughing Angels had won this round. The Righteous Ones hopes for a better tomorrow were hijacked by Green's lack of common sense. *Had he also become a brutal murderer?*

Chapter 24

Tony was surprised when Max urged him to see Stacey Blake. He reminded Tony that even after she was charged with committing multiple murders, many in the public still viewed her as a sympathetic character. They believed she was guilty, and should pay for her crimes, but they also recognized she was a victim of many circumstances that finally pushed her over the edge.

Tony said he would think about it. He was still haunted by Stacey. How she could go from a sweet and loving mother one day, to a cunning and brutal murderer the next, and then to a helpless child pleading for her father's love.

That night, Tony's nightmares came one after another. He envisioned himself locked up in a room with Stacey. She was as charming as ever, even as she began explaining her theories about the escort murders. Standing behind her was the ghost of Veronica Blake, Stacey's first victim, pleading with Tony to show mercy for Stacey. There was a strange bond between these two women. Veronica had forgiven Stacey for killing her, and even embraced Stacey for the loving care she gave to her sons.

As Tony watched in amazement, the two women joined hands. For a moment, they actually looked so much alike. They stared at Tony, and then spoke to him in one voice, showing the simplicity of their faith. *Jesus died for our sins. We have come to bring you home…*

Tony awakened in a cold sweat, his head and heart pounding. He began to hyperventilate and felt his blood rushing through his body. He got out of bed, staggered into the bathroom, took two aspirins and a glass of water, and went into the living room and dozed off on the couch. Although it was before sunrise when he woke up, Tony reached for the telephone. His first call was to American Airlines. It was still too early to call Max, so he left a message on his answering service.

"I'm leaving late this afternoon to see Stacey Blake," Tony said. "I already booked a flight to Detroit, and will stay at the Holiday Inn near the airport overnight. I'll rent a car in the morning and drive to Ferndale. It's only 15-minutes away, so I plan to fly back later that day. I still have to call ahead to the hospital and set things up, but I'm sure the Detroit PD will help if I run into any roadblocks. I'll call you when I get home to Bensonhurst. Don't worry. I'll be fine..." Then Tony laughed nervously. "The worst they can do is lock me up for observation!"

After a shower and a cup of very strong coffee, Tony's next call was to Dr. Boris Trotsky, Chief of Research Psychiatry at the hospital. Tony explained about the letter, and why he wanted to talk to Stacey.

Dr. Trotsky hesitated at first, angry that he did not know about the letter. But after hearing what Stacey had written, he told Tony he would be welcome.

"In fact," he said, "I'm looking forward to meeting you. When she first arrived here, Stacey mentioned you in some of our sessions. I'll agree to your visit, providing you allow me to monitor the session."

When Tony hesitated, Trotsky explained, "Please understand. Stacey is still in a very delicate state of mind, and anything she says might help in her therapy. That said, you don't need to worry about confidentiality. As Stacey's psychiatrist, I'm bound to keep your discussion in confidence."

"Agreed," Tony said. "I can be at the hospital tomorrow morning. Is 10:00 a.m. all right?"

"Just ask for me at the front desk. I'll let Stacey know you're coming. She doesn't like surprises very much, and she's been a bit agitated lately. Now I understand why. She's probably been waiting to hear from you. See you tomorrow, Detective Pinella."

"Tomorrow," Tony said. He hoped he was doing the right thing. For Stacey, and for himself.

The Laughing Angels sang out to the Righteous Ones with taunting laughter. "Want to come with us?" they asked. "This should be quite a show. Tony Pinella and Stacey Johnson Blake matching wits in a psychiatric ward. This is a sight even your God might want to behold."

Chapter 25

When Dr. Trotsky told Stacey that Detective Pinella was coming to see her, she expressed an objection when he said there would be a video camera in the conference room, and the presence of a nurse and Dr. Trotsky. "That was part of the deal," he said. "No camera, no visit."

Stacey's face grew red as she stood up and paced around the doctor's office. Dr. Trotsky was sure she was about to have one of her tantrums. To his surprise, Stacey kept very good control of her anger. She calmly sat down and remarked to Dr. Trotsky, "I'm glad you will be there. It will prove to you that I'm totally sane, and not the same Stacey Johnson Blake that did those horrendous things! Tony will see it right away, and he will probably ask that I be released to help him with his case."

"Well, Stacey," Dr. Trotsky said. "We certainly will keep an open mind. Let's just take this one step at a time. Detective Pinella will be here at ten o'clock this morning."

"That's only an hour from now," she said. Her face suddenly had the young and excited look of a teenager about to greet her prom date. "Is our session over, Dr. Trotsky? I need to get ready!"

"I'll call the attendant to take you to your room, Stacey."

"Oh, I need my clothes. I certainly can't see Tony in this dreary hospital gown."

"You know the rules, Stacey. You can wear one of the nice pink terrycloth robes over your gown. I'm sure you will look just fine to the detective. I'll tell the attendant to help you get ready."

"Thank you, Dr. Trotsky. This is a very special day…"

While Stacey was glowing at the prospect of seeing Tony, he was having breakfast at his hotel and wondering if meeting with Stacey was the smart thing to do. He knew the encounter could be aimless, frustrating, and probably very bad for his health. These days, it might not take much to totally drag him downhill. At the very least, he would probably end up with a migraine headache, and the worst with a heart attack. On the other hand, he also knew it was time to fight his demons and put an end to the nightmares. *Why let Stacey have such a hold on me?* Tony thought. *Why should I feel lost in a wilderness of guilt? How much time do I really have on this earth, anyway? And what right do I have not to listen to someone cunning enough to pull off a series of murders, and get away with it for so long? Maybe something Stacey says will break through the barrier Max and I have in linking Morris Green to the escort murders?*

Very early in his career, Tony was warned by his superior officers to be careful, not to step on anyone's toes politically. Now he was contemplating taking down one of the hottest political darlings of the decade. Despite his admitted indiscretions, many in the public, his political allies, and some very influential people, all bought into Morris Green's *mea culpa.* He still had enough friends in high places, encouraging him to keep his eye on a future in congress, or even the White House.

If there were even the slightest chance that Tony could finally rid himself of the demons that still followed him, he was willing to take it. As he got ready to leave the hotel, Tony began to feel strong and more confident. *This might be a golden opportunity to set things straight for me*, Tony thought, *and solve these murders—even if the truth will bring a tidal wave down on the political scene.*

As he drove the short distance to Ferndale and the hospital, Tony thought of something Dr. Trotsky told him. While still not able to function outside of a very controlled setting, Stacey would seem *like a new and different person*, as he put it. Tony would need to speak to her and listen to her differently. He knew this would not be easy for him.

Chapter 26

Having gone through all the security checks and barriers, Dr. Trotsky brought Tony into a small conference room, nicely decorated with beautiful paintings of landscapes on two of the walls. He also took note that on one of those walls there were a series of small windows placed too high to reach without a ladder. The windows had bars, which were covered by brightly colored sheer curtains that let in the sunlight. There were six chairs around a rectangular table with two plastic pitchers on a tray. One pitcher held ice water, the other iced tea. There was also a carafe of hot coffee, paper cups, plastic spoons, sugar packets, and powdered cream. If Tony did not know they were in a psychiatric hospital, he would have thought this was Stacey's dining room and he had been invited for lunch, except for the large mirror on one wall, which Tony figured was a two-way mirror and observation room with cameras and recording equipment.

Standing at the table were Stacey and a nurse. Just as Dr. Trotsky started to introduce the nurse, Stacey took charge. She reached out to Tony to shake hands. Dr. Trotsky quickly nodded to Tony, indicating it was all right to shake Stacey's hand.

"Thank you for coming, Tony. I see you've already met Dr. Trotsky." Then, gesturing towards the nurse, "This is Nurse Helen Spagnoli. Helen will also be joining us today."

"Thank you for the nice introductions, Stacey," Dr. Trotsky quickly interjected, even before Tony could say a word.

Tony hesitated, still somewhat in shock over how Stacey took over the meeting. He hoped he did not sound as nervous as he felt. "Nice to meet you Nurse Helen. Stacey, you're looking very well. Thank you for inviting me."

The entire scene seemed surreal to him, with Stacey looking as lovely as ever, even in a pink terrycloth bathrobe with the hospital insignia on it.

"Why don't we all sit down," Dr. Trotsky said, leading Tony to a chair at the table. Nurse Helen sat next to Stacey, both facing the two-way mirror, which was high enough on the wall behind Tony to clearly watch every move made by Stacey. Dr. Trotsky took a seat at one end of the table. Tony figured that way he could watch the entire session—and signal to the observers, just in case he needed some assistance.

Tony could not help staring at Stacey. She looked radiant and as beautiful as he remembered—certainly not like someone who had been incarcerated in a psychiatric hospital all these years. Although her face had matured, she still had those childlike qualities he found so endearing, especially when she smiled.

Stacey glanced just for a moment at Dr. Trotsky, who nodded that it was all right for her to speak.

"Thank you again for coming, Tony," Stacey said. "I think it's about time I thanked you for recommending to the court that I serve my sentence here, rather than a prison."

"I'm so glad you're getting the help you need."

"Oh, yes," Stacey said. "I meet with Dr. Trotsky several times a week, and work with other therapists every day. I keep pretty busy."

"That's wonderful, Stacey! I understand from your letter, that you read a lot."

"Oh, yes. I'm permitted to read the newspapers and books from the library. I really like the ones on self-improvement. Although mystery books are my favorite. I think I should write a book one of these days. What do you think, Tony? Maybe I should write a sequel to *The Salvation Peddler*."

Dr. Trotsky shot a concerned glance at Nurse Helen, and said, "Why Stacey, I didn't know the librarian was bringing you mystery books."

"Oh, yes, Dr. Trotsky," she said.

Stacey then turned to look at Tony. With a sly, almost threatening sound to her voice, she asked, "Did you read *The Salvation Peddler*?"

"Yes, I did," Tony said. Very cautiously, he added, "It was very interesting, Stacey. Did you ask me here to talk about that book?"

"No, not exactly... but as long as we are talking about it, it's too bad the author didn't have the decency to interview me."

Dr. Trotsky felt this was a good time for him to interject. "Stacey, *The Salvation Peddler* was a novel, a work of fiction. Why do you think he should have interviewed you?"

"Oh, you're right, Dr.Trotsky. The way it was written was fiction. Had he spoken to me, the murderer in the book would have been portrayed quite differently."

"What do you mean?" Dr. Trotsky asked.

Stacey turned and looked directly at Tony when she answered. "He never understood my—*I mean, her*—commitment to religion and morality, and how they go hand in hand."

Tony was doing his best not to comment. He felt a lump in his throat and a deep pain in his chest. With all the jury had learned, and what had been all over the news during her trial, Stacey was still trying to convince herself that those who are religious are also more moral than the rest of society.

"What do you think, Tony?" she asked. "About religion and morality? Certainly your years of experience as a detective have taught you something."

Dr. Trotsky had warned Tony not to challenge Stacey, but Tony was also mindful of how scheming Stacey could be. He knew she was leading him somewhere concerning the escort murders.

"Well, Stacey, if you really want to know what I think…"

"Yes, I do," she snapped back.

"When you talk about religion and morality, are you referring to all religions? And to all people?"

Stacey looked up at the sun streaming through the barred windows. She knew she had to tread carefully or Dr. Trotsky might call an end to this meeting, and rescind her reading privileges.

"I just wondered if you believe as I do that if one doesn't accept Jesus, it's nearly impossible to be moral. *What do you think?* I really want to know."

Dr. Trotsky signaled with his eyes to Tony that it was all right to answer.

"Okay," Tony said. He slowly leaned forward, poured a cup of coffee and took a sip, and then looked directly into Stacey's eyes. "I certainly don't believe that Christianity and morality go hand in hand. In fact, after everything you've suffered, I'm very surprised that you do. There's nothing to substantiate that those who are Christian are more moral than people of other persuasions. Think about all the evil and atrocities committed over the centuries in the name of religion."

Stacey seemed taken aback by Tony's blunt response. The tone of her voice changed. "You're right, Tony. I don't know what got into me. At times, I need so much to believe in absolutes, to not waver on my strong opinions. I'm not sure that's healthy for me. What do you think, Dr. Trotsky?"

Before Dr. Trotsky could answer, Stacey looked back at Tony. "Thanks for calling me on it, Tony. In fact, that's part of what I wanted to talk to you about. In reading about the escort murders, I think too many people are being absolute about how these poor women might have died."

"What do you mean, Stacey?" Tony was glad to bring the conversation back to the escorts. "I have to admit, in addition to being interested in how you've been all these years, I was curious as to why these cases interested you enough to write to me. We didn't exactly part on good terms."

Stacey sat back and laughed loudly. "No, we didn't. Although, I was always curious as to how you finally learned the truth, and why it took you so long. In the end, you were very gentle with me—and always showed concern about the welfare of my daughter and stepsons. I wanted to return the favor."

Dr. Trotsky listened to the banter between Tony and his patient with great interest. At first, he did not want to approve Tony's visit. Now he realized that psychotherapy and medication had only scratched the surface of this complex patient's problems.

Then Stacey caught him by surprise by turning her attention to him. "Listen closely, Dr. Trotsky," she said. "I may be a murderer, and maybe I am as insane as the court ruled. But I also see things that no one else sees, and sense what's really in the hearts of people who pretend to be *holier than thou.* Wealthy people, politicians—and, yes—religious leaders, who think they are above the law. I see the dark images within their souls, and they talk to me."

"How does this fit in with Detective Pinella's visit?" Dr. Trotsky asked.

"I knew weeks before the police arrested Amanda Wilson's boyfriend that he had nothing to do with her murder."

"What do you mean? What happened weeks before you heard about his arrest?"

"It's simple, Dr. Trotsky! After I watched Governor Morris Green's resignation performance, I kept seeing dark images of death. That's when I knew. Amanda Wilson's murder and Morris Green were connected. But I didn't know how..."

"Wait a minute, Stacey," Tony interjected. "What could possibly make you think there was a connection between Morris Green and Amanda Wilson? Her name was never mentioned during that press conference. Not in the televised speech, and not in the newspapers."

"Well, first off, Amanda Wilson and that escort Green was caught with, Angela *something or other*, worked for the same escort service."

"But no one's murdered Angela Robinson," Tony said.

"No, not yet," Stacey said emphatically. "So it's possible. It could still happen. Right, Tony?"

"I'm not going to say what I think about that, Stacey. But you do have me curious as to why you think Morris Green had anything to do with the Wilson murder."

At this point, Dr. Trotsky looked at his watch. "Detective Pinella, I think Stacey must be getting tired..."

"Please Dr. Trotsky. Please let me continue. Just another half-hour? I promise to be done before it's time for my lunch and therapy session."

Tony interjected. "I certainly don't want to tire Stacey, Dr. Trotsky. But the Amanda Wilson murder is a critical case. If Stacey can add any insights—well, as skeptical as I may be—it's important that I hear Stacey out."

"Well, all right. Just a bit longer. We can always have Detective Pinella come back tomorrow. Is that all right, Detective?"

"Thank you, Doctor. Yes. Just a little longer and then I'll come back tomorrow morning," Tony said. "Okay, Stacey? I think Dr. Trotsky is right. Your therapy session is important."

"All right, all right," Stacey said. The sound of her voice showed that she was growing too anxious.

"I was asking you why you think Morris Green had anything to do with the Amanda Wilson murder."

"I'm surprised at you, Tony. Didn't you watch the news conference? I'm not just talking about poor Amanda Wilson!"

"What do you mean?" Tony asked. "There was nothing I heard at that conference about Amanda Wilson, nor any of the three murdered escorts. Morris spoke only of his *inappropriate relationship* with Angela Robinson."

Stacey clenched her fists and pounded on the table. "That's the trouble with all of you," she cried out. "What you heard! But what did you see? Obviously, Green's wife and three daughters all *looked* hurt and frightened. They were in a room full of cameras, reporters, and probably millions of viewers."

Dr. Trotsky quickly leaned forward towards Stacey and spoke very calmly. "We're all listening to you, Stacey. Please tell us what you saw."

Stacey looked angrily at Dr. Trotsky. "I'm talking to Tony, Dr. Trotsky! I doubt you would understand. You always think my visions aren't real. I think Tony knows better... Don't you, Tony?"

"I'm very interested in what you saw, Stacey. Please tell me. I appreciate your help. We both do... Don't we, Doctor?"

With that, Tony shot a telling glance at the doctor, who sat back and crossed his arms over his chest.

"Yes, please Stacey. I'm sorry to have interrupted," he said.

Stacey gave him an icy stare and continued.

"Like I said, they all looked hurt when their father spoke, and frightened as the flashbulbs kept popping. But the eldest daughter... What's her name? Julia?"

"Yes," Tony said. "It's Julia."

"She had a gleam in her eyes. Not a frightened gleam like her two little sisters, but an angry gleam. It even frightened me for a moment."

"Why did it frighten you?" Tony asked. He did not know at this point if he were surprised or concerned that anything could really frighten someone who committed more than one murder.

"Julia reminded me of myself, how I looked in the mirror as I was planning Veronica's murder. For a moment, I even frightened myself. But you missed it, Tony. All those months, and even after the other murders, *a great detective like you missed it! Didn't you, Tony?* You, too, Dr. Trotsky. *You missed it, too.* I could see it in your eyes during our first session. You thought I was frightened, but not for the right reason. I was only frightened for the futures of my daughter and stepsons. At that time, I was still glad that Veronica was dead. The others were just *collateral damage.* Isn't that the term you detectives use, Tony?"

Tony answered, his voice now softer. "Yes, Stacey. *Collateral damage.*"

Dr. Trotsky looked at his watch and then at Tony. "Well, Detective Pinella, I think we are done for today. Is tomorrow morning at ten o'clock all right? It's time for Stacey to have lunch and our therapy session."

With that, the doctor stood up and shook hands with Tony. Stacey reached her hand out to Tony as well. When he took it, she clasped his hand with both of hers. "I'm so glad you're here, Tony. I think I can really help you...."

Nurse Spagnoli put her arm gently around Stacey. "Let's go to your room and freshen up before lunch. You'll see Detective Pinella tomorrow morning."

"Yes, thank you nurse," Stacey said. She glanced over at Tony with a look that made him shiver.

When the nurse and Stacey left the room, Dr. Trotsky quickly turned to Tony. "I hope you realize this may only be feeding on Stacey's delusions, Detective. I'm only agreeing to continue this visit because it shows me how much more there is to learn about this complex woman. I hope it will help me understand her better."

"I think she will also be helping me solve a series of heinous crimes, Dr. Trotsky. I appreciate your letting me come back tomorrow. I understand your concern, and hope these discussions also help Stacey."

Chapter 27

During her afternoon therapy with Dr. Trotsky, Stacey was pensive.

"Do you want to know what I'm thinking now?" she asked.

"Of course, Stacey. What are you thinking?"

"Instead of marrying Jason Blake, and playing the role of a minister's wife—and then a minister's mother when Jason Jr. started preaching from the pulpit—I might have expressed all my inner fears, hostilities and anxieties in another way, instead of murdering anyone."

"That's an interesting self-evaluation, Stacey. What would you have done, if not marry Jason?"

"I could have become a minister, or even a traveling evangelist, going from town to town—preventing others from going astray. I think I have a good understanding of human nature. I can even see it in people's eyes—whether they are good or evil."

"Did you have that ability before attending Jason's sermons?"

"Well, no. But I didn't think about murdering anyone either until I met Jason."

"So that was a real turning point in your life—attending Jason Blake's sermons."

"Yes, that and the nightmares."

"In all our time together, Stacey, you haven't mentioned your nightmares. Do you want to talk about them now?"

"I'm not sure. I still have them."

"It might help to talk about them."

Stacey turned to look out the window, and took a deep breath. Dr. Trotsky sat silently, waiting for her to speak. When she turned back to look at the doctor, there were tears in her eyes.

"I don't think anyone can do anything about my nightmares—*and I don't want to stop them,*" she said emphatically. "I now realize that I should have seen the change in myself, and have learned to recognize it in others... When the look of innocence and the sparkle of happiness in our eyes are replaced by a look of desperation and then a fierce stare, something evil is bound to happen—and then comes the dull look of emptiness. Our lives become meaningless. I think it was that look of emptiness that touched Detective Pinella when he arrested me."

"Is that why you want to help the detective now? To make peace with yourself?"

Just when Dr. Trotsky was feeling satisfied that maybe his many sessions had actually reached Stacey, she glanced out the window again, and then turned to him with a strange smile on her face.

"It's more like God wants to help me," she said. "God wants my life to have meaning—to mean more to my stepsons and daughter than a legacy of jealousy and murder. He now speaks to me—and uses the nightmares to help me."

"How do the nightmares help you, Stacey?"

"God gave me the power to visualize things others can't see. There's no escape for me, whether I'm locked up here or living on the outside. If that makes me insane, then so be it. I have been summoned by the Lord and accept the wisdom He shares with me in return for my sanity and freedom... I'm tired now, Dr. Trotsky. I have lots to think about before seeing Tony tomorrow morning."

After Nurse Spagnoli took Stacey back to her room, Dr. Trotsky dictated his notes: "As evident in the transcript of today's session with Stacey Johnson Blake, she obviously remains a very disturbed person. However, I will allow her to continue a dialogue with Detective Pinella, as it has opened up a new channel of discovery that I hope will help her—and help us better understand the full nature of her illness."

❧

The Righteous Ones were amazed at how far Stacey had come to understanding God's ways. This was a *win* in their eyes. It showed how much the Supreme Being cared about all his children. Even Stacey deserved a time to be in the sunshine, a time to be appreciated and accepted.

The Laughing Angels danced around with glee, celebrating the ignorance and misinterpretation of the Righteous Ones. God was finally showing himself to care more about the souls and egos of the sinners than the victims—just as he had always done.

The battles between the Righteous Ones and the Laughing Angels would continue, with Detective Tony Pinella still in the middle. *Oh, good,* the Laughing Angels thought. *The real fun is just beginning!*

Chapter 28

Before he left the Holiday Inn for the hospital, Tony checked at the front desk and extended his stay for another night. He had a feeling today's session with Stacey might run into the evening. He also changed his flight.

When he arrived at the hospital at 9:45 a.m., and checked through the secured area, Tony worried that something had happened to Stacey. He was not escorted to the conference room, but taken instead to Dr. Trotsky's office. He became more apprehensive when both Nurse Spagnoli and Dr. Trotsky were waiting for him.

"Is Stacey all right?" he immediately asked, before greeting either the nurse or the doctor.

"Yes, yes, she is fine," Dr. Trotsky said. He rose from behind his desk to shake Tony's hand. "We just thought we would fill you in a bit, as your time with Stacey brought out some interesting findings during her therapy session yesterday. Please sit down."

Now seated next to Nurse Spagnoli and across from Dr. Trotsky, Tony could not help still feeling anxious. "Are you sure she is all right?"

"Yes, Stacey is fine. Well, as fine as a paranoid schizophrenic with a messianic complex can be," Dr. Trotsky said. "I thought you should know, so there are no surprises during your meeting with her this morning. Stacey truly believes that she is acting as an agent of God in providing you with insights into the escort murders. That it is God's way of redeeming her for the sins she committed in the past. Normally, I would put a stop to this immediately, as it's generally not good to feed the illusions of such patients."

"But..." Tony said. "I assume there's a *but* coming."

"Yes, Detective, there is a *but*," Dr. Trotsky responded. "In trying to help you, Stacey is actually doing a self-analysis. She is looking inward at the circumstances in her own life that led her to becoming a murderer—and that self-awareness is a good thing, a very positive step forward in her therapy. That said, when she goes on about her messages from God, I ask that you don't, under any circumstances, encourage Stacey to continue having these conversations with God."

Tony took a moment to consider what the doctor said. "I have to admit, this is much more complex than I anticipated. Maybe it was a mistake to answer her letter. I certainly don't want to harm her in any way."

"I admit, I was dubious about this whole thing to begin with," Dr. Trotsky said. "When I saw your letter, my first reaction was to call and ask you not to contact Stacey again. Then, I wondered if this experiment was worth the risk—and it is! Stacey is opening up to me about her deepest thoughts as never before. What she says and proposes will help Nurse Spagnoli and I learn more about how to help Stacey."

"So what should I do?" Tony asked.

"Just let her talk without rejecting any of her ideas and suggestions about how to proceed with your investigation. Take notes, be appreciative, ask the same questions you usually would to a witness or anyone else coming forward with information about a murder. But, please, do not challenge her. Especially about her relationship with God. Leave any of that to me. I'll stay quiet, unless I think she is getting too agitated. Stacey is still quite prone to having tantrums, and I want to be careful you don't step over a line that suggests her ideas about the case are being rejected outright."

Dr. Trotsky got up from his desk and asked Nurse Spagnoli to make sure Stacey was ready, and then bring her to the conference room.

"We'll meet you there in a few minutes. Do you have any other questions, Detective?"

"No. I think I understand the situation, and appreciate everything you said. I just need your reassurance. Just as you have a doctrine of patient confidentiality, I also want to be sure that nothing Stacey says, and everything we discuss about the case—about the escort murders and Morris Green—remains confidential, including any videotapes or notes of Stacey talking about the case."

"I understand completely, Detective. As I mentioned to you earlier, you need not worry. Our files are locked and secured, and Nurse Spagnoli will also honor both your and Stacey's confidences."

Stacy and Nurse Spagnoli were in the conference room when Dr. Trotsky and Pinella entered. Stacey remained seated, but greeted Tony with an enthusiastic smile. He noticed she had a tall stack of note cards on the conference table, all in different colors.

"Tony! I'm so glad you came back. I was worried that you might not think my ideas would help you!"

"On the contrary, Stacey. I am very impressed with how insightful you are and want to know more about your ideas concerning Morris Green."

"Thank you, Tony! I have to give some credit to all the detective books I've been reading, and that wonderful British series, *Prime Suspect*, with Helen Mirren. I watched some of those episodes over and over on the video player. In fact, don't you think I look just a little bit like Helen, with my hair cut short?"

"Now that you mention it, Stacey, maybe you do look a little like Ms. Mirren...." As soon as the words were out of his mouth, Tony saw Dr. Trotsky frowning.

Stacey laughed as she caught the silent interaction between the doctor and Tony. "Don't let the good doctor intimidate you, Tony. He always frowns like that. But, yes, I am anxious to see what you think about my view of how this mystery ends. If I'm right, and I think I am, I may even write my own book, maybe a sequel to *The Salvation Peddler*. Imagine the publicity I'll get. It will bring my life full circle. Not only did I commit murders—but I also will solve murders, with God's help, of course."

"Let's get started then," Tony said. He decided not to comment on Stacey's remark about God.

Stacey's eyes lit up as she carefully organized her notes into little piles on the conference table. While they all silently waited, Tony shot his own glare in Dr. Trotsky's direction. He wondered why Stacey was even permitted to read books like *The Salvation Peddler*, or watch the Helen Mirren series. Dr. Trotsky seemed to have a very liberal approach to psychiatric therapy that might not always fit into what the criminal justice system would prefer.

Tony had done some online searches and learned that Trotsky was considered a real rebel. He did not believe in sheltering even the most disturbed patients from most aspects of the world outside the psychiatric hospital. Just the opposite, he wanted them to be in as normal an environment as possible, but also provided all the medical and legal precautions that were mandated for such criminally insane patients. In one of his many psychiatric research papers, he wrote: *Although most will be incarcerated for life, at least we will have done our best to provide them with some normalcy.*

Tony did not agree with this principle—nor did most other psychiatrists. However, it seemed that in Stacey's case—and given her insights into the escort murder cases—it was working to Tony's advantage. Trotsky's special research unit was set completely apart from the rest of the psychiatric department, with total and complete security, so there was never any risk to other patients. Doctors, nurses, and non-medical personnel all had to sign releases, stating they knew the risks of working with such dangerous criminals in the special research unit.

"All ready," Stacey looked up and proudly announced.

As she brought Tony through her scenario, it was easy to see why Trotsky gave the green light to their meeting. She was so well organized, quite unlike what he expected. Each escort had her own card color, and Stacey went from case to case, beginning with Stephanie Taylor in Chicago; Valerie Powell in Paradise Valley; and Amanda Wilson on the Lower East Side of Manhattan. She used other colors to show how the murders were linked. Her idea, she explained, was to come to a point where all the colors converged into black—where the name of the murderer would be revealed.

Tony could see by the looks on their faces that Dr. Trotsky and Nurse Spagnoli were in awe and surprised at how logical Stacey was in her analysis. So was he!

Stacey's conclusion was that two people were responsible for all three murders: Julia and Tom Rawlings, Julia's fiancé.

As Stacey looked around the table, she flashed a satisfied smile towards Nurse Spagnoli and Dr. Trotsky, which turned to a ferocious glare when her eyes rested on Tony.

While it was hard for Tony to admit, Stacey's detailed reasoning seemed to make perfect sense to him. She had created a reasonable scenario, actually a detailed psychoanalysis that explained Julia's motives, and even why Tom helped her carry out these heinous crimes.

The question for all of them was, did Stacey truly believe that God had led her to this conclusion, or was this just a devious ploy designed to show Dr. Trotsky how smart she was—and to get Tony's attention? Maybe it was Stacey's way to get back at him for uncovering her secrets and landing her in a psychiatric hospital!

Tony spoke up first. "You've given me a lot to think about, Stacey. It is extremely important that this entire meeting, everything we discussed, must be kept strictly confidential. Do I have your promise, Stacey?"

"Of course, Tony. I'll be waiting to hear from you. You're welcome to take my notes with you. Nurse Helen, I am rather tired now. Will you please take me back to my room?"

Dr. Trotsky nodded in agreement, and Nurse Spagnoli left the room with Stacey.

As soon as they were out of sight, Dr. Trotsky turned to Tony, "Let me walk you out, Detective. I'm not sure where Stacey's dramatic imagination will take you, but everything will be kept confidential. Please let me know if there is anything further you need from me. I'm not certain whether it's wise for you to see her again. But, obviously, Stacey has some attachment to you—and I will do whatever is necessary, so long as it helps her and does not interfere in her progress."

The ball was now in Tony's court. Stacy's scenario was intriguing—despite the fact that there was no solid evidence leading to her conclusion—only Stacey's analysis of Julia's possible motives.

How far should I take this, if at all? Tony asked himself. *If I do pursue Stacey's line of thinking, at what point should I involve Max Gold and David Kagan?*

Although he was always a risk-taker, looking like a total lunatic was not the way Tony envisioned ending his career.

❧

The Righteous Ones felt a sense of optimism that someone like Stacey Johnson Blake, who had committed such evil crimes and brought pain to so many innocents, would now help a person like Tony, who devoted his entire life to protecting the innocent. Perhaps, with Stacey's help, the families of the murdered escorts might find some peace in seeing those responsible brought to justice.

The Laughing Angels roared louder than ever as they saw the self-satisfied look on the faces of the Righteous Ones. *What hypocrites they are! Had the Righteous Ones forgotten that even Julia Green was a Daughter of God?*

Chapter 29

Two weeks had passed since Tony's meeting with Stacey. His investigation had taken a very unconventional twist. Obviously, Stacey could not be used as a witness—*and not only because of her home address.* Even if she lived at 1600 Pennsylvania Avenue, her visions would not be considered valid evidence. Messages from God would not influence any detective enough to get a search warrant for the Green household.

Tony would need to find another way to investigate Morris Green's family and Tom Rawlings, Julia's fiancé. It was time to call Max.

Max practically shouted into the phone after Tony told him about Stacey. "So you want me to look into the Green family based on Stacey's messages from God?"

He could hardly believe what Tony had said. In all his years as a journalist, Max never gave credence to anyone's story about messages from God. Although flexible in thought, and open to new ideas, attaching significance to Stacey's *messages from God* did not fit Max's beliefs in how the universe worked.

"Look, I'm not sure this is anything more than Stacey's wild imagination, but I'll check around," Max said. "I guess the Blake case left more scars on you than I realized."

"Even more than *I* realized," Tony answered. "Stay with me on this one, Max. It's just a desperate hunch. I don't think it's a *message from God.* But I do believe that Morris Green is involved in the murders, and maybe sniffing around his family is the only way we'll be able to draw him out. It's really burning me up that this guy landed on his feet, while three women are in their graves."

"You've got a good heart, Tony," Max said. "What the hell. I'm in."

What Max had been able to confirm so far was that Julia and Tom were in Chicago when Stephanie Taylor was murdered. That much was on the society pages of *The Chicago Tribune* when they were photographed at the opening of a new wing at The Art Institute of Chicago. Was it more than a coincidence that the day after Amanda Wilson was killed, Julia, Tom, and Green's wife Sally, were also seen attending a performance of The New York City Ballet at Lincoln Center?

What about the third murder? Where were Julia and Tom around the time when Valerie Powell's body was found in Paradise Valley, Arizona? Max was not able to find anything that supported Tony's hunch.

Tony would have to ask David to dig deeper—without ruffling any political feathers.

Tony had not spoken to David since his meeting with Stacey, so he would need to bring him up to date. He suspected that David would have much the same first reaction as Max.

In the meanwhile, despite the weak evidence pointing to his role in her murder, the police were still holding Amanda Wilson's ex-boyfriend in custody.

Max is right, Tony thought. *There's no way I can pass on to the police anything about my conversations with Stacey. They're liable to lock me up alongside her,* he chuckled to himself.

Tony needed more time to sort everything out, and then decide how to proceed. In the meanwhile, Morris Green was gaining more and more visibility.

"That bastard...," Tony told David when he called him. "That bastard is actually talking about running for the open senate seat from New York. He's on a real campaign to bolster his image. One day showing up to serve meals at a homeless shelter for women and children, supposedly unannounced, but with a pack of reporters close behind. Another day, calling on the press to watch him present a large check to a charity for some rare genetic disorder...."

"Calm down Tony," David said. "I'll do my best. It's a little harder in Paradise Valley. This is pretty much a small town with some very wealthy and influential people. It doesn't matter how many ads there are in newspapers and magazines for people needing escorts. No one here wants to acknowledge how big a business it is."

"Sorry for the soapbox speech, David. I'll appreciate anything you can find. I need something, *anything*, that shows some connection between the Green family and your neck of the woods at the time of Valerie Powell's murder—*and if it's Morris Green himself, that's all the better*."

The Righteous Ones hearts pained for Tony. They knew what it was like to feel the agony of wondering which side God was on. Was it the truly righteous, the good souls who lived, loved and died without doing harm to others? Or, was it only the powerful and wealthy, regardless of their deeds, who seemed to wield the same power on earth as the Supreme Being did throughout the heavens.

The Laughing Angels were stunned at the thoughts coming from the Righteous Ones. For centuries they had been waiting for the Righteous Ones to loudly scream out to God—*Enough is enough. How long can we justify sitting at your throne, watching so many honest, hardworking people suffer, while you consolidate your lofty position with only the powerful and wealthy!*

Chapter 30

Nineteen-year-old Julia Green and 21-year-old Tom Rawlings were considered two of New York's beautiful people—their photos frequently seen on the society pages of the local newspapers.

The Rawlings, like Julia's family, were from *old money*, and had been well established in the community, and involved in a variety of charitable organizations. The story was that Tom's grandfather made most of his money in the stock market, leaving a great fortune to his wife and only son. After his grandfather and grandmother's tragic death in a car accident, Tom's father, a physician in the Washington Heights area of Manhattan—with little interest in business management—lost most of their family wealth through several bad investments.

Nevertheless, Tom received a good education, and his parents were known to be very charitable. They were hands-on volunteers for several local programs that aided the homeless, and worked weekends collecting and distributing clothing, toys for children, and supporting programs that provided apartments and homes for the elderly and the disabled.

Tom was also known as a mathematical wizard, continuing in the financial footsteps of his grandfather, while also being very active in the community and in local politics. It was his interest in politics that led him to meet Julia Green at a rally for Morris Green when he ran for the office of Governor of the State of New York. Tom seemed devastated by the governor's recent revelations of *inappropriate relationships*, and visibly angry that Green put his wife and daughters in such a humiliating situation.

Tony kept all this in mind, as he considered Stacey's index-card assessment of the escort murders, and the possibility that Julia Green and Tom Rawlings were somehow involved. The years had taught Tony to always keep an open mind. Not to judge a book by its cover. Some people are quick to learn exactly the right words to say, to appear perfect on the surface—especially people with their eyes on a political future. As a young homicide detective, he learned to watch out for anyone with something important to lose, who is confronted with a stumbling block to their plans, and then forced to take an unexpected detour.

Tony had seen the most self-assured person flounder, while the less confident somehow found the inner strength to survive and even thrive on the challenge.

When Tony was promoted from detective to senior detective in the homicide section of the Detroit Police Department, it was following a murder case that involved corporate corruption and the involvement of some very high level city officials, men with enough political clout to put solving the crime in jeopardy.

Division Commander Sean O'Connor cited that part of Tony's success in solving the crime was due to his commitment to the independence of the police in searching for the truth—regardless of any political influence.

"Solving each case is always Detective Pinella's goal," Division Commander O'Connor said. "Always following evidentiary rules and not looking for the easy way out. Detective Pinella is a *cop*, first and foremost. *To Protect and Serve* is not just a slogan to him. *It is the very essence of Detective Pinella.*"

Tony recalled that day very clearly. Sean O'Connor was one hell of a cop. He really believed in the motto *To*

Protect and Serve. Integrity was everything to him. Just two months after Tony's promotion, O'Connor unexpectedly retired and *ate his gun*.

A week before his suicide, O'Connor had learned that a jailhouse confession of a prisoner had completely exonerated a young man O'Connor had arrested fifteen years earlier for murdering a Detroit bookie. Found guilty, based on the evidence presented by O'Connor, this desperate and innocent young man was murdered in prison soon after his incarceration, leaving a wife and three young children behind.

O'Connor further learned that the actual killer had been hired by a Detroit City Council member who had owed the bookie thousands of dollars. O'Connor made sure the older and now-retired council member was arrested, but it was fifteen years too late.

A life-long bachelor, O'Connor left a will, leaving his entire savings, $250,000, to the children of the young man he had arrested.

To Protect and Serve. Sean O'Connor had lived by those words—and died by them. It was those words and that commitment that kept Tony on the trail of Veronica Blake's murderer—and to Stacey Johnson Blake. It would be those words that would prevent him for going after Julia Green, Morris Green, Tom Rawlings, or anyone else, until he had indisputable evidence of their guilt. So far, all he had were Stacey's color-coded index cards and the hypothesis of a known psychopathic killer—and his and Max's hunches. *Not enough to ruin anymore lives.*

Chapter 31

Finally, the break Tony and Max were waiting for came from David. It was a long shot, but David checked to see if any major business or other special events took place during the week that Valerie Powell was murdered. The one that stood out, and made the most sense, was a national meeting of independent financial advisors and hedge fund consultants, and stock brokers that was sponsored by Fidelity Investments.

It only took one quick call to the local Fidelity conference manager to get a copy of the program. There it was! Tom Rawlings was listed as a panel moderator for two sessions during a four-day business conference at the Loews Ventana Canyon Resort in Tucson.

According to the conference schedule, a private speakers' welcome cocktail party on Wednesday evening was followed by a dinner for all registrants, with Rawlings as the keynote speaker. The conference sessions began on Thursday morning after an early buffet breakfast, followed by a variety of simultaneous workshops, a formal luncheon with a speaker, more workshops, and a more casual barbecue dinner for all attendees.

Both of Rawlings' sessions were held on Friday, one in the morning and the second right after a buffet luncheon. Friday evening's formal dinner included a local comedian as the entertainment.

Saturday morning included another round of workshops, after which attendees were free to lunch at their leisure, and sign up for golf or tennis, with no additional events planned until the closing dinner that evening—where a panel of Fidelity specialists gave their sales pitches.

Most of the attendees had early Sunday morning flights home. David found out that Rawlings had left New York on an early Wednesday morning Southwest Airlines flight out of New York LaGuardia Airport, arriving at Phoenix Sky Harbor at approximately noon. He was met by a private limo service provided by the conference organizers. Based on the time he checked in at the Loews resort, the driver had taken him straight to the hotel from the airport, arriving several hours before the scheduled six o'clock speaker's dinner. Rawlings was on a return flight from Phoenix departing at 10:15 a.m. on Sunday, and arriving at LaGuardia at about 7:00 p.m. Both flights stopped at Midway Airport in Chicago where he changed planes.

If he went to all the scheduled functions, and that's an *if* right now, David thought, the only time Rawlings would have had on his own was Saturday afternoon—when there was ample time to rent a car and drive from Tucson to Paradise Valley, kill Valerie, and drive back to Tucson for the closing dinner. The time frame was tight, as Nancy Powell had found her sister's body at around 5:30 p.m. David would have to interview the conference attendees and hotel staff on duty that Saturday, to see if Rawlings was seen during lunch or during any of the free-time activities—or if he had shown up for the dinner and Fidelity sales pitches.

At this point, he did not want to arouse any suspicions about Julia's fiancé without talking to Tony. The days matched, but it still was a long shot.

Tony was excited to get the news from David, but he also wanted to be cautious in his approach. He suggested that David bring a photo of Rawlings up to the Lowes resort and discretely talk to the resort manager, and then with the staff. Rawlings was a strikingly handsome man and liked to flash his money around—so Tony was sure someone would recognize his photo and maybe provide some answers.

"If that pans out, then move on to the good folks at Fidelity who were onsite at the conference," Tony said.

When David called with the news, Tony was ready to go into action.

"Tony, you won't believe it. Right after the dinner Friday night, Rawlings told a couple of the Fidelity people that he was feeling *a bit under the weather*, and would probably sit out the Saturday morning sessions. Rawlings said he wanted to be sure not to miss the final sales pitches Saturday evening.

"According to resort staff, he called down to the front desk early Saturday morning and asked that a pot of tea be sent to his room. He said that he would be resting all day, so to please hold all his calls."

So far, there was no evidence that Rawlings made the approximately 70-mile journey from Tucson to Paradise Valley. David had checked all the car rental services, private limousine and taxi services that worked in and around the Loews resort. David also called in a private investigator who Tony knew in the area, to check out whether Rawlings might know someone in Tucson who drove him to Paradise Valley and back.

David also spoke to a friendly front desk agent at the resort, who looked up the telephone calls Rawlings made during his stay. Outside of room service, he made no other calls—not even to Julia, which Tony and David thought was strange. Of course, he could have used a cell phone, but there, again, there was no evidence that would get them a warrant to take the investigation further.

As the days turned into weeks, Tony knew he had to work smarter and faster—or the case would get away from him. Max was getting on his back for quicker results. His story was growing cold as Morris Green was gaining strong public confidence and support. At the same time, fatigue began to set in for Tony. Life in New York was so much faster than he had grown used to in Newport, Rhode Island—and the daily pressure was no longer appealing to him. There were days when his arms felt so heavy, he worried about having a heart attack. Other times he was overwhelmed with feelings of loss, as he thought about the many loved ones and good friends from the neighborhood who had died in the past couple of years.

Now there was Stacey Johnson Blake, working with her color-coded index cards. She actually seemed happy in her highly controlled environment at the psychiatric hospital. She had such faith in God's plan.

Then, it was as if a light bulb went off in his mind. *Maybe Stacey had the right idea all along.* At that moment, Tony went into the closet and took out the jacket he wore when visiting Stacey. As she had left with Nurse Spagnoli that afternoon, Stacey discretely passed Tony a crumbled-up piece of paper—which he quickly stuffed into his jacket pocket so Dr. Trotsky would not see it.

Tony's head was so filled with anxiety when he left the hospital that day, he had forgotten all about it. *That was not like him,* he thought. There was a time when every little detail in his life remained clear, especially when he was working a case. Maybe this was another sign that he was growing weary.

Yes, he found the note, still crumpled in the pocket. Careful not to tear it, he un-crumpled the paper. He felt as if Stacey's scribbled words cried out to him: *Tony, please don't weaken. Don't let me down. You and I can see the truth right through them. They don't want to help us. They want us to die for their sins, without any meaning in our lives.*

Tony looked out the window at the streets of Bensonhurst, the place of his childhood where there was so much love and understanding. He thought of his days in Detroit, the good people he knew there, like the Kagans. He thought of Max's determination to expose the truth about Morris Green—and the bravery of Angela Robinson, and her eagerness to move on with her life. Angela, Stephanie Taylor, Valerie Powell, and Amanda Wilson deserved more than a dusty file in police archives.

Chapter 32

A 21-year-old coed from the University of Arizona in Tucson was the key to breaking news in the investigation of Valerie Powell's murder. David told Tony that Shannon Riley had driven Tom Rawlings from Tucson to Paradise Valley.

"This is great news! Who is she? How does she know Rawlings? Where did you find her?" Tony was full of questions for David.

"Take it easy, Tony. I'll tell you everything. Slow down," David said.

"Okay, okay... This is just such good news. How did you find her?"

"To start with, I didn't find Shannon. It was your private investigator friend, Eddie Johnson. He did some poking around the Lowes resort, and talked to the desk clerk, an older guy named *Ricardo*, who happened to be working the late shift that week and through the weekend—from midnight until eight o'clock in the morning. *It was just one of those lucky breaks, Tony!*"

"Okay... So?" Tony asked.

"So, Johnson takes out a photo of Rawlings, flashes a fifty dollar bill, and Ricardo remembers him right away! Rawlings was talking to a very pretty redhead in the lobby about 2:00 a.m. Friday morning, just outside the cocktail lounge. Ricardo overheard Rawlings say, *Thanks, Shannon. I'll meet you Saturday morning in front of the hotel.*"

"Is that all you have, Kagan? *Thanks, and I'll meet you Saturday morning?*"

"Hang on, Tony. There's much more..."

"So? I'm waiting..."

"Like I said, Ricardo was just going off duty at eight o'clock on Saturday morning, when he sees Rawlings and the redhead meet in the lobby and drive off in a silver mustang convertible."

"How did Johnson track down this redhead?"

"I'm getting to that, Tony. This time, Johnson asks Ricardo if he minds looking on the hotel's garage registration info to see if there was a silver Mustang registered on those dates. At this point, Ricardo is pretty curious and hesitated, saying he'll have to make a call to the garage attendant for that information. So Johnson flashes his PI license and another fifty dollar bill, and says the redhead's family is pretty worried about her dating this guy from out of town, and can Ricardo please help him out."

"And Ricardo fell for that?"

"Let's just say an extra fifty, and he went straight to the computer. There was only one guest with a silver Mustang—and that was..."

"Shannon Riley," Tony interrupted with a thunderous sound of satisfaction.

"Yup! Not only did he give Eddie her full name and a contact phone number, but she was here with a group of graduate students from the University of Arizona for a seminar—and you'll love this—on *Religion, Politics and the Law.*"

"I'll get a flight out tomorrow morning," Tony said.

Not even trying to hide his laughter, David said, "Let me know the flight number, and I'll meet you at the airport. I know how fond you are of Phoenix cabbies!"

"Very funny, Kagan. See you tomorrow."

At least for now, Tony decided not to let the NYPD, not even Max, know about Riley. All Tony knew so far was that he was worried about her safety, as well as the success of the investigation. Being able to pull Rawlings in for questioning was the break they needed—the key to linking Morris Green to the murders.

The best thing for Tony was to get back to Arizona as soon as possible. Another long plane ride was not something he especially looked forward to, but Tony got right on the phone. He was lucky to book a flight for early the next morning.

Tony called David back, and left a message on his voice mail with the flight number.

Chapter 33

Long flights, even short ones for that matter, were bothering Tony more and more. He made the reservation too late to get either an aisle or a window seat and would be stuck in the middle—a tough spot for a stocky man with long legs! The agent told him that maybe when he got to the airport, another seat would be available—but no such luck!

Tony settled into his seat, eager to get some rest during the long flight to Phoenix. The two people sitting next to him were an older woman at the window, and a middle-aged man on the aisle. Both were already quietly reading their magazines when Tony squeezed between them.

The plane was crowded, filled to capacity. As soon as everyone boarded and the plane took off, Tony put his head back on a pillow, and settled in for a nap. He did not put his seat back, conscious of not disturbing the much older man sitting behind him. *At least if he could sleep,* he thought, *the flight might seem shorter.*

Unfortunately, the young man sitting in the middle seat just in front of him had the same idea, but was not as thoughtful. He put his seat all the way back, put on his earphones, and was having a grand old time moving around in his seat to the beat of the music playing on his CD player, which was loud enough for Tony to hear.

It was one thing not being able to stretch his legs in the short leg space, but now his knees were being crushed and he was forced to listen to music that was not exactly soothing.

Tony's first inclination was to tap the guy on the shoulder and ask him to move his seat forward and lower the sound, but he hesitated—something he would not have done five, or even ten years ago. Age and its various infirmities had changed him. He used to wonder why his parents—as they grew older—were less likely to complain to the noisy people living in the apartment across the hall, or to ask the building manager for more heat during a cold winter. Tony had to step in to speak up for them.

It was the same thing in Detroit. Before Tony was promoted to detective, older people in the neighborhood he patrolled did not want to call the police when they were harassed by some of the tougher kids on the block, or when a neighbor was blasting the television late at night. Tony and Steve Kagan used to watch out for the older people of the neighborhoods as much as possible, and tried to encourage them to call the police—that they were there to help them.

Now here he was, stuck in a small seat with some young punk rhythmically and indifferently banging against his arthritic knees with every beat of the loud music—and no thought whatsoever for anyone else around him.

Tony kept trying to sleep, but it was no use, and he was getting more and more agitated. Finally, he tapped the young man softly on his shoulder, and said politely, "Excuse me, but would you please move your seat forward? I'm afraid it's banging pretty hard against my knees."

When there was no response, Tony repeated himself a little louder, and the young man turned around.

"Hey, I heard you the first time, mister. That's just too bad. I paid for my seat, just like you did."

Tony tried to hold his temper. This time, he pressed the guy's shoulder with some strength. "Well, how would you feel if the person in front of you put *his* seat all the way back?"

The only response Tony got this time was the guy turning up the music, which was already loud enough to cause the woman sitting in the aisle seat next to him to sigh loudly, and glare at the kid with a clear look of exasperation.

Now Tony was really pissed, but still did not want to cause a ruckus in the crowded plane. He decided to wait for the flight attendant, who was nearing his row with the snacks and beverages.

"Excuse me, Miss. Please ask the young man in front of me to raise his seat a bit. It's pretty squashed back here."

"I'm sorry, sir, but it's really busy right now. Perhaps you can ask him yourself," she responded and continued wheeling her serving cart up to the front of the plane.

Well that's just great, Tony thought. *The airlines just don't give a damn, so long as they get their money.* The flight attendant had forced his hand. He would have to handle the situation his own way, like he would with any punk on the street. Tony unfastened his seat belt, leaned forward carefully, and tapped the shoulder of the woman sitting next to the punk.

"Excuse me, ma'am. You seem very uncomfortable, and I wondered if you would like to stretch your legs a bit, while I visit with my friend sitting next to you? I'll just be a few minutes… "

Her smile showed obvious and grateful relief. "Thank you so much," she said. "I was just getting up to visit the rest room."

Tony slid into her seat, with the offender still oblivious to what was going on—until Tony pulled the earplug out of the kid's ear, and flashed his PI license and an old Detroit police badge he kept for such *special circumstances.* Then Tony whispered quietly but firmly, "This is your last warning, kid! Put your seat up and lower that music, and keep it that way for the rest of the flight. Do exactly as I say or the detective who's meeting me at the Phoenix airport will be happy to greet you as well!"

The young man did not have to say anything. The pale frightened look on his face said it all. He stiffened, put his seat up, and shut off the CD player that was in his lap.

"Good boy," Tony said as he firmly patted the young man on the shoulder and slid out of the seat. "Have a nice flight and enjoy your stay in Phoenix!"

Tony headed back to his own seat, just as the woman was returning to her seat next to the young offender.

"I think you can enjoy the rest of your flight, miss," Tony said with a knowing smile.

"Thank you so much. Who says chivalry is dead," she remarked with a bright smile.

Tony slept for the rest of the flight, feeling refreshed when he heard the captain's voice over the loudspeaker: *Welcome to Phoenix ladies and gentleman, where the temperature is a pleasant 104 degrees.*

Chapter 34

After showing his badge to the security personnel, David met Tony at the landing gate. As soon as he saw Tony, David quickly took the carry-on bag from his friend's hand, and noted that Tony did not resist the help.

"Tony, good to see you! How was your flight?"

"Well, if you don't count the lousy seating and the young punk sitting in front of me, not too bad! Let's just say that I'm looking forward to sitting in your nice air-conditioned car and meeting Shannon Riley. Are we seeing her this afternoon?"

"We're on with Shannon tomorrow. Let's just grab the rest of your luggage from the claim area, and get you back to my apartment for a cold drink—I'll fill you in on Shannon's story in the car. It's a real break for us, Tony!"

"Just my carry-on this time, Kagan. But I hope your car is close by. My knees are killing me!"

"My car's down the escalator, right outside the door. Another of the advantages to being a cop."

"Too bad first class plane tickets aren't on our list of benefits," Tony laughed. "Not even for high-class NYPD consultants, like me."

David realized the years were really catching up on Tony, as well as on himself. He wondered if the stress of this case, particularly, and the long flights back and forth to Phoenix, were too much for his old friend.

"Are you sure you're all right, Tony? Maybe you should have let me handle the Riley part of this investigation on my own?"

"Hey, Kagan. I may be a little older than you are, but when I came out of retirement to take on Morris Green, it was with a one hundred percent commitment. I may have a few more aches and pains, and my prostate never lets me forget my age… but I'm in this for the long haul."

"Take it easy, Tony. I didn't mean any harm… and my prostate isn't exactly letting me sleep through the night, if you catch my drift!"

Tony let out one of his guttural laughs. "Glad to hear we still have so much in common," he said. "Now fill me in on Shannon Riley. What's her background? On the phone, you said she's a student. Why can't she meet with us this afternoon? How did she get mixed up with Tom Rawlings?"

"One thing at a time, Tony. Yes, Shannon is a student and she has exams all day today. We're almost at my apartment. Let's wait till we're both sipping on that cold drink, and I'll give you all the background I have so far."

It was only about ten minutes later that David pulled into his parking space at the Cibola Apartments in Scottsdale, and carried Tony's bag up to the second floor. He left the air-conditioner turned down low, so the apartment was nice and cold.

Tony gave a great sigh of relief as he stepped through the doorway and into the cool apartment. "Ah, that feels great," he said. "Even going from your car to the front door made me start sweating!"

David laughed as he carried Tony's suitcase into the bedroom. "I think it's a good thing you retired to Newport, Rhode Island," he said. "My first few years in the desert heat were tough. I really missed those cold winters in Detroit. Now, I wear a jacket when the thermometer reads sixty degrees in the winter. I used to sleep with the windows open in Detroit when it was zero degrees! Life sure changes."

"Speaking of life changing, I'm going to the bathroom," Tony said. "Then I want that cold drink, and for you to tell me all about Shannon Riley and Tom Rawlings."

While David updated Tony on what he had learned so far from Shannon Riley, she was finishing up her exams and planned to head straight back to her apartment in Tucson, near the University of Arizona. Her plan was to drive the two hours to Paradise Valley early the next morning for her meeting with David Kagan and Tony Pinella at police headquarters. She was very nervous about her potential role as a witness concerning the murder of Valerie Powell, to the point that she felt physically ill. How could giving someone a simple ride to Paradise Valley, when she was going to visit her parents in Scottsdale, risk her life—and maybe even her parents' lives? *He seemed so nice,* she thought. He had introduced himself as an accountant attending a Fidelity Investments conference... *It was just a drink, not even a date!*

She never imagined she would start receiving threatening phone calls from Rawlings within weeks of giving him that ride back and forth from Tucson. After speaking to David, Shannon had *Googled* Rawlings and was surprised to see his name pop-up in connection with Julia Green and Governor Morris Green. *This can't be the same Rawlings,* she thought. Then she found a photo of Rawlings and Julia Green at a charity benefit for children. His hair was combed differently, but it certainly looked like the same guy.

Now, she was more frightened, and even more determined to make a formal statement about Rawlings' harassment and threats. For her own sake, and those of her parents, she felt an obligation to assist the police in any way she could.

Chapter 35

David and Tony arrived at the Paradise Valley Police Department at 9:30 a.m., an hour before Shannon Riley was scheduled to arrive. The conference room was already set up to both audio and videotape the interview. Captain Juanita Lopez would be observing from the adjacent room.

David knew Shannon would be especially nervous, so he had arranged for a more comfortable conference room, rather than the stark interview room that was usually used for suspects and other witnesses. The table was set with a variety of donuts and muffins, coffee, water and soft drinks.

Shannon arrived promptly at 10:30 a.m. David met her at the reception desk. When he brought her into the conference room, Tony walked right over and warmly shook Shannon's hand.

"I'm Tony Pinella, and I can't tell you enough how much we appreciate your cooperation, Ms. Riley. I know this is difficult, but I hope we can make you feel as comfortable as possible. Your help means a great deal to all of us."

"Thank you, Detective Pinella. Yes, I am nervous. But Detective Kagan has explained everything, and I know this is the right thing to do. I could not live with myself if the man I met in Tucson really is a killer, and someone else gets hurt because I did not cooperate."

"Then let's get started," David said. "Please sit down and help yourself to some coffee or soda and a pastry. Tony, why don't you start."

"Thanks, David. Shannon, will you please start by stating your name and telling us how you first met Tom Rawlings."

"Yes. My name is Shannon Riley and I'm a graduate student at the University of Arizona in Tucson. I was with a group of fellow students attending an evening seminar and dinner on *Religion, Politics and the Law* at the Loews Ventana Canyon Resort in Tucson. I met Mr. Rawlings on Friday night, when I stopped in for a drink at the cocktail lounge."

"What did you discuss?" Tony asked.

"It was all very casual. The usual things about why we were at the Loews, where we were from… nothing very serious. I told him I was from Scottsdale, and he said he had heard it was a beautiful area. I guess I was so comfortable with him, I told him that I was going there to visit my parents the next day, Saturday, and would be happy to drop him off somewhere and bring him back to Tucson later that day. That's what I did. We left the hotel on Saturday morning at about eight o'clock. I dropped him off about ten-thirty, and picked him up later that afternoon in the same place. We got back to the hotel late Saturday afternoon, about five-thirty or so."

The interview went on for several hours. Shannon told David and Tony that since that Saturday, when she drove Rawlings from Tucson to Paradise Valley and back, he had called her several times.

"At first," she said, "he just asked me not to tell anyone about the rides. He sounded a little nervous, even though nothing more happened than a drink in the cocktail lounge that previous Friday night. I figured he had a jealous girlfriend somewhere. I don't know—maybe someone had snapped a picture of us sitting at the bar. I'm not naïve, those things can innocently happen… I told him I hadn't mentioned it to anyone."

"Did he call again?" David asked.

"Yes, several times. Always being polite, and just asking how I was feeling. His later calls sounded more ominous, more like threats."

"What do you mean by threats?" Tony asked.

"One time, he said, *You're very pretty, Shannon. It would be a shame if anything happened to you.* I asked him what he meant by that. He just laughed and said, *Oh, you know. You ought to be careful who you give rides to...You never really know who they are or what they're capable of doing."*

"Did he keep calling you?" Tony asked.

"When I began getting hang-ups late at night, I was pretty sure it must be Tom. Then, just before David called me last week, Tom called again. This time he didn't hang up when I answered the phone. I quickly asked, *Is that you Tom? What do you want?* He said, *Don't do anything stupid, Shannon. I know where your parents live.* It was after that, when David called and asked me to make a formal statement at police headquarters. That's when I found out about you, and the other murders."

"You really have been a great help, Shannon. I know this isn't easy for you," David said.

"I'm frightened, Detective Kagan, but I'll cooperate with the police as much as needed. If Tom Rawlings really is a murderer, it's my obligation to help. Escort or not, no woman deserves to lose her life that way. From what I read in the newspapers, Valerie Powell was a good kid. It's not for me to judge the life choices she made. Let's face it. I felt no misgivings at all about having a drink with the guy! What if that evening, or the next day, someone had found my body?"

"You're sure?" David asked. He wanted to be one hundred percent confident he had a witness to tie Rawlings to Powell's murder—and possibly to the New York murders.

"I'm absolutely sure. I feel a responsibility. *But what about my parents? What should I tell them? Do you think they're in danger?*" she asked David.

"I'll make sure someone is discreetly watching their house, just in case," he answered. "What's their address in Scottsdale?"

"Should I let them know what's happening?"

"At this point, let's not alarm them. The car will be unmarked, and we have a special unit that knows how to handle these situations. Just one thing, would they let you know if you they were receiving unusual or threatening phone calls?"

"Oh, yes, they sure would. My mom calls me even if the Safeway delivery service sends a new driver! She watches all the television shows, like *Law and Order Criminal Intent*, and has read every true crime book that's ever been published. I'm sure she would let me know even if a stranger walked down their street!"

"Try not to worry, Shannon. We'll have another plain clothes officer watching your apartment, as well as the one watching out for your parents," David said. "Thanks so much for cooperating. You're a brave woman."

"Thank you, detectives. Thank you both," Shannon said.

It was obvious to David and Tony that she was trying to hold back her tears.

Chapter 36

Settled into an aisle seat on his flight back to New York, Tony looked over David's and his notes, and the copy of Shannon Riley's statement. There was no doubt in his mind that Tom Rawlings had both motive and opportunity for murdering Valerie Powell.

The newspapers described the premeditated murder of Valerie Powell as vicious, the work of a monster. It left Tony wondering just how far Tom Rawlings would go to protect his lifestyle, and Morris Green's reputation.

Tony was confident that Shannon would make a good witness. He was impressed with her strength of character and commitment to justice. Although it was obvious that she was frightened, it was just as apparent to Tony that Shannon felt strongly about her obligations to the young murdered women.

Although the crime scene had not provided a direct link to Rawlings so far, the CSI team was going over all the evidence samples one more time. Tony also had called ahead to his New York police contact, and his team would do the same for the murders of Stephanie Taylor and Amanda Wilson. *At least it was a start,* he thought. Between the hotel staff and Shannon's testimony, David had just enough to bring Rawlings in for questioning. He was not sure about Julia Green—not yet.

Paradise Valley was one thing, but would Rawlings have been bold enough to commit murder in New York, where his face is well known to the public? It would not be the first time someone with money, status, and power thought they could get away with murder. At the very least, if not by their own hands—Rawlings, Morris Green, or even Julia might have put up the money for the killings.

Lots to think about, and it probably was time to let Max in on the new information.

Tony was tired, and it was only an hour into the long flight home. He could not help thinking about the safety of Shannon Riley and her parents. Without her cooperation, it was possible that the murders might never be solved.

Shannon and Tony hit it off immediately. As they shook hands, the nervous look on Shannon's face softened when she told Tony that he had the same twinkle in his eyes as her grandfather. Although he did not tell her, Shannon reminded Tony of his first serious girlfriend, Jenny Vincent. Sweet Jenny he used to call her. When she was thirteen, Jenny had moved with her family from rural West Virginia to Bensonhurst. He recalled how lost Jenny seemed when they first met in the high school cafeteria. He could still see it clearly. Sweet Jenny standing there, next to his lunch table, not knowing where to sit. When he asked if she would like to sit down, she said *thank you so much*, in such a soft accent, he was immediately smitten. They remained good friends throughout high school. Now he wondered where she might be….

Tony's trip down memory lane ended abruptly when he overheard a heated discussion going on between the two women seated next to him. Being a detective all these years had left him with a few bad habits, one of them was listening in to other people's conversations! This time, the argument was on a topic he felt strongly about—the questionable relationships between television network newscasters and so-called analysts with big-time politicians. Evidently, it was an article in that day's newspaper that started the argument. NBC and its affiliates had already hired the daughters of two major politicians for a couple of vaguely described *special assignment* jobs: Meghan McCain, daughter of Senator John McCain, and Jenna Bush, daughter of George W. Bush. Now NBC was hyping it had hired Chelsea Clinton, daughter of Hillary and former President Bill Clinton, as a *special correspondent* for its new Prime Time News Magazine, *Rock Center with Brian Williams*.

"Never mind that not one of them is trained or even has any experience in journalism," the woman sitting by the window said emphatically. "None of them are journalists! Newspapers are shutting down all over the country, with highly skilled journalists left without jobs—while these three young women—with no relevant journalistic experience, are smiling into the cameras, and doing interviews with their families! Is that what journalism has come to? Network executives and their anchor people making points with the politicians they are supposed to be objectively reporting on? Give me a break!"

"Well, you're certainly right, Nancy," answered the woman sitting in the middle seat. "The president of NBC News should be ashamed of himself."

"He should lose his job!" Nancy screamed. "And don't forget about all the ambitious young students, who graduate each year from fine schools of journalism, like Columbia University in New York, and the University of California in Berkeley. The only jobs they can find are unpaid internships running errands and probably bringing coffee to McCain and Clinton!"

"It's not that I don't agree with you, Nancy. It just isn't worth your getting so angry and frustrated. You're not going to change anything about how these networks operate. You'll just get all upset, while Chelsea walks off with the $600,000 a year she's supposedly earning to interview her father and mother."

"You're right, Janet. After 25 years of friendship, you know me too well. I'm not only frustrated from a feminist's point of view. It's just so disappointing. Too many newspaper journalists aren't *journalists* at all. Many of them don't even know the basic elements of a hard news story, or what a lead paragraph looks like. I'm sorry to stand on my soapbox about this, but television news isn't any better. Those of us who tune in to hear objective news are faced with network anchors and their executives hiring unskilled men and women—just to gain access to influential people."

"It's the way of the world, Nancy. I don't want you having a heart attack over it."

Then Janet unexpectedly turned to Tony and asked, "What do you think about what my friend is saying?"

Tony hesitated, but this was one of his favorite topics. "Do you really want my opinion?"

"Yes, if you don't mind. We both would welcome your thoughts on this subject—a man's point of view. *Wouldn't we Nancy?*"

"Well, Nancy is right about NBC. You're right, too, Janet. No one should have a heart attack over it. It does seem like a losing battle."

"Is that all you have to say?"

Tony was not sure he really wanted to get into a heated conversation with these women. He was tired. *But what the hell*, Tony thought. *It's a long flight and I have a captive audience actually asking for my opinion.*

"Look, I have a problem with some of our journalists, too. Even the good ones go astray at one point or another. Have you ever heard a television journalist ask a politician, who is asking the American public to sacrifice, why he isn't willing to sacrifice his taxpayer supported pension? That would be a start."

"Do you think that would be fair?" Janet asked.

"Don't you?" Tony shot back. "Of course it's fair. In my view, government pensions, federal or state, should be reserved for the military, and for law enforcement officers and firefighters. They're the ones who risk their lives every day for all of us. What would be fair, is if members of congress and other federal workers paid into the Social Security system, just like the rest of us—and had to set up their own retirement accounts. Accounts not subsidized by the taxpayers."

"Well, you certainly have some interesting thoughts," Janet said.

Tony could feel his face growing red and his blood pressure rising. "Interesting! Good grief, woman!" he exclaimed. "Congress makes a big deal when they sacrifice a weekend to do the people's work, or work late into the evening so a budget is passed in time to make sure our brave soldiers and their families get their salaries. There are people who work longer hours for minimum wage, and then work overtime with no additional pay, just because they take pride in their work. Then their tax dollars go to pay the salaries of members of congress—not to mention the perks! That's far more than *interesting*, don't you think? Where are the journalists who are writing about that?"

Recognizing the discussion was taking an angry turn, Nancy quickly interjected in a soft voice. "I love your ideas, sir. Don't mind my friend. Janet's grandson is on our local city council in Dearborn, Michigan, so I'm afraid she's especially sensitive when it comes to the relationships between government officials and the public."

Tony took a deep breath and realized he needed to calm down. "Sorry if I was rude. I think I've done enough pontificating for one flight. I'll let you get back to your conversation."

"Yes, I think that's best," Janet said. "I'm sorry I disturbed you."

"It's been our pleasure," Nancy said. "By the way, you already know that I'm Nancy and my sulking friend here is Janet. What's your name?"

"Tony Pinella."

"Pinella. I *know* that name," Nancy said slowly. "Oh my God, don't tell me you're *that* Tony Pinella. The one who solved the Veronica Blake murder?"

"Yes, that's me"

"No wonder you know so much about how the press works. They were all over that story! Who was that one writer? I think his name was Max Gold. His articles were terrific!"

"Max did an excellent job," Tony said. "He's one of the few journalists that respects law enforcement officers and the difficult jobs and decisions they face every day."

"Well, I loved reading about that case, and you were terrific. I know this might sound strange, but you were very much responsible for strengthening my faith."

Tony perked up and could not resist asking, "That's very nice of you to say, but in what way?"

"You proved to the world that Jason Blake was not a murderer, while so many reporters had him tried and convicted as soon as that poor woman's body was found. It would have been terrible if an evangelist, a trusted man of God, were found guilty of murder."

"Not if he did kill his wife!" Tony sharply said.

"Well, I guess so," Nancy softly answered. "*Anyway,* you did a great job of clearing him."

Tony noticed that Janet had started to take an interest in the conversation, and he did not want to pursue a discussion about Jason Blake. He simply said, "I did my job and had a great deal of help."

This time Janet intervened, realizing Nancy was about to begin one of her diatribes about God's grace and absolution.

"Yes, Detective Tony Pinella! Now I remember... When you retired from the Detroit Police Department, there was a magazine article about you. The writer said you had received many commendations from the department, and that the officers you worked with considered you a great detective. If I'm remembering correctly, you weren't exactly popular among the local politicians," Janet said. "Now I understand why you feel so strongly about them—no offense intended," she quickly added.

"None taken, Janet. Believe me, I take that as a real compliment!"

"If you don't mind my asking, what are you doing now?"

"Mostly, I'm retired, but I do have a license as a private investigator and sometimes consult with various police departments."

"That sounds exciting! Were you in Phoenix on a case?" Nancy asked.

"Well, now, Nancy, I'm sure you can appreciate that even if I were traveling on a case, I couldn't share that with you."

"Oh, of course not. I understand. Do you have business cards for us? Never know when we might need a good detective."

Tony reached into his shirt pocket, where he always kept a few cards, and gave one each to Nancy and Janet. He was not sure that was smart, but who knew... business comes from all sorts of unexpected places. Who could have thought he would be traveling to Phoenix on a murder case involving a New York State governor!

Tony leaned his head back, closed his eyes, and finally dozed off. After an hour or so, he was abruptly awakened by a rough landing at LaGuardia. The bad weather had delayed his arrival, so it was after 11:00 p.m. when Tony finally returned to his Bensonhurst apartment. The next day would be a long one, so after a short hot shower, Tony set his clock radio for 6:00 am, and headed straight to bed.

Tired as he was from the trip, Tony could not sleep. His heart raced with anticipation and concern. Shannon Riley had given them a good lead towards linking at least one of the escort murders to Tom Rawlings. So far, it was the only break in any of the cases—but it was still only a lead. More evidence was needed to connect all the dots to actually place Tom Rawlings directly inside each escort's apartment.

Chapter 37

When the clock radio went off the next morning at six, Tony was groggy. On his nightstand was a copy of yesterday's *The Arizona Republic*, so it took him a few minutes to remember he was in his own bed in Bensonhurst, and not at David's apartment in Scottsdale.

When he looked at the front page, he remembered why he bought the paper at the airport. The headline was about the former Catholic Bishop of Phoenix, who decided not to accept an award from the Catholic Community Foundation. *I'll read that article later*, he thought. *I better get this day started!*

Dragging himself out of bed, Tony slowly showered and shaved. Getting his days going in the mornings were getting harder and harder. Showering took longer, as he was careful not to slip in the tub, and shaving around his sagging jowls was tricky. After cutting himself several times, he mumbled to himself, *guess it's time to turn in my old barber's razor for an electric shaver before I slit my own throat.*

With little shreds of toilet paper covering the cuts on his cheeks and neck, Tony sat down at his desk and picked up the phone. First on the day's agenda—even before breakfast—would have to be a call to Chief Detective Salvador Cedeno, his contact at the NYPD, to update him about Tom Rawlings. It was already after seven o'clock, and he was sure Cedeno would be on the job.

Tony learned that late yesterday afternoon Captain Juanita Lopez called Cedeno and was very pleased with the progress made on the Valerie Powell case. She agreed to coordinate their respective cases through Tony—who would now be the official consultant and liaison to both agencies on the escort murders. Cedeno was pleased. He stuck his neck out hiring the retired detective as a consultant on the New York cases, and then stretched the budget by sending him to Arizona twice. Fortunately, the trips to Arizona were fruitful. The information Tony brought back seemed to cinch the link between Tom Rawlings and the Paradise Valley murder. They were still checking on the murder of Stephanie Taylor in Chicago. All they had on the case was that Stephanie, like Valerie Powell and Amanda Wilson—and, of course, Angela Robinson—all worked for Leslie Stevens' escort service.

Now Cedeno wanted clear evidence that would place Rawlings directly at the scenes where the bodies of Taylor *and* Wilson were found.

Next call was to Max. As soon as Tony mentioned Rawlings' name, Max stopped him and suggested they meet for an early dinner at his favorite deli, so Tony could fill him in on all the details. Tony knew that Max would hold off on any articles until he got an okay from Cedeno. They did not want Green to get wind of the investigation too soon, and circle the troops around Julia's fiancé. Worse would be if Green realized that Rawlings was only the first target of the investigation.

Tony needed to find out if Julia Green *and* her father were also directly involved. The scenes at all three murders needed to be re-examined for even the slightest evidence linked to Rawlings. Even the best CSI teams might have overlooked something—maybe a small fiber, a splinter of glass… Tony did not want to take any chances.

Just as he sat down for a strong cup of coffee, the phone rang. It was only 8:45 a.m., and Tony had a bad feeling. *Maybe another escort has been murdered*, he thought. But, no—that was not the news.

"Tony, our game plan just changed," Chief Cedeno said. "Tom Rawlings was found dead in his apartment just after eight o'clock this morning. The officers who found him said it looks like a burglary gone wrong, and all I know right now is that he may have been killed sometime late last night or very early this morning."

"Who found the body?" Tony asked.

"A neighbor from across the hall. She said that when Rawlings came home sometime after eleven o'clock, she heard shouting coming from his apartment—and then very loud music. The building superintendant didn't answer her phone calls, so she just went to sleep. The music was still blasting early this morning. She banged on Rawlings' door, and when no one answered, she called the police. Evidently, the killer—or killers—turned the music up so the shot wouldn't be heard. I'm on my way over there now, and I have a forensic team on the way. I want you there, too, Tony."

"I'll be there," Tony said.

While sitting in the taxi on his way downtown, for a brief moment, he wondered what Stacey Johnson Blake might say in this situation. Probably that God, in all his mercy, had saved Tom from the possibility of many years in prison—or even the death penalty. Then his mind switched quickly to who knew that Rawlings was a suspect in the escort murders.

The first to know were Juanita Lopez, David Kagan, and Shannon Riley in Arizona. *No Morris Green connection there*, he thought. *It had to be someone in New York. What if Max knew his phone might be tapped? That would explain why Max didn't not want to hear the details about Rawlings over the phone.*

In New York, other than Cedeno on the NYPD, there was Don Lynch, an old friend. He was in Delaware at his niece's wedding and did not yet know about the Rawlings-

Paradise Valley link, and Fred Lewis, an officer attached to one of Cedeno's special units, who had been working on a potential link between the Stephanie Taylor and Amanda Wilson murders.

Tony had always been a little nervous about Lewis' assignment to the cases. Max told him that Lewis had spent some time in Morris Green's security detail during special public events. Without any evidence to support his suspicion, it was best to keep quiet about Lewis—at least for now. Cedeno trusted Lewis completely, so that was not Tony's call.

Tony had two bigger problems. He still had nothing that connected Rawlings to the Chicago murder of Stephanie Taylor. Without Rawlings, it would be harder to connect Julia Green to the escort murders.

Any evidence leading to Julia's complicity would have to be very strong. Her paternal grandparents were wealthy and powerful people, and they had a direct line to Commissioner Brennan, Cedeno's boss.

Even the public would be sympathetic to Julia, Tony thought. *The whole family was humiliated when Green was forced to resign as Governor of New York State. Was that enough for his daughter to commit murder? Even if she did go crazy, like Stacey Blake did, the public would certainly sympathize more with a young woman in Julia's position—and now her fiancé had been murdered. Unless,* he thought further, *she also killed Rawlings!*

By the time Tony reached Rawlings' apartment, Fred Lewis was already there with Cedeno.

"It sure looks to me like a robbery gone bad," Lewis told Tony. "The wall safe is open and empty, and it looks like someone rifled through the papers in the desk drawers. There may also have been some cash in there—and Rawlings' wallet, and the diamond cufflinks and Rolex watch he was wearing last night are missing."

"How did you find out so fast what Rawlings was wearing last night?" Tony asked.

"An invitation was in his suit pocket to a black-tie bachelor party at the Four Seasons on East 52nd Street. We sent an officer right over there, who confirmed with the hotel banquet manager that the party broke up early, probably around 10:45 p.m. or so. One of the waiters had recognized Rawlings and commented to the manager on his *flashy* jewelry. We also found out that the party was for Craig Rainford, one of Rawlings' big-time clients."

"It's only a few minutes by cab to this building, so the neighbor's time estimate is probably right," Tony said.

Tony then pulled Cedeno aside. "Even if this does turn out to be a burglary, someone must have known Rawlings would be at that party last night, and probably figured it would run much later than eleven o'clock. I'm still suspicious. Whoever was in this apartment when Rawlings came home last night wanted him dead. Breaking into the safe—even removing his watch and cufflinks—was to make it look like a robbery."

"Let's see what our CSI team finds," Cedeno said. "Lewis, have any of the family been notified?"

"Not yet," Lewis said. "We thought you would want to handle that."

"Yeah, thanks! Just what I'm looking forward to," Cedeno said. "Lewis, you and Pinella meet me back at police headquarters at noon. I need to get back now and update the commissioner. He'll want to arrange a press conference and get quick control of what information is released."

As soon as he left Rawlings' apartment, Tony called Max. "We have a lot to discuss, Max. Tom Rawlings has been murdered."

"My God, Tony! What happened?"

"Not now, Max. I'll explain everything later. I have to be at police headquarters at noon. Can you meet me at my apartment this evening at six-thirty? I'll order from Kosher Chow's down the street."

"Okay. I'll be there. This is quite a turn of events," Max said. "Right now, I'm headed over to *Public Corruption* to see what reports, if any, have come in on Rawlings' murder."

"Nothing yet, I hope," Tony said. "The chief wants to keep this under wraps until the commissioner has a chance to call the family, and arrange a press conference."

"Got it, Tony. See you later. Bye."

Chapter 38

Tony decided to walk back to police headquarters. It was a long walk, but he needed to clear his head, think about something else—and the exercise would be good for him. Not far from Rawlings' apartment was St Patrick's Cathedral on Fifth Avenue. Tony looked up at the beautiful building. He had only been there once, as a young boy, when his blessed mother took him sightseeing in Manhattan. Then he recalled the article in *The Arizona Republic* about the Catholic Bishop of Phoenix who decided not to accept an award from the Catholic Community Foundation. He had put that section of the paper into his briefcase before he left his apartment.

Tony looked at his watch to see if there was time for lunch before his meeting with Cedeno and the Rawlings' murder team. He was hungry and still feeling jet lagged from his trip to Arizona. He remembered a sandwich shop a few blocks from the police station, and stopped off for a cup of coffee and a grilled cheese sandwich. *Now I can read that article about the Catholic bishop,* he thought.

When the award was first announced, *The Arizona Republic* columnist, E.J. Montini, had written about the outrage of many in the Phoenix community when The Catholic Community Foundation announced that ex-Bishop Thomas J. O'Brien was one of three individuals to be honored at the Crozier Gala, the Foundation's upcoming annual spring fundraising event.

O'Brien, who served as the Catholic Bishop of Phoenix from 1982 to 2003, was listed as the event's faith honoree. As he continued to read the article, Tony was fuming. This was the same O'Brien who had received immunity from criminal charges in 2003 for transferring pedophile priests from one diocese to another. Soon after, O'Brien was arrested for leaving the scene of a car accident when his vehicle struck and killed a pedestrian. He got probation and only did community service for that crime!

Montini's column expressed the outrage felt by parents of children who had been abused. Of all people, how could they choose O'Brien for an award meant for *someone who has had an impact on the community with their commitment to the faith*? Tony could hardly believe it.

The article went on to say that after Montini's column appeared, and the invitations to the gala had been mailed, O'Brien decided not to accept the award. Donna Marino, the foundation's president, issued a statement apologizing to those who were hurt by the decision to honor the bishop. In an earlier statement, she also shielded the foundation by saying it was not the foundation itself, but a panel of volunteers who voted to give O'Brien the award—as well as foundation board members who evidently did not oppose the vote.

Tony wondered what these volunteers and the board members were thinking. *Would they cross themselves and pray for this bishop, a man who acknowledged shielding priests who were abusing children? Better they should pray for the children he abused, whose faith had been shattered—their lives and their families' lives—changed forever.*

All Tony's years of experience taught him that it did not take much for the innocent and unsuspecting to be injured, physically and emotionally, by people of all faiths who hid behind their cloaks of respectability.

Sometimes, Tony thought, *a newspaper columnist can really make a difference by opening the eyes of the pubic.* That is what he respected about Max Gold—and *The Arizona Republic* columnist E.J. Montini. Both had real guts.

❧

The Laughing Angels celebrated a monumental victory. Their understanding of human nature was once again confirmed by those who publicly professed their faith—while their actions rarely had anything to do with their beliefs.

Chapter 39

It was just noon, when Tony caught up to Salvador Cedeno, who was walking into the conference room at police headquarters. To their surprise, Fred Lewis evidently decided to start early. He took charge of the meeting—without either Tony or Cedeno present. Lewis was saying it was an open and shut case.

"Tom Rawlings' murder was obviously a burglary gone bad," Lewis said. "Most likely, it was someone at the bachelor party, or maybe someone who works for the caterer, who set up the burglary—not counting on it ending so early. Just Rawlings' dumb luck. Probably someone Rawlings gave bad advice to on an investment."

"Wait a minute," Tony interrupted. "That's a pretty hasty conclusion. We don't even have all the forensics back yet. We know there is a firm link between Rawlings' visit to Tucson and the murder of Valerie Powell. We're still re-examining the evidence from all three escort murders to see if there's a link to Rawlings. The *so-called burglary* could have been a set-up all right. Suppose someone had a reason to kill Rawlings? Something related to the escort murders? They could have known about the party and were waiting for him to come home. The jewelry and cash were taken to mislead us."

"Come on, Pinella. That's pretty far-fetched," Lewis snarled. "We all know you have it in for Greens. You think Rawlings and the Greens may have some link to the escort murders. For that matter, you've got a problem with most people in this city who wield some power. It's far more likely that if we do connect Rawlings with the escort murders, he acted alone."

"You're right about one thing, Lewis. I do think that people with power and money are able to get away with murder, the Greens included. That said, I don't disagree with you completely about Tom Rawlings. I think there is a connection between Rawlings and all the escort murders. If I'm right, it's still far too soon to say that he acted alone."

"I don't want to argue with you, Tony. But I know the Green family very well, and I don't think anyone in that family is capable of murder. It's more likely that Tom Rawlings took too many chances in the investment game. He could have messed up the portfolio of an investor who wasn't happy when the market dipped and Rawlings' advice went sour. The Greens are good people. Even if this wasn't a robbery gone bad, I think Rawlings acted alone, maybe to protect Julia as well as her mother and sisters from any more humiliation. The Greens had nothing to do with it. They've been shamed enough!"

Tony tried to calm the situation. "That was quite a speech, Lewis. I won't argue with you either, but I think everyone in this room realizes it's too early to assume that Tom Rawlings acted independently. With all due respect, your conclusion is based on conjecture. At least wait until all the evidence is in before you rule out other possibilities."

"Look guys," Salvador Cedeno interjected. "I think we all need to take a step back and wait for all the evidence to come in. Let's see what forensics comes up with from Rawlings' apartment, and not make any hasty decisions. We need to have the latest results from the murder scene here, and compare them to the murders in Chicago and Paradise Valley. At least for now, and with Rawlings dead, we shouldn't make any assumptions. I'll let you all know as soon as I have more information."

The meeting was over. Lewis confidently headed back to his office, turning around only to sneer in Tony's direction.

Tony patted Cedeno on the shoulder. "Sorry to get so hot in there, Sal. Guess I'm feeling pretty frustrated over Rawlings' death."

"Don't worry, Tony. Lewis always did look for easy answers. We'll get to the bottom of all this. Right now, I'm not willing to make any assumptions. Let's see where the evidence takes us. Three murders, three escorts who worked for the same agency, but in three different locations. Morris Green still has lots of clout in this state—*especially in this city*. We knew this wouldn't be easy. Be patient and just let me deal with the commissioner and his politics. For now, as far as this office is concerned, we're still looking at every angle."

Tony headed back to Bensonhurst. He wanted to make a few calls from home before his dinner this evening with Max. He was tired, physically and emotionally. He knew that Cedeno was still leaning in his direction—and so was Don Lynch. Whatever he said, Cedeno was between a rock and a hard place without scientific evidence against Rawlings, Julia, or anyone else.

Don Lynch agreed with Tony. He also thought there was a connection to Julia or someone else in the Green family, but had no control over the Rawlings murder case, or any of the murder cases. He was on his way to retirement. He had no influence over Lewis—and even if he did, it was obvious that Lewis was determined to ignore any connections between Rawlings' murder, the escort murders, and the Greens.

Tony knew Lewis could make a lot more money opening his own security firm, with Morris Green as his first major client. He certainly had more to gain by staying on the good side of Green, who was pondering a political comeback.

If he's not on the take, Tony considered, it was remotely possible that Lewis was acting on his own out of some obligation or real sympathy he may have felt for the Greens, especially Julia, who he referred to several times today as *grieving for her fiancé*.

Tony had seen it happen before. Someone, like Lewis, who had been a good officer for so many years, always faithful to his badge and his uniform—then tempted by one powerful person who finally got to him. Why work late into the night and early into the morning without great financial rewards? Why not take advantage of an opportunity to change his life, send his children to the best colleges, and buy that big house on the northern shore of Long Island that his wife always wanted? Why not enjoy the life that he thought would always stay beyond his means?

Whatever is going on, Tony thought, *not being able to interview Rawlings was definitely a major setback.*

The Laughing Angels were beginning to see an extra bright light at the end of the tunnel. Although they loved competing with Tony, it was conceivable he was getting too old for the job. They danced around the pensive detective, easily picturing him sitting in a rocking chair and living in a retirement home for aged cops—telling stories about how he caught the psychotic killer of Veronica Blake.

If they had anything to say about it, the Laughing Angels would make sure that Stacy was involved in Tony's life until the day he died!

Chapter 40

Max was outraged when he got to Tony's apartment. He had just returned from the commissioner's press conference about Rawlings' murder, where Fred Lewis was introduced as the lead detective on the case and spokesperson for the department.

"It made me sick," Tony. "Lewis called the murder *a horrible instance of a robbery gone bad.* He said that Rawlings had *walked in on a burglary and tragically lost his life.* He promised that the department would continue investigating the burglary, that they would find and punish the felon. Then he extended his sincere condolences to the Rawlings family, who were sitting next to the commissioner on the platform. Lewis never mentioned anything about Rawlings' possible link to the escort murders. Probably wanted to avoid a defamation lawsuit by the Rawlings family. In fact, he didn't even mention Julia Green, or Rawlings' relationship to the Greens."

"Was Cedeno there?" Tony asked.

"Yes, as well as the district attorney and the department's PR team. Cedeno looked uncomfortable. First time I've seen him like that. On the other hand, Lewis looked too confident, like the proverbial *cat that swallowed the canary*. It was disgusting!"

"Look, I know you're angry and frustrated, Max. So am I. In the meanwhile, Cedeno told me he had the commissioner's okay to order a complete re-examination of all three crime scenes and hiring an independent trace expert to go over all the evidence. I'm certainly going to keep digging. As for not mentioning Rawlings and the Paradise Valley murder, all we really have so far is that

Rawlings had opportunity because he was in the area the day she was murdered—and, *at least we think*, plenty of motive...That said, *and it didn't come from me*, a good investigative reporter may have more to say about the investigation, if you know what I mean..."

Tony and Max ate their dinner in silence and in a hurry.

"Thanks for the chow, Tony, but I better go. Looks like I've got a column to write in time for tomorrow morning's paper. It's time I gave Commissioner Brennan, Chief Cedeno, and Fred Lewis something to think about."

"Be careful, Max. We're dealing with some pretty tough guys—and we don't have much evidence yet to support our theory."

"You know me, Tony. I'll write first, and worry about it later. I'm really angry and that's the best time for me to write!"

"At least take home some of this food. Something to munch on while you put on your *Don Quixote* persona. Just don't ride your white horse into that windmill. I'm counting on you to look out for us little people for a long, long time."

"Thanks, *Sancho Panza*. I'll do my best not to let you, Angela Robinson, or those poor murdered women down."

Chapter 41

The next morning, Tony did not have to rip through the pages of *Public Corruption* to read Max's column. It was featured right on the front page. Tony grinned with satisfaction. As usual, Max didn't disappoint his devoted readers.

Money, Politics, and a Wrong Turn
that Led to Murder
Max Gold, Crime Reporter

They were all daughters of caring and concerned parents. During their young lives, they experienced both the pains and joys of growing up in a very complex society. As most of us know, we make our share of mistakes, go on with our lives, and try to do the best we can.

Valerie Powell, Stephanie Taylor, and Amanda Wilson all wanted to live life to its fullest. Yes, they made a wrong turn by working for an escort service—especially a service known for its very exclusive clientele.

It was easy to be enticed by the money. Money that could one day pay for a college education. Money that would not only secure their futures, but the futures of their brothers and sisters, and the financial security of knowing their parents could be well taken care of as they grew older. It was all very appealing, even glamorous, to wear expensive clothing and be seen at the best restaurants.

Too good to be true? Yes, it was! The dread set in when the events surrounding the liaison between Angela Robinson and the former Governor Morris Green unleashed a series of heinous events, not all of which reached the New York headlines.

New York City has a great police department. I'm proud that the majority of our officers are dedicated public servants.

So when something is not right, as a journalist, who has been fortunate to have gained the people's trust over these many years—and as a citizen of this fine city— I feel an obligation to speak up. Something is not right!

I'm afraid that in reporting the death this week of investment consultant Tom Rawlings, politics and greed took over for duty and responsibility to the public. Point man on the investigation of Rawlings' murder is Detective Fred Lewis. Lewis is also heading up the investigation of the escort murders. Stephanie, Valerie, and Amanda all worked for the same service as Angela Robinson, the escort named in ex-Governor Morris Green's inappropriate relationship scandal. You remember. The scandal that caused Green to resign.

Where does Tom Rawlings fit in? Rawlings was Julia Green's fiancé. It was Rawlings holding Julia's hand when Governor Green resigned. I have it from a good source that Rawlings has some connection to at least one of the escort murders, possibly all three murders—and that it's likely he did not act alone.

At yesterday's press conference, why didn't Fred Lewis mention the possibility that Tom Rawlings was murdered by someone who wanted to put a stop to any further investigation to his possible role in the escort murders? Granted, Rawlings is no longer here to defend himself. That leads me, among others, to think even more strongly that it was to someone's benefit to see him dead. Also, as I already mentioned, there is good reason to believe that Rawlings did not act alone. That he had at least one accomplice. Those sources also believe that's why Rawlings was murdered. It was not a burglary gone bad, it was a burglary designed to hide the truth.

Detective Lewis, why don't you do the right thing and recuse yourself from these investigations? You honorably worked in the security detail of ex-Governor Morris Green, and the word on the street is that you remain very close friends with the Greens. Hey, I understand that. So whether it's because of friendship, politics, or money, you clearly have a conflict of interest in anything that has to do with the murder of Tom

Rawlings, as well as the brutal slayings of Valerie Powell, Stephanie Taylor, and Amanda Wilson. They need justice—and so do we.

Chapter 42

Max's column gave New York City Mayor Jack Saunders and Police Commissioner Sean Brennan enough reason to have Fred Lewis removed from the escort murder case. The mayor, who was only fourteen months away from his re-election bid, made it clear to Commissioner Brennan that he did not want the Lewis uproar to become an issue in the campaign. The result was that Chief Cedeno *strongly suggested* to Lewis that he would be wise to recuse himself from both cases, to avoid any embarrassment either to him or to the department. Since there was a *possible link*, as Cedeno phrased it, between Rawlings and the escort murders—and because Lewis knew Rawlings when he had served on Governor Morris Green's special-event security service—it would be an acceptable decision. *Easy to explain if questions arose at an upcoming press conference about their progress on the escort murders.*

The new point man on Rawlings' killing and the escort murders would be Abraham Bloom, a respected veteran detective with a no-nonsense personality.

Later, on the same day that Max's column had appeared, Cedeno had the press officer call a press conference for the next morning.

Cedeno opened the conference. "Thank you all for coming on such short notice. We have some updates for you on how we are proceeding on Tom Rawlings' murder, and the ongoing investigation into the escort murders. I would like to introduce Fred Lewis, whom you all know has been leading the way on our investigation team on both cases. Detective Lewis..."

Fred Lewis stepped up to the microphone and briefly explained why he recused himself from the investigations. He thanked his team for their support and hard work and quickly sat down. It was not an easy moment for Lewis, but he was near retirement, and keeping his job for the next year—as well as his pension—helped him through the embarrassment.

Most of the press had read Max's column about Lewis, so they were not surprised. The room remained quiet as they all waited to see what came next.

Chief Cedeno returned to the podium, thanked Lewis for his contributions to the cases so far, and introduced Abraham Bloom as the new point man on both cases. Most of the press knew Bloom as a respected veteran detective with a no-nonsense personality. What they did not expect is what came next.

Bloom thanked Cedeno and expressed his appreciation to the team for their loyalty and hard work. His next words came as a surprise to the curious press.

"I would like to now announce a new member to our team. I'm sure the people of New York, and justice loving people everywhere, will be pleased to learn that Detroit's well-known, and retired detective, Tony Pinella, has agreed to come back to work as a consultant to the New York City Police Department on both Rawlings' killing and the escort murders. Detective Pinella brings an experienced *and objective* voice to the cases. I'm sure many of you in the NYPD, and the press, remember how Pinella solved Detroit's nationally reported murder of Veronica Blake. For those of you who don't remember the case, let me give you a little background on Tony Pinella.

"Veronica Blake was married to the popular and well-known evangelist, Jason Blake. Under great social and political pressure, and with a complex set of circumstances surrounding Veronica's murder, Detective Pinella solved the case—and arrested Stacey Johnson Blake—*who had married the evangelist soon after Veronica's death.* Stacey was judged guilty but mentally ill, and remains to this day in a psychiatric hospital.

"As a *Special-Assignment Operative* for the New York City Police Department, Detective Pinella reports directly to me—and he has access to all the information we've gathered so far, without any restrictions. Tony, it is my pleasure to welcome you to the NYPD. Perhaps you would like to say a few words to the press..."

As he listened to Bloom's introduction, Tony thought carefully about what he would say. He knew that Commissioner Brennan and Sal Cedeno were on the hot seat with Mayor Saunders because of the Fred Lewis situation. Cedeno's message to the team had been strong and clear: "It's up to you guys. We've got to bring confidence back to the public and the press—*and to the mayor and commissioner*. We have to show the public that the investigations will be completely transparent. No giving in to the political or social pressure sure to come from Morris Green's allies and the Rawlings family. I want the truth here, and I want the public to know we mean business."

There was a guarded amount of applause coming from the grim-faced press as Tony stood up and walked to the podium, wishing he had worn a more comfortable pair of shoes. His feet were killing him! He needed to walk a delicate line. *Tell the truth, but not tell so much that the investigations might be jeopardized*, Tony thought. He would leave no doubt to anyone sitting there, or standing against the wall in the crowded room, that the game had changed.

After he and Bloom shared a warm handshake, and Bloom sat down, Tony turned to face the press and quietly surveyed the room with a serious look on his face. Max was sitting in the last row. When they made eye contact, he nodded to Tony with a very satisfied smile on his face.

The press could tell right away, this man was not preoccupied with his own importance—Detective Tony Pinella was a serious no-nonsense cop. The officers sitting behind the podium, and others who Tony recognized standing in the back of the room, knew and respected his reputation. They were confident that Tony would restore the faith of those who had doubted the resolve of the NYPD to solve these cases, when Fred Lewis headed the escort and Rawlings' murder teams. Tony's work had been a model to many of the younger officers, the reason they became cops.

The soft buzz of voices stopped as Tony started to speak.

"I know you all have lots of questions, so I'll be brief. First, I want to extend my sincere appreciation to Mayor Saunders, Commissioner Brennan, Chief Cedeno, and, of course, to Detective Bloom, for welcoming me to their team. I have a deep respect for the work of the NYPD's dedicated officers, and have every intention of supporting their efforts and working closely with each one of them to solve both the Rawlings and escort murders. All of us before you today are here to see that justice is served for everyone in this great city. And now, Detective Bloom and I will be happy to take your questions...."

Tony was quick to recognize Janet Adams in the first row. He knew her as a veteran and objective reporter, who had written about many of his high profile cases.

"This must be a pretty complex case to bring in such a well-known detective like you, Tony, out of retirement. Did you get tired of fishing?"

"That's very astute of you on both counts, Ms. Adams. I'm here looking for bigger and *more deadly* fish. Like

Detective Bloom and the rest of his team, we have our biggest hooks in the water, looking to bring justice to the young women who were murdered, as well as to the late Tom Rawlings—and to their families."

"Two follow-ups, please, Detective. Including Tom Rawlings, there were two murders in New York City, one in Paradise Valley, Arizona, and another in Chicago, Illinois. Is the NYPD working in coordination with the departments in the other two cities? And doesn't that indicate that more than one murderer is involved?"

"I guess, since this is our first press conference, and the answer includes NYPD policy on interagency relations, I think I'll defer to Detective Bloom."

"Thanks, Tony," Bloom said as he moved in front of the microphone.

"The murders seem to have required some traveling, that's true. But since one of the murder victims, Amanda Wilson, was found in New York City, we are taking the lead—with Detective Pinella acting as liaison with local teams in Paradise Valley and Chicago."

"How did Pinella get involved?" someone sitting behind Janet Adams shouted.

"In fact, that's how Detective Pinella came to work with us. Frankly, it was Tony's work as a private investigator that led us to look into the link—and then to confirm the connection between the three escorts. All three women worked out of the same agency, which is based in New York City. It's no secret that police departments like to be territorial. Interstate agency communications aren't always as quick as we would like. We're fortunate that Detective Pinella has contacts in both Paradise Valley and Chicago that go back to when he worked on the well-known Veronica Blake murder case. It was actually his independent work that led us to bring him in as a consultant for our team—and enabled us to establish a possible link between Tom Rawlings and the three escort murders. *Back to you, Tony.*"

"Thanks, Abe... Janet, I think you had another question."

"Yes, thank you. So you think Tom Rawlings killed all three escorts?"

"We're still looking at the evidence, Janet. Let me tell you what we know so far. Yes, there does seem to be a possible link between Rawlings and one of the murders. We also know there's a definite link between the three escorts. What's not clear at this point is if Rawlings killed anyone. Like they say on all those new crime series on television, *we're following the evidence.*"

The aggressive audience began shouting questions from around the room.

"Hang on, hang on," Tony said loudly enough to be heard over the competing voices of the reporters. We'll try to get to all your questions. He pointed over the crowd to a young man who seemed to be struggling for attention, jumping up and down with his hand raised.

"Who is that with the turtleneck sweater and baseball cap. You, in the back of the room. Where are you from?"

"Dick Elliot of *We the People* magazine."

"Oh, yes," Tony said. "Isn't that the magazine trying to keep our politicians in line?"

"Yes, sir, that's us," Elliot said nervously.

The room erupted with laughter as the young reporter's face turned bright red. *We the People* was known around the city as an upstart student-run publication, six to eight pages stapled in the corner, and handed out for free around Washington Park, near the New York University campus, and on other local college campuses.

"What's your question, son?"

"I read your bio. You were raised in New York, but left to work for the Detroit Police Department. Is the police department here any different than the one in Detroit?"

Snickering could still be heard around the room.

"Hey, quiet down," Tony said sternly. "The public has a right to know who the city is paying to work on its behalf! There are some differences, and many more similarities. The NYPD is much larger than the Detroit force, and far more technologically advanced. Although, in the years since I worked for the Detroit office, I'm sure it has caught up a bit. That said, I'm very impressed with the personnel and the dedication of everyone I've met here in New York. Like all the departments I've been associated with over the years, the commonality is the devotion to the people—the total commitment of each and every officer to protect the citizens, whether the crimes are politically or financially motivated, small—or major—as it is with the cases we are talking about today."

Tony paused for a moment, wondering how far he could take his answer. Bloom was firm—*Don't say anything about Julia Green or anyone in the Green family. It would put them too much on notice. We don't have enough evidence to implicate them, at least not yet.*

Bloom was right, Tony thought quickly. This was not the time or place. *Then again...* when he glanced over his shoulder and saw the commissioner looking angry, while Cedeno and Bloom looked more frightened than angry, Tony just could not help himself.

"Well, if you don't mind, let me pontificate a little," he said.

The reporters laughed. When the room quieted down again, Tony continued. "These days many cities have a diverse population, and I'm glad they do. It's part of what makes our country great. But New York has one distinguishing factor, the United Nations."

Tony smiled broadly as he caught Max's eye again—the look on his face said, *Oh, no. Here he goes again with his shtick about the U.N.*

"New York City is home to the United Nations, and all its delegates with their staffs—individuals that come here with various political as well as financial agendas. For visitors, it is a very exciting and dynamic place to visit. To property owners of the highest priced apartments, and proprietors of the most expensive shops, it also makes for very appealing and lucrative opportunities—which also brings more tax dollars into the city and state. However, for our dedicated law enforcement agencies, the U.N. also presents the problem of any organization and its members, who think they are above the law. That's a problem that sometimes arises with powerful people throughout our society, the very wealthy, local, and national politicians, and so on—but with the U.N., it's worse, it's *diplomatic immunity*."

At that moment, Tony could feel a strained smile coming from Abraham Bloom, as he put his arm around Tony's shoulder, and moved closer to the microphone.

"Thank you, Tony. We are all fortunate you feel so strongly about the law being applied evenly across our diverse society. Are there any further questions for Detective Pinella?"

As more hands were raised throughout the room, Tony could see Max trying not to laugh. Tony then pointed to the very attractive redhead sitting in the front row.

"Thank you, Detective Pinella. I'm Rita Spencer of *Channel 42 News*."

Max held his breath and wondered how Tony would handle this one. Rita Spencer was thirty years old, and had developed a great following in her five years at the station. She was promoted to evening news anchor after only two years in the field. She was a tough and honest reporter, best known for asking confrontational questions to politicians and the police, and never one to sit behind a desk waiting for other reporters to do the legwork.

This should be good, Max thought.

"Detective Pinella, the rumor around town is that before Tom Rawlings was killed, he was going to be offered immunity for his testimony against other suspects in the escort murder cases. Then, after his murder, the rumor quickly changed—that he murdered all three young women. Earlier, you said it's possible that Rawlings is linked to one murder. It sounds like you suspect there's more than one killer involved in the escort murders. *Are there other suspects?* Is there a cover-up of some sort in play here? Just how far are you willing to go to solve these murders?"

"You certainly get right to the point, Ms. Spencer—and so will I. We heard the rumors about Rawlings, too. *Rumors don't solve murders! Moreover, they certainly don't do justice to the young women who were brutally murdered, or to Tom Rawlings, who may or may not have murdered anyone.* A link is just that—*a link.* It is only one small part of the evidence package. Rumors, at this point, rumors at any point in an ongoing investigation, show a blatant disrespect for all the hard work being done by law enforcement officers in three states to solve these murders…

"How far are we willing to go? As far as we have to…

"Let me add one more thing, especially because there are people in this room who do not know me, other than my work on the Veronica Blake murder investigation. My parents taught me to respect others, but never to be afraid of them. I've never been intimidated by pressure from the so-called *powerful people in our society*—and I'm certainly not going to start now! *Does that answer your question, Ms. Spencer?*"

"I think so, Detective Pinella. I certainly recognize your obligation to find the truth. I hope you understand that my obligation is to ask the questions that are in the public's mind, and to make sure I report the truth. Thank you for your candor, Detective."

Max could see everyone sitting behind Tony take a deep breath, while Bloom stood next to him, speechless. Tony Pinella had done it again. If anyone thought Tony was too old to solve a murder, or to face the contemptuous and always suspicious press, they were wrong!

Detective Bloom moved closer to Tony and began speaking into the microphone. "We have time for one or two more questions," he said.

Bloom then pointed to a young man he recognized in the second row. "Steve, you've been waiting a turn."

"Thank you, Detective Bloom. Steve Singer, *The Beacon Newspaper Group*. Detective Pinella, reporters in Detroit describe you as someone who always hears the voices of the victims."

"Thank you, Mr. Singer. I'm flattered that you've done some research on me. Now what's your question?"

"Many here in New York, and elsewhere, feel that using an escort service is a victimless crime. Something not important enough to prosecute. What do you think?"

"I'm not sure where you're going here, Mr. Singer, but breaking the law is breaking the law. There is no in between. When someone, anyone, breaks the law, and then tries to hide the violation, the cover-up often leads to an even worse result. For example, many would agree that the Watergate burglary was a crime, but the crime of the cover-up had an even greater impact on former President Richard Nixon and our country."

Max knew that Singer hit one of Tony's hot buttons. Would Tony dare to bring in the Morris Green situation? He could tell by Abraham Bloom's face, he was afraid of the same thing. Tony continued talking…

"Since one of the topics of this press conference is the tri-state murders of three escorts who worked for the same New York City escort service, are you implying that bringing a woman over the state line for sexual purposes may be considered immoral, but it's not a punishable crime? That it's a private matter?"

"Well, that is one of my thoughts, yes…"

"Let me be blunt, Mr. Singer. If something is against the law, it is not a private matter. In the present cases, it is very possible that wanting to keep these unlawful acts *private*, may have led to the murders of three young women."

As smart as Tony is, Max thought, Singer might have outsmarted him. Or did he? Maybe this is just what Tony wanted, to force the guilty to make another move that would expose them. *Where is this going*? Max wondered.

"Actually, Detective, that is my point. New York State ex-Governor, Morris Green, had sex with a New York escort that he brought to our nation's capital. Yes, he was forced to resign, but never prosecuted. Doesn't that show we have a separate set of rules for politicians?"

"The deals made by the attorney general's office don't need the NYPD's approval," Tony responded.

"Anyone else have a question?" Tony asked.

"Please, Detective Pinella. One follow-up question…"

Before Tony or Bloom could cut him off, Singer blurted out, "It's a known fact that Angela Robinson worked for the same escort service as Stephanie Taylor, Valerie Powell, and Amanda Wilson. Is that where Tom Rawlings fits into the story? He was Julia Green's fiancé."

Uh-oh, Max thought. *Singer's got them now.*

"At this time, I don't think we should make any assumptions. We should let the NYPD proceed with a full investigation of the Rawlings and escort murders. When that's done, and we've looked into every possible angle, we'll be sure to report the facts to the press and the public. One thing I can promise all of you. Throughout this investigation, I will be listening to the voices of Stephanie Taylor, Valerie Powell, Amanda Wilson—and Tom Rawlings. Now I think Detective Bloom has a few closing words."

"Yes. Thank you, Tony. And thank you all for your thoughtful questions. We'll get back to you when we have more information."

Tony went back to Bloom's office, expecting to get a tongue lashing for not backing away from Singer's reference to the Greens. Instead, Bloom firmly shook Tony's hand.

"Good job, Pinella. I wish more public officials would follow your example. I think this is the first time the commissioner realized there's just so much we can do to keep the Greens out of this case."

"Thanks," Tony said. "Look, we're all worried that by exposing Green's potential involvement in the murders only gives him more opportunity to go underground and call on favors from his political allies."

"You're right about that, Tony. But, like you—and our friends in the press—I think it's time for us to be more transparent. In general, it means making sure our politicians and their wealthy friends are subject to the same rules as the rest of us."

Salvador Cedeno had just entered the room and overheard Bloom's comments.

"Abe is right, Tony. I just left the commissioner's office and he thanked me for bringing you into this investigation. You have more support than you can imagine. The NYPD is proud to have Tony Pinella working with us."

The Laughing Angels loved seeing retired Detective Tony Pinella back in the action, and on the biggest stage of his career—larger than when he solved the Veronica Blake murder. *Would he succeed,* they wondered. *Or would he just end up a big flop on Broadway?*

This time the mighty Pinella was up against a more powerful opponent than Stacey Johnson Blake. She was smart and devious, but still a tender soul compared to the rich, politically connected, and hardened villains on this stage. At present, it was too early in the game to tell. *And let's face it,* they thought, *even if Pinella's mind was as sharp as in the old days, he did get tired faster—leaving him more vulnerable to the bad actors in this play. Morris Green still had friends in high places, both in the NYPD and in Albany.*

The Laughing Angels warned the Righteous Ones to hold on to their seats. The heavy curtains on this stage might come down right on top of Tony's head.

Chapter 43

While the investigations into the Rawlings and escort murders moved forward slowly, Julia Green seemed to be moving on with her life. She was seen at several social events with her close friends, as well as hosting a large charity event organized by Sally Green. Julia still shed a public tear or two when someone mentioned Tom Rawlings. Most of the public viewed her as a young woman, trying to pull her life together after grieving for her murdered fiancé.

In private, however, Julia did not miss Rawlings. She also did not worry about being a suspect in any of the murders.

For the first few weeks after his relationship with Angela Robinson was exposed, Morris Green said all the right things publicly and to his family. Although he tried his best to make amends to his loving wife and three daughters, it was not long before his ego took over.

Although the public still saw them as a family committed to the ex-governor, in private, Julia and her father were not getting along. Then one Saturday evening, during dinner with Julia and Sally, while the younger two daughters were at their grandparents for the weekend, Green dropped a bombshell. He was considering a political comeback.

"How many people have the ability to make a positive difference to society," he said proudly. "I was a skillful and successful governor. Why should I give all that up because of one slip-up? Our lives don't have to change. I've already made a comeback, and the public seems eager to forgive me. *I think we can do this together.* I've already made some contacts in Albany. They owe me plenty, and I'll have their support."

Julia became enraged. She threw her napkin on the table and stood up—infuriated that he would even think about a political comeback.

"After everything you put us through with your disgusting behavior," she screamed. "After publicly disgracing me and my sisters, to say nothing about mom—how can you even consider putting us behind a podium while you announce a political comeback? Don't you care anything about us? You've ruined our lives, but all you think about is your own desires and ambitions."

She started to sob and ran from the table. Sally Green glared at her husband.

"Now isn't the time," Sally said angrily. "I'll go and talk to her. I'm sure she'll come around. She just needs more time."

The Laughing Angels loved how the minds of politicians worked. Their arrogance never failed to disappoint them. They knew that more deception and hypocrisy was right around the corner. It filled them with energy and purpose, while it drained the Righteous Ones of their optimism.

With some empathy for Tony Pinella, the Laughing Angels knew he was ultimately doomed to fail in his lifetime fight for justice.

Chapter 44

This would be a short workday for Tony at the downtown headquarters of the NYPD. He was anxious to return to his apartment in Bensonhurst and take a nap. He had learned to pace himself, so he would be recharged after an hour of sleep in the afternoon—especially when he knew there was a long night ahead of going over notes from the team of detectives working on the murder cases.

The train had been hot and crowded, so the cool breeze of fresh air on his face felt good as Tony walked the few blocks home from the station. He was looking forward to getting under the covers—not anticipating the surprise waiting for him in the mailbox. It was a letter from Stacey Johnson Blake. He had tried not to think very much about Stacey and her predictions concerning the escort murders. She was still hopelessly psychotic, despite the frightening accuracy of her dreams. Even when she made sense, she would inevitably step over the line into insanity.

Dr. Trotsky had explained that Stacey was a perfect example of the mind's complexity. How someone with a fine intellect, and the ability to be thoroughly beguiling, could be hopelessly insane.

Finally, resting on the couch, he opened Stacey's letter. After reading the first paragraph, his chest tightened and he felt like his entire life passed before his eyes. All the good and evil deeds he may ever have committed were challenging one another for a place to rest. His personal *Book of Life,* a concept his blessed mother believed in, may be in its final pages—with no chance to change his destination. To his great regret and sadness, it appeared likely that Stacey Johnson Blake would play an important role in the final chapter.

It was also obvious that Stacey had managed to charm another nurse or an attendant to mail the letter without Dr. Trotsky's review of its contents.

Dear Tony,

I found your press conference about Tom Rawlings and the escort murders extremely disappointing. Although you were charming, you missed the opportunity to give me some credit for all the hints I gave to you about the escort cases. Instead of acknowledging my help, and making things right between us, you betrayed me. Don't ever forget that you were not a national hero until you became involved in the Veronica Blake murder case.

I thought you had enough self-confidence not to be intimidated by my ability to see and understand things that are not visible to others. Don't ever forget, there are few people who understand the family unit like I do, which is why I've been so successful in helping you.

Now let's move on. Please know that I still believe in your decency and sense of fairness. You came to visit me when I reached out to you, and I will never forget that. So, I have not given up on you yet, dear Tony. I think we have a special bond, an eternal connection, and that's why I'm still willing to help you. For people like us, life is never predictable and simple. The dreadful dreams of a life being taken never stops haunting us. We constantly hear the voices of the victims.

So, I want to share my latest dreams and visions with you. At this point, if he has any shred of a conscience, Morris Green realizes that his relationships with various escorts were not a victimless crime. Julia Green and Tom Rawlings are victims, too. Now Tom Rawlings is also dead.

Julia had dreams and so did Tom. Their dreams would be destroyed if any more escorts came forward with stories about Morris Green. If that did happen, there goes any remaining self-respect for Julia's entire family, starting with her father.

You're probably reading this and thinking, Stacey is right about everything. Let's face it, Tony. You're still far from solving these murders. I know you're thinking that Tom Rawlings was a convenient scapegoat for all three murders. He had no protection the way Julia does. She is the one with her father's powerful and wealthy connections. The Rawlings family had lost their wealth and influence many years ago, so the focus is clearly on the Green side of the story.

So where does all this really leave us? Who really killed Tom Rawlings and why? He certainly was an easy scapegoat. If Julia and Tom worked together to kill the escorts, his murder got her off the hook. Morris Green has enough connections to hire a killer. With Tom dead, and assumed to have acted alone to murder the escorts, no one would suspect Julia.

Maybe Tom had nothing to do with the escort murders. Did Julia kill Tom because of a romance gone bad? Was Tom going to leave Julia, her father's favorite, because of Morris Green's scandalous behavior? After all, Tom worked hard to achieve his status in the financial world. Why let a scoundrel like Morris Green ruin it all? Hadn't his family been through enough in the past?

Let me help you out here, Tony. My visions of Tom and Julia always show them madly in love with one another. Julia never would have killed Tom, just like I never would have killed my husband Reverend Jason Blake. But I would kill anyone who threatened my life with Jason, or who interfered with our children. In fact, I did—and still would—which is why I'll probably be in this institution forever. Julia may not show it, but she speaks to me in my dreams, and I know she was devastated by Tom's death. They would have done anything for one another.

So where does that leave us, Tony? I have the answer, but I'm not going to make it that easy for you. Next time you visit, I will tell you who murdered Tom Rawlings and why. I have a feeling at your next press conference you will sing my praises.

Best Wishes,
Stacey

Chapter 45

After reading Stacey's letter, Tony realized it was useless to try taking a nap. He knew Stacey was planning her next move in this chess game. His anxiety about seeing her again, and her frighteningly logical insights into Tom Rawlings' murder, made his entire body twitch. Now he understood why some people under great stress resorted to heavy drinking or taking sedatives. For him it was a long, hot shower, as he tried to cleanse himself from all the evil and insanity in the world.

Stacey is right, Tony thought, *there is a bond between them.* It began the day he realized she was the real murderer of Veronica Blake. Tony literally stalked Stacey until she finally broke down and confessed. For years, she appeared to the world as a smart, sophisticated, and charming woman—a good mother and a very loyal wife—who was actually a ruthless killer.

At the end, when Tony arrested Stacey for murder, she broke down completely. She looked up at him like a little girl with tearful eyes, and cried for her father. He now wondered if she meant her flesh and blood father, *or God.* Stacey would spend the rest of her life in a psychiatric hospital. Tony had no doubt about that. What frightened him most is that she also had great insights into the escort murder cases. *We are all daughters of God,* she had said. *She was right.*

While Tony's mind ran wild with these thoughts, Stacey was feeling very satisfied with how she had succeeded in maneuvering into a position of power.

Time is on my side, she thought, while laughing hysterically. *Where am I going, anyway? I'll be locked-up in this institution for the rest of my life. There is no ladder for me to climb and escape. Only the ladder to God, to my Father in Heaven.*

Stacey fell to her knees and cried out, "No one can defeat me, Father—not even your son, my brother. He still believes in turning the other cheek, and that confession cleanses the soul. What good did that do him? What good has it done for humanity? Has he stopped any wars, or is he responsible for starting them in your name?"

Stacey's loud cries brought in the attendant. The attendant on duty was used to Stacey's conversations with her *Father*, but this time, she had become so agitated, he called Nurse Helen Spagnoli to the room. "She's really in a rage," he told Nurse Helen. "I think you better come. Stacey trusts you."

Nurse Helen carefully approached the praying Stacey and gave her a sedative, and the attendant lifted her gently onto the bed. Just as she closed her eyes, she looked up at Nurse Helen and tightly gripped her hand. "Maybe I'm the only sane one. It's only me who can bring peace to all mankind—*not my brother.*"

As Stacey slept, the Laughing Angels danced around her bed. This is what they loved about sibling rivalry. Watching the brother diminished as the delicate, useless one, while the sister exerted a stronger and more aggressive stance. This time, let the Supreme Being turn the other cheek, while Stacey berated her brother without mercy. The Laughing Angels knew that God's son never really understood his sister's anger at the audacity of those in power. Was she really insane to think she could win over the Son of God?

Chapter 46

Tired after his shower, Tony put on his pajamas and fell asleep on the couch, listening to the beautiful voices of Linda Eder, Charlotte Church, and Kayt E. Wolf. The music touched him deeply and helped calm his shattered nerves. If only soothing melodies could also bring peace to the souls of Stephanie Taylor, Valerie Powell, and Amanda Wilson. Although he knew in his heart, that only justice would accomplish that mission.

The next morning, still physically and emotionally drained, he decided to stay home and rest—not even bothering to change into his clothes. He poured a cup of coffee, slathered cream cheese on a toasted bagel, and sat down to eat.

He must have dozed off after eating, because it was around noon when he heard the phone ring. He took a moment to shake himself awake and then picked up the receiver and heard Max's voice.

"Quick, turn on the TV to CBS—no time to explain. We'll talk later. Call me."

Tony grabbed the remote control and turned on the television—just as former Governor Morris Green stepped in front of the microphone.

What the hell is this, Tony thought. It took a moment for him to realize this was a live shot, not a rerun of the former governor's earlier resignation and *mea culpa* speech. Standing beside Green were his wife Sally and three daughters, just as they had before, still appearing to be the perfect family.

Tony felt sick to his stomach, as he heard the words spoken so confidently by Green:

"Ladies and Gentleman, thank you for coming today. I'll make my remarks brief. After very serious discussions with Sally and my lovely daughters, I feel an obligation, now more than ever, to serve the people of New York. As you can imagine, this was not an easy decision for me nor my family—and we all stand before you today, asking for another chance to serve you and the people of our great country."

The bulbs from the cameras immediately started flashing, as the press shouted questions from every corner of the room. Green stopped talking for a moment, and motioned with his hands for the noise to stop.

"Please, give me a chance to explain. I know you have many questions, and in the next few weeks, I promise to answer them all. For now, I want the citizens of New York to know that I deeply regret how much I disappointed them—and how sorry I am to have caused great embarrassment to myself and my loving and supportive family. Yes, I committed acts that betrayed my core beliefs, and I apologize to every one of you from the bottom of my heart.

"Today, I stand before you a humbled and better man, asking for another chance. My idealism has never wavered. In the past months, I have received wonderful letters, all expressing appreciation for the years I served as attorney general of our great state, and then as governor. Therefore, it is with great humility that I ask you to vote for me once again, so that I may represent you and the great state of New York in the United States Senate.

"Thank you all so much. God bless you and God bless America."

Tony's mouth was wide open in shock, as he leaned back on the couch in total disbelief. The phone rang and he knew it would be Max, but Tony was not ready to talk to anyone right now. He had to digest the unbelievable performance and utter audacity of Morris Green. Tony knew he needed to get a hold of his emotions. The days ahead would require him to be rational, objective, methodical, and totally focused on the investigations.

Tony considered all his years in law enforcement, his unblemished record of fighting for justice. Even when he was called *controversial,* no one ever questioned the integrity he brought to his job, and the love he had for our country. In all likelihood, Tony realized the Tom Rawlings and escort murder cases might be his last stand. He was determined that whatever it took, he would find out the truth behind the murders.

The phone rang again. Tony did not answer it. There would be ample time to talk later. Right now, he had to think.

Chapter 47

According to the latest poll, the people of New York were willing to give Morris Green another chance for political office. With three candidates in the upcoming democratic primary, Green was garnering more than fifty percent of the vote. Even with all his problems, he was at the top of his game, able to convey that he was the strongest and best candidate, willing to work tirelessly on their behalf.

The Green family was back in the headlines, and still the darlings on the society pages. Sally Green was admired by many women for her decision to stand by her husband. As a team, the Greens thought there was no limit to what they could accomplish together.

"Just think," Sally said to her husband. "One or two terms in the senate, and then a run for the presidency."

Unfortunately for them, a personal call to Morris Green from Commissioner Sean Brennan signaled the Green's problems might not be over. Brennan said it was just a *courtesy call* to let Green know that Tony Pinella and his team were interested in speaking to Julia about Tom Rawlings' murder.

"Look, Morris, they just want to question her, and it might be better if she volunteered to come in, instead of having two detectives show up at your home with the cameras rolling. You know—just to keep the reporters away." Brennan said.

Green had no idea that Tony Pinella and Abraham Bloom were sitting right next to Brennan as he made the call. They were not happy with giving Green advance notice, but Brennan convinced them that this was the best way to go.

"Let's not raise any alarms just yet," Brennan explained. "If you guys are wrong, and Julia had nothing to do with Rawlings' murder, we'll save the department from a lot of bad press. You know what I mean. We have to play this with some amount of political savvy. There's a lot at stake here."

Tony was not happy with the plan, but he also realized that Commissioner Brennan had Mayor Jack Saunders to answer to, and Bloom answered to Chief Cedeno. If this case went haywire, Tony could crawl back to Newport and be done with it. Brennan, Cedeno, and Bloom's careers were at stake, while Green remained a heavy player with lots of political clout.

❧

The Laughing Angels loved how the rich and powerful operated. Every disgrace offered a new opportunity. After all, they believed, God never aimed to provide the universe with a level playing field.

Let the rich and powerful have their fun for now, the Laughing Angels thought. *Eventually, everyone had a price to pay at some point. It's just a matter of time before they all fall down. The game was God's—and He would be the only winner.*

Even the Righteous Ones wondered what God had in mind. They cried out to the heavens, as they fought off their tears. *Whose side are you on? Have the Laughing Angels been right all along? Is everyone just a casualty in the game of life?*

God said nothing.

Chapter 48

The call came in late Thursday afternoon to Detective Bloom's office. Steve Kerry, Julia Green's attorney, informed him that Julia Green would come in for questioning first thing Friday morning.

Right after he hung up the phone, Bloom let the commissioner and mayor know. He then called Tony and Cedeno, and told them to be at the interview. Bloom told Tony that he and Kerry went back a long way, to a corruption case involving a small-time hoodlum, who Morris Green used as the state's main witness. It was Morris Green's first big case as New York State's attorney general.

Kerry, a young and idealistic street lawyer at the time, acted pro bono for the hoodlum—who testified that he saw an accountant take money from a known Brooklyn drug dealer. The accountant turned out to be the head of a major New York City investment firm, who was also helping launder money for a statewide prostitution operation. That case grew much larger, when it exposed the Brooklyn drug ring, and brought down the prostitution operation—along with a state senator and three Brooklyn City Council members.

Green was impressed with Kerry and hired him to handle a variety of cases throughout his term as attorney general. Kerry quickly gained a reputation for being honest and shrewd, Bloom explained. Like Tony, he was now semi-retired, and kept a small office in his apartment on East 90th Street in Manhattan, an older neighborhood, not far from the trendy Yorkville area and Gracie Mansion, the official residence of the mayor.

While he became a loyal friend to the Green's, always thankful for the business Morris Green gave him, he never forgot the *people of the street*, as he called them. Kerry was the first one to volunteer pro bono services to elderly tenants, who were losing their apartments to large condominium developers, and to the homeless when he thought their rights were being violated.

Tony was surprised at the choice of Kerry, but Bloom explained that he was like an uncle to Julia. Morris and Sally Green probably felt their daughter was better off with someone Julia trusted—and who knew how the system worked.

At nine o'clock the next morning, they met in the conference room, which Bloom thought would be friendlier and less threatening than some of the other rooms used for questioning. The room was equipped with a camera and recording system, so everything would be carefully documented.

Once all the introductions and handshaking were over, they all sat down. Julia eyed Tony carefully. He could see that she was trying to get a sense of him—the only person in the room she had never met. Although she appeared to have a somewhat sad demeanor, and held a handkerchief she frequently used to touch her tearing eyes, Tony had the sense she was far more self-assured. A product of private schools and probably well rehearsed for this day.

Bloom underestimated this young woman, Tony thought. The way she eyed him, he suspected Julia thought he was just a dumb cop who could be easily fooled.

They only had one hour, and agreed ahead of time that Bloom would ask most of the questions. But the answers always came from Steve Kerry, not Julia, who repeated several times that *Julia knows nothing about what Tom Rawlings might of done that got him killed.*

As the interview was ending, Tony felt frustrated. They had not learned anything. He was convinced that Julia knew much more. Then, to everyone's surprise—including Steve Kerry—Julia blurted out, "It just goes to show you how naïve I've been. I should have known better. I never thought Tom was capable of doing anything that would get him killed."

"Don't be so hard on yourself," Tony quickly interjected. "Who would think Tom had a motive to go around killing escorts."

Neither Cedeno nor Bloom said a word. The interview revealed nothing helpful. Maybe Tony had something up his sleeve and they should let this new scene play out. Kerry glared straight at Tony, quickly trying to assess his motives. He wanted to stop Julia from saying anything more, and gently put his hand on her arm. It was too late.

"What on earth are you implying?" she asked.

Tony responded quickly, carefully watching for Julia's reaction. "Maybe Tom was trying to please you."

Julia responded just as quickly and with an air of superiority in her voice. "That's absurd! Tom would never have thought that."

Kerry squeezed her arm tighter, trying to stop the conversation, but to no avail. He knew this young woman well, and feared Julia's ego had taken over. It was obvious that she was determined to match wits with Tony, someone she clearly thought was below her status.

Tony came right back at this cocky young woman. "What if Tom loved you so much, he decided to help you and your family by getting rid of the escorts?"

"I guess you also think that God created the world in six days, when he could have done it in only one day—or even one second!" Julia said in a mocking manner.

Julia's response puzzled Tony. He leaned across the table and asked her firmly but sincerely, "What does the Bible have to do with any of this?"

"That's exactly my point," Julia said triumphantly. "What you said about Tom has nothing to do with anything."

Then, to the surprise of the others in the room, Julia and Tony shared a hearty laugh. Bloom, Cedeno, and even Kerry, let out sighs of relief. These two shrewd people—Julia Green and Tony Pinella—had baited each other, and it was a draw!

After Julia and Kerry left the room, Tony sat down with a satisfied smile on his face.

"What are you smiling at, Pinella?" Bloom asked. "Clearly, we're just where we started."

"On the contrary. I thought that was a good meeting. Today was only round one," Tony answered.

Chapter 49

Within days of her interview about Tom Rawlings, Julia Green took a leave of absence from college to work on her father's senatorial campaign. She believed his election to the senate was important for her and the family. It would keep them focused on something positive, especially after all the months spent on allegations and ugly innuendos about escorts and murders.

After a particularly hectic week of reviewing campaign speeches and fundraising breakfasts and luncheons, Sally thought she and Julia needed a night out, a brief diversion from the political world. In a darkened movie theater, they could escape from the public's eye. They chose a film because it starred several of Sally's favorite actors: Susan Sarandon, Christopher Plummer, Gabriel Byrne, and Max Von Sydow.

Unfortunately, they did not look closely enough at the movie synopsis! By the time the film ended, both Sally and Julia were totally drained. Although they had spent many wonderful vacations sightseeing in France, neither explored the darker side of French history during WWII in German occupied France. The movie was about the Drancy internment camp, where French guards brutalized more than sixty thousand French, Polish, and German Jews—including approximately six thousand children—before they were packed onto railway cars and sent to their deaths in extermination camps.

Sally and Julia left the theater in stunned silence, walking hand-in-hand to a nearby coffee shop that was famous for its desserts.

All those times, enjoying the beautiful French countryside, and gaily shopping in Paris, they never once discussed the cruelty of the French government and so many of its people as they cooperated with Nazi Germany.

After they ordered from the menu, Sally took Julia's hands in hers and said very seriously, "Julia, we have to talk. We're facing something as a family that will have great impact on all our futures."

"I know, Mother. I guess I really take our lives for granted."

Sally was not sure what Julia was thinking. "What do you mean?" she asked.

"Seeing what all those people went through during that dreadful war... We are so fortunate to have a second chance with dad's run for the senate. Who knows? One of these days, we could be headed for the White House."

Sally was surprised at Julia's analogy. She always thought her eldest daughter was more sensitive than to compare the killing of millions of people to her father's relationship with an escort.

"Well, yes," Sally said. "That was a terrible time in history... But I certainly wouldn't even try to draw an analogy between the horrors of war and what our lives were like these past months."

"I'm sorry, Mom. I'm sorry I upset you. What do you want to talk about?"

"These past months, we've been through a great deal—that's true. As a mother and wife, I have to take most of the responsibility for letting this go so far. By staying supportive of your father, I've been called everything from an enabler of his *inappropriate behavior*, as he calls it, to a poor example to other women and to my own daughters. It's hurtful, but closer to the truth than I want to admit."

Julia reached across the table and took her mother's hands, and squeezed them affectionately. "Mom, you can't possibly blame yourself. Dad's been getting all the credit and accolades all his life, and now it's his turn to take the responsibility for his actions. I'm glad to say, I think he's doing that now. You have nothing to apologize about. We owe you for keeping us together. Look... I love Dad, too. I'm grateful for the life we have, and I'm happy to work on his campaign. If he wins, we all benefit. But what about you? You're the one who gave up a promising career to take care of my sisters and me! My God, Mom, it could be you running for a senate seat if it weren't for your sacrifices."

Sally began to cry and Julia got up and gave her mother a long embrace.

"Thank you sweetheart... I appreciate what you said. But now, please sit down." Sally smiled, "We don't want people staring. Next thing is you'll read in *The New York Post* how the two of us sat crying in a coffee shop!"

Julia laughed and returned to the seat opposite her mother. Sally Green tried to keep her composure, while at the same time realizing she could not get away from the excruciating pain she felt—her fear that the family she loved was in deep trouble. She watched her beautiful daughter dip into the hot fudge sundae the waitress placed on the table. Since she was a child, whenever Julia was nursing a scratched knee, or sad because her father was away on business, a hot fudge sundae always cheered her up.

Sally watched Julia lick the dripping hot fudge off the tip of her spoon. She looked just like the same little girl, always wanting to get the last drop of her delicious treats. While Sally did not want to bring it up, she knew it was time.

"Julia, I have to ask you a very serious question."

"What is it, Mom?"

"Why did Tom kill those three young women?"

Sally could see the immediate change in Julia's mood and tone.

"I'm not sure he did," Julia answered. She nervously dipped her spoon back into the ice cream sundae. "Do we have to talk about this now?"

"Yes, we do, Julia. The police say they had the evidence, and were just waiting for the arrest warrant, when Tom was found murdered. Please, Julia. *I think you know more*. You and Tom were more than an engaged couple. You were each other's confidants. I could see something was going on between you, some secret. At first, I thought maybe you were planning to announce your wedding date—then all this happened. Please help me understand," Sally pleaded. "Why did he do such awful things?"

"Mom, I thought this was going to be a nice evening together. A chance to set all this murder stuff aside. Can't you just drop the subject? Nothing I say, or you say, can change anything. What dad did to this family is a tragedy, for us and everyone else involved. Our lives changed drastically! I'm just thankful he wasn't sent to prison."

Sally Green looked around the coffee shop to be sure no one was listening to the conversation. She kept her voice down, but spoke very firmly to her daughter.

"Julia, your father wisely decided to go on with his political life. Right now, I'm concerned about you. *You have a life, too.* I don't think it's wise for you to get involved in his senate campaign."

"I can't believe you're saying this. Do you really think I have a choice? Dad needs our help. He's not like other politicians. Dad is very sensitive to the needs of the people.

Yes, he has human frailties. *We all do.* But his good points outweigh his unfortunately bad habits by a landslide—and from the looks of the polls, the public agrees with me."

"Julia, earlier you thanked me for giving up my career to take care of you and your sisters, and to support dad in his career and political aspirations. I appreciated that very much. But, given all that's happened, did it ever enter your mind that your father should also think about us? To perhaps get out of politics and support the ambitions of the rest of his family—*our family*?"

"That wouldn't be fair to him. Anyway, Mom, *this is what I want to do*. Besides, it's not too late for you to do whatever your heart desires."

Sally sat back in her seat and sighed heavily as Julia scraped the last bit of hot fudge from the bottom of the dish. Maybe Julia was right when she said this was not the best time to have such a serious conversation. At the same time, Sally also feared that time was not on their side. She had done her research and knew Tony Pinella was persistent, determined, and smart. He was not intimidated by wealth and power. He would keep on digging into their lives no matter how long it took.

"My darling daughter," Sally said with great affection and concern. "It's getting late, so let's talk about this tomorrow, after we get a good night's rest."

"Sure, Mom," Julia said. "That's a good idea. I do love you..."

Chapter 50

Tony was not looking forward to his next visit with Stacey Johnson Blake. It had been awhile since his last trip to the psychiatric research wing of the John Henry Hospital in Ferndale, Michigan. The last time he called to check with Dr. Trotsky on Stacey's status, he learned that her hallucinations were so intense, she was under sedation. That was weeks ago.

In her last letter, Stacey described her prior condition as being *under the weather*. "I'm now back to full strength," she wrote, and "we have so much to talk about."

Tony was not sure he wanted to continue down that path. His last visit put him on an emotional rollercoaster that took too long to shake off. *Then,* he thought, *Stacey always had a way of reaching his heart.*

In her letter, she wrote: "Thank you for the Charlotte Church CD. I especially loved her rendition of *Papa Can You Hear Me*, and her duet with Josh Grogan of *The Prayer*."

Stacey also wrote that during her years of therapy, she came to the realization that she was not seeking forgiveness.

"God revealed to me that the whole concept of forgiveness is just a bunch of nonsense proclaimed by members of the clergy, who themselves are sinners looking for redemption. One has to learn to live with our evil deeds. Yes, we must be remorseful, but God is not there to forgive us—that can only come from our victims."

Tony did not know what Dr. Trotsky thought, but it seemed clear to him that Stacey's self-evaluation was both a step forward and a step backwards. On the one hand, it was important that she recognized her crimes, and perhaps felt that helping solve the escort murders was a way of making amends to Veronica Blake, the woman Stacey killed. On the other hand, it probably was not healthy that she continued to proclaim herself as God's *chosen* daughter, the one he endowed with special crime-solving insights.

While Tony certainly did not feel guilty about putting away a violent and disturbed murderess, there was more than one side to Stacey. The *insightful* Stacey, who could recognize and respect true religious belief, and distinguish it from hypocrisy. The *sensitive* Stacey, who cried when listening to the tender sounds of *My Prayer*. What about the *little girl* Stacey, who never failed to touch Tony's heart? The one who yearned to be loved by a father figure?

Today, he hoped to see the *intuitive* Stacey, who seemed to have some real insights into the escort murders—and, maybe, the murder of Tom Rawlings.

While Tony continued to gear-up for his trip to Ferndale, Stacey was also preparing for his visit by reliving her past as a murderess, which she believed was the reason the escort murders had such an impact on her. *Why should her brother get all the credit for doing good deeds,* she thought. *As God's chosen daughter, I have a responsibility to the young murdered escorts—as well as an affinity to their murderers.*

The Laughing Angels were eager for Tony to arrive for his visit with Stacey. She was at the top of her game, they thought, and could not wait for Stacey to tell Tony her latest thoughts about Julia Green.

Julia and Stacey, Stacey and Julia, they sang while dancing around Stacey's room. Both of these were damaged women, betrayed by fathers they loved. The Laughing Angels were amused, but not surprised, that Stacey was the one person who figured it all out.

The Righteous Ones detested how the Laughing Angels derived so much enjoyment from the pain and suffering of so many. How they cackled with joy on those nights when Stacey knocked her head against the wall, compelled by her need to use physical pain to displace the emotional pain she felt for the dead escorts. She had come so far from her days of committing mayhem and murder. Even a minor disappointment could lead to a major setback. She had grown tough in those last days before murdering Veronica Blake. Now, she seemed more fragile—like a little girl, desperately seeking her father's approval.

Chapter 51

When Tony arrived at the hospital, he was led directly to Dr. Trotsky's office, where the doctor and Nurse Helen Spagnoli were waiting. Tony's first reaction was that something awful had happened to Stacey.

"Is Stacey all right?" he asked anxiously, as his heart pounded and he broke out in a cold sweat.

"Yes, yes, Detective Pinella," Dr. Trotsky said. "But there are a few things we need to discuss before I bring you to see Stacey."

"I'm listening," Tony said with a sigh of relief.

"Since her last letter to you, Stacey has become very vocal about theology and about her father—that is, her biological father."

"Well, that's not so unusual, is it? Hasn't that been her problem all along?"

"Yes, her needs for a strong father figure, as well as her obsession with Reverend Blake, are what led her to commit murder in the first place."

"So why are you so concerned? This isn't anything new," Tony said.

"That's true, Detective. It is also true that Stacey has always been very vocal about her visions and helping you solve the escort murders. In fact, she often refers to you as her *partner* in that effort."

"Is there a *but* here, Dr. Trotsky? Why are we having this conversation?"

"Yes, there is a *but*, and I ask that you be patient and hear me out. *My job is to protect and help my patient. Not solve your murders*," Dr. Trotsky said.

Tony was surprised by the obvious disdain in the doctor's voice.

"Hold on, Dr. Trotsky. I'm as concerned as you are about Stacy. For me, it's personal. Not part of some medical paper you'll probably write about her. And, yes… I'm also concerned about the three young women who were murdered. There's another killer out there who I want to stop before he kills again."

"My apologies, Detective. It's just that Stacey was making such good progress. Then, as soon as she learned you were coming, she became very secretive about the murders, and much more emotional and defensive when discussing her father. I think we may be close to a breakthrough. I just don't want her visits with you to interfere in her therapy. You want us to cooperate with you… Now I'm asking you to cooperate with us."

"I'm sorry, too, Dr. Trotsky. I didn't intend to be rude, and I certainly appreciate your cooperation, *but I am confused.* Isn't it a good thing that Stacey is opening up about her childhood relationship with her father? I thought that was the purpose of psychoanalysis."

"Yes, Detective, it is—and with that comes a danger point. Stacey gets very frustrated when she thinks we don't understand or consider her special relationship with God. She thinks that *you* are the only one who does understand her. Do you know anything about Freud's psychoanalytic theory of *transference*?"

"Why don't you explain it to me!"

"When a patient like Stacey does not feel satisfied with her analyst's role as a helper, she may see him as a reincarnation of an important figure from her past. Any feelings or reactions she had, or has for that person, are transferred onto the analyst. Are you following me, Detective?"

"I think so. Stacey doesn't see you as her doctor, but she thinks you're either her biological father or Jason Blake."

"That's *sort* of right. It really alters the entire analytic situation. In simple terms, as the patient sets aside the rational idea of becoming emotionally healthy, it allows her to concentrate on pleasing the analyst, winning his approval, even his love. This becomes a strong motivational force in gaining the patient's collaboration. She becomes well because she wants to please her father, her mother, her husband…"

Tony interrupted. *So... this transference is a good thing. It can help Stacey.*

"Not so fast, Detective. I'm trying to explain something in simple terms that's far more complicated. Transference can be positive, even affectionate. But it also can be negative, and very hostile."

Tony was quickly losing his patience again. He had murders to solve, and Stacey was miraculously being helpful. He did not have the time or patience to be lectured on what he generally thought of as *psychobabble*.

"Look, Dr. Trotsky, we both know that Stacey is never going to leave this place, so why not give her the little pleasure she seems to have by helping me solve a murder case? Like you, I try to understand people's motives—it's one of the ways we solve crimes. I don't think you really want to give me a detailed lesson on something that Sigmund Freud spent his whole life trying to explain. What's your bottom line here?"

Dr. Trotsky's face showed his frustration with the situation. He leaned forward and spoke to Tony with an obvious tone of annoyance in his voice.

"I'll make this as simple as I can, Detective Pinella. I think Stacey's transference is to you. Stacey sees you, not me, as the father figure—someone she desperately wants to please. At the same time, she still feels hostile towards you for arresting her."

"With all due respect, Doctor, I've known that all along. I have mixed emotions about her, too. But I'm not going to spend the rest of my life on a psychiatrist's couch to sort it all out—and I never murdered anyone. I know Stacey is very complex. At the same time, she's analyzed the escort murders in a way that's helping us zero in on the perpetrators of these heinous crimes. Any way you look at it... Whether she wants to please me, thinks it's messages from God, or believes she's competing with her brother Jesus Christ—*I need her help*. Who knows? Maybe she even wants to do some good after all the chaos she caused in the lives of her husband and children. So long as I'm not harming her in any way, I'm depending on you to let me get that help. Now, if you don't mind, I would like to see Stacey—or do I need to get a court order!"

The Laughing Angels danced around Dr. Trotsky's office with great delight. *So now,* they thought, *Pinella is a psychiatrist as well as a detective!* Would he be so bold as to battle the Righteous Ones for a seat at God's throne? Maybe Tony would come over to their side, and finally see God in the same light as he viewed most politicians and religious extremists—as hypocrites.

Chapter 52

When Tony entered the room, it was obvious that Stacey felt at the top of her game. Just the way she greeted him showed certainty in her voice. It was like the first time they met, and he found himself, once again, mesmerized by her. Unfortunately, the cost had been great, and he was still paying a price—feeling guilty about taking so long to solve Veronica Blake's murder, and being totally manipulated by a confident Stacey.

That would not happen this time, he silently resolved to himself. He would listen to Stacey closely, but always keep in mind that more lives might be at stake if she led him purposely, or even innocently, in the wrong direction with her theological adeptness.

At one point, after Stacey had spent about fifteen minutes talking non-stop about her responsibility as God's daughter, Tony's mind drifted—which did not go unnoticed.

"Tony," Stacey shouted with annoyance. "You need to listen to me closely. Your mind seems to be somewhere else."

"I am listening," Tony said, realizing he sounded too defensive.

Stacey did not respond at first, her face angrily contorted. "So you heard what I said about Sally Green?" she shouted.

Dr. Trotsky intervened, worried that Stacey might become enraged and need to be medicated. "Why don't you repeat what you said for all of us, Stacey. We know how important this is to you."

Stacey glared at Dr. Trotsky and then gave Tony an icy stare.

"You know, Tony... When I was a child, my father taught me a very important lesson," she said indignantly. "Daddy told me, when you go to school, you might as well listen and try to learn something. Since you decided to come here, you should make more of an effort to listen closely, so I don't have to repeat myself."

The atmosphere in the room remained tense. Dr. Trotsky scowled at Tony for having upset his patient. But Tony was quick, and tried calm the situation. In his most sincere voice he softly said, "Please, Stacey... Please... I apologize if I offended you."

Stacey's eyes suddenly filled with tears. The last thing Tony wanted was to hurt Stacey. "Your father gave you good advice," he said. "I promise, you have my full attention. Please do tell me again, so I can be sure my notes are correct."

"Thank you," Stacey said with a sly smile. "I wasn't really angry, just worried that your attention span is not like it used to be when you were younger."

"Don't worry about that, Stacey. I may have slowed down a little, but my years of experience and dedication to catching the bad guys have kept my mind alert. But thank you very much for your concern."

"Thank you, Tony," Stacey said. Then she looked at Dr. Trotsky, "Do we still have time, Doctor?"

"Yes, of course, Stacey. This is your meeting, and I'm sure Detective Pinella learned his lesson about who is in charge. Haven't you, Detective?"

Tony was steaming at Trotsky's innuendo, but let it go. He did not want Stacey to become a pawn in some ego battle.

"You have my full attention, Stacey. So let's go over this once more."

"Okay. Well, we know that Julia Green and Tom Rawlings were in New York and Chicago when each of the first two murders took place. We also know that when the third escort was killed, Tom was in Paradise Valley, Arizona. Do you have that, Tony?"

"Yes, Stacey. I have that in my notes. You were about to tell me something more...."

"Don't be so impatient, Tony," Stacey snapped. "It's not every day that someone in a place like this solves murders for a big-time detective. Don't forget, I know what it's like to be accused of murder, and then convicted. I feel a lot of empathy for Julia and her mother. Please don't take all this lightly."

"That's true," Tony said apologetically. "Please continue. Please tell the story in whatever manner you want. I'm very grateful for your assistance."

"Yes, Stacey," Dr. Trotsky interjected. "I'm sure Detective Pinella is *very* appreciative of your help. Isn't that right, Detective?"

"Yes, of course I am," Tony said.

"Thank you, Tony! I'm trying to build the scene so you can picture what happened to Tom Rawlings—just like I saw it in my visions."

Tony tried not to show the surprise on his face. "Did you see how Tom Rawlings was murdered?"

"Of course, I did. That's why I asked you to come here. I've solved that murder, too! Who do you think had any interest or a motive to kill Tom?"

"Please go on, Stacey. Who do you think killed Tom Rawlings—and why?"

"Sally Green, Morris Green's wife, was involved in Rawlings' murder!" Stacey said triumphantly.

"If Sally Green was involved, what was her motive?"

"One thing at a time, Tony. Sally realized that her daughter was implicated in the escort murders. The only way for the police to prove Julia's involvement was if Tom Rawlings decided to talk. Sally's only way to protect Julia was to make sure Rawlings was eliminated."

"How did you come to that conclusion, Stacey? Did you have a vision?"

"No vision this time, Tony. It was murderer's intuition, as well as knowing how a mother would feel if her daughter were threatened. I understand Sally's need to protect Julia and her sisters from another scandal, not to mention Sally's own lifestyle."

"I respect what you're saying, Stacey. But I'm going to need hard evidence."

Stacey laughed, and looked straight into Dr. Trotsky's eyes. "I know what you're thinking, Trotsky. *Oh, boy, is Detective Pinella seriously going to believe anything this crazy, convicted murderer has to say?*"

Then she looked over at Tony with a big smile on her face. "Don't worry about that, Tony. So far, I haven't steered you wrong on this case. Just remember it's me you're dealing with... *So, what do you say, Tony?*"

Tony was about to say something, but realized he needed to be very careful with his words. He could not risk Stacey flying into a rage if he questioned her visions. As crazy as this all seemed, the only reason he was here today was because everything Stacey said about the escort murders had been right. Whether it was her visions, or the mind of a murderer, she was on target. Nevertheless, he would need more than Stacey's visions to convince the district attorney to look at the possible involvement of Sally Green in Tom Rawlings' murder.

Stacey kept looking intently at Tony, waiting for his response. "Why Tony, I don't remember you ever being speechless."

"Well, I am surprised, Stacey. You certainly know how the criminal justice system works. So you also realize I need more to go on before I move on this. Not only do I have to be absolutely convinced, so does the district attorney, before we bring in Sally Green for questioning."

"I thought you would be more appreciative, more open to new ideas," Stacey said.

Tony was not taking any chances. Accusing Sally Green of any involvement in Tom Rawlings' murder would take hard evidence, not *gut feelings*. He needed more from Stacey, even if he risked losing her trust.

"I'm open to ideas, Stacey. I agree with your thought process, but I'll need more to go on."

"You see, Tony, this was all told to me in a dream. Well, not just my dream. Sally's dream—a vision God sent to her."

"I don't understand."

"God came to Sally Green and told her to *kill Julia*. Of course, Sally said *no*. Then God said, *kill your husband Morris*. Sally thought her husband certainly deserved to die, but she still said *no*. So then, God told Sally to kill Tom Rawlings, because he was the one who held the key to whether or not Julia might spend the next twenty years in prison. Sally thought that was a good idea."

Tony looked astonished, and so did Dr. Trotsky and Nurse Helen. This was bizarre, even from Stacey. Then Stacey began laughing hard enough to bring tears to her eyes.

"*I'm only kidding!* If all of you could just see the expressions on your faces! Do you think I'm crazy? *Don't answer that*! We all know I am crazy, *but I'm not stupid*."

"You really had us going there, Stacey," Tony said.

"I just wanted to remind you that I realize I have problems, but I haven't lost one bit of my intellect and intuition—intuition based on the solid fact that I am a murderer who almost got away with it because of my keen understanding of the human condition. I was, after all, a preacher's wife—and Sally is a politician's wife. We both gave up a great deal of our own personal fulfillment for the bigger picture promised to us by our husbands. True, my case is a little different. I committed murder in order to become Jason's wife. Both Jason and Morris are despicable. Nevertheless, Sally wants to maintain her lifestyle, and she loves her daughters. She would do anything to protect the status quo."

Tony, and even Dr. Trotsky, looked at Stacey with amazement at her clarity, her view of the situations. In her mind, she rationalized that she had been wronged and violated—and that made sense. Many women felt that way, but few would resort to murder. Neither Tony nor Trotsky were prepared for Stacey's next revelation.

"Don't ever forget that I'm God's daughter. He gave up on his son a long time ago. *Think about it!* Aren't more and more business owners turning their companies over to their daughters instead of their wayward sons? Why should God be any different?"

Dr. Trotsky stood up. It was apparent to him that was Stacey's last word on the issue. "I'm sure you have given Detective Pinella a great deal to think about, Stacey. Now I think it's time for Nurse Helen to make sure you have lunch and get some rest before your afternoon group therapy. Detective, may I show you out?"

"Yes, thank you, Dr. Trotsky. A special thanks to you, Stacey. I'll think very hard about everything you shared with me."

Chapter 53

Julia was helping her mother decide on the seating arrangement for an upcoming fundraising dinner for a local shelter for abused women, when Sally surprised her daughter by bringing up Tom Rawlings' murder.

"Julia, it's likely the police will want to interview you again about Tom's murder. I want your promise that you won't say a word to them, or to anyone, about the escort murders."

"What made you think about that, Mother?"

"Oh, just that my mind is on abused women, and it made me think of that detective, Tony Pinella, and something he said about those poor girls."

"So? What has that got to do with me?"

"Well, he's interviewed you once about Tom, and he might want to interview you again. You knew Tom better than his own family, and it makes sense he might think you can help the investigation. You know, Detective Pinella may look very low key and unassuming, even charming—but he has a reputation for getting deep inside a person's mind when he's looking for answers. I read that he'll continue to pursue a case, even years after other detectives have considered it solved."

"Mom, I think you've been watching too many old television re-runs of *CSI Miami*. When he and I spoke, Detective Pinella was very sensitive and considerate."

"I just want you to be prepared, Julia—just in case he seeks you out. Don't be fooled by his outward humility. Pinella is very clever, even charming in an awkward sort of way. More like Peter Falk in *Columbo* than David Caruso as

Lieutenant Horatio Caine in *CSI Miami*! Be careful what you say to him."

"Why, Mother, does dad know you have a secret crush on Tony Pinella?"

"That's very funny, Julia. Your dad has more important things to worry about… I'm serious about this. It's your secrets I'm worried about."

"Secrets? I don't have any secrets, Mom. I don't know what you're talking about."

"I just want to be sure you know that I'm here for you."

"I know that, Mom… and I'm here for you, too. I'm not a little girl anymore."

"No, no you're not," Sally said.

She leaned across the table and took Julia's hands, squeezing them tightly. She was trying hard not to cry, determined to provide her daughter with a strong sense of support.

Julia pulled back, eager to change the subject. "Well, now that we've got that all straightened out, I guess we better get this seating plan done."

Chapter 54

At the same time as Sally and Julia were putting seating plans together, Tony was on the phone with Max, who seemed to be struggling with the column he was writing for the next day's edition of *Public Corruption.*

"I'm not pulling any punches. Green's worse than a con man," Max shouted into the telephone. "Green not only duped the public, he deceived and humiliated his wife and daughters. He made them all look like fools in front of the entire country. Then he has the audacity to sucker the public in again by running for the senate—and they still applaud him. Well, not if I have any say in the matter. I'm sick of him and his kind."

Tony knew exactly how Max felt. It was not always easy to draw the line between one's own outrage and keeping an objective perspective.

"Hold on to those thoughts and express them in your column—just as you always do," Tony said. "Your readers, as well as your editor, trust you to tell it just like you see it."

"Thanks, Tony. I needed to get that off my chest. I don't want the column to sound more like a personal vendetta than genuine public outrage. Gotta go! I only have fifteen minutes to make sure this gets into tomorrow's issue. Hey… Thanks for listening."

Max's column appeared on the front page of *Public Corruption.*

Morris Green for Senator? You've Got to be Kidding!
Max Gold, Crime Reporter

Morris Green wants the people of New York to support his bid for senator of our great state. My question to you Morris Green is this: "What makes you think you have the right to ask for our votes?"

Without sounding presumptuous, let me guess what your answer will be: "Wouldn't the fine people of New York rather have someone like me, someone who admits to his human frailties? Someone who has the courage to fight for our city's needs, often against the odds? Someone who doesn't hide behind a false cloak of respectability, like those who wheel and deal behind the walls of congress, safe from public scrutiny? Morris Green is here to fight for you, with all my personal flaws exposed. I let my family down, that's true. But they have forgiven me. So, today, I ask you to join my family in supporting me for senator of the great state of New York."

That's not a bad speech. But it's not good enough for the people of New York! Your name should not even be on the ballot. Your name should be on the list of cases to be prosecuted by the current attorney general. Come to think of it, didn't you prosecute people for much lesser crimes?

I was surprised that you were given an undeserved break when the state chose not to prosecute you. What shocks me even more, is that you feel entitled to run for another public office—and so soon!

In the name of fairness and justice, I ask that you remove your name from consideration. After all the time, pain, money, and disappointment you caused the people of New York, it is the least you can do for us.

Chapter 55

While people all over the state were reading Max's column, Sally Green sat staring out of the bedroom window of their Gramercy Park townhouse in Manhattan. Her mind drifted to the earlier days of her marriage to Morris Green. They had purchased this townhouse when Morris' law practice had its most successful year. That was before he got involved in politics and became attorney general, and then governor. When they moved to Albany, and later into the Governor's Mansion, Sally had insisted they keep this townhouse as a getaway, their private family sanctuary.

She thought about how different and happy their lives would have been if it were not for the mess Morris created. Now he was busy with his senatorial campaign, oblivious to what his family was going through. Nothing seemed to get in the way of his ambitions. She learned too late that Morris' idea of sacrifice was that everyone else should accommodate his needs.

This is how Morris had always been, she thought, growing angrier and angrier with herself. *There was a time when his aggressive and ambitious traits, actually made him more attractive to me.*

Tears welled up in Sally's eyes, when she recalled how her heart swelled with pride when Morris asked her to be his wife. *Morris Green was a man destined for success*, she thought. *How proud I felt, being a part of his plan. I should have known better.*

Now it was too late. The damage was done. Sally still worried about the discussion she had yesterday with Julia.

Sally knew her daughter was in denial—not recognizing, or not wanting to face up to the danger ahead.

Just then, she was surprised when Julia walked into the room. "Mom, about yesterday, I think we need to talk more. I didn't tell you everything."

Sally stood up and embraced her daughter. "Yes, Julia. We do need to talk, and we may need some legal advice—but not from anyone associated with your father. What do you think about our visiting with Aunt Jan? We've been friends for more than thirty years. I trust her completely, and she is a well-respected criminal attorney. She loves you and your sisters as though you were her own daughters. You know, even though we're the same age, Jan has often teased me that she sometimes feels more like my mother than a close friend—*and she's right.*"

Julia began to cry and Sally put her arms around her daughter. She whispered, "Julia, I'm ready when you are."

"Oh, Mom, yes! Please call Aunt Jan. I don't think I can take this much longer."

"I'll call her right now."

The twenty-minute car ride to Jan Clark's office was very quiet. Sally recalled how much Jan disliked Morris. She never understood why Sally had such a crush on him. He was too sure of himself, and always bragging about how he would be a famous politician one day.

During their first year of law school, they started dating, and soon after announced their engagement. Jan warned her again. She called Morris *a political opportunist, who would say and do anything to get what he wanted—no matter who got hurt in the process.*

Years later, after her third daughter was born, Jan told Sally that she was surprised her marriage to Morris had lasted so long. That she hoped Sally and her children would never have to pay a price for her husband's mistakes. Now those words rang loudly in Sally Green's ears, as she was about to tell her friend the awful truth.

The Laughing Angels, riding in the back seat of Sally Green's Mercedes, were delighted. Once again, Plato's Republic had failed. The concept that *knowledge is virtue and virtue is knowledge* was based on a faulty premise. Plato never took into account how those who are well versed in the law can be the most devious.

The Righteous Ones were about to say something, but decided not to bother. They wanted to embrace Sally and Julia, to tell them everything would be all right. But they knew better. This time the Laughing Angels were holding all the chips. They based their conclusions on reality—not on the ideal.

Chapter 56

While Morris Green was at a campaign rally among a room full of supporters, the mood was very different in the reception area of Jan Clark's office.

As soon as she embraced her friend, Sally broke out in tears and Julia began to sob. In all their years as friends, Jan had never seen Sally so distraught. Even when Morris gave his *mea culpa* speech and resigned as the Governor of New York State, Sally still showed a glimmer of hope. Now, seeing their faces of fright and despair, Jan did not even imagine the story they had to tell.

"Hold all my calls, and cancel the rest of my appointments," she called out to her secretary, as she led them into her private office and shut the door.

Sally and Julia sat down on the sofa, and Jan sat on the chair next to Sally, not letting go of her hand. "What happened?" she asked.

Through her tears, Julia said without any hesitation, "Mom, I'm so sorry. I was involved with Tom in the murders of the three escorts!"

Jan looked thoughtfully at the two distressed women sitting before her. She had to remind herself, *think first as a lawyer and second as a friend.* "Hold on a minute," she said. "Hand me a dollar *right now*, so I'm officially your lawyer. Anything you say to me will be privileged."

Sally wiped away her tears, sat up straight, and took two dollars out of her wallet. "Here's two dollars, one for each of us." Then she turned to Julia, "My God, Julia. Do you realize what you're saying?"

"Yes, I do, Mom." Then Julia looked at Jan, who had not said another word, "I can't tell you what made me do it, except I had to do something. I couldn't let them destroy my parents and my sisters' lives. Now, I wish I had left it all alone."

Sally turned white as a ghost, with tears still rolling down her cheeks. It's true that she had suspected Julia's involvement, but hearing her daughter say it out loud, admitting she was actually involved in murdering three young women, was devastating.

"This is all Morris' fault," Sally shouted. "His total disregard for me and our daughters, just to satisfy his lust and need for power."

Jan tried to keep her voice steady and professional. "Let's take this one step at a time. Start at the beginning. You first, Sally."

"There's more..."

"More? What more could there be, Mom?"

"I'm so sorry, Julia. I've known for months about the murders. Tom Rawlings told me. I didn't want you to know, but he tried to blackmail me; he wanted one million dollars for his silence."

"Oh, my God, Mom! I was afraid he would do something like that, but he promised that wouldn't happen."

Up to now, Jan sat there quietly, anticipating what might come next—trying to keep a professional distance while her heart ached. She knew that a shrewd prosecutor, especially one with a grudge against Morris Green, would have a field day trying to set mother against daughter in this house of cards.

"Sally, tell me what actually did happen between you and Tom? Did you pay him?" Jan asked.

"I wasn't sure what to do. He said I could have a few days to think about it. The next evening, I called him on his cell phone. He was at some sort of party downtown. He said he would leave the party early and meet me at his apartment."

"What happened at his apartment?" Jan asked. "Try to think of everything he said and did once you were there."

"At first, it was very cordial. He offered me a drink, but I refused. He already seemed a bit tipsy, and I wanted my mind to be clear. He asked if I brought the money. I said that walking around with one million dollars in my purse wasn't smart, and asked if we could work something out. He glared at me, and said something like, *Don't mess around with me. Those designer clothes and diamond necklace you're wearing are worth at least half a million.* Then he laughed and grabbed at my throat, trying to rip off my necklace. I tried to fight back, but Tom pushed me against the bar in his living room—this time with both hands around my throat. When I managed to scream, he quickly let go of me and pulled a gun from his pocket. We struggled and I heard the gun go off. I thought I was hit. But when Tom staggered and dropped to the floor, I ran for the door and left."

"After you left, why didn't you call the police?" Jan asked.

"Call the police? I couldn't risk that! There would be too many questions. I couldn't risk getting Julia involved. What if Tom didn't care about his own guilt, and decided to incriminate Julia in the murders? I didn't know what to do. So I didn't do anything. I just left.

"I wore a scarf around my neck until the marks healed where the necklace ripped into my skin. Then, when I heard Tom was dead, what could I do? I certainly couldn't tell Morris. Even if I called you, and we went to the police and claimed self-defense, I didn't want to get Julia in any more trouble than she was in already."

The next hour was spent divided between moments of agonizing silence, tears, and discussion. Sally and Julia's secret worlds had come together, colliding with an impact that could destroy them.

It took all Jan's professional qualities to maintain her composure, while her heart was breaking for her dear friends. Sally and her daughters were family to Jan. Just the thought of what they had done, and the shock of it all, had her mind going in many directions. Now their very lives were in her hands. First and foremost was to be sure she had all the facts, and that would take some digging. Right now, both Sally and Julia were too distraught. Jan needed to maintain some calm and consider which steps to take first.

Jan reached out to hold Sally's hand. "Give me a day or two while I consider our options and work out a strategy. We need to proceed very carefully. Can I count on both of you to stay calm, and not to mention any of this to anyone? Not to the police, not to Morris—no one!"

"I promise," Sally said as she blew her nose and wiped away her tears.

"Me, too," Julia said. "Thank you so much, Aunt Jan. I feel so awful. How could I have been so stupid?"

"We'll find a way to work this out, Julia. Right now isn't the time for introspection. Now is the time to find solutions and the best way to approach the police—before they find any evidence pointing to either of you. I'll have to act quickly."

"Do you think we'll go to jail?" Julia asked. Her voice sounded so much like the four-year-old little girl Jan once held in her arms when Julia fell off her bicycle.

"Let's not get ahead of ourselves just yet," Jan answered as she held back her own tears. "For now, just remember, if you do get a call from anyone about the escort murders or Tom Rawlings, you say nothing without me present. Just call me and I'll be right there! I mean it. Talk to no one!"

"Even my father?" Julia asked.

"Especially your father!" Jan said sharply. "Like it or not, he's really in the middle of all this. I know it won't be easy, but do your best to go on with your usual activities. You can do it. I know you can!"

"We'll be fine, we both will," Sally said with surprising confidence. "This is one time that Morris will not come first!"

"Oh, and one more thing. Because I'm so close to your family, I want to bring another attorney in on this. We are dealing with two different cases here. Julia's involvement in the escort murders, which we haven't even discussed fully, and the murder of Tom Rawlings. Her name is Lorna Adams. Don't worry. Lorna will also be bound by absolute confidentiality."

"I've heard of her," Sally said. "Didn't she handle that big national case, when the mistress of a well-known Hollywood actor was accused of murdering his wife?"

"That's Lorna, all right," Jan said proudly. "When Johnnie Cochran wasn't available, Lorna got the call. Let's just say when Lorna walks into a room, the prosecutors start to perspire profusely!"

"Thank you so much," Sally said. "Julia and I will do anything you say. We've both made some dreadful mistakes. I don't know what we would do without you."

As the three women stood up, Julia put her arms around Jan Clark and hugged her tightly. "Thank you, Aunt Jan. I'm so frightened, but also relieved to have you helping us."

"I'll do my best. You know I will, and so will Lorna Adams. We'll all meet soon. Just give me a few days to sort things out. Now don't forget, not a word to anyone. If you get a call from a reporter, say *no comment.* If the police do call you in for any reason, just tell them you have nothing to say until your attorney is present. Keep my card and private cell phone number with you. I'm available to you anytime, day or night. I can't emphasize that enough. *Don't answer any questions without me there. Are we clear?*"

"Absolutely, Aunt Jan."

"Not a word," echoed Sally.

Jan walked Sally and Julia to the elevator and hugged them both.

"I'll call you in a couple of days," she said as the elevator door slid shut.

As she went back to her office, Jan stopped at her secretary's desk. "Martha, please hold my calls for a while longer. I need some quiet time."

Sitting back at her desk, Jan just stared out the window. The tears she was holding back flowed down her cheeks. Sally was such a faithful person, always willing to set aside her own needs for the people she loved, whether they were friends or family—they could always count on Sally.

Chapter 57

Sally Green awakened at five o'clock the next morning to find that Morris must have returned sometime after midnight from one of his fundraising dinners. He was in the study across the hall from their bedroom, sound asleep on the couch. She quietly closed the study door and went to check on Julia, whose bedroom was downstairs.

As she peeked into the room, she could see that Julia was also awake and sobbing softly. Sally quietly went to her side and sat down on Julia's bed.

"My beautiful daughter. I wish I could make all this better for you, like I did when you were a little girl afraid of the dark. I would hold you in my arms and tell you there was nothing to fear, that everything would be all right."

"You can't make this all right, Mom – but I wouldn't mind your holding me. I'm so frightened. What if Aunt Jan can't help us? What if we both go to jail?"

"I can't predict the outcome, and there will be hard times ahead for both of us, but I know we did the right thing by going to Jan. She will do her best to help us through the mess your father brought to our door. Together—and with Jan and Lorna's help—we'll get through this."

"But, Mom… we're involved in murder! Three escorts are dead because of me, and you left Tom's apartment not knowing if he were dead or alive. We can't change that!"

"Hush, hush, my darling. Don't forget, your father isn't the only lawyer in this family. I also know how the law works, and there are lots of gray areas in both our situations. Jan's handled harder cases than ours—and I know Lorna Adams is very skilled. Both of them know exactly which angles to use. Let's try to be strong and keep all this to ourselves, just like Jan said."

As Sally rocked her still sobbing daughter in her arms, she had no idea that Morris was standing just outside Julia's door, listening to every word. He was also restless and got up shortly after Sally. He was on his way to the kitchen, when he heard Sally's voice coming from Julia's room. He was about to walk into the room, to make sure his daughter was all right, when he heard Julia cry out, *What if Aunt Jan can't help us? What if we both go to jail? What if the police think we're also involved in killing Tom?*

The initial shock momentarily paralyzed him. Nothing in his past had prepared him for this—his wife and daughter were in real trouble. For the first time in his life, Green had to acknowledge that, not only was he responsible for their pain—they also chose not to come to him for help, even at such a desperate time.

He went back upstairs and locked himself in the study. He had to think. Green did not have all the details of Sally and Julia's involvement, but that did not matter. He loved his family and it was up to him to protect them.

It was my own stupid indiscretions that caused all this, he thought. *And there is something I can do about it, but it has to be fast*!

Up to now, he reasoned, all the evidence on the escort murders pointed to Tom Rawlings. *It had to stay that way*. As far as who killed Rawlings, like many others, Green thought Tom's shady dealings had finally caught up with him. Now, after learning that Sally was in legal jeopardy, Green thought further about what to do—how to place the blame on someone else—someone who was willing to take the fall for killing Rawlings. There was only one person who could help him—a guy whose skin he saved years ago, and who owed him big-time. He took his private cell phone out of the safe in the study and left a message for his contact. Within an hour, Green received a call back.

"I heard you have a problem," the husky voice said. "And I have someone to solve it."

"Who is he?" Green asked. "What does he want?"

"All you need to know is that the guy is deeply in debt. He's seriously ill with only months to live. His health insurance is tapped out and he has no life insurance. He's desperate and will do anything to guarantee that his wife and young children will be financially secure for the rest of their lives. Chances are he will not even live long enough for the case to go to trial."

"His confession will be solid?" Green asked.

"Yes, it will be. I just need one more thing…"

"What's that?"

"You and me…We're even now."

"Make the deal," Green said.

By noon the next day, 45-year-old Brian Grissom walked into the New York City Police Department and confessed to murdering Tom Rawlings.

The news traveled fast after Police Commissioner Sean Brennan released a brief statement to the department that a man suspected of murdering Tom Rawlings was in custody. More details would be available once a thorough interrogation was completed.

Sally and Julia were sitting in Jan Clark's office when she got the call from Lorna Adams—only hours before they planned to approach the district attorney about Sally.

"What should we do now?" Jan asked Lorna.

"Nothing," Lorna said. "Sally and Julia need to stay quiet until we have a better understanding of what's going on here. Tell them to go home and try to act as if nothing has happened."

Jan told Sally and Julia the news. At least on the surface, it looked like Grissom's confession could be a game-changer.

❧

Even the Laughing Angels saw this as one more opportunity to ridicule the Righteous Ones. *Cheer up,* they said. *Maybe Brian Grissom is your new Messiah!*

The Righteous Ones were saddened by what had transpired. *Was this the new American dream? Admitting to a murder that you did not commit, so that your wife and children would have financial security?*

Chapter 58

Within 24 hours after Detective Abraham Bloom called Brennan with the surprising confession of Brian Grissom, the investigations into the murders of the escorts and Tom Rawlings were officially closed.

Chief Cedeno advised Tony immediately that his services on the escort and Rawlings' cases were no longer necessary. His consulting contract and payments would remain in effect for the next six months, but *under no circumstances* was Tony to continue investigating either case—*they were closed, period.* Cedeno reminded Tony that his contract prohibited him from working with any other police agency on these cases without express consent of the NYPD—so that ended any official contact with either the Paradise Valley or Chicago Police Departments.

Tony was stunned when he received the call from Sal Cedeno and learned the details of Grissom's confession. His surprise quickly turned to anger. He was sure the fix was in—but not sure about the source.

"What's going on here, Sal?" he asked. "Who is this guy, Grissom? Why are you so sure he worked alone?"

"Look, Tony, my hands are tied. This comes straight from the top. The DA has checked it all out, and the confession is solid. The cases are closed and that's just the way it is! The press conference is tomorrow at noon. I want you to be there. You can stop by my office before the conference, and I'll have the papers for the six-month arrangement ready for you to sign."

Cedeno hung up the phone before Tony had a chance to respond. He was not ready to sign anything that would prevent him from working on his own. First and foremost, he was not about to be bought off by anyone. *Cedeno should have known that,* Tony thought.

Tony had to consider his commitment to Max. *Would Public Corruption still support the investigation into the murders or the potential involvement of anyone in the Green family?* Tony and Max would need to have an honest and candid conversation. *What about Angela Robinson? Even if Grissom was the killer, what if Cedeno was wrong, and Grissom did not work alone? Was Angela still in danger?*

Then there was Stacey to consider. *How much of an explanation, if any, do I owe her?* Tony wondered. *Surely, she deserves some closure, if the case is really closed.*

Tony called Max first and asked him to come to Bensonhurst that night. They needed to talk. Max had just received an email about the press conference, but the announcement only said there would be an update. He was shocked, and furious, when Tony told him about Grissom.

"I'll understand if you have to back off, Tony—but I'm pretty sure my editor will want more than what Cedeno's told you so far. She's a tough woman, and a great editor, totally committed to the truth. She'll let me go as far as necessary—until I'm one hundred percent satisfied that this is all on the up and up."

"I'm sure glad to hear that, Max. Right now, all I know is what Sal Cedeno told me, which is next to nothing. We'll talk more tonight."

Tony decided not see Stacey until he had a better view of the situation—after the press conference, when and if, he had made some decisions.

If I close the door on this investigation, I'm pretty sure Stacey won't be as understanding as Max, he thought. *I'm not even sure I would understand!*

❧

The Laughing Angels did not believe their good fortune. They laughed and jumped around the room with joy in their hearts. *What could be better than this*, they sang out. *Tony seems so tired. With all the air sucked out of him, the courage of his lofty convictions seems to have faded. Will he finally realize that the shadowy side of life has more advantages than always standing up for justice and righteousness?*

The Righteous Ones sat at God's throne, pondering the situation. They wondered if their roles as God's disciples were no longer justified. It was an old story, over and over again. The powerful of society took every advantage and always had the strength to carry on. *What difference does it make if good, but less fortunate people struggled for every morsel? Does God care if an innocent and honest man goes to his death in undeserved shame, so his family can survive?*

The Righteous Ones cried in shame, and the Laughing Angels danced in triumph—while Tony Pinella decided what he should do, if anything.

Chapter 59

Tony phoned Max the morning of the press conference.

"Max, I did some digging on my own, and from what I learned, I'm not satisfied at all with the so-called evidence against Grissom—and I won't let Cedeno pressure me into signing any agreements."

"What about the press conference?" Max asked.

"Well, Cedeno said to be there, so my plan is to show up only minutes before the rest of the guys, and take my place behind the podium as usual. As far as I'm concerned, when I step behind that microphone to answer questions, I'll try to be as candid as possible."

"What if they don't let you answer any questions?" Max asked.

"I think they know better than to pull that in front of a room filled with reporters, especially after making such a big deal to the press when they hired *the great Tony Pinella* as a special consultant. But just in case, you certainly have my permission to ask why I'm so unusually quiet."

"I'll do more than that, Tony. I'll ask if it's true that the evidence against Grissom is very weak, and say that I have information from a reliable source that Tony Pinella doesn't think Grissom murdered Tom Rawlings. That should raise a bit of a ruckus around the room!"

"Thanks, Max! I knew I could count you. Let's just hope it doesn't come to that. I'm leaving in a few minutes to check out a few more things about Brian Grissom with someone who knows him well."

"Just be careful, Tony. I want to be sure you're around to read my next column!"

Chapter 60

Abraham Bloom, lead investigator for the escort and Tom Rawlings' murders, stood at the podium, ready to make his remarks. Standing at his right were two of his top aides, Danny Tramutola and Esther Kramer. At Bloom's left was Tony Pinella, special consultant on both cases. Seated behind them were Police Commissioner Sean Brennan, Mayor Jack Saunders, and Chief of Detectives Salvador Cedeno.

The room was packed with reporters, some having to stand against the wall. They were promised that an important breakthrough announcement was pending.

Max stood at the back of the room, close to the door. He was glad to see Tony standing just where he planned. While those around him would think that Tony looked serious and determined, Max clearly saw his friend's displeasure at what they both thought was a travesty and an injustice.

Tony's mind was racing. He had no idea what would come out of Brennan's mouth. All he knew was that aside from the confession of Brian Grissom, the evidence they apparently had was too weak to hold up in any reliable way.

The mayor and the commissioner are in for a big surprise, if they think they can treat Tony Pinella like a hired hand, or some old man they no longer needed, Tony thought. He was not going to let anyone manipulate him or tell outright lies about the murders of the escorts or who really killed Tom Rawlings.

Max knew instinctively that no one in this room would ever forget this press conference!

When Abe Bloom began his remarks, the room grew quiet.

"Ladies and gentleman, thank you all for coming here on such short notice. As most of you already know, with the death of Tom Rawlings, the case of the escort murders is officially closed. The New York, Chicago, and Paradise Valley police agencies are satisfied that Rawlings killed Amanda Wilson, Stephanie Taylor, and Valerie Powell. Unfortunately, Rawlings himself was murdered only hours before he was to be arrested and formally charged with these horrific crimes.

"I'm also happy to announce that we have in custody Brian Grissom, who has confessed to Rawlings' murder.

"This ends the very difficult, and extremely thorough investigations into both the escort murders and the murder of Tom Rawlings.

"Before we take any questions, I would like to thank the many individuals who assisted in our great success, especially my aides, Officers Esther Kramer and Danny Tramutola. Their dedication and expertise are a model and fine example for police officers everywhere.

"My deep appreciation also to Detective Tony Pinella for his invaluable assistance in both of these very difficult investigations. Tony showed us why he is considered one of the elite investigators in the history of law enforcement. Thank you, Tony. Thank you so much."

Before Tony could say a word, Bloom turned back to the microphone. "As you all know, I am a great believer in a free and informed press, so we will be happy to take some questions."

A buzz of voices filled the room, as many reporters waved their hands in the air, hoping to be recognized.

"Frank, Frank Harrison of the *Journal American.* I think you're first."

"Detective Bloom, no offense intended, but this confession of Brian Grissom came rather quickly. Word on the street is that the department was in a particular hurry to close the Rawlings case."

"We wish we could close all our cases quickly, Frank. The Rawlings murder is no exception. No different from when a deadline forces you to complete an assignment. You still make sure the story is correct—at least we all hope so!"

"A follow-up, please Detective. I want my story on Rawlings to be correct as well. Exactly what evidence is there that Grissom actually murdered Rawlings? What was his motive? Was he a disgruntled investor? Was it a robbery gone bad, as was first reported?"

"Let me assure you, Frank—and all of you—first, we have clear evidence that Tom Rawlings acted alone when he killed the three young women. The evidence has been corroborated by our team, working with both the Paradise Valley and Chicago investigators. That case is closed and the files sealed in respect to the families of those unfortunate women. It needs no further discussion. Second, we have verified all the information provided by Brian Grissom. With respect to his family, and the family of Tom Rawlings, the district attorney has advised that all files related to the case will be sealed."

Max saw the feeling around the room turn from excitement to mistrust, as Bloom called on the next reporter.

"Dick Elliot of *We the People Magazine.* I think you're next."

"Thank you, sir. My magazine has a story about Brian Grissom scheduled for publication next week. From what his neighbors and past employers told us, Grissom is the perfect father and husband. They also said that he was recently diagnosed with an inoperable and rare cancer. There's nothing we've found that answers why someone like that would kill anyone. Why would Grissom, without any apparent motive, murder Tom Rawlings?"

"All I can tell you is that we have confirmed everything Brian Grissom told us, and we are obligated to follow the evidence. Yes, he has a tragic story—which is why the file was sealed by the district attorney's office—to protect his family."

"One more question, please?"

"One more, Dick. Then let someone else have a turn."

"Did Grissom have any relationship to Tom Rawlings through Morris Green's family? After all, Rawlings was Julia Green's fiancé. It sounds as if there's sort of political cover-up going on here."

The room fell silent, while Abe Bloom's face grew red with anger and frustration. Tony, who had pretty much given up on what would really come out of this press conference suddenly took more interest.

"Like I said, Dick. We followed the evidence and confirmed Grissom's confession. I'm very disappointed that you would even entertain such a comment. If there are no more questions…"

"Please, Detective Bloom. I do have another question. Rita Spencer, *Channel 42 News*."

"Okay, but this is the last question. Go ahead, Ms. Spencer."

"Actually, my question is for Detective Pinella."

Tony stood up and went to the microphone, gently displacing Abraham Bloom from the podium.

"Detective Pinella, when you first signed on with the NYPD to investigate the escort murders, and then the murder of Tom Rawlings, I asked how far you were willing to go to solve the cases. You said, and I'll quote you in part: *As far as we have to—and politics, money, nor any other sort of influence will not keep us from the truth about all four murders.* You also said: *Throughout my career, I have never done less."*

"You have a good memory, Ms. Spencer. I remember that very well. In fact, I also remember you asked what I would do if people in powerful positions were involved in the murder."

"Your memory also serves you well, Detective. What do you say now? Do you truly believe that this case should be closed?"

The room was silent as the reporters watched the looks of anger and distress on the faces of everyone on the platform, including Detective Bloom and Chief Cedeno. Everyone, that is, except for Tony, who smiled for the first time all afternoon.

"Well, Detective Pinella?" Rita Spencer said. "Do you think the cases should be closed? Do you feel satisfied that it was Brian Grissom who murdered Tom Rawlings, and that Tom Rawlings worked alone to kill all three escorts?"

Max watched with amusement as Bloom and Cedeno, who were standing at the side of the podium, moved back to confer with Commissioner Brennan. That did not stop Tony from answering Spencer's questions.

"No, Ms. Spencer. I do not think any of these cases should be closed! However, I also am not ready to accuse anyone of a cover-up. My opinion is that it's too early to close the cases."

"Will you continue to investigate the murders for the NYPD?"

Before Tony could answer, Chief Cedeno stood up and walked quickly to podium. "I think we've run out of time, Detective Pinella. Thank you all for coming today."

To everyone's surprise, Tony did not move away from the microphone. He glared for a moment at the chief, then continued to speak.

"With all due respect to Chief Cedeno and Detective Bloom, with whom I enjoyed working closely these past months—and to the fine team they assembled to investigate these heinous crimes—I will no longer be working for the NYPD. In my heart and mind, I believe these cases are far from being closed, and I intend to continue my personal investigation to find out what really happened. Thank you all for coming today."

With those words, Tony walked off the platform and headed for the door, badly in need of some fresh air.

Chief Cedeno seemed frozen in time, while the mayor and commissioner sat quietly, scowling at Cedeno. Bloom quickly returned to the microphone. "That's all for today, ladies and gentleman. Thank you for coming."

Mayor Saunders, Commissioner Brennan, and Chief Cedeno quietly walked off the platform. Detective Bloom was the last to leave. As shocked as he was to hear Tony speak up so boldly, Bloom agreed with him. In his mind, these cases were far from closed. The Grissom confession just did not fit, but his hands were tied. Bloom understood that Sal Cedeno had received immense political pressure from the commissioner, as well as from the district attorney's office. They wanted him to close the files on everything that pertained to the escort murders, as well as the murder of Tom Rawlings. As for today's press conference, at the very least, Bloom suspected he would be reprimanded by Cedeno for not finding a diplomatic way to get Tony off the platform. He might even be forced to retire early.

Max left right after Tony, eager to return to his office and write his next column.

Chapter 61

The sky was overcast with thick dark clouds and it started to drizzle. *Just the way I feel,* Tony thought. He did not look forward to his next task, which was a trip back to Detroit to see Stacey Johnson Blake.

If he had the energy, he would have walked back to his Bensonhurst apartment—but he was physically and emotionally exhausted. In the old days, the long walk was a cinch, but not anymore. Tony walked for about fifteen minutes, then hailed a taxi.

As soon as he got to his apartment, Tony tossed off his clothes and put on his favorite old flannel bathrobe. He boiled a pot of water, poured a mug filled with instant hot cocoa, and sat down on the couch with a jumbo bag of chocolate chip cookies. It reminded him of the days when a case was successfully solved, and he relaxed with a glass of hot Ovaltine® —the same brand his mother used to give him when he got an A-plus for *conduct* on his report card. Of course, her homemade chocolate chip cookies were not the kind that came in bags or boxes. She bought his favorite chocolate bars, broke them up into nice big chunks and added them to her own cookie dough recipe. On the top of each giant-size cookie was a whole Hershey's chocolate kiss. He loved watching the chocolate melt into the rich hot chocolate milk.

"Extra kisses for you, my little Tony," she would say, "for being a good boy at school."

Well, Mom, Tony thought. *I wasn't such a good boy to some people today. At least I spoke the truth, just like you always told me to do.*

Tony finished the bag of cookies and fell asleep on the couch.

Chapter 62

Up early the next morning, it was time for Tony to make that call to Dr. Boris Trotsky. *Might as well get it over with*, he thought. Dr. Trotsky approved the last-minute visit, and Tony was on the next flight out.

When he arrived at the hospital at three o'clock, Dr. Trotsky came right down to the reception area. The look on his face was grim. "We have a little problem, Detective Pinella," he said.

For just a moment, Tony thought Stacey might have harmed herself in some way. "What happened here? Did she try to kill herself?"

"Goodness, no! Stacey is far too determined to survive us all than to harm herself. However, she is very agitated over the news in the morning paper about Brian Grissom. We try to screen her reading material, but I'm afraid the attendant who brings her newspaper didn't look at it carefully enough, and didn't remove the section on *News from Around the Country*. There was a brief article about the murder of Tom Rawlings that included the confession of someone named Brian Grissom. I tried to call you back and cancel the visit, but you had already left for the airport," Trotsky said.

"I knew she would be upset. I had hoped to break the news to her myself. I would have come last evening, but I needed some time to figure out how to approach her. What to say and what not to say," Tony said very thoughtfully.

"Well, the damage is done. Stacey will probably be more upset if I don't let you see her. So please be very careful what you say to her. I'm afraid she feels betrayed, which could set her therapy back months. Nurse Helen Spagnoli is with her now in one of the smaller conference rooms, and we have an attendant standing by and prepared with medication—just in case we need to sedate Stacey. Let me go ahead of you, so Stacey doesn't think I've been advising you. I'll send someone for you in about five or ten minutes."

"Thank you, Doctor."

While he waited, Tony could not help wondering if this might be the last time he saw Stacey. It was an incredible feeling to finally admit that Stacey Johnson Blake had changed his life so much. He wondered if it were possible to achieve a sense of peace without finding true reconciliation with her.

About ten minutes later, an attendant came to bring Tony to the conference room. Tony was barely through the door, when it was apparent that Dr. Trotsky's warning was an understatement. Stacey had dark circles under her eyes and was sobbing softly. Nurse Helen's arm was around her shoulder, trying to comfort her.

"Look who's here to see you, Stacey. Detective Pinella came all this way just to talk to you."

Stacey looked up and quickly stopped sobbing. The look in her eyes turned from sadness to anger.

"You must be an impostor! The real Detective Pinella, my Tony Pinella, would never let this happen!" she shouted. "The real Tony Pinella believes in justice. He knows this Grissom person had nothing to do with murdering Tom Rawlings. Where is the real Tony, please… where is the real Tony Pinella? He knows there has been a cover-up."

Tony reached out to touch Stacey's hand, and Dr. Trotsky did not try to stop him. "Stacey, I do understand that you're very disappointed. I feel very badly about that, but I haven't given up on making sure true justice is served. I promise...."

His words seemed to calm Stacey down. "You really promise, Tony?"

"Yes, Stacey. I really promise, but it's going to take some time and you need to be patient," Tony said. Then, gently but firmly, he added, "Not everyone looks at this case the way we do. At this point, I'm not prepared to call it a cover-up. I need to move carefully, one step at a time."

Tony could see that Stacey's anger and suspicions were growing. "You sound just like Dr. Trotsky when he talks about my psychotherapy," she said.

"In a way, this is just like therapy—my therapy," Tony said.

"What do you mean?" Stacey asked.

"The police department decided that my services are no longer needed. I'm unable to officially continue this investigation without their approval."

"I can't believe what I'm hearing! The great Tony Pinella is going to let murderers roam the streets? *You must be an impostor*—not the Tony I know. My Tony could never live with that," Stacey said.

"I might have to, Stacey. I am getting older, and not every call is mine."

"It certainly was your call when you put me in prison. With your attitude now, I might still be walking the streets as a free woman. So what if they fired you! Are you going to do nothing? Is that how you prefer the system works?"

Dr. Trotsky was not sure whether to be glad or on guard that Stacey was showing her more aggressive, sarcastic self, and obviously in full control of her emotions. Tony, perfectly aware of what she was capable of, hoped the attendants were close by and ready for anything.

A few moments later, Stacey appeared to relax and leaned back in her chair, a sly smile on her face. "Wait a minute. You said you're unable to *officially* continue the investigation. What am I missing here, Tony? What aren't you telling me?"

"I guess I'm telling you that I'm going to take a breather and figure out a way to make sure that justice *is* served—even if it takes a while longer. Right now, I don't have the hard evidence I need to take to the police, and I have to play it smart, or the wrong people will win."

Stacey stood up triumphantly. "Now that's the Tony Pinella I know," she said. "If this case is the end of your career, you owe it to yourself—and to those poor murdered young women—to finish on a high note, with your integrity intact."

Dr. Trotsky and Nurse Helen were surprised at Stacey's clarity of thought. They would never have guessed that today's meeting with Tony would be a breakthrough instead of a complete breakdown for their patient. They had all been prepared for the worst-case scenario. Instead, it seemed that all Stacey's pain and anguish, her heinous crimes, and all of her past problems had taught her some very important lessons about life. Whatever the future held for this obviously psychotic woman, who saw herself as God's chosen daughter and the sister of Jesus Christ—she saw some things clearly. More than some rational people did.

Right then and there, Tony felt the spirit of his saintly mother beside him. He was right to reject what amounted to six months of *hush money*. He was right to stand up to Mayor Saunders and Commissioner Brennan by speaking the truth during the press conference—and he was right to visit Stacey today.

❧

As Tony sat in the airport waiting for his flight back to New York, the Laughing Angels, as always, danced around him with glee. Today took the prize! Not only was this aging and pathetic detective trying to find peace with the one he called *the God of my saintly mother,* now he was even trying to reconcile with a murderer who thought she was God's daughter. *Poor Tony,* they laughed. *He's finally going closer to the deep end, making it easier for those who seek to destroy him. Any closer and he will end up in a room right next to Stacey!*

The Righteous Ones made another effort to speak to God on Tony's behalf. *This is a compassionate human being,* they cried, *one who has never forgotten his roots. Oh merciful God, please do not forsake this good man in his time of need. Let him see your glory. Let him feel your sanctity. Do not let him fall victim to the Laughing Angels, as you have let so many millions before him.* Their pleas, like so many times before, went unanswered.

Chapter 63

It took nearly two weeks for Tony to feel strong enough to return to the battle. He still felt the anguish and frustration of knowing that at least one person was getting away with murder in the escort case. This realization contributed to the sad truth that he was at a time in his life when his need for rest frequently took priority over his pursuit of justice.

Max's editor gave him some flexibility with his other assignments to continue investigating the case, but that leeway would not last for long. With the case closed, so was Max's access to information. Brian Grissom was in a prison hospital. All requests to interview him were rejected. He tried talking to Grissom's wife, but she did not answer her phone, and he was consistently turned away from the Grissom home by a private security guard.

Both Max and Tony felt sure that Julia Green had assisted Tom Rawlings in planning the escort murders. Motive and opportunity were easy to prove, but direct evidence was another story. Grissom's confession resulted in the crime scenes being thoroughly cleaned and devoid of any potential evidence.

Abraham Bloom would not take Max's telephone calls. The response from Bloom's office was always and emphatically the same, *the cases are closed.* Even the usual scuttlebutt that generally surrounded such murders was completely shut down.

The one new lead Max had was a man who lived on Rawlings' floor. He was sure he saw someone who looked like Sally Green leaving Rawlings' apartment on the day of the murder. Someone must have gotten to him, because in the past few days, even he had clammed up and was not returning Max's calls.

Max urged Tony to try reaching Bloom. After all, they had forged a good working relationship while investigating the escort murders. Bloom had even asked Tony to call him next time he was in the city.

"That won't fly," Tony said. "Abe made it very clear that once the cases were closed, and Cedeno called it quits on our consulting arrangement, heads would roll if anyone on his team discussed the cases with anyone—especially me!"

"Can't you try once more, Tony? We just need a little more time…" Max pleaded.

"I'm really sorry, Max. As frustrating as this is to both of us, I just can't put Abe in that situation. Cedeno read him the riot act for letting me speak during the press conference. He ordered him to work on his other assignments and leave the escort murders alone."

"What if you call Cedeno?" Max asked.

"That will probably make matters worse, and get Abe in more trouble," Tony answered.

"What if I call Cedeno?" Max persisted.

"Look, Max, I've been in this business long enough to know what Cedeno meant. It was a warning to Ab*e—mind your own business.* Abe is a good guy and he's up for retirement in a couple of years. I don't want to rock his boat and risk the only income he's likely to have when that day comes."

"I understand, Tony. I really do… I'll just keep trying for as long as my editor gives me the flexibility. I'll keep you posted."

Tony could tell by the sound of Max's voice that he was not going to give up.

"Be careful, Max. It's hard for me to say this, but it all comes down to one inescapable fact: *Don't ask too many questions*. As disgusting and frustrating as it seems, the powerful people earned that title for a reason. The price of exposing them can put your own life in jeopardy."

❧

The Righteous Ones cried tears of sadness as the Laughing Angels cackled with confidence. *Had they finally defeated the great Tony Pinella?* Usually, Tony's secure roots in the ideals of his parents carried him through even the worst situations, never taking the easy way out. Somehow, he was always able to withstand the temptation of being like everyone else—he would not bow down to the threats of those in power.

The Laughing Angels shouted to the Righteous Ones. *What do you think now?*

The Righteous Ones walked away in silence. Tony had always been a voice for those who did not have one. The person who would not succumb to the evil and depraved among us—those deceitful ones who heaped praise on the Supreme Being, and then felt they deserved his favor.

Now it was God's turn to wonder why the Righteous Ones did not plead for his intervention.

Chapter 64

The Waldorf Astoria Hotel ballroom on Park Avenue was filled with cheering supporters of Morris Green, all celebrating his election to the United States Senate.

Most of the political pundits and experts predicted the embattled Green had no chance of winning. The majority of New York voters proved them all wrong. Green was overwhelmingly vindicated by his loyal followers. Some even waved *Morris Green for President* posters as they waited for him to take the podium—sure that his election to the senate was his pathway to the highest office of the land. In their eyes, Morris Green remained a man of the people, someone who represented their own hopes and dreams.

Watching the gala affair on television from their homes were Tony in Newport, and Angela Robinson in New York. They were bonded by feelings of disgust and dread. Seeing Morris Green strut onto the stage, Tony knew the anguish Angela must be feeling at this moment. He was sickened at the sight of Sally Green and the three Green daughters hugging Morris, and then smiling and waving to the crowd and the cameras as he walked to the podium.

Morris Green had engineered one of the greatest political comebacks in American history. His risky personal choices almost ruined him—but not quite. It certainly had a devastating effect on the lives of Sally and Julia Green, even if their involvement in the murders never came to light. Tony could only hope that Morris Green felt some remorse. That he had learned to restrain the questionable inclinations that led to his reprehensible behavior—or *mistakes*—as he referred to them.

The combination of his family's wealth and influence, and his time as a talk show host, alongside an attractive Pulitzer prize-winning woman journalist, certainly did not hurt his successful return to the political arena.

The crowd grew quiet as Morris Green stepped up to the microphone and began to speak. Green looked around the room, seemed to pause for a moment, and then proudly exclaimed, "New York, I love you. I love the people of New York. Thank you for believing in me and believing in our great country."

The crowd roared once again, as Green stood there smiling. He let them hoot and howl for a full minute and then signaled them with his hands to quiet down.

"Thank you so much for bringing us all to this moment of victory—*your victory.* I'm delighted to report that we won in every age group. We won with women and men. We won an overwhelming majority among independent voters. And we carried all the boroughs, suburbs, and Upstate New York."

The audience roared once more with wild enthusiasm.

"Yes, you all deserve to celebrate," Green continued. "We won by the largest majority in the history of New York State's senatorial elections. We accomplished what we set out to do. Not solely for my redemption, but for the opportunity to fix our state's and our nation's problems."

Green stopped to sip from a glass of water, giving the crowd a chance to applaud. Some raised their posters and shouted, *Morris Green for President.*

"Thank you, thank you," he said. "I greatly appreciate your enthusiasm. We all draw upon many sources for strength, especially during difficult times. In addition to my wonderful wife and daughters, I also feel the love and support of my beloved grandfather, who passed away so many years ago. The other night, he came to me in a dream. He spoke softly and earnestly. *Morris, it's time to move forward,* he said. *Time to leave a legacy to your children, my great-grandchildren, and to future generations. The people are giving you a new chance—and you owe them the peace of mind that comes only from doing what is right and just."*

At that moment, Green got teary-eyed and looked back tenderly at his family. It was their cue to stand up and join him behind the podium.

Tony thought he would toss up his dinner as he watched Sally kiss her husband, followed by hugs and kisses from his daughters. The crowd, however, was mesmerized, cheering and clapping as the loving scene played out before them.

Green then turned back to the microphone, wiped the tears from his eyes, and once again signaled for quiet.

"I want to thank my darling wife and our three precious daughters for their love and support. They stood by me during the most difficult of times. Like all of you good people, they believed in me—even when I doubted myself. For all this, I am eternally grateful and will take this new opportunity to make you all proud.

"God bless you all, and God bless America."

Chapter 65

Two months after his confession to murdering Tom Rawlings, Brian Grissom passed away. His memorial was a quiet affair, attended only by his wife Donna, their two sons, and a small gathering of friends, neighbors, and former co-workers. Max and Tony were the only outsiders Donna invited to attend.

Donna told the funeral director explicitly not to run an obituary, nor to provide any information to the public. Eager reporters, who located the time and place, were kept away from the memorial service by two cops who patrolled the beat near the neighborhood church, where the family's minister made some brief comments.

Grissom was cremated, so there was no graveside service—nothing that would draw a crowd of unwanted spectators.

When Max called to express his condolences, Donna requested that he refrain from writing a column on Grissom's passing. *At least not yet*, she said. Max was curious and tried to get some answers from her, but she was steadfast.

Donna spoke with a quiet determination. "One of these days, I hope the public will learn that my husband was not, could not, be a murderer."

"I promise you, I'll be here when you're ready," Max said.

When Max told Tony about Donna's curious statement, his frustration was more obvious. "Max, her story just doesn't hold. I don't believe that Brian was paid back by someone he helped during the good years—before he became ill. Maybe we need to dig deeper."

"We tried as hard as we could," Max said. "I interviewed dozens of people the Grissoms have known for years. I even dug deeply as possible into all of their backgrounds. No one they knew, past or present, could have given Brian or Donna enough money to get out of debt. None of them had that kind of money—and there's absolutely no evidence that anyone paid Grissom to kill Tom Rawlings."

Up to now, neither he nor Tony had been able to uncover anything new that contradicted Grissom's confession. It was as if an iron wall had been built around anyone who knew anything about the case. Max's editor warned it was time for him to move on to another story. Grissom was *old news* that ended with his death.

For Max and Tony, the question remained: *How was Grissom's wife able to pay the family's debts during the past few months?*

After the service was over, Tony told Max, "I'm going back to Newport for awhile. It's hard for me to say this, but all the rigors of these frustrating investigations have exhausted me more than I want to admit. I'm not giving up, but I need some time away from New York and all its politics. Maybe when I'm more rested, I'll be able to look at the situation with a different perspective—maybe come up with some ideas."

"I understand completely, old buddy," Max said. "Donna's even thinking about selling the house and moving. She said it might be better for the boys not to be surrounded by people's wagging tongues and being teased by kids at school."

"Sounds reasonable. But if you learn anything new, Max, I'll be on the next plane back to New York."

Chapter 66

Not everyone was saddened by Brian Grissom's death. Morris Green was proud that he had rescued Sally and Julia—as well as and his own political ambitions. His family settled into their new home in Alexandria, Virginia, where the freshman senator was already planning his ascension to the presidency.

There is nothing to stand in my way, he thought. *Now Morris Green will lead America to its rightful glory.* At least that was his plan.

Max was disgusted every time he saw a photo of the happy family at another charity event, or read a quote from Green—coming either from his senate office, or after a so-called *impromptu interview* on a golf course.

It was late Sunday afternoon when Tony heard Max's disgruntled voice on the telephone.

"Enough is enough, Tony," he said. "It's time for an article that will upset the status quo in Washington and New York. The citizens of New York deserve the truth about the political corruption that unraveled the escort murder case. It's time to bring justice to Brian Grissom and his family. Time to show the families of those dead young women that someone cares about their daughters. *Are you with me on this, Tony?*"

"Let's go for it, Max. I'll head back to Bensonhurst on Tuesday. As soon as I get in, we can work out a plan of action."

Tony hung up the phone and smiled with satisfaction. He was eager to get back into the fray.

For only a moment, he wondered how Stacey Johnson Blake was doing. He imagined that if the demons were haunting his dreams, it must be much worse for Stacey. More than anyone, she understood, even in her most delusional moments, how evil in the guise of holiness could destroy hardworking and well-intentioned people.

The Laughing Angels could not be happier with the current circumstances. Senator Morris Green's mind worked just as they expected for a self-serving politician. Every disgrace was just another opportunity to ask God for redemption, for his unwavering love and forgiveness. Cleansed of their sins, they would then move on to their next devious plan. Green's next plan was to reach the Oval Office, and he was confident that he would succeed.

As to be expected, the Righteous Ones were not so gleeful. They worried about the lack of integrity shared by so many in the nation's capital. It never took long for even the most idealistic among them to succumb to the temptations of power, and put their own interests above even the most basic needs of the people.

Morris Green was one of their biggest disappointments. There was a time, only a few years ago, when the Righteous Ones believed Green was the one person who would rise above political squabbles, selfishness, and total corruption. That he would be a righteous example to all those who prayed that America be restored to its role as the greatest country in the world.

Chapter 67

Tony packed one small suitcase and was ready to head back to New York. Just before he left for the airport, Max called with surprising news.

"*Tony, you'll never believe it. Donna Grissom just called.* She has a videotape that proves Brian's confession was false. She wants to go public with the information, *even if it puts her life at risk*. She won't go straight to the police; she doesn't trust them. She'll only show the tape to you and me."

"Are you sure Donna understands the risk she's taking?"

"I'm sure, Tony. Her exact words were, *I want people to know the truth, even if it puts my life in danger*."

"What about her sons?"

"She's arranged for them to stay with her cousin in another state, just in case there's trouble. Tony, this is the break we've been after!"

"I hope you're right, Max. I don't want my career to end with an innocent man's children growing up thinking that no one cared about the truth. If Brian Grissom was not a killer, his family deserves to see his name cleared."

"I am right, Tony. I feel it in my gut."

"Look, I've got a cab waiting for me, and I have to get going or I'll miss my flight. You can fill me in on the details when I get back tonight. Go ahead and set up a time with Donna for tomorrow."

Max made all the arrangements for them to meet the next morning at the Grissom home. With the murder cases closed, reporters were on to other stories, long gone from staking out Donna's house. That seemed like the best place, and she agreed.

For just a few moments after he hung up the phone with Donna, Max wondered if his editor might be right. Maybe Donna Grissom is just a grieving wife, still defending her dead husband. Was he leading Tony off on another wild goose chase? *No, that could not be it,* he thought. What could Grissom's wife have that was so compelling? Why did she wait so long to come forward?

Then again, everything Max and Tony found out about Brian and Donna Grissom pointed to how honest they were. Hardworking and dedicated to each other and their children. When tragedy hit, it was devastating to the family. All the investigations into their financial situation came up zero—they were broke. Of course, it was reasonable that friends and family came up with a little cash to keep them afloat. Yet, all the signs were that she was in the kind of serious financial trouble one might expect, even with the help of friends.

Max wondered if maybe the police were so eager to close the case, they did not look deep enough into the Grissom's finances. Where did Donna Grissom get the money to keep her house? There were too many unanswered questions and Max was eager to see Donna's videotape.

There was something very confident in Donna Grissom's voice. She sounded strong and determined, Max thought. He sensed that Commissioner Brennan and the prosecutor's offices, as well as the Green family, were on the verge of meeting their worst possible scenario—*and it was not just a grieving wife*—not if he and Tony could finally get the goods on the real story.

Max cleared his desk of all the notes and articles on the story his editor assigned him. All his senses told him that breaking news was right around the corner.

❧

The Laughing Angels were eager to watch God's reaction to the potential consequences of this new development. What would the Almighty do, they wickedly laughed, if the powerful were so concerned about their own survival, they lost the inclination to praise Him?

At the same time, the Righteous Ones were listening to Stacey Johnson Blake, as she paced around her hospital room in the John Henry Hospital psychiatric research wing.

Stacey pleaded to God. *Please make things right. Your son did not even try to stop me from committing terrible crimes—crimes I regret with all my heart and soul. This time let me—your chosen daughter—make amends for your transgressions, and your son's failures.*

Chapter 68

Donna Grissom was nervous about her meeting this morning with Detective Tony Pinella and journalist Max Gold. Out of all those involved in investigating or writing about the escort murders, Tom Rawlings, and her husband's surprising confession to murdering Rawlings, Tony and Max seemed to be the ones most interested in pursuing the truth. The ones who had an honest compassion for the victims of these horrible crimes—and she counted her husband as one of the victims.

How could all this happen? she sadly thought. *I never wanted any more out of life than being Brian's wife and the mother of our children.*

Now Donna Grissom was the widow of a confessed murderer—a good and loving man who never harmed a soul. He did his best to support his family and to be there whenever a friend was in need. Now she was in the center of a political scandal that could get her killed if anyone suspected what she was about to tell Max and Tony. She hoped and prayed she was doing the right thing.

I can't stand by and let these scheming politicians and their big-shot friends trample over my husband's good name—and the legacy he would have wanted for his sons, she thought. *Brian gave up what little was left of his precious life for us, bravely taking his last breath without his family by his side. Now it's my turn to be brave. To set the record straight, and make sure the public knows the ugly truth about the people they trust to uphold the law.*

Just then, the doorbell rang. At first, Donna hesitated.

"Mrs. Grissom? It's Max Gold and Tony Pinella. No one else is out here, I promise," Max said.

"Yes, yes… Just a moment…"

After a brief hesitation, Donna Grissom took a deep breath and opened the door. "Thank you for coming, Mr. Gold, Detective Pinella. Please come in."

Donna showed them into the living room where she had set a pitcher of lemonade, an electric pot of hot coffee, and a plate of homemade cookies on the cocktail table.

As they sat down, Tony next to Donna on the couch, and Max opposite them on a chair, there was a moment of awkwardness. It seemed like no one knew how to start the conversation.

Tony gently took Donna's hand and broke the silence. "I realize how hard this is for you, Mrs. Grissom, how hard it's been for your family. Max and I appreciate your asking to see us."

It was easy to see the pain and sadness in Donna Grissom's eyes, yet her smile was warm and gracious.

"Thank you, Detective Pinella." Please call me Donna.

"Only if you call me, Tony."

"Thank you… Tony. I appreciate both of you coming here this morning. Yes, this is difficult for me. But not as difficult as seeing my husband's name tarnished, while the real killers go on with their lives as though nothing has happened."

"I must say, I was surprised to get your phone call yesterday," Max said. "If you have evidence that will clear your husband, why did you wait until now to show it?"

"First, let me explain that the only reason we've been able to keep our home and, frankly, survive at all, is that shortly before his confession to killing Tom Rawlings—*his false confession*—Brian gave me eighty thousand dollars in cash. He said it was a gift from a very old family friend—someone who appreciated the help Brian gave him years ago, when he fell on hard times. He was insistent that Brian take the money so we could pay all the past due medical bills and keep up with our monthly home mortgage, as well as our day-to-day expenses."

"I don't mean to question your story, but didn't that strike you as a pretty large sum of money coming from an old friend?" Max asked.

"I was concerned and wondered what he might want in return," Donna said. "But Brian told me the only condition was that he remain anonymous. Frankly, I was so grateful and relieved... and I trusted Brian completely. I don't know how we would have managed without help."

Tony and Max looked at each other in disbelief, a look Donna noticed. Max set aside his compassion and let his journalistic instincts take over.

"If you had proof Brian was innocent, why did you stay quiet so long about this videotape? Especially if it exonerated Brian. And why didn't Brian put the money right into the bank?"

As Donna stood up and slipped the videotape into the machine, she said with a new confidence in her voice, "I understand that you're suspicious, Max. Please understand. At the time, we were so much in debt; I had no reason not to believe or to question Brian. In all the time we were married, never once did my husband lie to me. We both cried, and I just hugged him and thanked God for his friend's generosity. Brian said we should just keep the money in the house and pay our large expenses with money orders and cashier's checks, and pay everything else in cash."

She smiled sadly and added, "Brian never did trust bankers. He thought they were all crooks. I assumed he wasn't comfortable plopping that amount of money down on some bank manager's desk before he had time to think about it. Look, I realize you don't understand, but I never dealt with our finances before. Yes, I'm one of those women who cherished my life as a wife and mother. Brian and I were high school sweethearts. I never doubted him for a moment—and he never let me down. If Brian said to put the money away for awhile, that's just what I did."

Tony gave Max a look that clearly told him to pull back.

"You don't need to explain any further, Donna. My dear mother was proud to be a wife and mother. I respect women who make that choice—and I'm sure Max does, too. Please go on with how you came into possession of the videotape."

"Yes, please, Donna. I didn't mean any harm," Max said. "I'm only trying to understand how all this unfolded. Please go on..."

"Well... it was the very next day, that awful morning Brian falsely confessed to killing Tom Rawlings. Just after the boys left for school, Brian said he had some errands to run. He kissed me goodbye and told me to remember: *No matter what happens, never tell anyone about the money.* He said to use the cash when it was needed, but to pay all our bills with money orders. The next thing I knew, several hours later, the police were at the door with a search warrant and the news that *my Brian* had confessed to murdering Tom Rawlings."

"They didn't find the money during the search?" Tony asked.

"No. I thought they would! I hid it at the bottom of a trunk where we store old family photos. The police opened the trunk, but never looked underneath the photos."

"And the videotape?" Max reminded Donna. "When did you find the tape?"

"Just days before Brian died, I was finally allowed to visit him. I guess the nurse at the prison infirmary where they had him, took pity on us— because she gave us some time alone. Brian knew he only had weeks to live, maybe less. As he kissed me goodbye, he whispered in my ear: *After I'm gone, look in our secret place."*

"Your secret place?"

Donna smiled as she explained. "It's something we used to do on birthdays, holidays, and other special times. We hid love notes and little gifts when we wanted to give each other something privately—out of the boys' sight."

Tony could see the tears welling up in Donna's eyes again. "Do you want to stop for a while? We can take a break."

"No... I want to go on. I really couldn't think of much right after Brian died. When a policewoman came to the door with the news, all I could think about was the children and how to tell them. It took me a few days to remember what Brian said about our secret place. That's when I found the videotape."

"And the police didn't find it when they searched?" Tony asked.

Donna wiped the tears that had run down her cheeks, and smiled warmly before she answered. "No. But that's no surprise. Brian used to say Geraldo Rivera couldn't find that spot—not even if he thought it hid Al Capone's fortune!"

Donna's smile quickly faded. She cleared her throat and looked at Max and Tony with great determination. "Getting back to the reason I asked you here, before you watch the videotape, I'd like to read you the letter Brian left for me in the same package."

"Letter? You didn't mention a letter when you called me. There's a letter *and* a videotape?"

"Yes, Max. Brian left me a letter and a video. I didn't tell you because I wasn't sure you should see it. I think you'll understand when I read it to you. I'm only letting you hear it now, because I have to trust someone, and I guess I trust you and Tony more than I trust the police, or anyone else."

"We would never do anything to put you or the children in jeopardy," Tony assured her.

"I believe you," Donna said. "But please understand, the only thing you will leave with today is the videotape. It shows Brian saying the same words that are in the letter—*up to a point.*"

Donna took a deep breath and hesitated for a moment before continuing. "Brian knew I might one day have to use the videotape to expose the truth about his false confession—to make sure the legacy he left his sons would not tarnish their futures."

Tony could see that Donna was still hesitant about sharing the letter.

"We understand how important this is to you, and you have our promise. We will not share the contents of Brian's letter with anyone!"

"Tony's right, Donna. We would never do anything to jeopardize you or your sons. Just one more thing before you read us the letter. I want to assure you again. *We never thought Brian killed Tom Rawlings*. Just before you called me yesterday, I told Tony I wanted to do another column about the escort and Rawlings murders. Maybe whatever is in the video will help us expose the real killers."

"I hope so," Donna said. She took a deep breath and began reading Brian's letter:

My Dearest Donna,

You're the most wonderful wife and mother anyone could imagine. After I became so ill, and spent more time at home with our boys, I heard Brian Junior tell one of his friends that his mom is the greatest in the world. Little Johnny also put his two cents in. "She sure is! No one has a mommy as nice as ours!"

I'm so proud of our sons, and of you. You're the best mom in the world. No one could ask for a better wife or friend, and I've cherished every moment we've spent together.

Donna paused for a moment, and smiled as she read the next words. In her mind, she could hear the sound of Brian's voice and almost hear his laughter.

You even get along with my mother, and very few people can make that claim. I hope you're laughing, even just a little, as you read this letter. I wish I were there to see your beautiful smile and hear the laughter I always thought sounded like a sweet song. Please know that my love and spirit are with you forever, and with our precious sons.

I'm not there to take care of you anymore, but I did my best to be sure you and the boys will be able to move on with your lives. The video will explain. I hope and pray you will not be angry and understand that the only reason I took such unthinkable steps, was to secure your lives—for now and for the future. It's very important that you read what I say in this letter very closely. It carries more than the message in the video. I taped it only hours before I confessed to killing Tom Rawlings—a crime, my darling, that I did not commit!

As you know all too well, we've fallen on hard times. Until a few days ago, I thought we would lose our home. I would die knowing my wife and wonderful boys would suffer unimaginable financial hardships. Like too many people, this certainly is not what I envisioned for our lives. I knew we would never be considered wealthy, but we shared the wealth of a loving family. When the time came, we hoped to help our boys through college or trade school—whatever career path they wanted to follow.

I wish I could warn everyone what happens when people find themselves in such desperate and seemingly hopeless situations. Many will think what I've done is reprehensible. That because of me, the real murderer will go free. But I'm desperate, my darling. For the first time in our lives, I felt hopeless, with no way out. No way to help the loves of my life—you and our sons. Until I was approached by a stranger. He seemed to be waiting for me just outside the hospital, after one of my meetings with the collection department. He knew I was dying, and that we were deeply in debt. He also knew that the hospital was planning to sue us. I don't know how he knew, but he did. He said he could help us—all I had to do was listen to his offer and not ask any questions.

Please understand, my love. My soul wouldn't rest if I didn't do everything I could to save you and the boys from losing our home, and all the suffering that would follow. So I got into his car and listened—and said yes to his offer.

That's where the eighty thousand dollars really came from. There was no old friend—no one to help us.

Please forgive me for not telling you the truth until now. I know you have questions, my darling, but I cannot tell you who hired me to come forward with a false confession. I was warned that telling anyone would put your life in jeopardy.

At the very least, you have this video and letter promising you and our sons that the only crime I committed was to accept money in exchange for confessing to a murder that I swear to you, I did not commit.

Also to keep you safe, when you watch the video, you will see that it ends pretty much at this point. The rest of this letter is for your eyes only—and for the same reason.

Here is what you, and only you, need to know. Deeper in our secret place is another envelope. It contains the name of a bank in Scotland where there is a numbered trust account set up for you. That account has in it two million dollars. That's right, my sweet Donna, two million dollars. The envelope I left for you has all the paperwork you need to draw on that account, including the name of a contact at the bank. Everything is in the envelope, so you will have no problems getting the money.

I know it may sound complex, but it's not. Even if someone learns about the account, I was assured there is no way to trace where the money originated. When the eighty thousand dollars runs out, there are instructions how you can make cash withdrawals from the account, open separate checking or savings accounts—whatever you choose to do. You will be financially secure for the rest of your life, and our sons will have the educations we always wished for them.

So my beautiful Donna, as I say goodbye to the love of my life, please know that I am grateful to you and our children for giving me a lifetime of happiness. You will always be my true soulmate—and I cherish you from here to eternity.

Your loving husband,
Brian

When she finished reading Brian's letter, Donna hit the play button on the remote control. Max and Tony watched and listened sadly to the last spoken words of Brian Grissom.

Chapter 69

As Tony and Max waited in the reception area of Jan Clark's law office, their minds raced. They had to tell her there was proof that Brian Grissom did not kill Tom Rawlings. They would measure each word, not wanting to reveal too much, especially until they could see how she reacted to the news.

After waiting ten minutes, the receptionist brought them into Jan's office. She looked even more smashing than Tony remembered, classy and beautiful in her bright purple St. John's suit. At fifty-five years old, Jan was even more of a knockout than thirty years ago, the first time Tony had met her.

Jan gave Tony a warm hug. She thought of him as one of the good guys in law enforcement, a person of integrity. She knew that Tony's goal was to make sure the innocent went free, the bad guys went to jail, and victims and their families received justice.

Tony knew that Jan must be feeling cautious, especially because he was here with Max—and he was right. Jan knew there must be trouble ahead. When Tony called to set up the appointment, he only told her there was something important he needed to discuss—and he was bringing Max Gold with him. When Jan reached out to shake Max's hand, Tony could tell she was on-guard.

Jan led them to a small round conference table that had a great view of the Manhattan skyline.

"Please, let's sit down. It's always nice to see you, Tony. It's so nice to meet you, Max. I'm a big admirer of your columns. It's obvious you're committed to the truth, and a master at digging for it!"

Tony laughed to himself at how well Jan was hiding her real dislike for the press. She did not trust them for a moment. He wondered how much she would like Max after she learned why they were here!

After a few minutes of pleasant small talk, Jan leaned forward and turned to Tony, speaking in her *I mean business* voice.

"While I'm happy to see you, I don't think you and Max are here to discuss the old days. I can only assume that your visit has something to do with one of my cases. Why don't you just tell me what's really on your minds."

Without hesitation, Tony looked right into Jan's eyes. "We wanted to tell you in person that Brian Grissom did not murder Tom Rawlings."

"I don't understand, Tony. Why are you telling me about this? Anyway, isn't that case closed?"

"I'll answer your second question first," Tony said. "Yes, the police have closed the case, but Grissom's confession was false. I advised them very strongly that it wasn't time to close the case, that Grissom's confession just didn't sit right with me."

Tony could tell that Jan was apprehensive. "And what about my first question?" she asked. "Why come to me with that information?"

"I'd like to answer that," Max said. "We know you're very close to Sally Green and her daughters..."

Jan snapped back before Max could continue. "Yes, I am. I've known them a long time. What does that have to do with it?"

"I'm going to be very straight with you, Jan. This is really a courtesy call," Tony said.

"A courtesy call? I still don't understand what you're getting at... But if you have information about Brian Grissom, why aren't you going straight to the police?"

Max and Tony looked at one another before Tony responded to Jan's question. They both noticed that she was agitated, which—in their minds—indicated they were on the right track.

"Going to the DA, or the cops right now, is premature. Remember, I was part of the escort and Tom Rawlings' murder investigations and, as you said earlier, those cases are both closed."

"You know what I think, Tony? You and Max are fishing for something, and I'm surprised at you. Surprised at Tony, that is. I would expect you to be more straightforward if you had proof that Brian Grissom was innocent. As for you, Max... I know you're a good journalist. If you had solid evidence of something, and the district attorney wasn't interested, you would just write a column. You wouldn't be sitting here. My guess is that you don't have anything of substance to report to the police."

Tony could tell by Jan's face that she was fishing for information, worried that Max knew something more about Brian Grissom and who killed Tom Rawlings.

"I respect you, Jan. That's why we're here," Tony said. "We thought you might want a heads up to what's coming down the road. A chance to tell your clients, *or friends*, that if they do know something about the murders, it might be in their best interests to speak up now. We have a video and access to a letter from Brian Grissom stating he had nothing to do with the murder of Tom Rawlings."

Jan sat back and laughed nervously. "The prisons are full of murderers who claim they are innocent."

Tony did his best not to get annoyed at Jan's *lawyer-speak*, as he liked to call it. She seemed a little too nervous, so he knew he was on to something, likely much more than he and Max even suspected.

"There was no evidence implicating Brian Grissom. All the police had was the confession of a man deeply in debt, with only months to live, and a wife with two young children. In fact, there is nothing at all that links Grissom to Tom Rawlings," Tony said calmly. "I told that to the police, but they went ahead with the indictment anyway, hoping Grissom would never live long enough to stand trial."

"Look, Tony, even if there is a letter, who knows if it's legit. Maybe Grissom's wife is looking for some sort of compensation because her husband died while in prison."

Max sarcastically answered Jan's question. "You have a point, Jan," he said. "Just remember one more thing. Grissom also left a video."

Jan hesitated for a moment before she asked, "May I see it?"

"Not today, but maybe soon," Tony answered.

"So the two of you came here today, a smart detective and an acclaimed journalist, to give me this information—just because you know I'm friends with Sally Green. How do you expect me to react to all this?"

Tony smiled confidently. "I know you're a smart lawyer. My guess is that you'll call Sally Green, and her daughter Julia, and suggest they return to New York to tell their side of the story."

This time, it was Jan who was sarcastic. "And what story would that be?" she asked.

"The truth," Tony said. "That Tom Rawlings was blackmailing Sally, and that he might have been killed by accident—very likely in self-defense."

"That's quite a story you have there, Tony. So let me ask you a question."

"Shoot!" Tony said.

"If you think Sally *might* have been in a compromising situation with Tom Rawlings, what does Julia have to do with it?"

"Let me tell you what I think, Jan," Max interjected. "May I, Tony?"

Tony leaned back and nodded his approval to Max, while he watched as Jan was obviously feeling very defensive.

"All indications point to Julia and Tom, together, planned and executed the murders of Stephanie Taylor, Valerie Powell, and Amanda Wilson."

Jan hesitated before speaking. Tony could tell her next words would be piercing, and they were. "Not so fast, Max. You've made quiet an accusation. A case I handled recently, and quite successfully I might add, was about a woman who casually mentioned to her boyfriend, *If only my husband would disappear, life could be so beautiful.*"

"And…," Max said.

"And, *the boyfriend killed her husband*, which was not my client's intention. The boyfriend was later convicted; my client wasn't even considered as an accessory to the crime, nor of aiding or abetting, and she wasn't charged."

"But, Jan, your client's husband did disappear, just as she wanted him to."

"That's right, he did. However, my client did not *aid another person who committed the criminal act.* Nor did she *willfully get someone else to commit a crime on her behalf.* She did not, in the words of the law, *aid, abet, counsel, command, induce, or procure the commission* of her boyfriend's crime."

Before either Tony or Max could comment, Jan quickly added: "To make it even clearer to you both, let's say Tom was attempting to blackmail Sally by fabricating a story involving Julia in the escort murders. There was no good reason to believe he was telling the truth. Look, even if Julia said to Tom one day, *I wish everyone attacking and accusing my father would just disappear*. It only proves that another young woman, like many young or even older women, misjudged what her boyfriend might be capable of doing. Bottom line, Julia would have no culpability at all if Tom, for whatever reason, decided to murder the three escorts. Maybe he was just looking for a way all along to use Morris Green's tenuous situation as a way to blackmail the Greens. Maybe one of his investment schemes put him in jeopardy and someone threatened him. Who knows why he killed those escorts? I could probably come up with a dozen scenarios."

Tony was disgusted. Lawyers were not his favorite people anyway, but he thought better of Jan. The stories she had right at the tip of her tongue made him angrier and angrier.

"You have an answer to everything, counselor," he said. "I forgot how protective you are of your clients. Of course, assuming Jan and Julia are your clients."

"That's part of my job description, Tony. I'm sure you can appreciate the sacred obligation I have to my clients—just like you have to yours."

"Yes, Jan. Most of the time I do. Other times, the moral considerations of a case become more important. I'll make this simple. I think it's best, either as their friend or their attorney, that you contact Sally and Julia and advise them to come back to New York."

Jan challenged Tony right back. "So far, you haven't given me a good reason why I should."

"Well, I guess this meeting is over," Tony said.

He gave a nod to Max, then stood up and headed for the door. Just before he reached the door, Tony looked back at Jan, who was still seated. "Here's one reason for you, counselor. Brian Grissom was paid a large amount of money to confess to killing Rawlings."

The look of surprise on Jan's face was obvious. "Wait a minute...He said that on the video?"

This time, it was Max who answered Jan. "Yes, he said *that*—and that's exactly what the public will learn if we haven't heard anything from Sally and Julia by three o'clock Wednesday afternoon. I think your friends *or clients* would appreciate knowing the truth about Grissom's confession before it becomes public."

Max and Tony did not say another word, to Jan nor to each other, as they left her sitting in the conference room. It was not until they were a block away from her office building that they sighed in relief.

"Boy, Tony. You really took a chance in there," Max said. "We have no hard evidence that Sally killed Rawlings, just a nosy neighbor's description. As for Julia's involvement in the escort murders, placing her in New York and Chicago when Amanda and Stephanie were murdered, well... that might provide opportunity—and we know she had motive—but she also has a father with a direct line to Commissioner Brennan's office."

"It was a shot, Max. Did you see the look on Jan's face when I guessed what happened? And then when I told her about Grissom's video? I would say we hit a home run on what really happened."

Max smiled. "Well, maybe a triple. I'll put down my bet when Jan calls to tell us Sally and Julia want to talk. In fact, my bet is she went right to the phone and called Sally as soon as the elevator doors shut."

"I'll take that bet, Max! Right now, I think it's time we move Donna Grissom to a safe and well-guarded location. The boys are already in a safe place. We don't really know who we're dealing with here. If someone hired Grissom to take the fall on Rawlings' murder, we may also be dealing with some pretty bad people."

"You should know, Tony. Who would have thought a petite, pretty woman like Stacey Johnson Blake could commit such brutal murders."

"Let's just play it safe for now," Tony said. "I'm pretty sure Donna will agree to a safe-house for awhile—just as a precaution. My guess is that whoever put up that two million plus dollars probably won't want any complications. I'm actually hoping that no one comes forward, so Donna can keep the money. Let's see what we hear from Jan in the next couple of days."

"What's your best guess?" Max asked.

"I'm counting on Jan encouraging Sally and Julia to come back to New York and tell their side of the story. But with or without their cooperation, we need to keep this all very quiet. Any move now that brings our case to the public only contradicts the NYPD and brings some very powerful politicians into the spotlight. That will assure putting Donna and her boys in danger—at the very least jeopardizing the money Brian went to such lengths for her and the boys to have. We're taking enough of a chance, and so did she by calling us. I don't want to take any further risks."

"You're right, Tony. We still don't know for sure who we're dealing with. Morris Green may be in with some pretty tough characters, and I'm not talking about the police brass."

"The next thirty-six hours will be crucial, so my job now is to make sure Donna and her sons are safe, and hope to hear from Jan," Tony said.

"While you're doing that, I'm heading back to my laptop," Max said. "Whatever happens, I want to have a column ready. I've got a variety of possible angles in mind.

The version that goes to my editor will depend on how badly Sally and Julia want to get out of this mess."

The Laughing Angels were so excited, they danced up and down the streets of Manhattan. They believed the powerful forces on the dark side of the human condition were capable of squashing these two naïve old-timers. There was only one thing Tony was right about. His opponents would do anything to protect their interests—*and any scenario was possible*. They could try to eliminate Donna and her sons, and kill Tony and Max in the process. They might decide to stay quiet and go deeper underground, letting Donna keep the money.

Whatever happened, the Laughing Angels knew the real losers were the three escorts. Nothing would bring them back. Evil won out, no matter who took the blame.

The Righteous Ones knew the Laughing Angels were right. No matter how fervently they pleaded to God for justice and compassion, He never seemed to intervene.

Chapter 70

The deadline passed at three o'clock Wednesday afternoon with no word from Jan Clark. Tony and Max had hoped for a better result from their meeting with Jan, but also realized events do not occur just because they want them to. If justice were to be served, it would take even more determination and staying power to overcome the many obstacles ahead of them.

When Jan did call, later that afternoon, it was only to tell Tony that Sally and Julia saw no reason to return to New York. She did not answer Tony when he asked if Senator Morris Green had some influence in that decision.

"Look, Jan, let's talk more about this," Tony said calmly, trying not to show his anger nor his disappointment. "I have a feeling you're not one hundred percent happy with your clients' decision. Are you available tomorrow to meet once more with Max and me? Let's give it one more try..."

"Tony, I really don't think this is going anywhere. My clients are starting new lives in Virginia, away from the questions and rumors. As far as they're concerned the escort and Tom Rawlings' cases are closed, just like the DA said."

"The cases may be officially closed, but those rumors—and the questions—are going to remain unless Max and I get some answers. I'm only asking one more time. If you're really concerned about your *friends*, it's time to forget they're clients and think like their friend. I think it's in your *and their* best interests for us to meet again."

"Okay, Tony, once more. But that's it! Two o'clock tomorrow afternoon at my office."

"Thanks, Jan. We'll be there."

After Jan hung up the phone, she sat there feeling very mixed emotions. She loved Sally like a sister, and felt the pain that she and Julia must have felt when Morris Green's escapades not only put the spotlight on his family, but also brought Julia's fairytale romance with Tom Rawlings to a crashing end.

Jan knew Tony's reputation, and Max's, well enough to realize that if Sally and Julia were going to be safe from further problems, she had better agree to another meeting. They were her friends and clients, but Morris Green was not! Jan did not want Sally and Julia to suffer any further from Morris' lack of judgment—or possible criminal behavior.

Whether Tony had made a good educated guess, or he had even more information than he told her, Jan thought the next meeting would be critical—critical enough that she might need to call in some heavy-hitters of her own.

As soon as Tony hung up the phone, he called Max. "We're on with Jan for one more try at working something out. This may be our last chance before this whole thing blows up in our faces, and then drifts away without any meaningful progress."

"I only agree with you on one point, Tony. I don't want anything to blow up either, and I'm not about to let it drift away. One way or another, this story isn't over for me. We both have an obligation to Donna Grissom and her children to clear Brian's reputation. *And don't forget about Angela*. She's the one who put us onto this story. She knew those escorts. It doesn't matter whether you or I, or anyone else, disagree with their life choices, their families deserve to know the truth about who killed them. Even Tom Rawlings' family deserves better!"

Chapter 71

When Max and Tony arrived at Jan's office, the receptionist brought them directly to a conference room where Jan was waiting with another woman. Max recognized her immediately as Lorna Adams, one of the most respected criminal attorneys in the city.

"Tony, Max, I'd like to introduce Lorna Adams, a member of our firm."

"Very nice to meet you. I'm quite familiar with your work," Max said.

"Same here, Ms. Adams. It's good to meet you," Tony added. When he shook Lorna's hand, her grasp was strong, tight enough to hurt. Maybe a message that she was confident and ready to do battle, if necessary.

"I'm very happy to meet both of you... *and please call me Lorna.* I'm well aware of your reputations—and your interest in two of our clients. I understand we have a lot to discuss."

"Yes, we certainly do," Jan said. "Please sit down."

Tony and Max sat next to each other, opposite Jan and Lorna. It was obvious to Tony that Lorna and Max already looked ready to do battle, so he was glad when Jan opened the discussion.

"Let me start by saying I'm very sorry that Sally and Julia were not able to meet yesterday's deadline. I spoke to Sally a short time ago and she is considering your request. I'll be talking to her later today with an update. If she and Julia decide to meet with you, I thought it best that we have a chance to review the entire situation with Lorna first."

"That sounds reasonable—and I guess answers the question of whether you're representing Sally and Julia as their *friend*, or as their attorney," Tony said.

"Yes, I am their lawyer—at least for now," Jan said. "If representation is actually needed, Lorna will take the lead. Of course, you understand, I'm in no way implying that Sally or Julia need representation. So far, you haven't provided me with anything that warrants either of them needing a lawyer."

"Right now," Lorna interjected, "we see this as a way for you and Max Gold to harass our clients. At this point, our role is to protect them from anyone spreading false and damaging information—and to take legal action, if needed, against those who try to harm them by publicly smearing their names in the press, and that includes Donna Grissom."

Lorna could see that her direct message had its desired effect on Tony. It took him totally by surprise. She was right. Tony tried not to show any distress, but his chest was pounding and he wished he could get up and run. A part of him wanted to tell Donna she should just take the two million dollars and start a new life for herself and her sons.

Max could see Tony was disarmed, and spoke up directly to Jan—disregarding Lorna altogether. He knew the one thing attorneys hated more than losing a case, even if they knew their client was guilty, was to be ignored.

"Jan, no one here said they wanted to defame anyone. We came to you first, rather than going directly to Sally and Julia, *because you're friends and would look out for their best interests*. Obviously, Morris Green looks out for himself first. He would be the first to turn his back on anyone, including his wife and daughters, if he thought it would hurt his political ambitions. He also has strong connections to

Police Commissioner Brennan, which is another reason we came here rather than go straight to the police."

"Max is right," Tony said. "If Sally or Julia know something that incriminates Morris Green, it's best they talk to us."

Before Lorna could respond, Jan spoke up quickly. She respected her colleague, but also knew she could be abrasive, and there was obvious tension in the room.

"Let's go back to the beginning for a moment. Right now, all we really know is that you want to speak to Sally and Julia because of a videotape Brian Grissom *supposedly* recorded. A tape claiming someone paid him to confess to murdering Rawlings. Is that right?"

Tony made the obvious move of placing his briefcase onto the conference table. "Yes, that's right. We've brought the tape with us. Right here, in this briefcase. All we're asking is that you view the video, tell Sally about it, and ask her and Julia to come to New York to meet with us. We need to know how much they know, what they did—if anything—and how we can move on from there."

Tony could see that Jan was not convinced, and neither was Lorna. "This isn't a trick of some sort, counselors. We've verified that the tape is genuine and not doctored in any way. *I think you both know enough about my reputation, and Max's, to realize that neither of us ever tried to pull a fast-one or slander anyone.*"

Max turned his attention to Lorna, who he could tell was growing impatient. "Frankly, Lorna, I resent your implications that we have any intentions of tarnishing anyone's good names. If that were the case, Tony and I could have gone straight to the police—which we might have done if we trusted the top brass to act honorably."

"We think a fix was in somewhere along the way," Tony added. "Brian Grissom may not have killed

Rawlings. We also think that Sally—or Sally and Julia—know much more about the escort murders and the murder of Tom Rawlings. Are they involved in the murders? If not, are they afraid of the truth? Are they covering for someone? Was Morris involved? Whatever they're afraid of, we think they hold the key to some questions: If Brian Grissom did not kill Tom Rawlings, who did kill him and why? Did Rawlings really kill the escorts or is there still a killer on the loose?"

Max watched quietly as Tony spoke. He thought Jan was visibly upset about Tony's questions. Lorna, on the other hand, showed no emotion. It was obvious to Max that she had no personal connection to either Sally or Julia, and might not have cared whether they were involved in the murders or not—probably why Jan called on her for help.

"That's quite a speech, Tony," Lorna said. "I don't think we should say anything more until you play the video for us."

"There's a videotape player in the corner," Jan said.

Tony took out the tape and slipped it into the machine, while Jan, Lorna, and Max swiveled their chairs around to face the screen. Tony hit the play button and then sat back and watched Jan and Lorna closely as they watched Brian tell his story.

Although Jan tried to hide her emotions, the impact of seeing Grissom's face, and hearing him describe every detail of how he was approached and why, it was obvious to both Tony and Max that she was persuaded by Brian's compelling story. It was more difficult to get a read on Lorna's reaction. She was more accustomed to convincing juries that hardcore criminals were innocent, so she might need something more persuasive. That's where the interviews with Sally and Julia would come in.

While Tony removed the videotape and put it back into his briefcase, Lorna recognized Jan's apprehension and decided to go on the attack.

"That was a very nice performance. But if Grissom is telling the truth, why doesn't he say who gave him the two million dollars?"

"I have that information in a signed affidavit," Tony snapped back at her.

"Signed by whom?"

"The messenger who delivered the money to Grissom."

"And that's it? You're not going to tell us who actually put up the two million."

"Not yet," Tony said. "We'll do that when Sally and Julia are present."

"What if they decide not to meet with you and Max?" Jan asked.

Tony's answer was firm and confident. "I'll call a press conference. And believe me—it will be standing room only."

"Before notifying the police? I don't believe you," Lorna said.

"Like I said, we think there's much more going on behind *NYPD's blue wall.* Sally and Julia—and you and Jan—have a choice. Talk to us now, or you can read all about it in one of Max's forceful, fully documented, and credible columns."

"Are you threatening us?" Lorna charged.

"Take it any way you want to, counselor," Max shot back.

"Where does this leave Morris Green?" Jan asked.

"Let me answer that," Tony said. "If I were you, it's Sally and Jan I'd worry about. We all know how well politicians survive unscathed, while many other lives are destroyed. Who knows? Senator Green might decide to go for the sympathy vote when he runs for president!"

"Your sarcasm is not appreciated," Jan responded.

"Neither is your hesitation to advise Sally and Julia that it's time for them to look out for their own interests, instead of their steadfast support of Morris Green's political ambitions."

Max looked over at Lorna, sure she was losing her cool demeanor and ready to explode with anger. But he underestimated her self-control.

With a cold stare at Tony, she asked, "What's the best Sally and Julia can hope for?"

"As their attorneys, you and Jan can answer that question better than I can—but I'm glad to give you my opinion," Tony said.

"Please do!"

"From what I surmise so far, Sally could reasonably claim she killed Rawlings in self-defense."

"What about Julia?" Jan interjected.

Max, who was fixed on the emotions around the room, could tell that Jan was still shaken by the image of Brian Grissom on the tape. Her question to Tony about Julia had been filled with the emotion of someone who was clearly worried. On the other hand, Lorna's eyes showed a lack of compassion. He could see she was setting the stage for a full frontal attack. The sound of Tony's voice brought Max back to the conversation.

"Well, Jan, that's a little more tricky. Like you said at our last meeting, it's possible that Julia quite innocently remarked to Rawlings something like, *If only those escorts would just disappear, instead of preying on my family and threatening to write tell-all books, and appearing on talk shows around the country!*"

Lorna recognized that Jan was feeling too emotional about Julia, and stepped right in. "So you're saying, if Julia said something like that in the heat of the moment, then she didn't ask Rawlings to do anything. There's also another point here; actually a question: Why would Julia ever assume that Rawlings was capable of murder?"

Tony was quick to answer. "You're the high-priced lawyers, so I'm not going to speculate on what Julia might have been thinking, or what she knew about Rawlings."

"Are you prepared to cut them some slack?" Jan asked.

"That's not up to me. Let's just see where my interviews with Sally and Julia take us. Right now, I'm looking at all possible scenarios. As I've said from the beginning, I think Sally and Julia know more than they're telling—and I want to get to the truth, and so does Max."

"We're all interested in the truth, Detective. Part of that truth is how Sally and Julia's lives were shattered by all the allegations against Morris Green—and then the murders," Lorna said.

There she goes, Max thought. *Already preparing the defense.* Tony could see that Max would welcome a real battle with Lorna, but could not stop him in time.

"Evidently, not shattered enough to cause Sally to leave Morris," Max blurted out.

"My, my, Max" Lorna shot back. "For someone who praises himself for always seeking the truth, aren't you being a bit judgmental?"

"I'll answer that." Tony said. He was quick to intercede before emotions took over. "Max is only reacting to what you said. Four people are dead, murdered, all linked to Morris Green in one way or another. What about their families? *Their lives were also shattered.* Until we have the truth, solid answers about who really killed them and why, they certainly cannot move on. At least not the way Morris

Green and his family are doing. Frankly, the way too many disgraced politicians and their families always walk away with barely a scratch on them."

"Maybe not," Lorna said. "But those escorts knew the dangers, the risks that go along with taking money for sex."

Now it was Tony's face that grew red with rage. "Now who is being judgmental? Don't go down that road with me, Lorna. Three young women are dead, most probably because of so-called *respectable men*, like Sally's husband. You and Jan, from everything I've read, call yourselves *feminists*. Where is the *feminist* in a woman who stays with a husband who has humiliated her in front of the whole country—just to maintain her own social status? What kind of example does that set for her daughters and other women? Where is her empathy for the escorts—the *other women* in their husbands' lives?"

Max was relieved to see Tony finally let into Lorna. He also knew this was one of Tony's hot topics and decided to cool things down before he had a heart attack, or Lorna reached across the table to slug him!

"Okay, okay. I think we're all getting a little too hot under the collar. Look, we can argue for hours about who is and who isn't a feminist, or why some women choose to let their husbands get away with murder. *Sorry, no pun intended.* We need to get back to the problem at hand," Max said.

Tony calmed down, but it was not easy for him. "Max is right. We have evidence that Brian Grissom did not murder Tom Rawlings, and that he was paid to give a false confession. We also think that whatever their involvement, or non-involvement, Sally and Julia Green know more about the escort murders and who really killed Rawlings. They need to talk, and soon. How about setting up a meeting for Sunday at noon?"

Lorna looked over at Jan for an answer.

"It's already Thursday," Jan said. "That doesn't give us much time."

"The deadline was yesterday. I think Max and I are being very generous in holding off any further action, even for one more day."

Lorna looked at Jan and nodded. Jan was still reluctant, but agreed. "Sunday at noon is fine. We'll see if Sally and Julia can make it."

Tony's reaction was swift and to the point. "Jan, you know that's not good enough. We *expect* Sally and Julia to be here!"

Chapter 72

Tony did not sleep well that night. He was headed back to visit Stacey the next day, and was not looking forward to seeing her. It was a promise he made after receiving a call from Dr. Trotsky. Stacey was feeling lonely and abandoned, and it was affecting her progress. At first, Tony said *no*. He really wanted to distance himself from any added stress, especially since he was now *unofficially* back on the escort and Tom Rawlings' murder cases. Dr. Trotsky persuaded him that, like it or not, he was an integral part of Stacey's therapy—and her psychiatric state was becoming far more erratic. Her days of self-confidence were becoming fewer than her days of outrage about not being recognized by society as the chosen Daughter of God. He recently had to increase her medications to higher dosages than he preferred, and thought a visit from Tony would help.

Tony arrived at the hospital in Ferndale, Michigan, at two o'clock, hoping to be there no longer than one hour. Surprisingly, he found Stacey very upbeat, as if she did not have a worry in the world. She was confident and energetic, and certainly did not seem depressed and lethargic, or outraged, as Dr. Trotsky had described. Her smile was warm and welcoming.

This Stacey was in full control of her emotions. Just like the Stacey from so many years ago, the first time he had met her. Maybe the high doses of medication were helping, Tony thought. It made him feel cautious and on guard. After all, Stacey's sweet smile had fooled him many times in the past.

"Tony, I'm so glad to see you. I know you've been working so very hard on the case. Don't worry. I won't compromise you by asking any questions about it. Well... I'll try not to."

"I appreciate that, Stacey."

Stacey laughed in a way that was frightening, even to Dr. Trotsky and Nurse Spagnoli.

"Don't thank me yet, Detective. I have some advice for you."

Tony was taken aback and not able to hide the sarcasm he felt at that moment. "Really, I can't wait!"

Stacey quickly snapped back. "Don't be so funny, Tony. I think we both know how much I helped you on this case."

Tony looked at Dr. Trotsky, whose face indicated he should show interest in what Stacey had to say.

"I'm sorry, Stacey. I didn't mean to be rude. I guess I'm a little tired today. You've been a big help and I'm eager to hear your ideas."

"Thank you, Tony. Now listen closely. Keep in mind that people, especially powerful people like politicians, clergymen, and even their families, use delay tactics for their own advantage—always giving themselves more time to come out on top of a situation."

"Yes, Stacey, I think we both share that opinion. So what are you getting at?"

"I see you don't have much patience today, Tony, so I'll get right to the point. I don't trust Morris Green's wife..."

Tony leaned across the table with obvious interest. "You've got my attention, Stacey. *What are you thinking?*"

Stacey looked at Dr. Trotsky again, with one of her *I told you so* glares, then back at Tony. "From the day she met Morris Green, Sally made concessions in her life—first to become his wife, and then to remain married to that awful man. His power was her power, and she would not let anything stand in the way of that lofty position."

Dr. Trotsky could not help himself from interposing a question. "Do you feel that's what happened with you and Jason Blake?"

Stacey turned her head and looked at the doctor with obvious annoyance. "I'm not talking to you, Dr. Trotsky!"

She turned back to Tony with a determined look in her eyes. "But, yes, Dr. Trotsky is right. That's one of the reasons I recognize it so well in other people. I loved that power—*and so does Sally Green*. Of course, Sally doesn't have the added advantage that I have."

"What advantage is that, Stacey?" Dr. Trotsky interjected again.

Stacey gave a big sigh of annoyance, and once again turned her attention to the doctor. "Well if you must know, Dr. Trotsky... With Jason, I was misguided in thinking my power came from him, and it caused me to do dreadful things."

"And now?" Dr. Trotsky asked.

"And now... I'm more sure than ever that my power comes directly from God, as his chosen daughter."

Stacey's eyes began to tear as she turned to face Tony. "That's why I needed to see you so much."

Once again, Tony could not help feeling sad for the little girl he now saw before him, a victim of her own delusions.

"Why is that?" he asked.

"I'm worried about you, Tony. You're much older now, and you no longer have the support of anyone powerful. I don't want you to get hurt."

Taking a cue from Dr. Trotsky, Tony reached out and tentatively took Stacey's hand. "Stacey, you know I can take care of myself."

"Please, Tony," she said, wiping the tears from her face. "Sometimes when people get older, they tend to judge a situation the same way as when they were younger. They don't always recognize the danger. It's like forgetting that you can no longer run up the stairs, two steps at a time, or sprint across the street moments before the light turns red."

Both Tony and Dr. Trotsky were astonished by the clarity in Stacey's voice and thoughts.

"Dr. Trotsky, I'm tired now. Thank you for coming, Tony. It was very nice of you to visit me. I always cherish our time together."

"It's good to see you, too, Stacey."

As Tony got up to leave, Stacey suddenly rose from her chair. "Please hug me goodbye. No one has done that in such a long time."

Tony quickly glanced over at Dr. Trotsky, who nodded in approval. As they embraced, Stacey whispered to Tony: *Take my advice and be careful. The Daughter of God has an obligation to warn all her followers when danger is near.*

The Laughing Angels returned to Bensonhurst with Tony, mumbling to each other along the way. Even they were amused at how Stacey, a mere mortal, had figured out how the world worked, how evil men and women so easily rationalized their actions. On the other hand, maybe she is the Daughter of God. *A daughter who God kept secret, even from the Righteous Ones.* Why not? He had already used an innocent Jewish mother and her charismatic son to appeal to the masses.

Chapter 73

Max was eating his second generous slice of coffee cake and third cup of coffee, while Tony enjoyed a cheese pastry and large glass of cranberry juice. The restaurant was only a couple of streets from Jan Clark's offices, where they were scheduled to meet at noon, only one hour from now.

"Tony, do you think Sally and Julia will be there?"

"We haven't heard otherwise from Jan, so I'm hoping they show up!"

"I have a feeling we're in for another disappointment."

"I guess that could happen," Tony said. "We certainly don't have any control over their decisions, but it's how we react that's important. We need to be prepared. If Sally and Julia aren't there, and Lorna and Jan ask for another meeting, my feeling is that we should set another date—but under no circumstances tip them off to our plans."

"What do you mean?"

"If they want to schedule another meeting, we'll agree to it. At the same time, we'll continue to move forward. We've given Sally and Julia every chance to tell their side of the story. Enough is enough!"

"I'm glad you said that. This may all have been a delay tactic set up by Jan and Lorna—trying to call our bluff, or forcing us to give up our sources, with no intentions of letting us interview Sally and Julia. They don't give a damn about Donna Grissom and her need to save the reputation of her late husband. Like all defense attorneys, the truth is only second to shielding their clients. They couldn't care less about wasting our time."

"You won't get any argument from me. What I do regret is that any time I've hired a lawyer, they seem to have cared more about how many hours they can bill me, rather than my needs!"

Max laughed heartily, until he saw the pain on Tony's face.

"I get it, Tony. It must be especially hard for someone like you, someone who believes sincerely in law enforcement and in uncompromising *justice for all.* Unfortunately, it's no secret that anyone who is powerful, wealthy, or politically connected has lawyers that work by a different set of rules."

"You've got that right. Are you all set to go with your column, just in case?"

"Damn right! Ready to go with Thursday's edition. What about you? When will you call the press conference?"

"If Sally and Julia aren't at today's meeting, the press conference will be on Tuesday."

Max seemed surprised. "That's two days before my column. Are you sure? How will you position it?"

"My plan is to give the press their first view of Donna Grissom, and their first real look at Brian through the eyes of his grieving wife. She wants to show the videotape herself."

"Brilliant!" Max exclaimed with a big smile. "For an old fogey, you're pretty devious."

Tony laughed and ate the last bit of his cheese pastry. "Let's get out of here and go to our meeting. This *devious old fogey* is ready for action."

Chapter 74

Like most Sundays, the office building was very quiet when Tony and Max arrived. The guard at the security desk checked their IDs and sent them right up to Jan's office. She met them at the elevator and showed them into the conference room, where Lorna was waiting.

The conference table was set with a carafe of coffee and a pitcher of ice water, and an assortment of muffins, pastries, and bagels. The only things missing were Sally and Julia Green.

Jan motioned for Tony and Max to take a seat. "Let me start by saying that Sally and Julia could not make it today. I only learned they weren't coming an hour ago, and I sincerely apologize for this turn of events."

Tony did not say a word. He poured a cup of coffee, and passed the carafe to Max, indicating that he should do the same. Lorna sat quietly, as she spread cream cheese on a bagel and proceeded to take a bite.

What struck Tony most, aside from the absence of Sally and Julia, was their obvious arrogance. Jan and Lorna acted like there was no way their clients could be facing prison time, and that he and Max were fools who could be easily manipulated.

It was hard not to show their anger and frustration, but Tony and Max were ready for them. They had agreed to remain composed and even-tempered, no matter what happened.

Tony smiled at Jan and asked, "Are you thinking about arranging another meeting?"

Caught somewhat off-guard by their unruffled behavior, Jan and Lorna exchanged a quick glance with one another. Just as Tony and Max hoped, they seemed to think they were tossed a gift, a delay without any argument or ultimatum.

"Yes," Jan replied. "Lorna and I really appreciate your understanding and would like to reschedule. How about Wednesday at noon, back here? Will that work for both of you?"

Tony looked at Max. "Can you make it?"

Max calmly reached for a blueberry muffin. "Sure... that sounds fine."

It was hard for Jan to hide the look of relief on her face. Her friend *and client* had dodged another bullet. Lorna also seemed relieved that they were amenable to another delay, but Tony also sensed both these shrewd attorneys were up to something.

"That's great. We really appreciate your flexibility," Lorna said.

After an awkward silence, Jan casually changed the subject. "Tony, I understand that you had retired some years ago to Newport, Rhode Island. Is that a nice place to live?"

Tony kicked Max under the table, and had to keep from laughing. He had warned Max in the ride over to Jan's office that she would try to change the subject, probably to something personal. His plan was to play along, no matter what she asked him.

"Actually, I'm only semi-retired. I do a lot of consulting and stay very active as a private investigator. I'm surprised at your question, though. Are you considering retirement?"

"Oh, not for me," she laughed. "My father is retiring in a couple of months, and I wondered what life is like in Newport."

"What are his interests?"

"He's worked at the same bank for the past thirty years, commuting from Connecticut to New York."

"If you don't mind my asking, does he have any outside interests? And what about your mother? Does she have any special interests?"

"My father's life has been consumed by his work. Mother says he's not interested in anything else. She wants to travel, but father made it clear that he has no interest in traveling. He seems happy just to spend his time at the country club playing golf."

At this point, Max was trying not to laugh. Tony had been right about Jan. He wondered where this conversation was headed. He assumed Tony had something up his sleeve. But what? At least, he thought, the muffins were good, as he reached for one with chocolate chips on the top.

On the other hand, Lorna seemed a bit surprised and restless. *What's Jan up to by engaging Tony in such a personal conversation*, she thought.

Tony casually poured himself another cup of coffee and leaned back in his chair. He would play along, see where Jan was headed, and make his own point when he was ready.

"I'm sure your parents have many choices," he said. "After all, I gather money isn't a problem. I chose Newport because it was economical and a nice place to live."

The sarcasm in Tony's voice was so obvious, Jan hesitated answering. "No… you're right. Money is not a problem. Still—I think a change would be good for him. He's much older than most of his colleagues at the bank. Once he's retired, I'm not sure his banking friends will be so available to him. I thought at your age, you faced a similar problem—you know, being out of the mainstream."

"Okay, Jan. I deserved that! I guess your father will need to find something he enjoys. Like I did!"

"What do you enjoy, Tony?" Jan seemed to ask sincerely.

"Well, first, as I said earlier, I'm only semi-retired. I still have much work to do."

Max sensed something in Tony's voice that he was about to make his point. If Jan or Lorna had thought this personal discussion was arranged to catch the great Tony Pinella off-guard, they were about to learn a lesson! *Here it comes,* Max thought…

"I have a mission, Jan. Would you and Lorna like to know what that mission is?" Tony said in a taunting manner.

At this point, Lorna glared at Jan and both women stopped eating and sat up straight. Max sat back and enjoyed his chocolate chip muffin.

"What is that mission, Tony?" Lorna asked with a stare that might freeze most lesser men.

Tony stared right back at her. "My mission is to challenge the status quo whenever necessary."

"That sounds quite noble," Lorna said sarcastically.

Tony looked intently at Lorna before he answered. "Being noble is only a myth that many lawyers use to describe their purpose in life, while they live a privileged life thanks to the hourly fees they receive from their well-connected and powerful clients."

Lorna remained cool and calm as she responded. "Just keep in mind that the *well-connected and powerful* are very often on the right side of the issue—and the law. Don't penalize them for being smart and working hard."

"I'm sure if I forget that, you and Jan will be the first to come forward to set me straight. One thing you can count on. Each person I work with, each case I take on, is handled on its own merit. When I know someone isn't well-connected and powerful, someone who is less fortunate than many of your clients—I will see that they also get justice, legally *and* morally!"

The conference room grew quiet and Max decided this was the perfect time to end the meeting. He knew how emotional Tony could be about the need for an even playing field, especially where justice is concerned.

Max stood up and motioned for Tony to do the same. "So, I guess we're all set for our meeting on Wednesday?"

"Yes, we are," Jan said. "Again, we really appreciate your patience and flexibility."

"No problem," Tony said. He shook hands with Jan first, and then Lorna. "Thank you for the conversation and refreshments. We know our way out."

If Jan or Lorna were waiting for a nasty closing comment, or a threat, they would be disappointed. This time, Max and Tony had agreed ahead of time. They would not say or do anything that would raise suspicion. They rode quietly down the elevator, without any doubt that Jan and Lorna were already discussing their strategy for the coming week—a strategy that did not include bringing Sally and Julia to their Wednesday meeting.

Chapter 75

First thing Monday morning, Max sent out a bulletin to a select group of New York-based print and television news reporters. He invited them to meet him the next morning at ten o'clock in the private dining room of The New York City Press Club on Lexington Avenue. The purpose of the meeting was to give advance notice that a big story was on the horizon—*a story so important, Max felt an obligation to share it with his colleagues, even before his own column was scheduled to appear.*

Max's reputation was such that not a person he invited had any doubt they should be there. The last time Max called his own press conference was six years ago, just before an announcement by the NYPD about the arrest of a local city council member who had been acting as a mole for the Mafia. His own column and perspective came later.

As a columnist, Max felt his job was not to break the news, but to explain it—to help people think critically about the city they lived in and the world around them. He went beyond the hard news, the basic *who, what, where, when* and *why* that was expected of good journalists. Max answered what he called the philosophical questions: *What else should the readers know? What does this mean?*

Other journalists respected his attitude and always read Max's columns to gain more perspective, which often led them on the trail of another hard news item!

As soon as she received notice of the meeting, Rita Spencer of *Channel 42 News* called Max to see who else would be part of this special press conference. "I've heard through my sources that Tony Pinella is still nosing around the Tom Rawlings murder. Will Pinella be there?"

"All I can say, Rita, is I think you'll want a front row seat. As I recall, you have a special interest in the subject!"

"Thanks, Max. That's good enough for me. I'll be there with my cameraman!"

Max called Tony to let him know that since his notice went out, the phone had not stopped ringing, including a call from Rita Spencer.

"She mentioned hearing about you *nosing around*, as she put it, the Rawlings murder."

"That doesn't surprise me," Tony said. "We've kept this pretty quiet, and I'm pretty sure Jan and Lorna haven't been talking to the press. Rita Spencer is the closest thing to you when it comes to exposing the truth. I'm surprised she hasn't called me yet. Just in case, I don't plan to answer my phone for a while. If you need to reach me, leave a message on my machine. I'll call you right back."

Tony felt the pressure of the situation. He knew his conscience and moral duty went beyond what is expected of a detective. It was a part of himself he liked! Something his parents would respect and cherish about their son. Regardless of the risk, he had a duty to help Donna and her sons. Again, a part of him wished Donna had done what Brian wanted, move away and use the money to assure a good life for her and the boys. It was not that simple for Donna. She decided that Brian's good name was more important than the money, and Tony respected that. Now he had to make sure, no matter what, that Donna and her sons were protected, and that their futures were secure, just as Brian wanted.

The problem was, Tony trusted politicians and their spouses even less than he trusted attorneys like Jan and Lorna. For only a moment, he was tempted to call Abraham Bloom for help. He had gained a great deal of respect for Bloom, and suspected he was just as frustrated and suspicious when the mayor and police commissioner closed down the Tom Rawlings case so quickly. He was too good a cop not to see through Brian's confession. However, getting the NYPD involved was too much of a risk, in addition to creating a conflict for Bloom.

Now, Tony—with Max's help—would have to play this one out the way Donna saw it. His mission was to expose the truth with as little risk as possible to Donna and her sons.

Chapter 76

Tony had arranged for private security guards outside the press club, at the private dining room entrance, and in key spots around the room. Tony had personally selected each guard, ex-cops he knew well and trusted. Donna Grissom's children were in a safe place, also guarded by Tony's team.

In order to be admitted to the conference, members of the press had to show their credentials.

At the front of the room was a table set on a platform with three microphones and three chairs. A large video display was on one side of the platform and two loud speakers.

As soon as the doors closed, Max walked onto the platform and sat in the middle seat. Tony came out next, followed by Donna Grissom. Max looked at each of them and smiled. When he moved closer to his microphone, the loud buzz of voices grew silent. The only sound was the soft hum of the *Channel 42 News* cameras.

Every person in the room was eager to hear what Max had to say. His last column had been about the New York City public school system, which hardly required this experienced journalist to be so secretive about the topic of this press conference. But it was Max Gold who called this conference, which meant something big was about to break.

Rita Spencer had been among the first to arrive with her camera crew and sat right up front. She was not surprised to see Tony seated to the right of Max, but who was the woman on his other side?

Max began his remarks:

"Thank you all for coming. I know everyone is anxious to know why I asked you here today. The answer to that question will be obvious in a few minutes. What you see and hear this morning will change the lives of many people, not only in New York, but everywhere that citizens have the right to expect our law enforcement officials to uphold the law, protect the innocent, and preserve justice.

"I'm sure many of you recognize Detective Tony Pinella. Tony worked closely with the NYPD to find the person, or persons, who were responsible for the murders of Stephanie Taylor in Illinois, Valerie Powell in Arizona, and Amanda Wilson and Tom Rawlings, right here in New York.

"We all know Tony as someone who perseveres in the fight for justice. He believes in total and complete transparency from our elected and appointed officials, and will not hesitate to turn over every rock and pebble, until he is absolutely convinced that justice has been served. He will not stop searching for the truth, even after a dedicated police department, like our own NYPD, has been pressured and coerced to end an investigation because of political pressure."

Max stopped for a moment, while whispers began to echo throughout the room.

"If you will just bear with me a while longer, I'll explain."

Everyone's attention quickly turned back to the front of the room.

"Seated next to Tony is Donna Grissom, wife of the late Brian Grissom. As many of you know, Brian sadly passed away of advanced cancer shortly after confessing to the murder of Tom Rawlings."

One eager reporter shouted out a question to Max…

"Please guys, I know you're anxious and have lots of questions—but if you wait just a little longer, everything will become very clear. Tony will explain everything, and Donna has agreed to say a few words. Tony, the microphone is yours..."

The room went completely silent as Tony moved closer to the microphone.

"I'm very grateful you all came today—even without knowing what this press conference would be all about. I could not have overturned all those pebbles without Max's strong commitment to uphold the highest standards of journalism. So let's get right down to it!

"My primary purpose is to clear Brian Grissom's name, which is why Donna Grissom is here with us. Donna wants everyone to know that her Brian was not a murderer. He was a loving husband and devoted father who fell on very hard times.

"I already know what many of you are thinking: *It's natural for many wives to think their husbands are innocent!*

"I don't blame you. *I expect a good journalist to question everything.* We've all seen how the wives of politicians and business leaders deny the guilt of their spouses, even after they've admitted to *errors in judgment,* as they like to call them. While that may be true in some cases, I think you know my reputation—and trust Max enough—to realize that neither of us would be here today without proof, and—I might add—at great risk to ourselves and to Donna, which is why the security today is so tight.

"What you're about to see and hear is a videotape secretly recorded by Brian Grissom, a man who knew he had very little time to live—the man who confessed to murdering Tom Rawlings. Brian left the videotape for his wife to view privately, and only after his death. At great risk to herself and to her children, Donna Grissom wanted the public to know the truth about her husband. To know that he was not a killer—but was paid a large sum of money to give a false confession to the murder of Tom Rawlings."

At that moment, the lights in the room dimmed, and the large screen showed the image of Brian Grissom speaking passionately to his wife.

As Tony was introducing the video, Jan Clark and Lorna Adams were working in their respective offices, unaware of what was happening only blocks away at the New York City Press Club.

Jan's secretary was making a pot of coffee in the office lunchroom, when a bulletin flashed onto the small television screen, which was set to *Channel 42 News*. She caught the end of Tony's introduction and quickly called Jan and Lorna, who ran into the room and saw the image of Brian Grissom explaining why he took money to falsely confess to killing Tom Rawlings. There were tears in Brian's eyes—and his sincerity and obvious ill health were overwhelming.

At the end of the video, the *Channel 42 News* cameraman briefly spanned the room, which was full of reporters asking questions of Tony and Max. Their even bigger surprise was Donna Grissom, seated between Tony and Max, and answering the questions shouted out by the eager press.

Lorna was shaken by this new complication, and angry with herself for underestimating Tony and Max. "I'm afraid we have some damage control to do," she said. "Jan, you're closer to Sally. I think it's better for you to call her and make sure that she and Julia stay calm."

"I'll get right on it. Those bastards! I guess they knew we didn't intend to bring Sally and Julia to New York. No wonder they were so cool the other day, and so accommodating to our rescheduling. I certainly should have known better. *Never underestimate your opposition, especially when they have the truth on their side.* We can't let those two old men fool us again!"

"One thing for sure, I guess our meeting with them for tomorrow is off," Lorna said.

"No kidding! I'll be here anyway, just in case they show up. I'm through playing games with those guys."

Jan went to shut off the television and head back to her office to call Sally.

"No, leave it on," Lorna said. "I want to hear the questions the press throws at them, and how they respond."

Tony called on Phil Scott, of *Public Accountability Magazine,* to ask the first question. "Mrs. Grissom, please accept my condolences. It took a lot of courage for you to be here today. Now that you have shown us the tape, what's going to happen to the two million dollars?"

Donna looked over at Tony for guidance. "Let me answer that," he said. "At this point, we'll have to wait and see if anyone comes forward and wants their money back."

"A follow-up then," Scott said. "Does Mrs. Grissom actually have possession of the money?"

"Let's just say that it's in a very safe place until we can get this all straightened out. Right now, it's doubtful that anyone will want to claim it!" Tony responded.

Scott was quick to respond, unable to hide his sarcastic humor—something he was known for among the press corp. "I wouldn't hold my breath, Detective Pinella. There's obviously so much more to this story."

"Yes, there is," someone shouted from the back of the room. "Alice Jankowski, *Radio New York.* If Brian Grissom is innocent, as his video claims, who did kill Tom Rawlings—and why?"

"Right now, I can't comment on that," Tony answered.

The questions started coming fast and furious, just like Tony and Max had hoped.

"Lance Crawford, *East Side City News*. Are the police going to reopen Tom Rawlings' case?"

"Well, I certainly would," Tony answered. "I guess you'll have to ask that question to someone over at the NYPD."

"Do the police know about the video?" Lance asked.

"I guess they will now!" Tony said with a wry smile. "I haven't spoken to anyone over there since the case was closed."

"Rita Spencer, *Channel 42 News*. Weren't you working closely with Detective Abraham Bloom? Do you know that he retired last week?"

"Yes, I was working with Detective Bloom. He's a good man. I knew he was nearing retirement age—but, like I said, I haven't been in touch with anyone at the NYPD since they closed the case."

For another forty-five minutes, the questions came one after another from local and national newspapers. Donna seemed to be getting tired, and Max did not want to add further to her stress. He also did not want to field any more questions about where the money might be. It was a good time to shut things down.

"I think we need to wrap things up, folks," he said.

"Just one more question, please. Jackson Parker, *USA Today*. Detective Pinella, it's obvious you're continuing to investigate Tom Rawlings' murder on your own. Since Rawlings was considered the chief suspect in all three escort murders, are you also re-investigating those cases? Do you think those killings have something to do with his murder?"

"Yes, Jackson, I am. My mother always told me, *when you begin something, be sure you finish it.*"

"Where do you go from here?" Rita Spencer shouted.

"I hope to be able to answer that question by tomorrow afternoon," Tony said.

Max thought this was a good time to stop. "That's it folks. Thanks again for coming and asking such good questions. I'm glad to see we still have an independent press with a commitment to keep the public well informed. When we have more information, we'll be sure to share it!"

Lorna shut off the television and angrily pulled out the plug. The press conference had run a full two hours. She carried the small television into her office to keep an eye out for any more news reports. The office staff would have to watch their soap operas another day.

She checked with Jan, who had been unable to reach Sally.

"I left a message for her, but haven't heard back yet," Jan said.

There were no urgent messages on Lorna's desk. *So far, so good,* she thought. She and Jan told their secretaries to hold all their calls for the rest of the day. They now anticipated that Tony and Max would show up tomorrow, most likely thinking they had the upper hand. Jan and Lorna needed to get their act together and be ready for anything.

Chapter 77

Tony and Max arrived at Jan's office a few minutes before their noon meeting and were escorted directly into the conference room. It was obvious by the expressions on Jan and Lorna's faces, the best Tony and Max could expect was a modicum of civility—and even that would be only out of necessity. This time, there were no pots of coffee or even a pitcher of water on the table.

Without the pretense of small talk, Jan started the conversation. "I suppose I owe you both an apology for stringing you along the past few weeks."

"You did what *you* thought was best for your clients," Tony said defiantly, "and then we decided what *we* had to do, what would enable us to learn the truth about the murder of Tom Rawlings."

"And whose truth is that?" Lorna angrily blurted out. "Donna Grissom's?"

"Hold on there, Lorna," Max interjected, his face growing red with anger. "Donna Grissom *and her husband* are victims of a deadly plan, a plan that *your clients* may know something about!"

Tony tried to calm things down. "Hang on both of you. We won't get anywhere if we start shouting at each other."

Jan sat back and took a breath. She was worried Lorna would get angry and storm out of the room. "Let's start over. Obviously, Donna Grissom is now part of this entire situation. Is it possible for us to meet with her?"

While Jan, along with Tony, were trying to hold the meeting together, Lorna was visibly furious that Max and Tony had grabbed the upper hand.

"Yes, that's right!" Lorna shouted at Max. "Is Donna Grissom as willing to meet with us, as she apparently was to speak at a press conference?"

"No," Max replied, just as defiantly.

This time, it was Jan who tried to bring some civility back to the meeting. "Look, guys. Shouting at each other isn't going to get us anywhere. Let's look at the facts. Putting Donna Grissom in front of the cameras opened up an entirely different can of worms. How did you think we would respond?"

"I'm sorry, Jan, but these two hot-shots have gone too far," Lorna shrieked. "I'll tell you how I plan to respond. I have some powerful friends in this town that might want to arrange their own meeting with Donna Grissom. All you did was assure she could easily be slapped with a charge of withholding evidence."

"I have no doubt you have powerful friends," Tony shot back. "But I suspect none of them will help you much where this case is concerned. As for withholding evidence, I'm sure there is someone in the district attorney's office who *would* like to speak with Donna—and she is ready to do just that! Your intimidations don't mean anything to me, or, for that matter, to Donna Grissom. In fact, there is some question as to why the case was closed so fast without interviewing Donna! Maybe one of your powerful friends would like to answer that question. No one in the NYPD followed the evidence in this case, none of which led to Brian Grissom!"

In another effort to lower the intensity around the table, Jan tried to mediate. The situation was getting out-of-hand, and she was beginning to worry if bringing Lorna onboard to represent Julia was a mistake. "Hold on, Tony—*and you, too, Lorna!* Accusations from you, Tony, and veiled threats from you, Lorna, won't accomplish anything."

Tony quickly agreed with Jan. He wanted these two heavy-hitting attorneys to know they were no longer in control, but he also realized that a duel between them would accomplish nothing.

"You're right, Jan," he said. "We all need to calm down and get some answers."

Lorna followed Jan's lead, but not as sincerely as Jan would have liked. "Yes, I apologize, Tony. I certainly didn't mean to offend you or Max."

"Apology accepted," Tony said.

Max kept quiet, not at all satisfied with Lorna's attitude—and feeling very uneasy about what she was really thinking.

"So, what are your plans now?" Jan asked.

"What do you mean?" Tony responded. "The only thing we have been asking is to meet with Sally and Julia. We thought that was the most respectful way to go."

"Yeah," said Max. It was obvious his anger was still on the surface. "I could have just shown up at their front door in Alexandria with a camera!"

Tony glared at Max, who was not going to let go of his anger so easily. "Take it easy, Max. I don't know about showing up on anyone's doorstep. But Max isn't all wrong. Let's be honest. We tried working through you, and didn't get any cooperation. As for our plans, like I said, we'll do what we think is necessary."

"Tony, we did try to cooperate. We did our best," Jan said.

Max was glad to see that Tony had reached his own boiling point.

"Your best?" Tony shouted. "Your best would have been to bring Sally and Julia to the table."

"We can still try to do that!"

"You can *try*? I'm afraid it's too late for *trying!*"

"What do you mean?"

"All I'm going to tell you is this. We have a signed affidavit that Morris Green made all the arrangements to transfer two million dollars to Brian Grissom."

The room went quiet as all the color drained from Jan's face. Lorna sat there glaring at Max and Tony.

"May we see it?" Lorna asked.

"Eventually," Tony answered.

Lorna's face grew red with rage, as she leaned forward and challenged Tony. "You can threaten us all you want, Detective. But there's nothing you can do! The DA closed the Rawlings case, as well as the escort murder cases. Do you really think the tearful wife of a confessed murderer, one who returns from the dead in a video tape, is going to convince anyone that Morris Green—who wins the people's vote every time— paid for Grissom's confession?"

Tony smiled broadly and leaned back into his chair. "Think whatever you want, counselor. Max and I will do what we always do, continue to fight for justice. The people responsible the all the murders will eventually pay a price."

Tony could see that Lorna was about to say something else, but he stepped in and spoke first. He knew that it was time to end the charade all of them had been playing.

"Max and I kept our commitment and came here today. We know that it took some very influential people to close down the escort and Tom Rawlings investigations. Hopefully, sometime in the future, they'll all answer for their interference."

Tony backed his chair away from the table and stood up. "Let's go, Max. We're done here."

As Tony and Max headed for the door, Jan stood up and called out to them.

"Wait! What if we can get Sally and Julia to agree to a meeting?"

"As far as I'm concerned, that window of opportunity is closed," Tony replied. "On the other hand, if they want to give Max an exclusive interview, that's up to him."

"What about it, Max?" Jan asked.

"If it's ever sincerely offered, then I'll consider it. But that offer is not open-ended."

At that point, Tony and Max left the room and headed for the elevator, leaving a very stunned Jan and Lorna in their conference room.

Chapter 78

Tony's morning cup of coffee never tasted better. It was a day of reckoning that would change many lives. Throughout New York, and other parts of the country, people were reading and discussing Max's column.

David Kagan, who Tony had been keeping up-to-date on everything, already called from Paradise Valley to congratulate him and Max on a job well done. "I knew you would never give up, Tony. I don't think there's a politician alive, or any of his rich pals, that can hide when Tony Pinella looks for justice. I can't wait to see what happens next!"

"I'll keep you posted. I'm sure you and I haven't fought our last battles yet," Tony said with a hearty laugh.

While David and Tony talked about the possibility of getting together in Newport during David's next vacation, Jan and Lorna sat in Jan's office discussing Max's column. It was hard for them to understand why none of their usual tactics worked to intimidate Tony and Max.

"We need to move fast," Jan said. "I have to call Sally Green. I hope she hasn't seen Max's column yet."

Lorna's response sounded more dispassionate than Jan would have liked. "I'll let you handle that," she said. "I'm going back to my office. I'm due in court later this morning for another case. I don't think your clients are being honest with us. Let me know when you have something more solid and I'll consider coming back on board."

At the same time, Abraham Bloom read Max's column and felt vindicated at having hired Tony to lead the investigation. It validated his controversial decision to bring in an outsider, someone known for his objectivity and integrity.

In Alexandria, Virginia, Sally Green was preparing breakfast, unaware of what the public was reading about her husband, and the escort and Tom Rawlings' murders. When she answered the telephone, Jan 's voice signaled the news was not good. Sally began to sob hysterically when Jan told her about Max's column.

Jan tried to sound composed and very much in charge of the situation. "I know this sounds devastating, Sally, but you must calm down and listen closely. Do just as I say. Are you listening to me?"

"Yes, yes. I'm listening. What do you want me to do?"

"First, keep your answering service on, but neither you nor Julia should answer any calls—unless you hear my voice. If anyone does get through, don't answer any questions about Max Gold's article, *or any questions for that matter*. Stay away from the windows and don't respond if you see or hear anyone outside your home or at the door. Is Morris there?"

"No. He's on some fact-finding mission in Venezuela for two weeks. Should I call him? What should I say to him? My God, Jan, What should I do? Where should I go?"

"You and the girls are coming to New York to stay with me. Are the girls home now?"

"Yes, I was just making breakfast when you called."

"Good. I'm sending a car from our Washington office to pick up you and the girls. Here's how it will go: The driver and a security guard will pull into your driveway in about half an hour. The security guard's name is Tim and the driver is Albert. I've worked with them for years. Tim will call me when he's at your back door. Then I'll call to let you know he's there. Tim will bring you to my place and escort you to the apartment next to mine. I also own that apartment, and it's fully furnished. I'll be waiting there. You and the girls will be comfortable and safe while we work everything out."

"Won't other residents be suspicious? What if they call the newspapers?"

"Don't worry about that. It's not unusual for me to have guests staying there. Just pack a couple of small bags for you and the girls."

"Okay. What should I tell Morris?"

"If you can reach him now, tell him you're going to New York. That you'll explain more later. You'll probably get his voice mail anyway, so I wouldn't worry about that."

"Jan, I'm really frightened."

"We'll get through this, Sally. I love you and the girls."

"Oh, Jan. We love you, too. I'm so sorry to have dragged you into this mess."

"Hey, messes are my specialty. You just get ready and wait for my call."

When Jan hung up the phone, she put her head down on the desk. *How could all this be happening*, she sobbed to herself.

❧

The Laughing Angels were delighted with how this new chapter in Tony's life was unfolding. While he sipped his coffee and felt satisfied with his pursuit of justice and the day's events, Morris Green's wife and daughters—victims of Morris' escapades and ego—were going into hiding.

Just look at you, they cackled as they taunted the Righteous Ones. *You still believe that Morris Green and his rich cronies would resign in shame from their lofty positions, and hide away somewhere. What a laugh! Morris is gallivanting around South America, while his wife and daughters are cowering in a corner in New York.*

While the Righteous Ones were proud of Tony and Max, they had to admit the Laughing Angels made some good points about the rich and powerful relying on being too big to fail. But they still believed that people like Tony and Max, and fervent believers like David Kagan, would never give up fighting for moral and legal justice—even during those times that the Almighty seemed to have lost his way.

Chapter 79

As Jan waited in her apartment for Sally and the girls to arrive, she reread Max Gold's column. She needed to work quickly on her next move. Maybe a nuance in something Max wrote provided a hint to what that move should be.

Here We Go Again...
Max Gold, Crime Reporter

When ex-Governor Morris Green asked the people of New York to give him another chance—they did.

Many of my readers commented that I should believe more in redemption, that it is not my place to be Green's judge and jury. They write that we should be thankful that someone who is so bright, and has such wealth of his own, cares so much about the citizens of New York.

The people of New York spoke out to me, and to the country, when they sent him to the senate. With all my heart, I hoped the people were right. I hoped that Morris Green learned from his mistakes.

I admit, I also wanted desperately to recapture the idealism of my youth, to believe that everything is possible. That even a scoundrel like Green could find his way back. After all, we all make our share of mistakes, and want to be forgiven. So why not give Green the benefit of the doubt?

I'll tell you why. From the day he assumed the job of New York's attorney general, Morris Green never ceased to perplex me. As attorney general, he showed a total disregard for everyone but himself. Frequently, to satisfy his own agenda, he intimidated and harassed innocent individuals into cooperating with his office—even when he knew they and their families would be in harm's way. He showed over and over again that his needs to succeed politically were more important than anyone else's needs.

Okay, you say. That was in the past, when he was a prosecutor and attorney general. So he let being a governor go to his head a little. So what if he made a mistake dating an escort? Didn't he pay a price by resigning? If his wife and children forgave him, so should we!

NO WE SHOULD NOT… and I'll tell you why. Morris Green wanted to find someone to take the blame for murdering Tom Rawlings, who the police suspected of being the escort murderer. Brian Grissom, an upstanding citizen of our state, learned he was dying of cancer. When too weak to work, he lost his job and his health insurance. When medical bills drained his savings, he fell behind on his home mortgage. Then, with only months to live, Grissom found himself desperate to find a way to secure the financial futures of his wife and two sons.

Enter Morris Green. In Brian Grissom, Green found the perfect scapegoat.

I don't know if Green thought he was doing Brian a favor. After all, Brian was dying anyway. Maybe Green thought what difference did it make if he died in jail, at home, or in a hospital. His family would have the money, and all he had to do was admit to a murder he didn't commit. In fact, Brian Grissom didn't even know Tom Rawlings.

NO my fellow citizens. Morris Green should not be given a pass. Not this time, and not ever again!

As governor of our great state, Green schemed to transport an escort from New York to Washington, showing no regard for the law, and no respect for the high office he held. And no respect for his constituents, or for his wife and daughters. That escort worked for the same service as the three young women who were brutally killed. The NYPD wants you to believe that Tom Rawlings, and Tom Rawlings alone, murdered them.

Now that we know Brian Grissom did not kill Tom Rawlings, who did? And why? I would like to know! Wouldn't you? I would also like to know why Senator Green wanted Brian Grissom to confess to that killing. Surely, it wasn't because he wanted to help the Grissom family. He could have done that by giving the money to the Grissom family with no strings attached.

There's more you should want to know. Who in the NYPD wanted both the escort murders, and Tom Rawlings cases closed with the death of Brian Grissom? Other than his bought and paid for confession, there was not one shred of evidence that Brian murdered Rawlings. It is only due to the persistence of Detective Tony Pinella, who worked on his own the past few months, that we even know the truth—what the NYPD and Senator Morris Green did not want us to know!

Regardless, we do know that somehow Morris Green is involved, at the very least in bribing a dying man to make a false confession. For that alone, Green should resign immediately from his senate seat.

Given our current knowledge, whether or not Green is guilty of anything else is for the police to investigate.

You and I, my fellow citizens, are also culpable. It is up to us to tell our law enforcement leaders, loudly and clearly, that no one should be shielded from our laws and justice system just because they are socially or politically connected.

Brian Grissom died in a prison hospital. Tom Rawlings died before he could name his possible accomplices in the escort murders. *And three young women are dead.* Let's give them the justice they deserve.

Chapter 80

As the three girls were comfortably settled in the adjoining apartment, Sally and Jan had a heart-to-heart conversation reminiscent of their days at university together.

Jan pleaded with Sally. "You have to forget about what's good for Morris. Your priority now is saving yourself and Julia. We need to work on a plan where your daughters don't lose their mother, and Julia doesn't spend years in prison."

"I know that, but..." Sally said.

"*But?* There is no *but!*" Jan shouted, no longer able to hide her anger. "In all likelihood, Morris will be forced to resign from the senate. If he pleads guilty to bribing Brian Grissom, and there's no guarantee he will, I'm certain he'll face at least some time in prison."

"I know, but he'll be so shattered and defeated. I want so much to help him in some way."

Jan stood up and walked to the window, just staring outside for a moment. It was beyond her comprehension that Sally would even consider Morris' feelings, when her own life and her daughters' lives were about to be destroyed. She turned around and faced her friend. "Well that's just too bad. Let's forget for a moment that I never liked Morris. The facts are this: One, his actions caused a national public humiliation for you and the girls. Two, he should have gone to prison for transporting Angela Robinson across state lines. And three, he didn't even have the smarts to use a condom when he had sex with Angela—and who knows how many more women!"

Sally was stunned by Jan's words and lack of compassion. She cried out, pleading to Jan. "He's my husband. The father of my daughters."

"Your husband? A father? My God, Sally. Please grow up! I'm not making a moral judgment. This isn't like our college days when HIV was not an issue. This is a life and death, as well as a legal issue. Was Morris thinking of himself as a husband and father when he jeopardized your life by not using a condom? Was he thinking as a father when he had a young woman brought from New York to Washington to satisfy his ego and sexual appetite?"

"Okay… Okay… What do you want me to do?"

"I've already spoken to someone about your confessing to self-defense in the Tom Rawlings matter. We're hopeful for no prison time."

"Do you really think that leniency is possible under these circumstances? What if they want to make an example of me?"

"I can't promise anything. You did leave the scene without reporting it, and you said nothing when Brian Grissom admitted to Rawlings' murder. There's also the coroner's report that said Tom didn't die immediately. If you had called 911, Tom's life might have been saved. Still, I'm hoping that if you come forward, the DA will consider a much lesser sentence with no jail time. But I can't promise that."

As Sally once again started to sob, Jan embraced her. "In all the time we've known one another, this is the first time you've done something really, really bad. I've always admired your self-discipline, as well as your genuinely loving nature. I love you and the girls, and we'll face this together. *That's all I can promise.*"

"Thank you, Jan. Thank you for sticking by me all these years. You warned me about Morris when I told you he'd proposed. I think you said something like, *Be careful. He's ambitious and might put that ambition before his love for you.* Turns out you were right."

"I wish I had been wrong. Now you must be strong for Julia and her sisters, as well as for yourself," Jan said in a more comforting tone. "I promise to work on a few more ideas tonight. Tomorrow morning, I'll have a long talk with Julia. Then you and I will discuss our next steps."

Jan walked Sally back to the apartment next door, and then returned to her own apartment.

As Sally rested in bed, it seemed that all the exhaustion and anxiety of the past months caught up with her. She thought of the day, so long ago, when she stood under the marriage canopy with a young and confident Morris Green. How happy and proud she felt then, as Morris spoke their wedding vows. She knew this wonderful man was destined for greatness, and she would be at his side.

When Morris asked Sally to stop working so they could begin a family, she thought he made so much sense. An idea she embraced without ever imagining that he was capable of destroying the entire foundation of their family and faith.

Jan told her to get some sleep. *How can I sleep,* Sally thought, *knowing that my decision to stay with Morris brought such pain to my daughters, especially to Julia. My darling Julia, who adores Morris so much. As a mother, I was a failure. I set a bad example by staying with Morris, even after I learned the truth about him.*

Chapter 81

Max told Tony that police officers were harassing him. It started with phone calls at all hours of the night. The phone would ring, and the caller would hang up as soon as he heard Max's voice.

"Are you sure it's the cops?" Tony asked.

"It's the cops all right. Since my last column ran, I've been stopped on the road several times, and for no reason. I've been *breathalized*, my license and registration checked, even accused of running a stop sign on a street that doesn't have one… Believe me, the calls are all part of it. My readers are more open when they don't like what I've written. They're usually all to eager to sign their names to letters, and generally call my office with their threats, not my private home line."

"I'll give Abe Bloom a call. He's retired, but still has plenty of contacts in the department. In the meanwhile, you be careful."

"Thanks, Tony. You be careful, too. I'm pretty sure we've made some enemies, with the police as well as a few politicians. Morris Green has long arms and lots of friends, and not all of them wear a badge."

"I'm sure of that. I'll get back to you if I learn anything."

As soon as he hung up the phone, Tony called Abraham Bloom. There was no way Bloom would be involved in anything like this, so he felt safe in contacting him.

"Most of our guys are on the up-and-up, but it's like anything else," Bloom said thoughtfully. "You get a few who forget what the blue uniform is all about. I'll give Sal

Cedeno a call. He's got pretty good instincts when it comes to uncovering these problems, and he has something to lose if any of his men go astray."

"Thanks, Abe!"

"No problem. If there's anything going on, I'll let you know. But, look, you be very careful not to let your own guard down."

"You sound like this doesn't come as a surprise. What's up?"

"Didn't you wonder why I resigned earlier than I planned?"

"Yes, I did. But then I also realized how much I wanted to resign right after that whole situation with Jason Blake and Stacey."

"Yeah, that was quite a time."

"So why did you resign early?"

"Something just smelled funny with that whole Tom Rawlings situation, and the Grissom confession. I knew it wasn't right, but my hands were tied. I was glad to see you follow up on your own, but don't tell anyone that!"

"I won't, but please tell me what finally made you go."

"Let's just say that too many people in power were too eager to see the cases closed. Your press conference, at least to some extent, might have made them less dangerous—and at least cleared an innocent man. But you and Max Gold also made enemies, and they might be worried about what you guys will do next. If they feel their positions are threatened, who knows how desperate they will be—and they have the power and money to wreak havoc on anyone who gets in their way."

"Thanks for the warning, Abe. I will be careful, and you be careful, too."

Right after speaking to Tony, Bloom called Chief Cedeno and let him know what was going on, and was not happy with his attitude.

"Tell Pinella not to worry," Cedeno laughed. "You know how our guys can get when they think someone is making them all look bad because of a few rebels. I'll check into it."

"Listen, Sal. Max Gold and Tony Pinella are two of the good guys. Always supportive of the police—and Pinella is one of us. I wouldn't take it so lightly if either of them thinks there's a problem. If it goes any further, Pinella will head straight to the mayor's office."

"Okay, okay. I'll get right on it..."

When he hung up the phone, Bloom thought the chief's response was too casual. He decided not to wait, and called Mayor Jack Saunders to brief him on the situation.

"Thanks for the heads-up," Saunders said. "I'll quietly see what I can find out. Let me know if there are any more problems. I know how easy it is for a few unsavory characters to tarnish the reputation of dedicated and honest women and men, who put their lives at risk each and every day."

At the same time Abe Bloom was talking to the mayor, Tony was back on the telephone with Max. "Something isn't right," he said. "I know we're probably fighting an uphill battle, and we need to be extra careful. But I'm especially worried about you!"

"*Why especially me?*"

"I just got off the phone with Abe Bloom, and he's looking into your harassment situation. He hinted there might be more than just a few angry cops involved. Your recent column might have scared some people with the money and power to pull strings at the highest political levels— people who will do anything to save their power and influence."

"We've fought the charlatans before. Do you think this is different?"

"All I'm saying is there might be people who are desperate enough to resort to drastic measures. From here on, and especially after your interview with Sally tomorrow, watch your back."

"I wish you were coming with me."

"No, I think Jan was right in suggesting I don't come. This is purely an interview for getting Sally's story out. If I'm there, it's too much like a police interrogation, and Sally might back out."

"Okay. You just watch *your* back… I'll be fine."

Chapter 82

Max's interview with Sally Green took place as scheduled in a conference room at the law offices of Jan Clark and Lorna Adams. He used his own video equipment. Max reaffirmed on the videotape that there would be no preconditions. Sally Green and her attorneys agreed that he could ask any question relating to the murder of the escorts and Tom Rawlings, and that Sally would answer on her own, without the interference of her attorneys. He also re-affirmed that Sally, nor her attorneys, would have any rights to see or edit his article before publication.

With their agreements on the tape, Max began the interview.

Q. Please tell me your full name.

A. I'm Sally Green and my husband is Senator Morris Green.

Q. Why did you ask for this interview?

A. I wanted to clear up certain issues about Tom Rawlings' death, and to tell my side of the story.

Q. I want to be sure you realize that some of the questions I will ask you today are for the benefit of readers who might not have followed this story.

A. Yes, I know. That's your job, and I understand.

Q. Is it true that you have agreed there are no preconditions to this interview? It is strictly up to you whether or how you choose to answer my questions.

A. Yes, I understand.

Q. Did you know Tom Rawlings?

A. Yes, I did.

Q. When and where did you meet him?

A. We met approximately one year ago. He came to our home to pick up Julia. She was dating him at the time.

Q. How long had they been dating?

A. About six months.

Q. Why did they stop seeing each other?

A. Julia found some of his behavior to be erratic, but she didn't stop seeing him.

Q. Erratic in what way?

A. He began arriving late for dates, and other times he would show up when she wasn't expecting him. A couple of times, he didn't show up at all, and then called the next day with an excuse.

Q. What kind of excuses? Give me examples.

A. Things like an important client asked to see him, or he didn't feel well and fell asleep, or he had to go out of town unexpectedly. Little things like that.

Q. Is that all?

A. Well, he was always that way. It got worse about a month after we had all that trouble, when my husband resigned as governor.

Q. How did it get worse?

A. Tom became very jealous and possessive. When Julia went shopping or had lunch with a girlfriend, he would get angry—accuse her of seeing someone behind his back. Things like that. Julia told him that his behavior was unacceptable, and he stopped for a while.

Q. What finally caused the break-up?

A. I guess it was about two months later. Tom and Julia were at a cocktail party, when John and his girlfriend walked over to say hello.

Q. Who is John?

A. Julia's ex-boyfriend. She broke up with him after meeting Tom Rawlings. In fact, they all knew each other from the various charity events our families attended. Anyway, it was natural for John to give Julia a warm hug. Tom grabbed Julia's arm, rudely said it was time to leave, and pretty much pulled her out of the room. She was so embarrassed! On the way home, Julia asked why he acted that way. Tom said he would feel better if she never mentioned John's name again, that he wished John would disappear altogether.

Q. What was Julia's reaction?

A. That's what I asked her when she got home that evening. I remember her exact words: *I told Tom that's how I feel about the escorts. Angela already did her damage. Now more escorts will probably come out of the woodwork.* Then she put her arms around me and cried and cried. She finally let out all the pain she had been feeling about the entire escort situation.

Q. But she continued to date Tom?

A. Yes. At that point, she had been through so much with Morris, I think she just didn't want any other changes in her life. Tom represented some security to her.

Q. What finally caused her to end her relationship with Tom?

A. His jealousy continued, and it made her nervous. When he told her he was out of town, he would suddenly turn up when she was having dinner with a girlfriend. He even showed up one evening when we were at the ballet. It was during the intermission, and there he was shouting at her for seeing a ballet that he wanted to see with her. It was bizarre. That was the night she told him never to call her again.

Q. How did he take that, when she broke up with him?

A. Tom kept calling and making threats, hinting that she would regret treating him so badly. He said it was all because of her father's predicament—that she was so worried about Morris, she no longer had time for him.

Q. Anything else?

A. She stopped answering the phone, so Tom started leaving these awful messages.

Q. *What kind of messages?*

A. One time, he said that the escorts were the problem, that they were ruining everything.

Q. *Did he say how they would ruin everything?*

A. Yes. He said if any of the escorts sold their stories about Morris to the newspapers or magazines, Julia's life would be ruined. When he left that message, he also cried into her answering machine—really sobbed—and said he only wanted to protect her. He said he would do anything, to prove he really loved her, and begged her to give him another chance. Julia was so upset!

Q. Did she see him again?

A. Unfortunately, yes. Julia had been moping around the house for weeks, so I asked her to join me at our tennis club's annual luncheon.

Q. Was Tom there?

A. No, but his mother was! She went on and on about how much Tom missed Julia, and how sad she was that they had broken up. I wish we had never gone. Days went by, and Julia being Julia, she worried about Tom. She felt responsible, that maybe Tom was right. What happened with Morris did affect the way she felt about Tom.

Q. So they got back together?

A. Yes. Tom was taking a trip to Chicago for his friend's engagement party, and asked Julia to go with him. He said it would be a good chance to get away from everything going on in New York—a chance for a fresh start. I was nervous about it, but she seemed so happy, happier than I had seen her in months, so I said all right. If I had just said no, we wouldn't be sitting here today.

Q. What happened?

A. The way Julia described it, they were having a good time. Tom was attentive and polite—and everything seemed fine, until they got back to their hotel room. Without warning, Tom started screaming at her, accusing her of flirting with his newly engaged friend. He said that he had sacrificed everything to make her happy, and this is how she thanked him! She was so frightened. She tossed her clothes into her carry-on and left the hotel for the airport. She was able to get on a midnight flight back to New York.

Q. Did she have any contact with Tom after she returned home?

A. He kept calling and leaving the same bizarre messages. Julia finally changed her personal telephone number, and we thought that would be the end of it. Until he called me!

Q. What did he say?

A. Not so much *say*, as *threaten*. He asked me for a large sum of money, and said if I didn't pay up, he would destroy my family. *He would go to the police and tell them that he and Julia killed the three escorts.*

Q. How did you respond to his demand?

A. I felt trapped and frightened for my daughters, especially for Julia. I agreed, and asked to meet him at a coffee shop near his apartment. I was afraid of him, and wanted to meet in a public place.

Q. Did he agree?

A. No. We did meet, but he insisted I come to his apartment. When I hesitated, he said something like, *the choice is yours. My apartment or I go straight to the police with my story.*

Q. So you went to his apartment?

A. Yes. He met me there after some party he attended that evening.

Q. What happened when you got there?

A. Tom seemed very distraught, and it was obvious he had been drinking too much. He started to tell me how sad he felt since the breakup with Julia, that he still loved her so much.

Q. How did you respond to him?

A. I was a little afraid because he was so upset. I tried to sound understanding, and said that all relationships are complex—sometimes hurtful things happen. When they do, it takes time to heal.

Q. What did he say?

A. He got even more agitated. I'll never forget the look in his eyes when he said, *I will never heal from how much she hurt me. It's Julia I want... Julia or nothing!*

Q. Then?

A. I was frightened and wanted to leave. I headed to the door, but he blocked it. He repeated how he would lie to the police about Julia and the escorts. He would tell them that Julia planned the murders and then he killed them.

Q. What did you say or do then?

A. It was obvious he wasn't going to move from the door, so I tried to stay calm and reason with him. I asked him, *Why would you want to hurt someone you love so much?*

Q. Did he answer you?

A. Yes. He said Julia hurt him so much, he didn't want to go on without her. The way he said it... He frightened me.

Q. Did he move away from the door?

A. No. He took a gun from his pocket. I think it was with his right hand. I was so afraid he would either kill himself—or me. I don't know what I was thinking. I grabbed his arm and tried to push him away from the door. We struggled for a few moments, when I heard the gun go off. *I thought maybe I was shot*—but then Tom slumped to the floor and I saw blood all over his shirt.

Q. Why didn't you call 911?

A. I panicked. I know I should have called for help—but I was so afraid he might still try to shoot me. All I wanted to do was get out of that apartment and pretend it didn't happen.

Q. And now? What do you think now?

A. I never should have agreed to meet Tom at his apartment. I should have told Morris and we should have reported the blackmail threat to the police.

Q. You weren't worried that Julia would be implicated in the escort murders?

A. *Of course not! Julia would never do anything like that!*

At this point during the interview, Sally looked over to Jan and Lorna, seemingly looking for guidance. Jan just nodded, and Lorna smiled—their agreed-to signal that Sally was doing fine and should rely on her own instincts.

Q. Let's take a minute and go back to something you said earlier. Julia recalled that when she mentioned her prior boyfriend's name, Tom said, and I'll quote you: *He would feel better if she never mentioned John's name again, that he wished John would disappear altogether.* Then Julia said: *That's the way I feel about the escorts.* Is that right?

A. Yes.

Q. So, are you implying that Tom thought Julia was hinting for him to kill the escorts?

A. I'm not *implying* anything. Julia would never say anything she thought would cause such a horrible thing to happen. Just for the record, her ex-boyfriend is alive and well.

Q. But you did say that Tom was distraught. Don't you think he might have misinterpreted what Julia said, and that's why he murdered the escorts? That he loved her so much, he wanted to please her?

Again, Sally looked to Jan and Lorna, not sure what to say. This time Lorna shook her head, indicating that Sally should bypass this question.

A. I have no idea what Tom thought. I am not going to speculate on his motives.

Q. Let's change the subject just a bit. So long as you mentioned Morris... I'm sure the public is curious. After you learned about his relationship with an escort, why did you stay with him?

A. First of all, it wasn't what I would call a relationship.

Q. Okay, maybe it wasn't a relationship. But it was reported that when your husband had sex with the escort, he risked your life by not using condoms.

Once again, Sally did not answer Max. She looked at her attorneys, not sure what to say.

"Max, you covered a lot of ground today," Jan said quietly. "Sally answered all your questions. Unless you have any more to ask about Tom Rawlings, this interview is over."

Max responded without showing any annoyance or anger. "Our agreement, and I would be happy to replay our opening comments, is there would be no limitations to my questions—I expect that to be honored. But I'll rephrase my question. Is that all right with you, Mrs. Green?"

"Yes, of course. I want to get to the truth as much as you do."

"Thank you. We won't be too much longer."

Q. Mrs. Green, is there anything that would compel you to leave your husband?

A. Well, yes. If Morris ever hurt our daughters.

Q. So you don't think his actions with the escorts hurt them?

A. Morris has been and remains a caring and loving father, and my marriage remains strong!

Q. Just how far would you go to keep your marriage together?

A. Just what I said in my wedding vows—*for better or worse*.

Q. What about murdering Tom Rawlings?

A. I would never do anything illegal. I certainly wouldn't murder anyone!

Q. Even if the end justified the means?

A. I don't know what you mean.

Q. You say that Tom Rawlings threatened your family... that he was blackmailing you... that you felt trapped.

A. I could never kill anyone!

Q. But you did.

A. It was self-defense. Tom pulled a gun and I tried to get out of his apartment. There was no intention on my part to shoot him.

Q. But you are relieved that he's dead, aren't you?

A. It was the worst day of my life! I wish and pray I could live that day over again, with a different outcome. Is this interview over?

Q. One more question, please. Will your husband claim the two million dollars used to convince Brian Grissom to falsely confess to killing Tom Rawlings?

Jan Clark abruptly stood up. "Don't answer, Sally. Max, I think that question is more suitable for Senator Morris Green to answer!"

Chapter 83

Max's interview with Sally Green, including Jan Clark's closing comment, ran in its entirety as a special section of *Public Corruption*, with a headline featured on page one. The tabloid sold out within an hour on all the New York City and Washington newsstands. By the end of the day, Morris Green, still in Venezuela, cut his visit short and was on a private plane headed back to Washington.

It was not business as usual at any of the congressional offices that day, as most people read and re-read every word of the interview. Tony thought Max's introduction was riveting:

Politics, Power and Murder: A Tragic Betrayal of Trust
The Real Story of the Escort Murders
and the Killing of Tom Rawlings
Max Gold, Crime Reporter

For many months now, I have been writing about the tragic murders of Stephanie Taylor, Valerie Powell, and Amanda Wilson. As most of you already know, just before Tom Rawlings was killed, he was to be arrested for all three murders. Then you read that a man named Brian Grissom, a man dying of cancer, had murdered Rawlings. That story was proven false, thanks to the fine detective work done privately by Tony Pinella, as well as the bravery of Donna Grissom, Brian's wife, who brought forth incontrovertible evidence that Brian's confession was false. A false confession bought and paid for by an unknown person, who obviously had access to a great amount of money.

The first thing journalists are taught is their obligation to tell readers the facts as they are known. The so-called *who, what, where, when, and why*. When the escorts were murdered, we knew *who, what, where, and when*. We never really knew the *why*. The same thing happened when Tom Rawlings was murdered.

When Brian Grissom confessed to killing Rawlings, we thought we knew *who, what, where, and when*—but, still, not the *why*. Then we found out that we did not even know the real who.

That, readers, is what this special supplement is all about. This past week, I was given an exclusive interview with someone who has the answers to all the questions, the who, what, where, when, and why three young women and Tom Rawlings were murdered.

My interview with Sally Green, wife of ex-governor and now Senator Morris Green, took place in the law offices of her attorneys, Jan Clark and Lorna Adams. Clark and Adams were there to observe. In providing you with a verbatim copy of that interview and discussion, you will have been there, too.

Chapter 84

"I just finished reading your interview with Sally Green. Max, it was terrific!"

"Thanks, Tony. I was worried you might think I didn't press her hard enough, especially towards the end, when I asked her about the money Brian received from Morris Green."

"She may seem distraught, but Sally Green is a tough woman. She's guarding the lifestyles of her daughters as well as her own. You went as far as possible, especially with her lawyers sitting there, ready to pounce! Now to the bigger issue. Do you think Sally was telling the truth with her *self-defense* story?"

"All I can say now is that she sounded believable. Unfortunately, we'll never hear Rawlings' side of the story. One way or another, she made sure of that. She certainly knows the law well enough to have called 911 when she realized that Rawlings was shot. I can understand her panicking at that moment. But why not come forward sooner? If her story is entirely truthful, why all the delays in talking to us? Did Morris convince her to wait, that he would fix everything?"

"Anything is possible, Max. I believe she would protect her daughters at all costs. Part of protecting her family means maintaining their lifestyle, her own lifestyle included."

"Well, she has two high-priced attorneys working for her. That also helps. So your guess is that she will never be charged with murder?"

"The most might be manslaughter—and that will never get to court, not with Jan Clark and Lorna Adams representing her. *Of course, we don't know what they may be hiding. If only the police would get back on the case,*" Tony said thinking aloud.

"What do you mean? Like what?"

"No one has mentioned the gun! Did Tom Rawlings even own that gun? According to the early forensic report, there were three sets of fingerprints on the gun. Tom's and Sally's—which she could claim got there when they struggled—and an unknown. Just before the case was closed, when I asked for the gun to be re-examined, it had mysteriously disappeared from the evidence box."

"Are you saying Sally may have gone there with a gun? That suggests intent. Her whole story falls apart if she had a gun with her, or if someone else was in the apartment with Tom."

"Think about it, Max. None of the escorts were shot. They were all stabbed, and violently—which generally indicates a very angry killer. Unfortunately, none of the murder weapons ever turned up. The stabbing patterns were similar enough to have been done by one person. Not exact enough to point to one killer—especially because a different knife was used for each murder. That could mean that the killer, or killers, planned each murder and knew what they were doing. Bottom line is that we needed more time to investigate each murder and to look for the weapons. My gut screams at me that those murders are connected. They were carefully planned and passionately carried out. These were all things we were looking into—including the gun that killed Rawlings—until Brian Grissom confessed and all the cases were closed."

"Where do we stand with Morris Green?"

"He's on his way back to Washington. I'm sure he'll have an answer for everything. He always does."

"How will he answer to the Brian Grissom letter, and the signed affidavit concerning the link between Morris Green and two million dollars?"

"The Grissom letter is one thing, but I haven't been able to locate Gary Edwards, the man who signed the affidavit and set up the account."

"Good grief, Tony. That was our only direct link between the Grissom confession and Morris Green!"

"I know, I know. At least the money is in Donna's name and safe—that's a fact!"

"True. Obviously the money had to come from someone rich, as rich as Morris Green. But is that enough to draw a link between the two?"

"Max, I'm doing my best to find out what happened to Edwards. He's a cagey character, well-known and trusted for carrying out high-priced deals like this. All I know is what he told his current girlfriend, *and I really want to leave her out of all this*. He said he was going to a very important meeting out of the country. It was his biggest deal ever, one that would change their lives. He never came back, and she hasn't heard from him since she kissed him goodbye! It's possible that Edwards was also killed, or he's living on some tropical island with his own fortune, his payment for taking care of the bribe and setting up the account for Donna."

"I don't like this, Tony. Not at all..."

"I realize that, Max. Look, I have to catch a plane to Detroit. Something's come up with Stacey, and I need to see her."

"Well, I just hope whatever it is, she'll have some of the answers we need. I'll take anything right now—even a dream from a psychotic murderer."

"I wish so, too. Don't be so hard on Stacey. I'm not making excuses for her crimes, but don't forget, she did provide the insights that led to our thinking about Sally and Julia."

"Yeah, she did. Sorry about my outburst, Tony. Go catch your plane… Have a safe flight."

❧

The Laughing Angels could not be happier with the current circumstances. The great Tony Pinella finally messed up big-time. His one sure link to getting the best of Morris Green—a symbol of power and corruption—might be sunning himself on a beach somewhere, while Tony was flying off again for *insights* from some loony woman, a convicted murderer, who called herself the true Daughter of God. They could not wait to get there and watch the show!

The Righteous Ones saw the scene differently. Stacey might not have answers for everything, and went a bit too far in her theological conclusions—but at least she still believed in the merciful powers of the Supreme Being.

You have to be kidding, the Laughing Angels screeched out. *Is that the best you can do? With all the pain in the Universe, you truly believe this one insane woman is proof that God is merciful?*

Chapter 85

Tony learned this might be his last visit with Stacey Johnson Blake. Dr. Trotsky was concerned that the longer Stacey believed her visions helped solve crimes, the stronger were her delusions that she was the true Daughter of God.

This saddened Tony, but he also felt a sense of relief. He knew Stacey would spend the rest of her life in a psychiatric facility. The one thing he hoped was that her final years would bring her some sort of peace. Perhaps Dr. Trotsky was right; he was feeding into her psychosis, not helping her. Guilt had been haunting him for months, and it was time for it to end.

This time, Tony was brought right to Stacey's room, where it was obvious she was heavily medicated, but awake. Nurse Helen sat at her side.

When Stacey saw Tony, she sat up and smiled at him. Even though she was groggy from the medication, there was an excited look in her eyes.

"I had an incredible dream last night," she said. "I asked God if it was all right to reveal the whole truth to you about the escort murders. I told him you were one of the good guys, that you deserved to know everything and receive your due credit for solving these awful crimes."

Tony could not help but feel a warm spot in his heart for Stacey. She wanted so much to please him, to have his approval, in a way that her father never understood.

"Thanks for the plug, Stacey."

Stacey laughed hysterically. "You can't fool me, Tony. I know you're skeptical about my relationship with God. Everyone here is. I can hardly think straight with all the drugs they're giving me. At least you listen to me, and admit my visions have helped you. Otherwise, why would you keep coming back to see me?"

Dr. Trotsky, who was sitting on the other side of the room, nodded to Tony—his signal that it was all right to agree with Stacey.

"I try to keep an open mind, Stacey."

"That's good enough for me. Now let's get down to business. I think it's obvious that Sally Green is a pathological liar. Trust me, that's something I know about. Sally's goals were always to have a wonderful family. An important, prosperous, and loving husband, beautiful children who adore her. At a critical moment in her life, she agreed with her husband to sacrifice her own professional success to achieve these goals.

"It was great while it lasted. She knew her role as Morris Green's wife, and she played it very well—until she began to doubt her husband's own willingness to make any sacrifices in his own life. At first, Sally tried to reconcile his behavior with the stress of his growing responsibilities, both at home and as a public official. Then she realized some of the responsibility was hers. She made the decision to remain with Morris, even after learning the extent of his actions."

Suddenly Stacey stopped talking and asked Nurse Helen for a glass of water. There were tears in her eyes.

"Are you all right, Stacey?" Tony asked. He wondered if she were rethinking her own life and the deadly steps she took to achieve the family unity she desperately wanted.

"Yes, I'm fine,Tony. My mind just drifted for a moment."

She took a sip of her water and handed the glass back to Nurse Helen.

"I'm all right now. For a moment, I felt sorry for Sally. How terrible it was that she had sacrificed the well being of her daughters for the comfort and privilege she craved."

Dr. Trotsky quickly interjected. "Are you talking about Sally Green's experiences, or your own?"

"Well, maybe my own. But only partly. To be fair, I murdered someone's wife so I could live the life I wanted with *her* husband. I thought my relationship with God made me far more suitable to stand by Jason Blake's side as he ministered to the people. It was me, not Veronica, who could help Jason in his quest to reach political as well as religious heights. That's what God wanted for his chosen daughter."

Tony saw the look on Dr. Trotsky's face. It was obvious that he was right about Stacey's state of mind. She was slipping more and more into her psychosis, recognizing her crimes—yet still justifying them with her special relationship to God.

Stacey glared at Tony with a sarcastic smile. "Well, Tony? Do you have a question about anything I've said so far? You look puzzled."

"I'm just wondering... Do you still believe that Tom Rawlings and Julia Green carried out the murders of all three escorts?"

"Yes, I do. I think that Julia knew how to manipulate Tom to do whatever she wanted. Tom and Julia were in Chicago when Stephanie Taylor was killed, and in New York when Amanda Wilson was murdered. We can place Tom in Paradise Valley at the time of Valerie Powell's murder, but not Julia."

Stacey kept that sly, sarcastic smile on her face when Tony asked, "Who killed Tom Rawlings?"

"Isn't it obvious? Sally Green intentionally killed Tom Rawlings. She went to his apartment, thinking it was the only way to save her family—especially Julia."

"Why are you so sure?" Tony asked.

"Simple! It's because I would have done the same thing under those circumstances. Sure, it's wrong! But that's what you do once you make the decision to stay married to a scoundrel—you find yourself acting like one."

"Interesting."

"Interesting? Is that all you can say?" Stacey asked very aggressively. "Tony, I hope you're not being too harsh on me. I always thought you were the one person who really understood, even when you arrested me. Now, all of a sudden, you're being judgmental. What happened to the man with a soul, the one who had tears in his eyes when they dragged me off to prison?"

It was now even clearer to Tony that Dr. Trotsky was right in putting a halt to his meetings with Stacey. He was sorry he asked for her input in the first place. At first, his guilt brought him to visit her. Then he thought her own background might actually give her—and him—some insights into this complex case.

Stacey now sat quietly, her face twisted in wicked satisfaction. She was getting even with him, while still understanding the leading suspects in this drama. Stacey had been playing him all along. Now it was his turn to play. He would get as much valuable information from her as possible, then close the door forever.

"So what do you think about the two million dollars? Did Morris Green really put up the money?"

"Of course, he did," Stacey said with conviction. "Morris overheard Sally and Julia taking about the mess they were in. Like any good father and husband, he knew what needed to be done. He contacted one of his sources and paid them to find some poor soul to confess to murdering Rawlings."

Stacey sat there in bed, looking triumphant.

"Why are you so sure?" Tony asked.

"Tony, don't you understand at all? I'm God's daughter, *the chosen Daughter of God.* He tells me everything. He gave up on his son a long time ago. Just like he's given up on you!"

Dr. Trotsky stood up abruptly, which was Tony's signal it was time to leave. "Let me walk you out Detective Pinella. Helen, I think it's time for Stacey's medication."

As Tony left for the airport, he realized Dr. Trotsky was right. Stacey was getting worse, trapped by her own plot to seduce him into thinking her visions would help him solve the murders. How naïve he was to allow his compassion for her to take priority over his common sense. That was her plan all along. What she had not counted on was that her own devious personality and weaknesses actually put him on the right track!

Chapter 86

When his flight from Venezuela landed at Reagan National Airport, Morris Green headed right to the private plane that would take him to New York City, where his staff had arranged a press conference at the Park Lane Hotel on Central Park. He knew the New York press, as well as his constituents, were waiting to hear directly from their senator.

The questions about the two million dollars, and the involvement of his wife in Tom Rawlings' murder, came fast and furious—but he was prepared with the answers.

Rita Spencer from *Channel 42 News* called out loudly, even before the senator reached the microphone. "Did you give Brian Grissom two million dollars to confess to Tom Rawlings' murder?"

Green answered in the sarcastic manner he liked to use with the probing press: "If it was my money, I'd ask for it back! I might be rich, but there's a reason for it. I've worked hard all my life, and I know better than to waste it on someone trying to extort money from me."

"Marco Rodriquez, *New York Hispanic Life.* Do you believe your wife killed Tom Rawlings in self-defense?"

"Nice to see you Marco," Green said with a smile. "You've interviewed my wife at several of the charity events she's hosted. Do you think she could hurt a fly unless she was threatened? *Of course it was self-defense!* Sally has always stood by me and I will stand by her. She's a wonderful and compassionate woman, a great mother and wife."

"Jim Harding, *New York Times.* What about Julia's involvement with Rawlings?"

"Julia is a special young woman, very much a romantic, like her mother—which sometimes clouds her choice of men. Unfortunately, Tom Rawlings was charming as well as devious. Julia did not see through the charm. She is a very caring, loyal, and moral person—she would never be part of the crimes Rawlings was accused of doing."

"Susan Graham, *Newsday.* Some at the NYPD think Tony Pinella went down the wrong road, wasted too much of the taxpayer's money in his investigation of the escort and Tom Rawlings' murders. Do you feel that way, too?"

"Tony Pinella is known for his superior investigative skills, and has been in the business for many, many years—maybe too long," Green said with a wry smile on his face. "He may want to think about spending his senior years writing fiction."

"A follow-up, senator. What about Max Gold? Do you think he has some sort of vendetta against you?"

"Max is a great journalist, who apparently is running out of exposés. He may want to join Tony Pinella and write that novel. Let's face it, they both have vivid imaginations!"

Morris Green was at his best. The mainstream reporters, even the good ones, were eating up his message. The room filled with laughter, too much laughter, Max thought. He stood against the back wall of the room, keeping quiet at the behest of his editor, who had already heard from her corporate attorney, as well as Green's lawyer.

Tony thought the press conference was a circus—a bunch of clowns watching the whip-cracking ringmaster in action. Except for a few experienced journalists, the room was filled with young reporters, who had not yet learned how to recognize a charismatic charlatan from an honest politician. *If there are any honest politicians left!* Tony thought.

One week later, Abraham Bloom did some checking. He let Tony know that Sally Green—quietly and in an unpublicized private hearing in the DA's office—got off on her self-defense plea. And there was no follow-up on Julia being involved in the escort murders.

Sally and Julia went back to doing charity work, with word on the street that the head of a major television network was courting Julia for a job in its news division as a *Special Correspondent* for a hefty $600,000 a year.

Back at *Public Corruption*, things were not going well for Max. His editor was run through the ringer by her publisher, who was under great pressure from the owners of *Public Corruption* and their attorneys. Max was told to lay off the senator and his family. No more columns about Morris Green, and no more time spent on the escort and Tom Rawlings' murders—or Max was back to covering school board meetings and building code violations.

"At least for now," he told Tony, "I'll have to keep my head down."

"Listen, I know it's hard, but don't give up altogether. Something will break on this story," Tony said trying to sympathize with Max, while his own anger was growing. "Maybe when the Greens feel safer and let down their guard.... Let's just play it cool and keep our eyes and ears open."

"Yeah, I will. Now comes the harder part. Letting Angela Robinson know our heads need to be in the sand for awhile."

"Let me know how she takes it."

"I will. Hey, take it easy, Tony. By the way, I might need that extra room at your place in Newport."

"Any time, old buddy. Any time... But I'm not leaving New York just yet. I'm not through with Green, and that's not for publication!"

❧

The Righteous Ones cried tears of joy, and their hearts swelled with pride, when they saw Tony leave his apartment in Bensonhurst and walk to the little Catholic Church his mother loved so much. They quietly followed him there and watched as he lit a candle and then knelt in one of the pews. They listened to Tony pray—not to God—but to the soul of his saintly mother, asking her to give him the strength to continue his fight for justice.

The Laughing Angels followed and danced up and down the church aisles with glee. *This is one more sign that the Almighty has lost another round; His so-called holy place is not being used to glorify Him—but to honor a mortal woman's soul.*

Not so fast, the Righteous Ones cried out. *A mortal she may have been, but she is still a Daughter of God.*

Chapter 87

Angela Robinson had just completed her sociology term paper. She was about to pop a frozen cheese lasagna dinner into the microwave and watch the evening edition of NBC News.

So far, she was excelling at all her evening courses at Brooklyn College's School of Humanities and Social Sciences. Her life experiences drew her to major in sociology. She wanted a better understanding of human life through its literature, conflicts, and philosophy. Her goal was to obtain a PhD, find a teaching job, and eventually write books and give seminars that would help others understand the critical matters that effect their daily lives—beginning with the book she started about her experiences as an escort, the one that was crushed by Morris Green's family connections.

By day, Angela was a waitress in a small restaurant in Flatbush. It was owned by Sophia and Giuseppe Amato, an Italian couple who lived in Bensonhurst, friends of Tony's from *the old days*, as he liked to call them. Without her make-up, by changing her hair color and style, and using her mother's Italian maiden name, *Angela Bertolini* had no trouble keeping her real identity a secret and signing up for night school.

Any happiness or satisfaction she felt, quickly turned to anger as she watched the television screen. Facing her was the smiling face of Julia Green, making her debut as NBC's newest *Special Correspondent*.

Angela could hardly believe it. There was Julia, talking about her upcoming series of reports on *Innocent Victims—Political Families in the Spotlight*. "My series of interviews with the wives and children of members of congress, will show how the seemingly privileged lives they lead are so unfairly turned upside down by the prying eyes of the press and the public. You will hear their personal stories of how their rights to privacy end when the campaigning begins...."

Angela almost choked on the piece of Italian bread she was chewing, and dropped the plate of lasagna onto the floor. Although she thought things were going well for the Greens, this was an outrage.

"What kind of crap is this," she shouted. "Has the whole world turned a blind eye to the truth?"

She shut off the television and picked up the phone to call Max, but hung up when she heard his answering service. Max had phoned her weeks ago with the bad news about how the Greens seemed to have worked their contacts well, and might be off the hook. *That was bad enough*, she thought, *but damn it, this is too much. I have to do something...*

Angela decided to write Max a letter, logically explaining her disappointment, and even exploring options for preventing Green's apparent clear path to the White House. Max already knew how her book contract had been abruptly cancelled, and it was obvious by his most recent columns that his editor had kept her word by pulling the plug on the Morris Green exposés. He was probably just as frustrated as she was about seeing Julia on the network news.

She cleaned up the lasagna mess, poured herself a glass of red wine, and sat down at her computer.

Dear Max,

It was depressing and disheartening to learn that the escort and Tom Rawlings' murder cases were closed, probably for good. Still, I went on with my studies and will be forever grateful to you, Tony, and the Amato's that I'm able to maintain my privacy, pursue my dream to obtain a degree in sociology—and then (hopefully) go on to get a PhD. I'm optimistic that one day my full story will come to light. I want to help others who might be swayed to go down the same hurtful past that will always be part of my life.

As I look back, ironically, the Greens actually did me a favor by convincing that publisher to cancel my book contract. Instead of getting the large advance I counted on, I had to work at a legitimate job, and pay attention to furthering my education. At least for me, a curse turned into a blessing. I only wish that Stephanie, Valerie, and Amanda could have had the same opportunity. They didn't have Max Gold, Tony Pinella, or the wonderful Amatos in their corner.

Yes, I still get disillusioned whenever I see photos and news clips of the Greens playing host at one of Morris' fundraisers. It makes me sad that the public is so forgiving of a wayward politician, but so judgmental of the women whose lives they may have ruined.

Yes, it still hurts when I read the articles I saved for my book about the way the press treated me, and the awful names Sally Green called me one moment, and then looked adoringly at her husband the next.

I live with those memories—and fully intend to use them to help other young women follow a different path. I also want to show those cruel and enabling political wives that one day it could be their daughters caught in the same trap. My book will be published! Maybe not next month or even next year.

My story will be told, my way, and in my time frame. That day will come!

What bothers me most at this moment is seeing Julia Green smiling into the cameras as a "special correspondent" (whatever that means!) for NBC. It's enough to make any reasonable person sick to their stomach. As a skilled and dedicated journalist, you and your colleagues must be especially disillusioned—or maybe you have come to expect that type of behavior by the less dedicated industry executives.

So why am I writing to you? I don't think the pathway to the White House should be so easy for Morris Green. Maybe it's not the time for my personal story, but it is the time to stifle Green's ambitions.

I would like to meet with you and Tony, if we can work that out. The sooner the better. You have my phone number and can reach me after I get out of class, at ten 'clock weekday evenings. Please call me!

Sincerely,
Angela

The next day, before Angela left for work at the Amato's restaurant, she dropped her letter off at Max's office. She took a deep breath, and hoped she would hear from him before the next weekend.

Chapter 88

When Max called Angela on Monday evening, the same day he received her letter, she sounded nervous, but determined. They planned to meet late the next evening at Max's apartment, right after Angela's last class.

"I've already called Tony, and he'll be there, too," Max assured Angela.

Angela was already at Max's apartment when Tony arrived at ten-thirty Tuesday evening. "Sorry I'm a little late," he said. "Even at this hour, the traffic coming into the City from Bensonhurst makes for a slow ride."

"No problem," Max said. "Angela and I haven't seen each other in a while. She's been telling me how nice the Amatos have been to her, and how appreciative she is that you reached out to them on her behalf."

"Glad I could help!" Tony responded. "I guess we better get right to it. Max said you were very anxious to see us. That you have important information for us about Morris Green."

"I'm not sure how to begin," Angela said. "We may be the only ones who can block Morris Green's path to the presidency—and he really frightens me!"

"Let me help you, Angela," Tony said. "You're with friends. Nothing you tell us goes outside this room, unless you say so—and unless we can assure your safety. Right, Max?"

"Absolutely! No column, no police contact, nothing—until you're ready, Angela."

"Why don't you start at the beginning," Tony said as he gently touched Angela's arm.

"Okay. Here goes. From the start, I haven't told you and Max everything. It all began when Morris paid for an entire evening, something he didn't do very often. Not with me, and not with any of the other escorts. I guess it just wasn't his style."

"Do you know why?" Max asked.

"No, and I didn't ask. That was one of the agency's rules, *don't ask any questions.* Anyway, that night Morris had a terrible nightmare. He screamed and woke me up. I tried to awaken him, but he didn't get up. Then he started to talk in a voice that was even more frightening than his scream—as though he were talking to me. His eyes were open, but I knew he was still asleep. I was so scared, all I could do was lie quietly and listen."

"What did he say?" Tony asked.

"He called me Dorothy. Then it was like he was calling out to her. *Dorothy, Dorothy, I'm so sorry, but you didn't listen to me. I warned you. I told you how sad I would be if you tried to leave me—how much I count on you to be there for me.*"

"Anything else?" Max asked.

"The next morning, when we were having coffee, I was so stupid! I broke Leslie's rule and asked a question. *Who is Dorothy?* Morris just glared at me with a look I'd never seen in his eyes before."

"Did you feel threatened? Did he hit you or attempt to harm you in any way?" Tony asked.

"No, no. It was just the look on his face when he asked, *I said Dorothy?*"

"Then what did you say?"

"I had to say something. *You had a nightmare and mentioned her name. That's all.* I was afraid to say anything else."

"How did he respond to that?"

"I don't remember his exact words, but his face was stone cold. He said something like, *I paid for your services, and the agency guaranteed absolute privacy—even if I talk in my sleep!* I was petrified. I promised I would never tell anyone."

"Did that satisfy him?" Tony asked.

"If it had, I don't think I would still be so frightened."

Max was puzzled as to why Angela waited until now to tell him about the Dorothy incident.

"Why tell us now about Dorothy? Why didn't you tell us earlier, when the escort story first broke?" he asked.

"I thought if he had something to do with the missing escorts, the police would find out everything—and Morris, or whoever he hired, would go to jail, and I would feel safe. I never expected him to become a senator or run for president! Look, my life has changed. I want to help other people, and I want to see justice done. It's apparent that's not going to happen unless I do something... Do you really think I want to open all this up again?"

"But you have, Angela," Tony said.

Tears were rolling down Angela's cheeks. "I know, I know... But when I heard from Max that the escort and Tom Rawlings' cases were closed for good, and then saw Julia as a special correspondent on the NBC News... I realized it isn't fair to Stephanie, Valerie, and Amanda—and it's not fair to Dorothy—for me to move on with my life. Their lives ended! Maybe if I had spoken up about the Dorothy incident sooner... I'm so sorry I didn't tell you everything."

Tony tried to hide his frustration with this frightened young woman. "It's not your fault. We all thought Morris and his family would pay the price. We'll work this out," he said.

"Yes, it is my fault. I was so sure it would all come to light. I was saving the details for after he was safely put away in jail. Then I was going to come forward, just before my book was published. Now I feel guilty. I'm so, so sorry."

Tony wondered, *is there another murder victim out there?*

Max could tell what Tony was thinking. He was thinking the same way. "We understand, Angela. Now is your chance to help us make sure the whole truth comes out. To do that, we need to know more about *Dorothy*," Max said. "Please don't be afraid. You've gone this far. Tell us everything you know or heard."

"Max is right," Tony said. "We need to know everything if we're going to get this guy. Is there more?"

"Yes, there is more. After I promised not to tell anyone about Morris' nightmare or anything about Dorothy, he kept that cold, really evil look on his face— and he threatened me."

"How did he threaten you? Can you recall his exact words?" Tony asked.

"He looked me right in the eyes and said, *People who meddle in other people's business have been known to disappear without a trace.* Then he took his bag and left the room. That was the last time I saw Morris before the escort story came out and he resigned."

Tony was still suspicious that Angela was holding something back. "So you don't know anything more about *Dorothy*?" he asked.

Angela hesitated before she responded to Tony's question. "Yes, there is something else. During his nightmare, before I woke him up, Morris cried out to Dorothy. I don't recall his exact words, but he seemed to be sorry for burying her in *that shabby shed* instead of somewhere more exotic."

"Where, Angela? Did he say where?"

"No, but after everything that's happened, I decided to find out more about *Dorothy*. I did some research, looked at lots of old newspaper and magazine articles for photos of

Morris at events. You know, who he might be standing next to... that sort of stuff."

"Did you find anything?"

"Nothing recent. I did find an old copy of Chappaqua's Horace Greeley High School yearbook for the year Morris graduated. He was captain of the boys' tennis team, and a cute redhead named *Dorothy Westlake* was one year behind him—a star tennis player on the girls' team. The Monday after Morris graduated from high school, Dorothy Westlake was reported missing. I checked her address, and she lived not far from the Green's old estate."

By now, Angela's look of fear and guilt about holding back some of the story had totally evaporated from her face, replaced by the excited look Max often saw on the faces of young reporters about to break their first big story. Tony, on the other hand, was still feeling unsettled. Angela was right. Lives might have been saved if this information had come out sooner.

"Angela!" Max said. "You're turning out to be quite a little sleuth. I'm almost afraid to ask... What else did you find out?"

"The Greens had a grand graduation party at their home for Morris the Sunday evening after his high school graduation. It was sort of a graduation party combined with a celebration of the Green's wedding anniversary. They were leaving the next morning for a cruise to the Greek Islands, and Morris was going with them as part of his graduation gift."

"What about Dorothy? Was she at the graduation party? Did she ever resurface?" Tony asked.

"I don't have any of that information, and certainly didn't want to contact the police to see if the Greens were ever interviewed. But I did find out one thing."

"What's that?" Tony asked, unable to hide his frustration.

"I took a ride up to Chappaqua to look at Morris' old home. It still has a shed towards the end of the property, beyond where it's all landscaped."

Max looked over at Tony, who he thought would have a heart attack right then and there. He knew Tony was getting angry, even while he felt some sympathy for Angela. He would want to move ahead and make some contacts with the New Castle Police Department in Chappaqua. Max thought he might need to slow him down a little.

"Angela, this has been so helpful. You're very brave telling us all this. I know you've been through a lot this past year, and Tony and I are grateful you're still willing to help. Aren't we, Tony?"

Angela realized that she might have reached the limits to Tony's sympathy, as his hard-core detective experience took over from his sympathetic mind.

"It's all right, Tony. I understand how you might be feeling right now. I'm feeling awful, too. I really am." Angela hesitated and then added, "There's one more thing you should know."

"What's that?" Tony asked.

"The Westlake's bought the Green's Chappaqua home ten years ago, when Morris' parents decided to buy a swanky pre-war condo on Sutton Place, the one they still own on East 57th Street. It's possible that, until the Westlake's financial problems and foreclosure of the Chappaqua home, Dorothy was near her family all along."

"Angela, you've been a tremendous help," Max said quickly, before Tony could explode. "Now I want to be sure. You haven't told this story to anyone else. Is that right? It wasn't in the proposal you made to that publisher?"

"No one until now, Max. I was too afraid to discuss this part of my story with anyone. It was going to be the surprise ending of my book."

"Okay. As soon as we check all this out, and decide what our next move should be, we'll call you. For now, you go back to your job at the Amato's restaurant, and attend your night classes as if nothing has changed. Promise?"

"I promise. Tony, I'm so sorry. Please don't hate me."

"I don't hate you, Angela. Right now, all I want to do is keep you safe—and bring the Westlakes some peace. Then we'll get that bastard. It may take some time, but we will get him!"

Chapter 89

It was only six-thirty in the morning when Jan Clark unlocked the door to her office and heard her private telephone line ringing. She ran to the desk and quickly hit the speaker button. She recognized the hysterical voice as Sally Green's.

"Morris is going to be arrested for murder!"

"Sally, calm down," Jan urged. "I just walked into my office. Hold on while I take my coat off."

Jan's heart beat rapidly. She tossed her coat on the couch and sat down behind her desk, took a deep breath, and picked up the receiver. "Okay, Sally. Give me all the details."

"Dorothy Westlake!" Sally screamed. "The police say he killed Dorothy Westlake. You have to do something!"

"I will, Sally, I will. Get a hold of yourself. I know it's hard. But I need you to think clearly and answer some questions. Okay?"

"Yes, okay. I'll try…" Sally sobbed.

"Let's start with Dorothy Westlake. Who is she?"

"Dorothy Westlake went to the same high school as Morris, and her family lived not too far from the Greens in Chappaqua."

"Did Morris know her well?"

"She was a year behind Morris, but they were friends. So were their parents. Morris was on the boys' tennis team, and Dorothy was on the girls' team. She went missing the evening after Morris' high school graduation. In fact, she was at the big party the Green's held for Morris that night. All the students at the high school were interviewed, and the teachers. For a while, they even suspected one of

Dorothy's uncles, her mother's brother. He was visiting at the time."

"I would think that Morris and his family were the first to be interviewed."

"Yes, they would have been. But that didn't happen until weeks later. The morning after the party, the Greens took Morris with them on a cruise to the Greek Islands. It was part of their wedding anniversary celebration and Morris' graduation gift."

"So Morris was interviewed when they got back?"

"Yes. Morris said all he remembered was that she must have left early with some of the other kids. By time the party broke up, he was going to walk her the few blocks home, but she had already left. At least that's what he recalls. They had all been drinking pretty heavily, and there were more than fifty kids going in and out of the house until just after midnight, so he certainly wasn't keeping track of everyone."

"That was so long ago. A real cold case," Jan said thoughtfully. "Why are they accusing Morris now?"

Sally started to cry again, and mumbled something that Jan could barely hear.

"Please, Sally. You have to calm down. I didn't hear you. They found Dorothy's remains?"

"Yes... Underneath the floor of a shed on the Green's old estate in Chappaqua!"

At first, Jan could hardly respond to Sally's answer, and Sally was crying hysterically. "You said something else, Sally. Please stop crying so I can hear you."

"When the Greens moved to their Sutton Place condo, they sold the Chappaqua house to the Westlakes! Not long after, the Westlakes made some very bad investments and ended up filing for bankruptcy. They lost pretty much everything—including the house. It's been in foreclosure and the Westlakes are renting a small apartment in New Rochelle."

"Oh, my God!" Jan exclaimed unable to hide her emotions. "So her body was right near them all that time!"

"What are we going to do? What am I going to do? You have to help Morris!"

"One step at a time, Sally," she said. "What happened that made the police look for Dorothy's body after so many years, and why in that particular spot?"

"It's a long story, and I don't know all the details. What I do know is that Max Gold and Tony Pinella have been hounding my husband since the escort story came out. They're the ones behind this..."

Jan was beginning to lose her patience with her friend. She thought Sally should have left that scoundrel a long time ago. "Come on, Sally. You must know more than you're telling me. You either trust me or not!"

"It seems that on one of Morris' *overnighters* in Washington with that *Angela woman who started all these problems*, she heard Morris scream out in his sleep. She said he yelled out some sort of apology to *Dorothy*, and...well, sort of apologized for burying her in a shed."

"For crying out loud, Sally! How long have you known about this?"

"Honestly, Jan... Only a few hours. Morris got a call about four this morning from someone in his New York office. Truly, that's all I know. I didn't want to call you until he left the house for the airport. He left here about six, and I called you at six-thirty, knowing you usually get to your office about that time. He was so upset when he left. He said he wanted to get out of the house—just in case the Virginia police come early."

At that moment, Jan could hardly speak. She leaned back in her desk chair, looked out the window, and tried hard to remember once again that she was Sally's lawyer.

Before she could comment, Sally spoke again. "I know it sounds crazy, especially with everything he's put us through. But, please... I have to do something to help Morris. I need to find some way to save him, save our family. It was such a long time ago. Isn't there anything you can do to help him?"

"Stop right there, Sally! I'm going to be straight with you, as I always have—as your friend and as your lawyer. I will not allow you to sacrifice anything more. You gave up your career, you almost gave up your life when you confronted Tom Rawlings."

"But, Jan..."

"*No buts*, Sally. This is it! This is outright murder and if I have anything at all to say about it, Morris Green is going to take full responsibility for his actions! If you don't go along with me on this, I swear, I'll resign as your lawyer. You can find someone else to represent you."

"So, I shouldn't do anything to help Morris?"

"That's right. It's time to think about your future and the futures of your daughters. Obviously that's the furthest thing from Morris' mind."

Sally was quite for a moment. "There's more..."

"More? What more can there be?"

"Morris said that if I don't help him, I could go to prison for leaving the scene of a crime."

"Don't listen to that scoundrel, Sally. You were lucky! The Rawlings case is closed forever! Enough is enough."

"Do you really think the girls and I can still have a good life?"

"Yes, I do. I don't think the escort or Rawlings' cases will ever be re-opened. Lorna and I feel confident of that.

We're sure the authorities are satisfied that Tom Rawlings acted alone. Your self-defense claim is solid. No one is going to come up with any new evidence sufficient to open any of those cases. At least I hope so!"

"Please, Jan. Isn't there anything you can do for Morris?"

"I'm your attorney, not Morris'—and there's nothing I can or want to do for him. He's a disgrace and hurts everyone close to him. Like too many politicians, Morris used his family for photo-op benefits with no regard whatsoever for the pain and humiliation you and the girls have suffered. Do you really think he will change if he's elected president?"

"You've always been a true friend, Jan. I appreciate your honesty so much. I feel like such a fool."

Jan sat back and took a deep breath. It was hard for her to believe Sally was still worried about Morris Green.

"One more thing, Sally. Tell Julia to call me. It's important that we talk before Morris gets to her. She needs to keep her distance from him. She's finally getting her own life in order and planning her future. It's time for you and the girls to focus on yourselves and to stop being victimized by Morris' ambition, lack of concern for others, and poor judgment—and that's saying it mildly."

"I'll talk to Julia as soon as we hang up. I think she has her head on straight—more than her mother! There is one more thing you should probably know."

"What else could there be?" Jan asked.

"It was Morris who handled the sale of his parents' Chappaqua house to the Westlakes. He said that even though their bid was much lower than another potential buyer, he wanted Dorothy to be near her parents."

Chapter 90

Morris Green's flight back to Washington from New York had gone smoothly; it arrived thirty minutes earlier than scheduled. His faithful driver, Moe Scoby, was there to greet him. Everything was in place for Senator Green's ride home to Alexandria.

An hour earlier, Gary Edwards had left his furnished Washington apartment and headed for the airport. Edwards was dressed in the only suit he owned, dark blue polyester, with a white shirt and burgundy tie. He was carrying a bag that he held very close to his body. He hailed a taxi and declined the driver's suggestion to put the bag into the trunk.

"I'll just keep it on the seat beside me," he said casually.

Edwards was pleased that soon he would be part of a major news story. It had been difficult for him, waiting in hiding all this time, but he was now ready to take center stage and tell the world how Morris Green had given him two million dollars—the money he then put into secret accounts for Brian Grissom's wife.

A deal had been made at New York State's highest political and law enforcement levels. Morris Green would give himself up to the FBI at his Virginia home, instead of in the State of New York, where he allegedly committed at least one murder. He had already phoned Sally, to let her know that everything was all set. He told her that his attorney, and the FBI, would be waiting outside the house to take him into custody as soon as he arrived. He asked that she take the girls to a movie.

"I don't want them to see me in handcuffs," he said—*and Sally did as she was told.*

When Edwards arrived at the airport, he learned that his flight had been cancelled. Nothing else was available until much later that afternoon. Already on edge, he decided to head for the bar and have a drink, holding tightly onto his suitcase.

As soon as he walked into the bar, he saw that most of the patrons were glued to the overhead television screen. Several different photos of Senator Morris Green were being flashed, one-by-one, as a network news anchor from ABC was reading a bulletin.

This just in from Alexandria, Virginia. A car carrying Senator Morris Green and his driver exploded into flames just streets away from the Green home. It's believed that both Senator Green and his driver were killed instantly. No word yet on the senator's wife and daughters, who neighbors said left the Green home about an hour ago. We hope to have more on this great tragedy in the next hour. Now back to regular programming.

Edwards stood there in disbelief, clutching his suitcase and feeling disoriented. After a few minutes, he decided to return to his apartment and devise a new strategy. He left the airport terminal, waited on the cab line, and headed home. The traffic was heavy. It gave him time to think, his mind racing from one idea to the next.

By the time he reached his apartment building, Edwards came to what he thought was the best and safest conclusion. This was his opportunity to take the money he was paid for the Grissom confession job, build a new life for himself, and move away from Washington and the shadows that seemed to follow him.

Edwards was smiling as he took the keys out of his pocket and started to unlock the door. He barely heard the large explosion as a wall of flames hit him. He died in the ambulance on his way to the hospital.

Everything in Edwards' one-room apartment was destroyed, along with both of the adjacent apartments. The newspapers reported that the other apartments were empty at the time, and no one else was injured in the blast.

The fire inspector determined that the oven must have been left on in Edwards' apartment. A single cigarette and melted disposable lighter were found just inside the door, and the smell of gas was apparent. Edwards must have left the oven on when he left the apartment, and lit a cigarette just as he returned home. That's what caused the explosion. There was no further investigation, no suspicion of arson, and nothing to indicate that Edwards had been murdered.

❧

The Laughing Angels were silent. No words could do justice to the events before them.

The Righteous Ones were distraught and disillusioned. They were determined, now more than ever, to pray with even greater fervor to the Almighty.

Epilogue

Julia Green was never charged for being an accomplice in the escort murders. *Tom Rawlings*, her fiancé, was thought to have acted alone.

The district attorney accepted *Sally Green's* statement, that she killed Tom Rawlings in self-defense. She was not charged for leaving the scene of a crime.

Jan Clark, at the urging of Morris Green's parents, is considering a run for their late son's seat in the United States Senate. They offered to financially support her campaign.

Donna Grissom was not compelled to return the two million dollars. No one credible ever came forward to claim the money.

Angela Robinson attends graduate school and is close to receiving advanced degrees in psychology and sociology. *The Journal of Clinical Psychology* accepted for publication her research paper on *The Impact of Corrupt Political Power: Its Devastating Effects on Society*.

Max Gold received a Pulitzer Prize for his series of articles on *Corruption in Politics*. He left his job at *Public Corruption* after receiving a grant to examine the lack of fair and balanced reporting in newspapers and on television news shows. One of his focuses is to look at how reporting changed after large business conglomerates began buying controlling interests in newspaper publishing companies, and television network and cable stations. His premise is, it led to rampant bias and a breakdown of journalistic ethics.

Tony Pinella is semi-retired, but is frequently called upon by police departments around the country to consult on complex cases. In his spare time, Tony is still trying to solve the murders of Morris Green and his driver, and looking more closely at the death of Gary Edwards. He believes that Edwards' death, the murders of Green and his driver, the escort murders, and the death of Tom Rawlings are all part of a larger conspiracy.

Stacey Johnson Blake remains hospitalized in Michigan and under the care of Dr. Boris Trotsky. The last time Tony checked on her status, Dr. Trotsky told him that Stacey still believes she is the true *Daughter of God*, and remains preoccupied with how Sally and Julia Green got away with murder. She is sure they will strike again...

"The past is never dead; it is not even past."
—William Faulkner

About the Author

Jerry Marcus is internationally acclaimed for his ability to create compelling fiction about thought-provoking issues such as anti-Semitism, political intrigue, and religious hypocrisy.

For several years, Marcus worked at a public relations firm in Washington, D.C., where he wrote press releases, position papers and speeches for political candidates.

When writing about challenging issues became his focus, Marcus left Washington and headed for Chicago. He wrote about politics for a local independent newspaper, as well as working at a variety of jobs (sales, loading trucks, waiting tables, and behind the counter at the well-known Mort's Delicatessen). He also began writing his first novel.

Marcus' hard work was rewarded in 1982, when *Abraham, Isaac, Jacob and Zev* was recommended by the American Jewish Congress, and later adopted as required reading for a humanities course at The State University System of Florida. His second novel, *The Salvation Peddler*, earned him the title of "Master of Suspense." *The Last Pope* continued Marcus' talent for turning out thrilling, religious-based fiction. *Broken Trust - The Murder Of Basketball Star Jack Molinas* explored the killing of basketball great Jack Molinas, and created a murder mystery that combines religion, politics, sports and gambling.

Marcus' 2013 novel, *Shoshana's Song*, was a finalist in the Arizona-New Mexico Book Awards.

Born in Israel of American parents, Marcus was raised in New York. He currently lives in Arizona, where he recently completed writing a collection of short stories, and is now working on his next novel.

About the Author

Novels by Jerry Marcus

From Brittany Publications, Ltd.

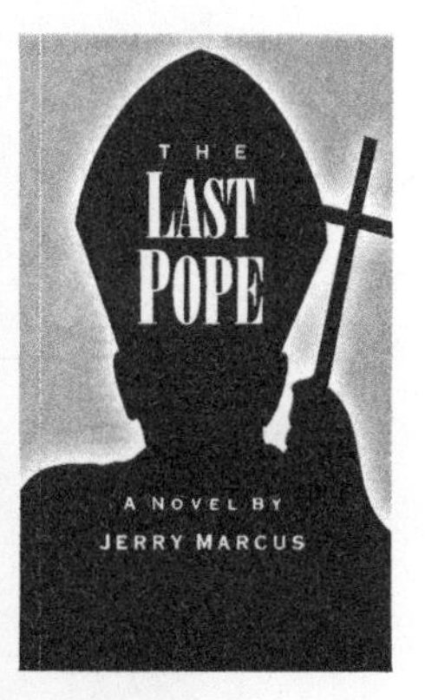

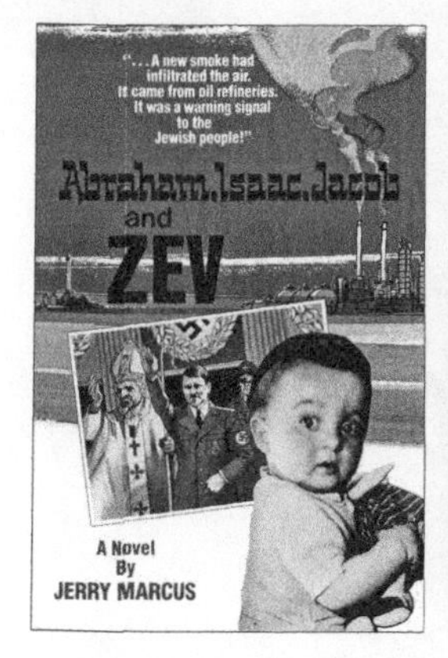

Available from Amazon.com and
www.brittanypublications.com